THE DISAPPEARANCE

Audrey Bailey will never forget the moment she met Ralph Templeton in the sweltering heat of a Bombay café. Her lonely life over, she was soon married with two small children. But things were never quite what they seemed. Now approaching 70, and increasingly a burden on the children she's never felt close to, Audrey plans a once-in-a-lifetime cruise around the Greek isles with twins Lexi and John. The Templetons set sail as a party of three – but only two will return. Audrey goes missing hours after she tells the twins they stand to inherit a fortune. As the search widens, so does the list of suspects...

THE DISAPPEARANCE

THE DISAPPEARANCE

by

Annabel Kantaria

Magna Large Print Books
Long Preston, North Yorkshire,
BD23 4ND, England.

British Library Cataloguing in Publication Data.

A catalogue record of this book is
available from the British Library

ISBN   978-0-7505-4472-6

First published in Great Britain 2016 by Harlequin Mira,
an imprint of HarperCollins*Publishers*

Copyright © 2016 Annabel Kantaria

Cover illustration © Hayden Verry/Arcangel by arrangement with
Arcangel Images Ltd.

The moral right of the author has been asserted

Published in Large Print 2017 by arrangement with
HarperCollins Publishers Ltd.

LP

Magna Large Print is an imprint of Library Magna Books Ltd.

Printed and bound in Great Britain by
T.J. (International) Ltd., Cornwall, PL28 8RW

For Maia and Aiman

18 July 2013, 10 p.m.

Captain Stiegman's gaze swept around the ship's library, shifting like a search light until it had touched everyone in the room. He took a deep breath, steadied his hands on the back of a chair and spoke. 'The search has been called off.'

I pressed my hand to my mouth, stifling a sob. Even though I'd been primed to hear these words, the sound of them left me winded: until now I'd still held out hope. There had been a mistake; Mum had been picked up by another ship. She'd been brought aboard, cold, weak, wrapped in a silver blanket, but alive. She'd floated on her back; she'd clung onto some flotsam; she'd been rescued by a lifeboat. Failing any of those scenarios, her body had been recovered. Anything but this; this inconclusive conclusion.

Captain Stiegman stood motionless. He was waiting for a response. I looked at John. He didn't meet my gaze. He was looking at the floor, his thin lips pressed in a hard line, his expression inscrutable. The only part of my brother that moved was his hand, his fingers tapping a rhythm on the arm of the stuffed leather armchair. I wanted to speak but there were no words.

Captain Stiegman paced the library floor, his steps lithe in his rubber-soled shoes. Doris, the cruise director, stood awkwardly by the book-shelves, a walkie-talkie in her hand, her lipstick

11

rudely red. Outside the picture window, small whitecaps topped the ocean like frosting. I imagined my mother's arms poking desperately up from the crests of each wave, her mouth forming an 'O' as the lights of the ship faded into the distance. In the library, you couldn't feel the low rumble of the ship's engines that permeated the lower decks, but snatches of a Latin beat carried from the *Vida Loca* dance party taking place on the pool deck outside. Doris's walkie-talkie crackled to life then fell silent.

'The decision has not been taken lightly,' said the captain, his English curt with a German accent, his words staccato. 'We have to face the facts. Mrs Templeton has been missing for over forty hours. The ship was sailing at full speed on the night she was last seen. We have no idea when she went overboard, nor where – the search area covers thousands of square kilometres.'

He paused, looked at John and me, then – perhaps heartened by the absence of tears – continued, ticking off points with his fingers as he spoke. A band of dull platinum circled his wedding finger.

'As you are already aware, I did not turn the ship. This was because, with Mrs Templeton missing for thirty-nine hours before the search was initiated, I felt there was nothing to be gained by retracing our route. It is my belief that Mrs Templeton did not fall overboard shortly before she was reported missing, but many hours prior to that, most likely in the early hours of the sixteenth of July.'

I opened my mouth to speak – this was pure

supposition – but the captain raised his hand in a request for me to be patient. 'However,' he said, 'tenders were dispatched from both Mykonos and Santorini, which is the area in which the ship was sailing when Mrs Templeton was last seen. A fleet of tenders traced our route from either end.' Now he paused and looked at each of us in turn once more. I gave a tiny shake of my head, eyes closed; there was nothing I could say to change what had happened.

'The Coast Guard was informed as soon as the ship search yielded nothing,' continued the captain. 'Two helicopters were scrambled and all ships within a thirty kilometre radius of the course we took that night were asked to join the search.' He paused again, looked at his shoes, then up again. 'I believe there were five vessels involved. The search has been fruitless. Mrs Templeton could now have been in the water, without a floatation device, for up to forty-eight hours. She was...' he searched his memory ... 'seventy years old?' His voice trailed off and he looked again at John, then at me, his eyebrows raised, the implication clear: she could not have survived.

John closed his eyes and nodded almost imperceptibly. Captain Stiegman echoed the nod. I opened my mouth then shut it again.

'Thank you,' said the captain. He bowed his head; looked up again after a respectful pause. I felt the thump of the music from outside. 'With the engines on full power, we should make Venice by dawn. I'm obliged to inform local police we have one passenger lost at sea. They will come aboard. They will talk to you. In a case like this,

13

it is a formality.' He removed his captain's hat, held it to his chest, his eyes closed again for a second. 'I am sorry for your loss.'

PART I

Before

December 1970

Tilbury, England

Audrey Bailey is on deck as the *SS Oriana* finally begins to ease her way backwards out of the dock. Someone's given her a streamer, but she's holding it clenched in her fist as she stands cheek by jowl with the other passengers and stares silently at the crowds on the quay. Everyone's waving flags, calling and shouting to friends and relatives. A band's playing onshore, and she can hear the rousing rhythm of sea shanties. The din is unbearable.

Then, as Audrey stares at the mass of humanity below, she catches sight of something that takes her breath away; the shape of a man, the colour of his hair, and the way he moves his arm as he waves a white hankie at the ship. Reflexively, Audrey raises her hand and waves back, knowing even as she does that it can't be; it can't be her father.

'Bye,' she mouths, the words silent on her lips. 'Bye Daddy.'

Audrey's hand remains in the air for a second or two as she turns her eyes to the sky, overcome with emotion. Then she turns abruptly and pushes her way back through the crowds, no longer willing to witness the ship's departure. She walks until she finds a deck that's less populated, sinks into a deckchair and tries simply to exist. All that is her, all that is Audrey Bailey, is gone. Her body is a shell, the softness inside her decimated. She sits in the deckchair for a long time, her head bowed; her eyes closed, just breathing. In, out, in, out, in, out. *If I do this enough,* she thinks, *this day will end. And then I will do the same tomorrow. I will get through this. One day at a time.*

Oblivious to her surroundings, Audrey does nothing but exist.

After some time – maybe an hour; maybe more – Audrey feels the rhythm of the engines move up a notch; she senses faster movement. She opens her eyes slowly and looks up. Her hair's whipped by a fresh breeze and she sees that the ship's already at sea. Slowly, she walks to the railing and stares down at the murky grey-brown water.

There are plenty more fish in the sea.

Audrey tries to see through the water; tries to seek out something – anything – of the sea life that must swim far beneath the shipping lane.

So where are they – these famous fish? If I had a penny... Audrey shakes her head to stop the thought. She's had it so many times she doesn't even need to complete the sentence: if she had a penny for every time some well-meaning person's given her arm a sympathetic rub and told her that Patrick 'clearly wasn't the right one for you, dear' and that there are 'plenty more fish in the sea', she'd have been able to afford proper nursing care for her dad, and given herself a bit of a break. Maybe then Patrick would have stayed. It's a circular thought; one that's now so familiar it's become part of the fabric of her being.

Audrey looks up. In the distance she can see land. It's still England, she presumes, and she feels a curious detachment from the leaving of her homeland for the first time in her life. *There's nothing there for you anymore,* she tells herself. *Nothing.* She's adjusted as much as anyone can to losing her mother at a young age; now her father – her rock – has gone, too: a stroke, a painfully slow recovery, and then another, massive stroke.

Audrey swallows a sob. Since the funeral, Audrey's been haunted by dreams – cruel dreams in which both her parents are still alive – and then she wakes, sweating, in the early hours, plagued by the terror that she's suddenly alone in the world. But, rather than lie in bed panicking, Audrey's learned to get up – at 3.30 a.m., at 4 a.m. – and to pace the worn-out carpet of her rented studio. She tries to outwalk the fear of being alone: no parents, no fiancé, no plans, no life.

Now, standing on the deck of *SS Oriana,* she takes a deep breath. Her life is changing. Changing for the better. She rummages in her coat pocket and pulls out an aerogramme, the thin paper covered in loops of blobby blue biro.

'*Dear Audrey,*' she reads, although she's read it so many times, spent so many nights thinking about it, she knows it off by heart. '*My parents told me about your father. I know we haven't been in touch for a while, but I wanted to reach out and let you know I'm thinking of you. I'm so sorry. I just can't imagine what you must be feeling.*

'*I hear you're a legal secretary in London. I always knew you'd get a good job: you were always top of the class. I'm based in Bombay now – yes, Bombay! I know! I work for a shipping firm and I like it here very much. But what I wanted to say is if you ever feel a*

19

need to get away; if things get too much for you in England, come to India. The P&O line sails to Bombay from Tilbury and Southampton. I'd love to see you – and sometimes a change of scene can really help.

'*Much love, Janet*'

Audrey looks up from the letter, a picture of Janet's face in her mind's eye. Dear, sweet Janet. *It's fate,* Audrey thinks. She has the sense that, somehow, from beyond the grave, her father has pulled strings to get this invitation to her because sailing to India is the right thing for her to do. Her parents met and married in Bombay and Audrey's grown up with stories about this exotic land of palm trees and British buses, of *chai wallahs* and Rupees – she's always felt a pull. So, yes, today Audrey is sailing away from England. It might just be for a holiday – but, equally, it might be forever.

November 2012

Truro, Cornwall

It started the day Mum crashed her car. It was a Saturday morning and the rain was coming down so hard it didn't look real; it was special-effect, Hollywood rain. Outside the supermarket, but still undercover, I stood for a moment and surveyed the scene: the clouds were so low they looked like they were trying to land on the trees. The tarmac was slick with rain, and cars circled like sharks, wipers swishing as their drivers hunted for somewhere to park – it was nearly lunchtime and, inside, the supermarket had been teeming.

Already I was tired, feeling a little faint; hoping with all my heart that the faintness could mean something other than my having skipped breakfast. With my mind on the tiny life that I wanted so badly to believe was growing in my belly, I took a deep breath and, shopping bags banging my shins, dashed in the direction of my car, fat drops of rain plastering my hair to my head. By the time I reached the row where my car was parked I was soaked. A car crawled at my heels, eager for my space, and I jerked my head towards where my car was, willing the driver to be patient.

I opened the boot and threw the shopping bags in, slammed down the lid, and slid into the driver's seat, trying to shrug off my wet coat as I went. I fastened my seatbelt, started the engine, shifted gear, then put the car into reverse. The phone rang and my body reacted viscerally: a quickened pulse, a catch of my breath. I'd waited all morning for a call from the doctor.

My eyes snapped to the dashboard display: not the doctor. John.

'Really?' I sighed. I almost didn't pick up, scared I'd miss the doctor's call if I did. But John must be calling for a reason; my twin never phoned just for a chat. With a sigh, I tapped the Bluetooth to connect and started to reverse the car out of the space.

'Lex? Is that you?' John's voice filled the car. 'I've been trying you for ages.'

'I'm out,' I said. 'What's up? Is Mum okay?'

'Well, that's why I'm calling.'

Out of the parking space, I eased the car through the congested car park and onto the road.

'What? What's happened? Is she okay?'

'She's had a car accident.'

'Oh my God! Is she all right?'

'I've just spent half the night and most of this morning at the hospital. But she's all right. Ish.'

'What do you mean "ish"? She's either okay or she's not okay!' My voice rose.

'She's fine. No broken bones. It happened late last night. I tried to call you but your phone was off. What were you *thinking* letting her drive back from Truro so late? You should have asked her to stay – or at least dropped her off yourself!'

Mum and I had gone to an exhibition of old photos of India the night before. I hadn't seen the attraction myself, but Mum had lived there for a bit when she was younger and still got a bit misty-eyed about it. She'd asked me to go with her, given it was within walking distance of my house. John had refused point-blank to drive her up from St Ives; I'd half-heartedly offered to come down and pick her up but she'd insisted on driving herself and, distracted by the thought I might finally be pregnant, I'd given in – way too easily, I realised now.

'I did ask her to stay! When I realised how late it was, I asked her to stay! She refused. You know what she's like.'

John tutted. 'At the very least, you could have kept your phone on.'

I started to argue then remembered that the battery had gone flat and I'd fallen into bed ex-hausted when I'd got back, forgetting to put it on

22

to charge. Mark and I didn't have a landline.

'Oh God,' I said. 'Flat battery.'

'Well, that's very convenient,' said John. 'So it was me they called in the middle of the night. They took her to hospital. Kept her in overnight.'

'You said she was okay! Why did she have to stay in?'

'She hit her head; strained her neck; got a few bruises. They just wanted to observe her.'

'Did you stay with her?'

'No. She didn't want me to. Anyway, they discharged her this morning on condition that someone stays with her tonight. She's been in shock and may have whiplash. They don't want her to be alone.'

'Okay.' I waited for John to tell me he was going to stay with Mum. It made sense given how much closer he lived.

'So, that's why I'm ringing,' he said. 'Can you come?'

'Me?'

'Yes, you, Lexi. I can't stay with her any more. I've done my bit. The twins are at a swimming gala this afternoon and Anastasia will kill me if I'm not there.' John pronounced his wife's name with a long 'a' and a soft 's', emphasis on the middle syllable: Anna-*star*-seeya. Never 'Anna-stay-zia'. It still blew my mind that my rather unemotional and unspontaneous brother had come back from a holiday to Estonia not just with a beautiful wife and two ready-made children, but with his new mother-in-law, too.

'But…' I thought about the call I was waiting for from the doctor. I had a mountain of marking to do and all I really wanted to do was curl up on the sofa and nurture the life I was convinced was growing inside me, not drive down to St Ives in the pouring rain and play nursemaid to Mum.

'Please can you do it, John?' A sob caught in my throat. 'Please?'

John sighed. 'I'm asking you nicely, Lexi. But it really is your turn.' There was a silence. 'Look. Isn't this why you moved to Cornwall? So you could help out a bit, too?' The implication was there: until Mark and I had moved to Truro six months ago, John had borne the brunt of looking after Mum while I 'ignored my responsibilities' – John's words – up in London.

Knowing he had the moral high ground, John continued almost seamlessly. 'How quickly can you be there? I dropped her off just now, so the sooner, the better, really.'

'You left her alone? Fantastic.' I slammed the brakes on as a car pulled out in front of me.

'I had to go, Lexi,' John said, his voice slow and deliberate. 'I have a family, remember? I've already spent half the night with her at the hospital. And then I scrapped our plans for the morning. I sorted out the insurance. I organised her car to be picked up, I took her home from the hospital and now I've made her comfortable. She's not very chatty – she's on the sofa, looking a bit dazed. I left her with a crossword. She'll be fine until you get there.'

Silence hung heavy on the line. A silence in which I realised that I had no choice. I indicated and turned into my road, the car's tyres swishing through puddles.

'Are you driving?' John asked.

'Yes.'

'Oh. You can call me back when you get in, if you want.'

'No it's okay. Hands-free.' I paused. 'Okay, I'll come down.'

'Thanks.'

I pulled into a rare parking space right outside my house, sending a silent thank you to the gods as I did so.

'By the way,' said John. 'While you're there, can you observe her a bit? I mean, more than usual? I thought she was acting a bit odd, like she wasn't all there. She was just sitting there this morning, staring into the distance. It's like she's in a different world. I'm worried the hospital might have missed something. You know – with the bang on the head.'

'Sure. But I can't go for an hour or two. I need to speak to Mark and he's not due back for a bit.'

'Okay,' said John. 'Thanks, Lexi. Bye.' The line disconnected and my phone buzzed at once: a missed call from the doctor's number, followed by the beep of a text message asking me to call. I dialled in.

'Mrs Scrivener,' the doctor said when my call was put through. I heard papers rustling; imagined her looking for my test results. 'How are you feeling?'

'Fine, thank you,' I said. 'A bit tired.'

'Okay. Well, the results of your blood test are back.' She paused.

'And?' I said.

'Your hCG level is very low.'

'What does that mean? Am I pregnant?'

25

The doctor sighed. 'Well. It's really too low for a healthy pregnancy.'

'What do you mean? I might not be? The test I did at home was positive. I did two really sensitive tests! Both were positive!'

The doctor's blood test was supposed to be a rubber-stamp of news I already knew. How could it not be certain when the over-the-counter test had been?

The doctor sighed. 'It's possible that something started and is now failing. A lot of pregnancies fail very early on, before many women even suspect they might have been pregnant. Sometimes, testing very early can backfire...' Her voice was gentle. She paused and I didn't say anything.

I'd been so certain. I'd even felt faintly sick this morning. I thought about the tiny babygros I'd just been stroking in the supermarket just now; the white Moses basket I'd picked out online. White because, although I hoped for a girl, I didn't want to know the sex.

'I'm very sorry,' said the doctor.

'I ... just ... I wasn't expecting this.'

'I know. It's very common, though. More common than you'd think.'

'Is there anything I can do? To increase my chances next month?'

'Just be kind to yourself. Eat well, exercise. Get enough sleep. Take it easy and try not to worry.'

Try not to worry! 'Okay,' I said. 'Thank you.'

I pressed disconnect and let my forehead slump onto the steering wheel as I wrapped my arms around myself. I'd been so sure this time! How could I not be pregnant? Even though it was very

26

early days, I'd felt all the classic symptoms. The last thing I felt like now was driving down to St Ives to look after Mum. As soon as I'd thought it, guilt washed over me. John had done his bit and I'd still expected him to do more. But that guilt was nothing compared to the guilt I felt about the pregnancy. Why couldn't I give Mark a baby? What was wrong with me?

Deep down, I knew the answer: at forty-two, time was hardly on my side.

January 1971

Bombay, India

When Audrey wakes up, the first thing she notices is the stillness. The small room in which she's lying in a tangle of sweaty sheets isn't by any means silent – the din of Bombay is alive right outside the window – but the absence of the rumble of the ship's engine rings louder than it ever did on the ship. A week after she's arrived, Audrey's still acclimatising to being on land. Truth be told, she's slightly terrified of Bombay and has hardly ventured out unless Janet's there, literally to hold her hand, to guide her across the streets, to fend off the beggars and street hawkers that swarm around them, and to flag down rickshaws the two of them use to get anywhere too far to walk.

But today Audrey has a plan. Today is the first day she's going to take on this strange city alone;

to conquer a corner of it. On the small table that counts both as Janet's dressing and dining table, there's a copy of Audrey's parents' wedding certificate, which names the small church in which they were married. Janet's asked around for her at work, and Audrey now has a hand-drawn map showing her how to find it. For the first time since she's arrived in Bombay she gets up with a purpose in her step. She washes quickly and dresses, makes some toast, and steps out into the chaotic street, where the warmth of the January air hits her.

Audrey stands still for a second, feasting her eyes on the dusty palm trees that look so exotic to her, their heavy fronds dancing like drunken spiders in the breeze. *This is home now,* she thinks, even while her senses revel in everything that's unfamiliar: the smells, the furious honks of car horns and the shouts in Hindi, Marathi, and a tangle of other languages – a gabble of sound she's unable to decipher.

Audrey's memorised where she needs to go – it's not far – and she walks as quickly as she can, trying, but not always managing, to stick to pavements while avoiding pedestrians, traffic, and holes in the road. Ahead of her there's a commotion and she sees the traffic's come to a halt as a couple of cows amble about in the middle of the road. Janet's explained to her that this is perfectly normal, and it's exactly how she imagined Bombay would be, but she still can't believe her eyes. Someone's trying to lead the cows off the street so traffic can pass, but no one except her seems to bat an eyelid at the strange juxtaposition of cows, cars, bicycles, and bullock carts that makes up this pungent traffic jam. As Audrey watches, one of the cows lifts its tail and deposits a steaming cowpat in the middle of the road. Audrey turns down a side street just before the smell hits her.

At first she doesn't see the church. It's not big, and it doesn't stand out from the dirty buildings surrounding it. She double-checks her map, then stands back on the other side of the street and scans the facades to be sure she's in the, right place before she goes in. Yes, it looks nothing like the churches she's used to back home, but there's a steeple peeping out from behind a dusty tree. It's definitely the church. Audrey takes a deep breath, closes her eyes, and imagines her mum arriving for her wedding, picking her way down the street in her finery knowing her groom was waiting inside the church. Holding the image in her head, she pushes open the heavy wooden door and enters.

It takes a minute for Audrey's eyes to become accustomed to the gloom of the interior after the bright sunshine outside so she stands still, taking in the sparse wooden pews – perhaps only seven or eight rows – and the small altar at the front. Dust motes dance in the sunbeams that penetrate the stained glass windows. When her eyes have adjusted, Audrey walks slowly down the aisle, picturing her mum doing the same on her wedding day, a small posy of garden flowers clasped at her chest. At the altar she stops, closes her eyes, and stands in silence, feeling the moment.

'Can I help you?' A woman's voice cuts in and Audrey's eyes snap open. She spins around.

29

'Oh, hello,' she says. 'I hope you don't mind …
I … I think my parents were married in this
church and I just wanted to come and see it.'

'Lovely! Welcome.' The woman waves her hand
at the church's interior. 'Please stay as long as
you like. When was the wedding? I could possibly
dig out the record for you.'

'Oh, could you? That would be fantastic! They
were married in 1940.'

The woman looks thoughtful. 'Yes. I'm sure we
have those records. I'd need a day or so to find it
but I could definitely get it out for you. Do you
know which month?'

'Yes – June.'

'Okay, well, if you'd like to pop by again tomorrow I'll have it ready for you.'

'Thank you so much! It's incredible. I'm here
now, where they got married. I can almost feel
them here.'

'Have they been back themselves?'

'No – they're – they passed away.'

'I'm so sorry to hear that. Well, you're most welcome. Whenever you like. Just come. The door's
always open.' The woman gives Audrey a kind
smile and turns back to the ante-room from
which she came. Audrey sits gingerly on the front
pew and closes her eyes. As the peace settles
around her, Audrey can feel the essence of her
dad. It's as if a part of him is here in this church.
She's grown up with stories of him coming here
every Sunday; of him wading through the monsoon rains or sheltering from the sun under an old
umbrella on his weekly walk to this very place.
This church has been a part of her childhood and

now here she is. A smile washes over Audrey's face, and, perhaps for the first time since her father died, her whole body relaxes.

March 1971

Bombay, India

Audrey and Janet walk arm in arm down Church-gate after dinner. In the distance, they spot a busy café, and the sound of its resident jazz trio floats to them on the night air. The street is alive with sounds, smells, and people. Audrey breathes deeply, inhaling the scent of this exotic city and revelling in the warmth that still comes as a surprise to her every time she steps outside. In England it'd still be coat weather. Janet looks long-ingly at the crowd of suited and booted punters that spills into the café's front terrace, even at this late hour. She lets go of Audrey's arm and dances a few jazz steps in the street, then turns back to face Audrey.

'They say this place makes the only genuine cappuccino in town. We've got to try one, Auds. What do you say?'

Audrey looks at her watch. She starts her new job in the morning but, equally, she doesn't want to disappoint her friend. Janet has been so kind.

'Umm,' she says.

'Come on! It's only a coffee. *Carpe diem!*' Janet grabs her arm again. 'I *still* can't believe you're here! And we'll be working together from tomorrow! Don't worry! I'll look after you!'

'Okay, just one, though. A quick one.'

Audrey allows herself to be drawn towards the café. She still remembers the mix of shock and delight on Janet's face when she'd turned up unannounced at the address given on the aerogramme. Aside from her visits to the church, her first few weeks in Bombay are a blur. Until very recently Audrey's still had moments when she wakes up in the morning not knowing where she is nor why; mornings when she wakes expecting to be in her bedroom in London, then realises with a jolt that she's on the other side of the world. She still has mornings when the grief is too raw, too painful, and she's capable of doing nothing but lying, numbly, under the sheet, where Janet finds her when she comes home from work. But, in the last few weeks, the fog has started to lift and Audrey's beginning to realise that she feels an affinity with the crazy, chaotic, noisy city that is Bombay.

The two women walk into the café and seat themselves at an empty table. Janet looks at Audrey and smiles.

'I know I've said it a million times, but I'm so glad you came,' she says. 'It's done you good. You look human now, compared to the ghost who turned up at my door.'

'Thank you,' says Audrey. 'You've been amazing. I don't know what I'd have done without you.' She smiles at her friend. 'But I do still feel a bit lost.'

'Of course you do.'

Audrey's eyes suddenly fill with tears. It happens at the most inopportune moments – times

32

when something reminds her of her dad: a smell, a sound, the shape of a person, a voice. She can neither predict nor control it.

'I'm so sorry,' she says, dabbing at her eyes with the fresh hankie she keeps on her at all times. It's one of her mother's: good cotton, with a bright flower embroidered in one corner and, as Audrey lifts it to her eyes, she sees her mum tying it around her little knee to stem the blood after she'd fallen in the park.

'Your dad was the best,' says Janet gently. Audrey nods. Although it's painful, especially to hear him mentioned in the past tense, she likes that Janet knew him; likes that she can talk to her about him.

'Ignore me,' Audrey says, flapping her hand at her face. 'I'm okay. He was the best, wasn't he? I'm not just being biased.'

'I was always jealous of you and your dad,' says Janet 'I know you missed your mum, but you seemed so happy. It's like he was the captain of the Bailey ship, always sailing forward with his eyes on the horizon. I loved that.'

'Me too. He was my rock.' Audrey smiles through her tears.

Janet reaches out and touches Audrey's hand. 'And that's how you must remember him.'

'I do. I will. Thank you.'

'My family was such a shambles.'

Audrey got her tears under control. 'Don't do them down,' she says. 'I used to love coming to yours. There was always that bowl of sweets on the hall table. I always nicked one. We never had sweets at home.'

Janet laughs. 'Oh yes. The Murray Mints! God,

I can still taste them!' They fall silent as the waitress brings over their coffees. Janet looks at the froth on the cups and raises her eyebrows at Audrey. 'Look at that: the real deal. Apparently they've got a huge machine just to froth the milk.'

'Cool beans,' says Audrey, and they each take a sip, delicately dabbing the foam from their top lips. 'Very nice. Good call.'

With the buzz and the music in the café, it was never going to be just one coffee. As Janet and Audrey stir their second round of cappuccinos an hour or so later, Janet looks around the terrace.

'So many men,' she breathes, hamming it up for Audrey. 'So little time.'

Audrey smiles. Janet's never hidden the fact that she's on a mission to find a wealthy husband; she has told Audrey about some of the scrapes into which she's got herself, the frogs that she's kissed as she searches for 'the one'.

'You should try to find someone, too,' Janet says. 'We're not spring chickens anymore. We'll be twenty-seven this year. The shelf is looming! Maybe a husband is just what you need.'

Audrey sighs. 'If it's meant to happen, it'll happen...'

'I don't know how you can be so relaxed about it!'

'Well ... you know I used to be engaged?' Audrey's tone is mild.

'What?' Janet presses her hand to her chest and gasps as if she's having a heart attack, her eyes wide. 'How did you keep this from me for so long?'

34

Audrey laughs. 'I guess we had more important things to talk about.'

'I guess – but *engaged?*' Her eyes slide to Audrey's left hand, then back to her face. 'Did you get married?' Audrey shakes her head.

'What happened?'

'He wasn't the right man for me.'

'Um, would you care to elaborate on that?'

'It's quite sad, actually. I thought he was lovely. A real catch. He was Irish. Patrick. Loved the ground I walked on. Or so I thought.'

'I feel a "but" coming on.'

'Well, it was quite simple in the end: when Dad had his first stroke and it became apparent that I'd need to move back home to take care of him, he dumped me.'

'What?'

'I suggested we move the wedding back a bit but he kept pushing for a date and I couldn't commit. I didn't know how long I was going to be needed at home – so he called the whole thing off.'

'Couldn't you have been married but live at home with your dad? Loads of people do that to start with. Surely?'

'You would have thought so, wouldn't you, but apparently not. "No wife of mine's living with her father," he said. I do understand.'

'I can imagine your dad being quite foreboding towards his daughter's fiancé.'

'He never liked Patrick. Didn't think he was good enough for me.'

'Find me a man who doesn't think that about his only daughter and I'll show you a liar.'

'I guess. But it seems he was right. Better to

35

find out before it's too late.' Audrey sighs and looks about the terrace, too. 'So, anyone you've got your eye on here tonight?'

'Funny you should mention it,' says Janet, 'but yes. Grey suit at three o'clock.' Audrey follows her friend's eyes and sees a tall man, classically attractive. He's wearing a slick suit with a white tie, and his dark hair is greased back from a prominent forehead.

'Not bad,' she nods. 'Looks the part.' Audrey knows the rules. Janet's marriage will not be about love, but about money. Janet's seen the society ladies with their jewels and their dresses being escorted by men in black tie, she's seen the cars with turbaned drivers waiting outside, and she's decided that's what she wants.

They watch the man in the grey suit for a minute or two. Audrey has to give it to her friend: he's very handsome but there's a sense of something else that almost makes her shiver and she can't put her finger on what it is. As she watches, the man turns around; Audrey doesn't look away in time and he stares back, openly assessing her.

Audrey drops her eyes to the table. It's power, she realises. Power and confidence.

'What do you think?' Janet asks.

Audrey says nothing. The man in the grey suit is still watching them. With his eyes still on Audrey, he gets up and makes his way over. Janet pats her hair and rolls her lips together to spread her lipstick.

'Good evening, ladies.' Grey Suit towers above their table. Audrey can feel the heat of him, and something tugs in her belly.

He has sharp cheekbones and his small eyes are not only bright, they're looking Audrey up and down in a way that makes her feel like she's something he'd like to devour. She's wearing a one-shouldered shift dress in vibrant pink. It's a dress she made herself and she knows it shows off the delicate bones of her clavicle while the colour sets off her auburn hair, but now she feels unsure. Why is he staring? Has her mascara smudged from crying? Is the dress so obviously home-made? Is the colour too loud – or is he really leering quite so openly?

'Ralph Templeton,' he says, placing a business card on the table in front of Audrey. He doesn't acknowledge Janet simpering across the table. 'Perhaps you'd allow me to take you out to dinner one evening?'

'Oh, I...'

The man looks at her while he waits for her to finish her sentence. He's older – distinguished – and, under his gaze, Audrey feels girlish and lacking in substance. There's no doubt about what it is he wants from her. She blushes and looks down, her sentence left hanging.

'May I take your number?' The man produces another business card and a pen. The cold weight of the pen tells Audrey it's expensive. She balances it in her hand for a second, toying with the idea of writing the wrong number. But there's something in Ralph Templeton's demeanour that suggests that refusal is not an option and Audrey finds that confidence compelling. She doesn't dare make eye contact with Janet as she writes her new office number on the back of the business card.

37

'Thank you. I'll have my assistant call you,' says Ralph Templeton, picking up the card and slipping the pen back into his breast pocket. Then he reaches out his hand and touches Audrey's hair.

'Beautiful,' he says. He runs a finger through a curl, then gently draws it down her cheek. He looks one more time at Audrey and melts back into the crowd. Janet's hand is clamped over her mouth.

'Oh my word! Talk about reeling them in! I need lessons from you!'

Audrey barely hears. She can just about make out the back of Ralph Templeton's head as he rejoins his table, and she can't tear her eyes away. Her cheek tingles where he's touched it and her body is electrified. The physical pull of Audrey's feeling towards Ralph Templeton takes her by surprise. She, stares at the business card as if to memorise every tiny detail.

November 2012

Truro

I was on the sofa with a cup of tea and a pile of marking when I heard Mark's key in the lock. Within seconds, he appeared in the living room doorway, filling it completely with the bulk of his frame. I looked up at him feeling, as always, a surge of love for my husband and noting at the same time the flicker of hope in his eyes.

I dropped my gaze back to the marking, willing him to know I wasn't pregnant without me having to spell it out. Mark crossed the stripped floor-boards in three strides and bent down to drop a kiss on my hair, his fingers stroking my cheek as he did so. He dropped onto the sofa next to me. His hand found mine and he interlaced our fingers.

'Hi darling,' he said, giving my hand a squeeze. 'How was your morning?'

I squeezed back.

'Did you hear from the doctor?' Mark asked, his face alive with expectation.

I turned to look at him, pressing my lips together, and nodded slowly, unable to articulate the words. Mark pulled me against his chest with his free arm. I felt my eyes well up; a prickling at the back of my nose. I squeezed my eyes shut and tears spilled onto Mark's sweater.

'It's okay,' he said, rubbing my back. 'It's okay.'

I pulled away and looked stared at his face in despair. 'But it's not okay! How is it okay? How can it possibly be okay? I was so sure this time! I'm getting older. It's not going to happen!'

'Lex. Lex, Lex, Lex. We've been through this. Yes, a baby would be nice, but we have each other. It's enough. It's *you* I married, not a child who doesn't yet exist. It's *you* I want.' His voice cracked. 'I wish you would believe me.'

I closed my eyes. 'I know you mean it now. But what happens in five years? What if you change your mind? You can...' I didn't say it. I'd said it before; Mark could leave me and have a baby with someone younger. It was my deepest fear; that I wouldn't be able to give him what he

39

wanted and he'd leave.

'That's not going to happen. You've got to stop beating yourself up about this, Lex. Please.'

I knew he was right and I did believe him. It was my guilt that kept bringing me back to this place: guilt that I'd wasted my child-bearing years in a dead-end marriage with a bully of a husband; guilt that I'd been too scared to leave. If I'd walked away five years sooner – if I'd met Mark five years earlier – maybe we'd have a nursery upstairs; the sound of tiny feet pattering overhead. It was a train of thought that Mark consistently refused to entertain. 'Everything happens for a reason,' he'd say. 'Maybe I'd have been a bastard to you five years ago. You can't live life thinking "if only".'

I sat back up and wiped my eyes with the back of my hand. The baby conversation – the same hopeless one we had every month – was going nowhere. 'Mum had a car accident last night,' I said. 'John called to tell me. It's not been a good day.'

'Whoah, sweetheart. What happened? Is she okay?'

'I think so. Bumped and bruised but nothing broken. She's shocked and might have whiplash but they've discharged her on condition someone stays with her overnight. John's asked me to go.'

'Okay.'

I sighed. 'It's just ... with all this...' I flicked a hand over my abdomen, 'I just...' My face crumpled again.

'I know, sweetheart. I know. But it's your mum, and she needs you.'

'I wish John could do it.'

'Have you told him about ... you know? Does

he know we're trying?'

I shook my head.

'Well, then you can't expect him to be sympathetic, hon.'

'I know, but...'

Mark looked at the floor. I knew him well enough to know he was trying to compose a sentence that I wouldn't necessarily like in terms that he hoped I might accept.

'He can't always be there for your mum, Lex. He's got a family,' Mark said carefully. He held up his hand, anticipating my argument. 'Yes, I know the twins aren't his. But Lexi, you've got to get over this. He's married their mother and adopted them. They are his responsibility now.' Mark paused to check he still had my attention. 'And we both know it's the *prima donna* who wears the trousers in that marriage.' He smiled at me. 'When she says *"jeté"*, he *jetés* over the bloody moon and back!' I couldn't help but crack a smile at the image of my po-faced brother flying over the moon in a ballet tutu. 'His life is way more complicated than ours, sweetheart. He's being torn in so many directions.'

I sighed and picked imaginary fluff off the arm of the sofa.

'And this *is* why we live here,' Mark continued. 'So you can help out. Can you imagine if you had to come down from London? It's so much easier now.' He paused and I didn't say anything. 'Shall I help you pack?'

'It's okay. Thanks. I've already put some stuff in a bag.'

'Good. Anyway – I have some good news today.'

41

'Really? What?'

'Fanfare please!' Mark pretended to play a trumpet. 'I should have a payment coming in this week!'

'Really? A big one?'

He nodded. 'Yep. It won't do anything daft like buy a car, but it should cover our outgoings for a couple of months. Give us a bit of a breather.'

Even as he said the words, I felt the tension I'd been carrying since we'd realised that it wasn't going to be as easy as we'd hoped for Mark to find a job in Truro release a notch. For the past few months, we'd been living hand-to-mouth on my teacher's salary, which barely covered the mortgage payments, plus the few odd jobs that Mark could do.

'That's fantastic.'

Mark smiled. 'And there's more. I've got a lead on a job that looks promising.'

'Wow! It'd be so good to have you back on a regular salary.'

'Tell me about it.' Mark leaned over and kissed me. 'Now. What else can I fix for you today, madam? Burst water pipe? Faulty boiler?'

I nodded my head towards the marking. 'Do you feel like marking eighty Year 6 assessments while I'm away?'

'I can't help you with that, I'm afraid: you're the smarty pants. Why don't you take them to your mum's? You're bound to get a chance to do it there.' He paused. 'But, please, darling, please don't make her feel bad about you going down.' He lifted my chin with his finger. 'I know what a little martyr you can be.'

March 1971

Bombay, India

Audrey's new job is in the office of the shipping firm where Janet works. She's far too busy on the first day, meeting the other staff and learning the ropes, to think about Ralph Templeton. But, as she starts to settle in over the next few days – as she answers the phone, types the invoices, and franks the mail – she finds her thoughts returning to the handsome stranger who'd taken her number, and she's surprised to realise that she's hoping he'll telephone.

'How about we go back to that jazz café tomorrow after work?' she says to Janet as they chat over their hot tiffins in the tea room almost a full week after their night out. She traces her finger over the Formica countertop that's stained with rings from mugs of tea. The smell of old cigarette smoke hangs in the air and a ceiling fan circles lazily overhead.

'Sounds like a plan,' says Janet. 'Any particular reason why?' She raises an eyebrow at Audrey.

Audrey focuses on her *dal bhat,* the simple dish of spiced lentils and rice that she's come to love. 'I thought the cappuccinos were amazing.'

'Just the cappuccinos?'

'Yes, just the cappuccinos.'

'Because I suspect there's another reason you

want to go back. A tall, handsome reason in a grey suit, perchance?'

Audrey feels heat rush to her cheeks. She licks her spoon and, once she decides to talk, finds that the words spill out of her. 'Okay. Maybe you're right. You have to admit, there was something about him. But it's not that I want to see him. I just want to know why he hasn't called. I mean, why make the effort to come over and give me his card and get my number if he's not going to call?'

'Oooh!' teases Janet. 'I do believe the lady's got her knickers in a twist!'

'I have not!' Audrey flicks a piece of *chapatti* at Janet. 'It's just – why did he ask if he's not going to call? Do you think I gave him the wrong number by accident? I've gone over it a hundred times.'

'No. I saw what you wrote. It was right.'

'Well, what then? Do you think it was a dare? Or did I say something wrong?'

'No, no. It's not you,' says Janet. 'He's just a chancer. Probably got a better offer. Sorry. Ignore it. Move on.'

'Whatever you do, don't tell me there are plenty more fish in the sea!'

'Well, there are. It's just that maybe we're not fishing hard enough.'

'I'm not fishing at all. I'm hoping the right fish will offer itself up on a plate for me when the time's right. With chips and dill mayonnaise!'

'So romantic! But, Auds, we're twenty-seven. I hate to tell you, but the fish are offering themselves to girls a lot younger than us. To some men, an unmarried twenty-seven-year-old is a scary proposition. We're going to be thirty soon. Thirty! They imagine all we want to do is tie them down and get ourselves pregnant.'

'Seriously?'

''Fraid so. I've heard it from guys. Sometimes I pretend to be twenty-three because, as soon as they find out how old I am, they run a mile. I worry about it. I worry that I'll never meet the right one. That I'll be a mad old spinster with only cats for company.'

Audrey skims off the fine skin that's formed on her *chai*, then breathes in its comforting scent of cardamom and cloves. 'There's nothing wrong with that from where I'm sitting. It beats sitting around waiting for the phone to ring.'

Ralph Templeton eventually calls. But not on the phone. When Audrey and Janet step out of the office on Friday evening a week later, there's a grey Daimler parked outside, a crowd of beggars teeming around it, pawing at its sleek paintwork and tapping at its windows. As Audrey approaches, the back door of the car opens and Ralph Templeton climbs out, a bouquet of brightly coloured flowers in his hand. His suit is immaculate and there's something commanding about him as he straightens up to his full height. Filthy street children scatter out of his way.

'Miss Bailey,' he says, holding out the flowers. 'I wondered if you'd do me the honour of accompanying me to dinner tonight?'

It takes Audrey a second or two to understand that Ralph Templeton is here in person, to ask her out to dinner.

'Tonight?' she says. She looks down at her clothing, more office than night out. 'It's just I... I'm not...'

'You look beautiful,' says Ralph. 'But if it makes you feel better, I took the liberty of choosing a few dresses. They're in the car. You could pick one and change at the hotel.' He lets this sink in. 'I have a dinner reservation at the Taj.'

Audrey looks at Janet. Janet widens her eyes. 'Fish,' she mouths, and Audrey turns back to Ralph, bobbing her head as she replies, 'Yes please. I'd be delighted to join you. Thank you.'

Ralph opens the car door wide once more. 'After you,' he says.

April 1971

Bombay, India

On the back seat of his Daimler, Ralph Templeton puts his arm around Audrey and pulls her close to him. She breathes in the now-familiar scent of his cologne and rests her head against his chest. He strokes her hair almost absently, letting it twine itself around his fingers, and Audrey sighs, her mind full of images of this man – this stranger – who's shot into her life like a bolt of lightning. Was their first date really just three weeks ago?

Audrey feels her cheeks flush as she remembers the way Ralph had devoured her with his eyes over dinner that evening; the way his gaze had made her feel so gauche despite the expensive dress she'd picked. Maybe she is a little younger, less sophisticated, than the women Ralph's used to, but he seems charmed by that. She bites her lip: thinking back, she can't believe she'd actually given him a real phone number in the café instead of transposing a couple of digits like she usually did when men pushed for her number; she can't believe she'd agreed to go out to dinner that night he'd turned up at her office. How life turns in an instant, she thinks.

After their first date, Ralph had bundled her onto the back seat of his Daimler and nuzzled her face until his lips found hers, then he'd kissed her all the way back to her tiny studio flat. Despite his protests, she'd refused to let him in. It'd been the right strategy, Audrey reflects now, because he hasn't been able to get enough of her since, pursuing her with a fervour that almost verges on the indecent.

In the car now, Ralph's hand moves from Audrey's hair to her cheek. Applying a little pressure, he turns her face to his, stares into her eyes as if he's searching her soul, then places his lips gently on hers, the softest of kisses that melts her. When he finally pulls away, she's breathless.

'Come home with me tonight, Red,' he says.

Audrey notices, all of a sudden, that the car's not on the usual route to her flat and a ripple of fear runs through her. She's in the back of a car with a man she's known less than four weeks, in a part of Bombay with which she's unfamiliar. No one in the world bar Ralph Templeton and his chauffeur knows where she is.

'Where are we?' she asks, sitting up straight in her seat and trying to get her bearings.

Ralph takes her hand. 'On the way to Juhu. I asked the driver to ... please, Red. Come home with me.'

Audrey buys time by fiddling in her handbag. Does she have reason to be afraid?

'Look at me,' Ralph commands. He takes her chin into his hand, turns her face to his and stares into her eyes. Audrey holds his gaze, mesmerised by the apparent depth of her suitor's feeling. 'Nothing will happen, not if you don't want it to,' Ralph says. 'This is not about sex. But please come home with me. I just want to have you there with me. To hold you.' His voice breaks. 'Red, I need you.'

He lets go of her face and turns away, his hand brushing at his eye and the very core of Audrey melts. There's something about this man that makes her feel she'd run to the end of the earth if he asked her to. She leans across and places her lips on Ralph's ear.

'Okay,' she whispers.

November 2012

St Ives, Cornwall

To say that John and I were surprised when Mum left London for Cornwall would be one thing; what was even more of a surprise was the house that she'd bought on the outskirts of St Ives. The large, stucco-fronted villa we'd grown up in in Barnes had been built in 1845. After selling it four years ago when our father died – far too quickly because she'd under-priced it, if you listened to my brother – Mum had eschewed the type of picturesque stone cottage we'd all envisioned she'd go for and bought a completely unremarkable box of a home that dated back to the seventies.

Moving with a speed and certainty that had taken us by surprise, Mum had allowed us each to choose any furniture we wanted from the Barnes house, then made the move to St Ives. 'It's got a subtropical microclimate,' she'd told anyone who asked her why she was moving there. 'Why wouldn't you?' There was also, I suppose, the fact that John lived in nearby Penzance, though I'd long suspected that was more coincidence than intent.

I took in Mum's house now as I parked behind her car in the driveway, gathered my things, and made my way down the steep slope to the front door. It was a low building, painted white, with double glazed windows and a neat front garden that Mum had lined with geraniums in pots. They added a certain something in summer, but not quite enough.

The rain had cleared but I still heard the irregular plop of drops falling off the trees and bushes. The garden was saturated. I knocked on the front door: two smart raps of a silver-toned knocker that made a hollow sound on the thin door. While I waited, ears straining for the sound of footsteps, I bent down and examined the front step. I'd noticed a while back that a brick had come loose and was wobbly to stand on. I'd asked John to cement it back down. He hadn't: the step still wobbled. I straightened up again, put my finger on the doorbell and pressed. Big Ben rang out electronically and I cringed inside, remembering both the substantial door and the majestic ring of the bell on the house in Barnes. After waiting another moment, I realised that Mum might not even be able to make it to the door. Kicking myself for being so stupid, I walked around the side of the house for the spare key, my shoes squelching on the wet gravel path.

I paused for a moment on the threshold of the garden. It was around the back that Mum's house came into its own: by itself, the small garden was unremarkable – it was only once I'd seen the view that I understood why Mum had fallen in love with the house. I drank in the view now: the sandy reach of Carbis Bay lay below and, curving into the distance, I could see Lelant and subsequent coves: the scalloped edge of England. Even on a dismal November day it was something really special. Today the sea looked grey-green but, in summer, it was an endless sweep of azure blue that was more Mediterranean than Atlantic. The previous owner of the house had installed decking that wrapped around the sea-facing aspects. Mum had bought some nice outdoor furniture and she claimed to spend part of every day out there, no matter what the weather. My city-dwelling mum, it turned out, loved the sea.

I scrabbled under another plant pot for the spare key, then let myself in the front door, dropping my bags and slipping off my wet shoes in the hall before padding quietly into the living room. Mum was on the sofa, propped up on a pile of cushions, her laptop open on her lap. She looked fragile, her face as pale as the brace that circled her neck, but, aside from that, I could see no physical evidence of an injury; no bruising, no extra bandages. I walked across the room to her and looked down at her. I couldn't tell if she was asleep or awake.

'Mum?' I asked softly.

She slowly she lifted her eyes to meet mine. 'Alexandra. Hello! How lovely to see you. You really didn't need to come.' She tapped the mousepad a couple of times, then closed the lid of the laptop.

I perched on the edge of the sofa and looked at her. 'Of course I was going to come. John said someone had to stay with you and it was my turn. How are you feeling?'

Mum touched the neck brace. 'I'm fine.' I raised my eyebrows at her. 'Really, I am. This is just a precaution. In fact, I've got to go back tomorrow and have it taken off. They're just playing it safe.'

She gave me a bright smile. 'It looks worse than it is. I promise you I'm absolutely fine or they wouldn't have let me out.'

'I'll take you in tomorrow.'

Mum nodded. 'Thank you.'

'You're welcome. You look a bit pale, but I suppose that's the shock. Are you in pain?'

'No.'

'Mum. Don't lie.'

She sighed. 'Okay, well, maybe just a little. It aches a bit, that's all. I feel as if I've been knocked about a bit in a road accident.' She laughed.

'Mother! This is a serious thing. At your age! You're so lucky nothing was broken. What happened?' I tutted. 'I should never have let you drive back last night. Were you tired? You didn't seem tired.'

Mum didn't reply. She was staring at the wall, then she turned to look at me.

'Was I a good mother?' she asked. 'To you and John?'

I leaned back on the sofa. 'Whoah! Where did that come from?'

'I just wondered,' Mum's hands fretted at the fringe of the sofa blanket. 'Seeing those pictures last night ... it brought it all back. My time in India ... when you were babies ... coming back to London.' Her voice trailed off. 'Did you feel loved as you were growing up?'

I hesitated – a whisper of a moment – but Mum appeared not to notice. 'Yes, of course,' I said. 'We never wanted for anything.'

And it was true – to an extent. Mum had done everything by the book when John and I were growing up. It was as if she'd read a manual on how to be the perfect mother. She cooked and cleaned and picked us up from school; she sewed, helped us with our homework, and took us to the park – but I'd always felt as if she'd wrapped her heart in cling film. I'd always felt it was as if, when I hugged her, I wasn't ever touching the real her; as if there was always something of herself that she held back.

'But...' Mum looked at me so intently I felt she could see what I was thinking.

'But what? What's all this about?' I asked. 'Are you worried we've turned out badly?' I laughed.

'No. No, it's nothing. Forget I spoke.' Mum shook her head and gazed off into the middle distance.

I stared at the carpet. Mum and I never had conversations like this. 'So what happened?' I said finally. 'The accident? Was it because you were tired?'

She looked at me as if only just realising I was in the room. 'Oh! No. No, I was fine... I stopped at a roundabout and some clown drove into the back of me. It wasn't my fault.'

'Is that what the police said?'

Again Mum didn't reply. She was staring at her hands, examining her fingers.

'So – did you stop suddenly or something? At the roundabout?'

'What?' said Mum.

'Did you stop suddenly?'

'Oh, yes. Yes. I was approaching the big roundabout near home. You know the one? I was about to enter it and then I don't know what happened. Someone came flying around. I don't know where he came from. I suddenly saw him. I braked but the guy behind didn't stop in time.'

'So he rear-ended you?'

'Yep.'

I imagined Mum's head whipping forward and back. 'Okay, well. If he rear-ended you, it's his fault.'

'Yes, that's what the police said.'

'Good. And it's good they put you in the brace. At least for tonight. I'm glad you're okay.' I stood up and stretched, bending my neck left and right. The traffic down to St Ives had been stop-start the whole way and my shoulders ached. 'Can I get you anything? Have you eaten? I'm going to make myself a cup of tea and, if you don't mind, I've brought some marking to do. If I don't do it tonight, I'll be in trouble.'

There was a silence. I looked at Mum – she was staring off into the distance again. I felt for my phone, thinking I must text John about this. He was right. Mum was clearly not herself. Whether or not this was related to the accident I had no idea. I was ashamed to realise I hadn't been down to see her for over two months.

'Mum? Would you like anything? Some tea?'

Mum gave herself a little shake. 'Yes, thank you. A cup of tea would be lovely.'

'And what about food? Shall I get some stuff in for you? Easy things for your dinners?'

'Oh, no need for that, dear! I'll be right as rain in a day or two.'

'But – I don't know. Should you be driving? Carrying heavy bags? Wouldn't it be easier if I nipped out and got you some bits that you could

54

just bung in the microwave for this week?'

'I'm not helpless.'

'No, I know. But can you please just admit it would be easier if I got you some ready meals? You can get good ones these days. Fresh. Almost like home cooking.'

Mum bowed her head. 'Thank you.'

'Okay. So what do you like? Curries? Indian? Thai? "Chicken or beef"?' I smiled like cabin crew.

'A shepherd's pie would be nice, maybe. And, yes, why not a curry or two? Spicy, thank you, dear.'

'Do you need anything else while I'm there?'

Mum shook her head.

'How about milk? You've got eggs. You could make an omelette one night?'

'Oh yes. Maybe some milk. To see me through. Thank you. And I think I'm low on cheese.'

I smiled. 'Back in a bit.'

'Thanks, dear.'

As I headed to the front door, I looked back at Mum and immediately wished I hadn't: lying on the sofa in her neck brace she looked small, and so very frail.

Back in the car I texted John. *'You're right. She's not herself. V vague. Gazing into distance.'*

He texted back at once. *'Told you.'*

'But is this the accident? Or was she like this anyway? I don't remember.' I put the blushing Emoji.

'Bit of both. She's getting old.'

'70 next year.'

'I know.'

July 1971

Bombay, India

'You've changed.' Janet taps her teaspoon on the saucer of her coffee cup and looks thoughtfully at Audrey across the table. They're once again in the jazz café – it's become their regular post-supper haunt, with Janet making no secret of the fact she hopes that she, too, will meet her own rich lover among the clientele.

'In a good way, I hope!' Audrey laughs, but even she hears the question in her voice. She lifts her cup to her lips and takes a tiny sip.

Janet pouts thoughtfully. 'You're more confident.'

'That's a good thing, isn't it?'

'Yes. Yes, of course. And you look amazing. You're glowing.'

It's the sex, Audrey thinks. She looks at her coffee. 'Well, I do feel better than I have in months. Years! Oh Janet, he's the best thing ever to have happened to me. Honestly, I always used to think how could so many terrible things happen to me – surely it was my turn to have some good luck – and along came Ralph!'

'I'm so glad you're happy,' Janet says, but Audrey sees a hardness in her friend's eyes. She looks at her closely; it's not jealousy – it's something else.

'Thank you,' she says. 'He's just so...' Audrey

56

waves her hand in the air, struggling to articulate how she feels about Ralph – how different he is; how her love for him consumes her. 'I don't know: perfect?'

Janet touches Audrey's hand. 'Just be careful. All right?'

'What do you mean "careful"? I'm on the Pill.'

Janet tuts. 'Not that kind of careful. Well – that kind of careful too. Just don't lose yourself in all this.' She stops talking but Audrey doesn't reply. 'It's just – there's something about him. I don't know.'

'Something about him? Looks, personality, charm – where do I start?' Audrey tinkles a laugh.

'Not like that. I mean, he's too good to be true. Men like him just don't exist. Trust me, I've a lot of experience.' Janet gives a rueful laugh.

'But he does exist, and he really is that good. I've been to his house. Many times. What you see is what you get with Ralph.' Audrey looks around the café, keen to change the subject now it's taken this turn. 'Look! Did you see that chap over there? What a dreamboat...'

Janet gives a cursory glance then turns back to Audrey. 'Men like Ralph Templeton ... they usually have something to hide,' she says. 'Really, Auds. I'm sure there's something he's not telling you.'

Audrey sucks her teeth and stares at her friend. The noise of the café behind her – the sounds of conversation, laughter and jazz – falls away as she realises that she's at a crossroads in her life; that this conversation is somehow seminal – something she'll look back on in years to come. She badly wants her friend's approval but she knows, too, that her relationship with Ralph is bigger than her friendship with Janet will ever be, and that, should she be forced to choose, her lover will be the one who'll win.

Audrey sighs. How can she explain to Janet what it is that Ralph Templeton does for her? How could she explain what it feels like to have no one in the world who loves her? How she misses having her father there to keep everything under control, and to offer advice and comfort? Would Janet understand if she told her how her insides know an emptiness that goes beyond life itself? Ralph Templeton is her antidote; he fills her veins with hot, red blood; he brings life back to her. Janet herself has noticed how Audrey's changed – blossomed – since she got together with him. And on top of that, he's so knowing, so worldly wise, so confident – he fills a little of the gap that yawns inside her. Just thinking about Ralph makes her shiver with anticipation of when she'll next see him.

'He takes such good care of me,' she says.

'That's nice,' Janet's voice is sarcastic. 'But don't you find him controlling? The way he calls you "Red"?' She shudders and Audrey recoils: her dad had called her mum 'Mousie' and she'd always thought it was sweet. But Janet is on a roll. 'The way you always do what he wants? You never get to choose where you go or what you do. The way he drove you to his house without asking you till you were right outside? Even the way he came over demanding your number that day. It's like he won't take no for an answer.'

'I quite like that,' Audrey says.

'You want to be careful, though.' Janet points her finger at Audrey. 'One day controlling, the next you're not allowed out. It's almost like he sees you as a possession.' She shakes her head. 'The way he sends his car to pick you up all the time. My word!'

Audrey closes her eyes and recalls the cool, leather interior of the Daimler. It's nice that Ralph sends the car for her. Especially when the rain's throwing it down as it has been this month. Really, she has no problem with that.

15 July 1971

Bombay, India

Audrey's grateful that the driver Ralph's sent to pick her up for her birthday dinner isn't one of the chatty ones. The drive to the Taj Mahal Palace is a long one and she turns her head and stares out of the window, watching as the car passes through the teeming street life of Bombay.

She watches beggars, cripples, cyclists, cars driving four abreast on what should be a three-lane road; sees pedestrians throwing themselves into the teeming traffic with little regard for life or limb. Whenever the car stops – which it does frequently given the road is permanently choked with traffic – filthy children swarm the windows, their hands tapping at the glass, thumbs rubbing against fingers as they beg for a coin, a bite to eat, something, anything. It's rained heavily and the car cleaves through standing water; the beggars are up to their ankles in it, but Audrey shakes her head at them and looks away, as she's learned to do. It's not that she doesn't see the scrum of life outside the car; it's not that she doesn't feel sorry for the beggars – rather that she accepts it, understands that it's part and parcel of life here. England seems so very distant these days. She can barely remember what life was like there. Cold. Ordered. Lots of rules and a place for everything.

She can barely remember life before Ralph, either. Audrey sits back in her seat and smiles to herself as she thinks about the nights she's started spending in his sprawling villa on Juhu Beach – nights in which she's slept with his arms wrapped tightly around her, her heart brimming with a love like she's never known as the rain drums down on the roof. It's as if heaven has sent the perfect man for her and, again, she wonders if her dad somehow had a hand in it.

'I'm so glad you found me,' she tells Ralph in bed as she strokes her fingers across his chest and drops butterfly kisses on his arm. 'That day – when you saw me. You came over to Janet and me so decisively. It was as if you knew what you wanted.' She shivers at the memory. 'Did you just "know"?'

'Yes,' Ralph says. 'I watched you for a while. I watched you talking to your friend and I saw something in you that made me want to protect you forever.'

Audrey wonders where it's all heading. She's allowed herself to dream about a future with Ralph; about carving a permanent life in Bombay, and she's surprised to find she's happy at the thought of it. Here, in India, there's a contentment in her soul that she doesn't remember feeling in England. Part of it, she's sure, comes from her regular trips to the church, where she sits silently in a pew and holds silent conversations with her father.

The driver pulls into the hotel's driveway and the car comes to a standstill adjacent to the front steps. Audrey pulls some notes from her purse and offers them a tip. The driver steeples his hands to his chest, nodding his thanks to her, and the hotel's doorman opens the car door and wafts Audrey up the steps to the Taj's impressive interior.

'I've something to tell you.' Ralph reaches across the table and takes Audrey's hand in his.

'Yes?' She looks expectantly at him. The waiter's taken their orders and they're sitting with their drinks. Ralph looks down at Audrey's hand and strokes it. Then he looks up at her with such a depth of emotion behind his eyes that she has to swallow.

'Red. I care about you very much. I need you. I need you in my life.' He pauses. 'But there's something I have to tell you.'

Audrey's blood runs cold. If her hand wasn't clasped in Ralph's she'd snatch it back. Janet's words come back to her: *he's married*, she thinks, and tears prick behind her eyes. With her free hand, she dabs at her eyelashes, her lips trembling as she tries not to cry. What a chump she's been to think a man like him would be seriously interested in the likes of her.

'No, don't. Don't tell me,' she whispers. 'I don't want to know.'

'Please. I have to tell you.'

Is that the beginning of a smile on Ralph's lips? Audrey stares at the tablecloth and waits. Waits to hear what a fool she's been. Waits to hear about the delicate wife he doesn't love but can't leave; waits to have her birthday dinner ruined.

'You don't know who I am, do you?' Ralph asks. He doesn't wait for a reply. 'You didn't see the story in the papers?'

Audrey shakes her head.

'I used to be married,' says Ralph. *Used to!* Audrey looks up, barely daring to meet his eyes but he carries on before she can say anything. She watches his lips – those lips she loves to kiss – as he speaks. 'Alice – my wife – died.'

Audrey's gasp is too loud. There's a stir in the restaurant as other diners look over. 'I'm so sorry!'

Ralph, oblivious to the attention, looks at the tablecloth for a minute, takes a deep breath; continues. 'She … she was swept out to sea. They think it was a suicide. It looked like suicide. She couldn't swim. She walked into the sea deliberately. She left her clothes on the shore – as a clue, perhaps, because … why else would she take them off if she was planning…' His voice falters.

'I'm so, so sorry.'

Ralph lowers his eyes and nods his acceptance of her sympathy. He sits back and breathes deeply and Audrey has the sense that the world is tilting. 'They think she had postnatal depression,' Ralph says. 'We had children, Audrey. Twins. John and Alexandra. They were three months old at the time.' Audrey covers her mouth with her hand.

'No, no! Those poor babies.' She shakes her head vigorously, feeling pain for the babies she doesn't know. And then a thought strikes her: 'But where do they live, the twins? When I stay over at your house, where are they?'

'They live with me in the house. But I'm often out so they have an *ayah* – a nanny. Their nursery is close to the *ayah's* room. You won't have heard anything from upstairs.'

'I had no idea,' Audrey breathes, suddenly re-imagining Ralph's huge house as a family home. 'But I suppose it makes sense. Why have such a large house just for you?'

Ralph nods. 'Indeed. But there's a reason for me telling you all this. Look, Red. I'm a single father to nine-month-old twins and, hand on heart...' As he says this, he presses his free hand to his chest and looks deeply into Audrey's eyes, 'I'm struggling. They need a mother. Normally I wouldn't move this fast but ... well, I think you know me quite well now, and ... what I wanted to ask you tonight was: will you marry me?'

Audrey lets out an audible squeal. In the last thirty seconds she's gone from thinking she's lost the man she loves to a proposal of marriage. In the last heartbeat, she's been offered something she'd thought might elude her forever: the possibility of a husband and children – a family to call her own – and, in this moment, she realises how desperately she wants it. She flaps her hand up and down, fanning her face. She can't stop herself from grinning.

Ralph gets up from his seat, reaches into his pocket and pulls out a red velvet box. He clicks it open and turns it to face her. Inside, there's a brilliant diamond solitaire. He gets down on one knee, takes Audrey's hand in his and asks her again: 'Audrey Bailey. I love you and I need you. Will you do me the honour of being my wife?'

'Yes,' breathes Audrey. 'Yes, yes, yes!' And Ralph takes her left hand and slides the engagement ring onto her fourth finger, kissing it as he returns the hand to her.

'Waiter!' he calls. 'Champagne!'

November 2012

Penzance

John lived in what I imagined estate agents would call a 'delightful barn conversion within striking distance of the Penzance seafront'. I always wondered, given he was presumably worth millions, why he didn't upgrade – move to a bigger place closer to the sea – rather than use every available square inch of space to accommodate the twins and Anastasia. Now, as the sun began its return journey towards the horizon, I approached the door of John's house. It was pretty, I'd give him that.

'Hi,' said my brother, opening the front door. His brown hair was cropped short and he'd lost weight since I last saw him a couple of months ago, his jeans hanging off his hips, his neck scrawny under the collar of his striped shirt. He looked me up and down, too, and I wondered what differences he saw in my own appearance.

'Come in,' he said. 'Mind the bikes.'

The hallway was chock-a-block with the detritus of family life: not just the twins' bicycles propped up against the walls, but a Michelin man of a coat rack laden with the family's outerwear; a shoe rack stuffed with more shoes than I imagined four people could ever own; and, on the floor, violin cases, school bags, riding boots, and sports bags, presumably also belonging to the twins. I picked my way behind John through to the living room, trying as I did so to block the unwelcome image of my brother's mother-in-law, Valya, lying dead on the hall floor, her neck twisted, lips blue, after falling headlong down the stairs and I wondered if he thought of her every time he crossed the hall.

In the living room, John picked up a few tatty pony magazines and stacked them on the coffee table – a small gesture that did nothing to take away from the sense of clutter that threatened to overwhelm the room. He flopped into an arm-chair and I sat down on the sofa next to a curl of sleeping cat. I knew better than to expect an offer of tea or coffee. Hospitality was not John's forte. This was just a fleeting visit anyway – a quick catch-up before I drove back to Truro.

I nodded at the empty living room. 'Where is everyone?'

'Swim-squad training.'

'Ah, okay. How are they? All good?'

'Fine,' he said. 'Everyone's fine.' He didn't ask after Mark, but then I didn't expect him to. There was something about Mark not having a job that made people not want to talk about him. Besides, when it came to John and me, it was understood that I was the one who had to make the small talk. John just didn't.

'How's she been since Valya ... you know?' I didn't want to say the words out loud, but I felt the question needed asking since this was the first time I'd seen John in the hall. Would her eyes have been open? I shivered.

'As good as can be expected,' John said. 'It was a blessing, I suppose. Good timing. We were on the cusp of putting her into a care home.'

'Because of her dementia?'

'Yes. It had got quite ridiculous. She didn't know who Anastasia or the twins were, let alone me. She had no idea where she was.'

'I'd no idea it had got so bad.'

'Why would you?'

'True.' I couldn't remember the last time I'd even seen Valya. Months and months ago. 'So – how's work?'

John did something with computers, though I'd no idea what. He'd worked his way up the IT departments of various blue-chip companies before quitting his job as CIO to run his own company. Although he always looked stressed, he was usually busy, which I presumed was a good thing.

John ran his hand through his hair. 'Same shit, different day,' he said. 'How's Mum?'

I exhaled hard through my teeth: a big sigh. Where to start? 'Physically she's fine,' I said. 'The hospital gave her the all-clear – took off the neck brace. No signs of shock. She's a bit stiff and achy, but nothing to worry about.' I paused.

'Okay. And?'

'Well, as I said in my message: you're right. There's definitely something different. She's vague. I don't know ... like, staring into the distance as if she's miles away, and not hearing me? I had to say quite a lot of things twice.' I paused. 'Do you think it's the accident, or is she always like that?'

John rubbed his upper lip with the side of his finger. 'I don't know.' He frowned. 'She's going that way, definitely. Whether the accident's made it worse, I don't know.'

I looked at the floor, then back up at John. 'I should know, shouldn't I?'

His look said yes, you should. 'Don't you speak to her every week?' he asked.

'I used to. I don't know what happened. It just kind of petered out when we moved down here. I guess I thought I'd see more of her so I stopped calling...'

'But you don't see much of her, either.'

'I know. It's just ... argh. When I did see her, I got the feeling she didn't particularly want me there. That I was interrupting her weekend. She almost used to tell me off for going down and that's the last thing I want when I've fought my way down the bloody A30 just to see her.' I ran my hand through my hair. 'God. I've got so much going on at home. So much to cram into the weekends. I guess I just stopped.'

I looked at John. I was hoping for empathy; some sort of understanding. There were a hundred things begging for my attention these days: work, finances, keeping things normal while Mark was unemployed – not to mention the all-consuming desire to conceive. I'd become almost obsessed with the idea of how it would feel to hold a tiny, living, breathing human being in my arms; the baby-scent of his or her skin. When I saw women out with prams, it was all I could do not to lean into them and scoop up the babies; to hold them against my shoulder and gaze at their tiny little features.

'I know. We're all busy. But you should try, Lexi,' John said. 'It takes – what – an hour to get there?'

'I know ... it's just ... you know.' I almost said it. I almost told him about the difficulties I was having conceiving but, as the words formed in my mouth, so much emotion swelled inside me that I couldn't get the words out. John wouldn't understand. He'd tell me to adopt, like he had. 'You know how it is.' I pressed my lips together, suppressing the secret that was eating me alive.

'And you don't even have kids.' John gave a bitter laugh. The words pierced me with a physical pain in my uterus. I inhaled, took a moment.

'What's it like, adopting?' I asked. 'Is it the same as ... you know, having your own?'

John gave another bitter laugh. 'I can't really answer that, never having had my own.'

'But do you love them?'

'Of course I do. I'm officially their father.'

'But do you *feel* like their father?'

He folded his arms. 'What is this? Twenty questions?'

'Sorry. I just – y'know. I wonder sometimes.'

John raised an eyebrow. 'Are you and Mark considering...?'

'What? Adopting?' I made a great show of shaking my head. 'God, no!' I laughed to show how silly the idea was. And, to be fair, it was. Mark and I had discussed it. While he was happy to support whatever I wanted to do, I think we both knew that, if we couldn't have our own children, our hearts were not in adoption. But sometimes, as the dream of a baby of my own slipped further away, I found myself wondering: could I do it? Could I love someone else's baby as my own?

'Anyway,' I said. 'About Mum. What do you think?'

John exhaled, fiddled with a newspaper lying on the coffee table. 'I don't know, Lex. It seems to have suddenly got worse. I think we should watch her – *we*, Lexi, not just me – and see how it goes.'

'Okay.' As I said it, I vowed to be a better daughter, to take better care of my mother. I would do it. I would.

'And,' said John, turning his gaze onto me, 'if things don't get better, I think we should start thinking about trying to get her to move into some sort of sheltered housing.'

'What? She's not even seventy!'

'I've just been through all this with Valya. Trust me, having scrambled around to find the right place for her at the eleventh hour, I know it's better to have plans in place.' He looked at me but I didn't reply. 'She's not getting any younger,

Lex. If we start looking at places now and get an idea of what's out there ... you know, before we know it she'll be in her seventies. I'd just like to know what we're going to do, moving forward.'

'Hmm.' I drummed my fingers on the armrest.

'She can't live on her own in that house forever. It's only a matter of time before something happens. There are some really nice places out there. I'm not talking retirement homes. Of course not! But there are some lovely residential developments where the oldies buy a place – like a one or two-bedroom apartment, or even a small house – and there are social clubs and restaurants. It's nice. Honestly.'

'I think you'll have your job cut out getting her to move. She loves her house. She loves that garden. The view...'

'I know, Lex. But I'm just thinking about her safety and her health. She crashed her car. For how much longer do you think she can continue driving? Being independent? It's not going to go on forever.'

'I don't know, John. It seems awfully premature.'

John groaned and buried his face in his hands. 'Then you've got to help me,' he said, looking up again, his voice desperate. 'With the physical stuff, not just phoning her. I can't do it all! I'm running around like a headless chicken trying to keep on top of Anastasia and the kids, not to mention work. There aren't enough hours in the day! The last thing I need is to worry about Mum going doolally.' He looked at me. 'Are you willing to pull your weight a bit more?'

'Pull my weight a bit more?' I snorted. 'Mark

and I moved from London to be closer! He now has no job. We have no money.' My voice broke. Even as I spoke, I realised John was right: the effort to conceive had taken over my life and, when it came to neglecting Mum, I was guilty as charged.

'Lexi, if you don't make the effort to see Mum, you may as well be living in Timbuk-bloody-tu,' John said.

I held up my hand. 'I'm sorry. I'll try. I promise to call her more often and go down more often? Okay?'

John took a deep breath. 'Thanks. Maybe we can come up with a rota where we take it in turns to visit her. But, meanwhile, I think we should start looking at those home places. I really do.'

July 1972

Bombay, India

Audrey Templeton examines herself in the mirror: she's pleased with the way the sleeveless silk sheath dress Ralph's tailor has made for her has turned out. The neckline reveals her collar bones, and the slit at the front reveals just enough leg to be daring but not vulgar. An opening at the back dips almost to her waist, making onlookers wonder how she could possibly be wearing a brassiere – the answer is that, tonight, she's not.

Although the dress is a soft white, it is almost

entirely consumed by large navy flowers and, as Audrey looks at herself in the mirror, she ties a silk sash in matching navy around her waist. She opens her jewellery box and selects from the jewels within a discreet pair of pearl stud earrings. She slips her stockinged feet into a pair of navy pumps and slides her hands into her favourite off-white evening gloves that reach way beyond her elbow.

As her fingers wriggle into place inside the soft silk gloves, Audrey hears the shrill cry of a baby. Arm still extended, she holds her breath, as if by holding herself still she can will the baby to stop crying, but the noise not only continues, it ramps up a gear. Audrey can tell, by now, that it's John, not Alexandra. The girl's voice is softer, less shrill. Audrey slips off her gloves and shoes and dashes across the expanse of the galleried landing to the nursery.

'Hush now. Hush, hush,' she whispers. John is sitting up in his cot, his face wet with tears. When he sees Audrey, his screams get louder. Ralph tells her the babies are too young to remember their mother – he's made her swear that she'll never tell them – but Audrey knows that, on some level, they know. She leans down into the cot and strokes John's hair but he flinches away.

'What's wrong?' Audrey whispers. 'Did you have a bad dream? You want Mummy to hold you?'

The screaming gets louder and Audrey stares helplessly at John.

'Ssh!' she soothes. 'You'll wake your sister!' She looks over at the other cot, where Alexandra is already starting to stir.

72

'Mama!' screams the boy. 'Mamaaaa!'

'Mama's here!' She reaches into the cot to try and touch John again, but he backs away to the farthest corner. 'Mamaaaa!'

Audrey's forehead flops onto the cot rail.

'What do you want?' she sobs. 'What am I supposed to do? Please stop crying!'

'Madam,' says the *ayah*, suddenly behind her. 'I try.'

Audrey spins around. 'Oh, Madhu. Thank you. I ... I just don't know what's wrong with him.'

Madhu reaches into the cot and picks up the screaming baby. Audrey slips out of the room and listens at the door. Within seconds the crying simmers down and Audrey hears the rhythmic step of the *ayah* walking up and down the nursery floor and the soothing hum of her voice. Why can't she do that?

Audrey steps silently down the polished staircase in her stockings. She walks across the parquet floor of the drawing room to the bar, where she pours herself a neat gin and adds a dash of Angostura bitters: a little sharpener. She takes a sip, then carries the glass back up to the bedroom, where she puts her shoes back on, selects a perfume and sprays it liberally on her neck and wrists, then looks in the mirror one more time.

She looks good. She looks, as Janet would say, 'the part.' She's now got used to the sophisticated woman with the expensive clothes and the tumbling red curls who looks back at her each time she passes a mirror. The new look was Ralph's idea: it was he who briefed the hairdresser and the tailor on how he wanted his wife to look and she likes the results. But it does take an increasing amount of effort to remember what Audrey Bailey, London legal secretary, used to look like. Ralph won't hear of letting her work.

The bedroom door opens behind her. Audrey turns a fraction so he can see she's braless.

'Nice,' says Ralph. 'Nice dress.' He stares at her, his eyes dark with desire. 'Come here.'

Audrey knows what's coming and she feels the familiar pull in her belly. But this is a game. She knows what Ralph likes. She extends her arm and looks at the little gold watch on her wrist, her expression inscrutable. 'Darling, we're due at dinner...' She turns towards the door as if to leave.

'Come here,' repeats Ralph, but he doesn't wait. In an instant he's across the room and he catches Audrey from behind, his hands roaming over her body as she leans back against him and turns her head to meet his kisses. Inside the dress his hands find her bare breasts.

'Red, what do you do to me?' he says, his mouth against hers. Audrey moans. She's known nothing like this in her life; Patrick was always so pedestrian, so strait-laced. Ralph scoops Audrey up, drops her on the bed, and wrenches up her silk dress. He undoes his trousers, tugs her knickers to one side, and pushes himself into her. She writhes under him, pushing her hips to meet his, then turns her head to one side as Ralph rains kisses on her face and neck.

'The *ayah*,' she breathes. 'The door...'

'So what?'

'But...'

Ralph is moving faster; he's not going to stop.

Out of the corner of her eye she sees the new nursery door open; Madhu steps quietly out and walks across the landing and down the stairs, her eyes averted. A moment later, Ralph climaxes with a moan and collapses on top of her; he's come too fast for her to keep up but she doesn't mind – there'll be another chance later. She strokes his back softly while his breathing returns to normal. *Are all marriages like this?* she wonders.

When he's caught his breath, Ralph props himself up on his elbows, strokes Audrey's hair back from her face, and stares into her eyes.

'I love you,' she whispers.

Ralph leans down, kisses her forehead, and rolls off her. He goes to the bathroom. Audrey sits up and rearranges her dress. She hears the toilet flush and the tap run, then Ralph strides back into the room.

'Hurry up, Red,' he says with a wink. 'We don't want to be late for dinner.'

The good mood unfortunately doesn't last. The traffic on the way to the restaurant is worse than usual and Audrey watches as her husband gets increasingly worked up, snapping at the driver to go this way and that in an attempt to avoid the snarls.

'It's okay,' she murmurs, taking his hand and giving it a squeeze. Ralph echoes the squeeze but then pulls his hand away, running it through his hair as he stares out at the gridlock, his jaw working as he clenches his teeth.

'I can't bear to be late!' he snaps without turning around and Audrey realises that she herself is too late: she's lost him to one of his black moods – his 'funks' as she's come to think of them – and her birthday dinner, when they arrive, takes the hit. Although the restaurant is softly lit, the tinkle of a piano barely breaking over the gentle hum of expensive conversation, it's as if a veil's suddenly come down between the two of them. Audrey uses every single one of her conversational skills to try to get her husband to give her anything more than a monosyllabic reply, but he's a different person to the one who ravished her in the bedroom. She asks coquettishly if he likes her dress. She talks about what she did all day with the children and she chats about the unseasonal weather Bombay's been experiencing – always a good topic – but even that gets little more than a grunt.

The tables are filled with beautiful ladies and well-dressed gentlemen and Audrey's painfully aware that she and Ralph are being watched; that maybe these people remember the story of Alice Templeton; that the little scenario playing out at their table is being talked about. In this room full of people, with her husband, on her birthday, Audrey has never felt more alone. As the waiter clears the plates from their main courses, Audrey decides to give it one more shot.

'Mmm,' she says, looking at the dessert menu. 'They all look so good. What are you going to go for?' No response. 'Hmm, darling? Does anything take your fancy?'

Ralph looks up. 'Sorry? Did you say something?'

'Yes!' snaps Audrey. She cracks the thick menu shut and bangs it down on the table with enough force to make the glasses jump. Ralph's hand shoots out to steady his glass.

'I'm terribly sorry if I'm disturbing you, Mr Templeton,' Audrey says, her voice shriller around the edges than she would have liked, her breath coming fast, 'but I just asked if you'd like anything for dessert. On second thoughts though, I retract that question. I'm calling it a night. Good night.'

She pushes back her chair and stands abruptly, putting her hands on the table for a moment to steady herself. Ralph looks up at her.

'Red,' he says sternly. 'Don't make a scene. Sit down.' His mouth is a straight, hard line, a picture of concealed anger, and a ripple of fear runs through Audrey's body.

'If you hadn't noticed, you've been making a scene all night by not speaking to your wife.' She says the words, quietly even, but she doesn't move from the table. Ralph passes a hand through his hair.

'Audrey,' he orders, and she quivers at the sound of her real name. 'Sit down.' He glares at her, as if willing her to sit with his eyes.

But still Audrey stands, debating her choices. Tonight was supposed to be a lovely evening – not just her birthday, but the anniversary of their engagement – and she doesn't want to ruin the evening. But, as she stands there, she realises that Ralph has already wrecked it by refusing to celebrate with her. Audrey stares at her husband and it occurs to her that he's spoiled her birthday evening deliberately; that he's enjoying manipulating her emotions. Maybe Janet was right: Ralph does like to control her. Like the sex, it's almost as if this is another game for him. Suddenly, Audrey feels like a pawn.

'Good night, Ralph,' she says. 'Enjoy your dessert.' She turns smartly and walks out of the restaurant into the humid stench of the Bombay night.

The restaurant doesn't have a taxi rank and Audrey regrets at once that they weren't dining in a hotel with a bell boy to summon a car. As she stands on the pavement, her hand raised, watching the oncoming traffic for vacant cabs, her sixth sense picks up that someone's approaching from behind. She assumes it's Ralph and a little smile plays on her lips as she realises she's won: he's come outside. Then her head snaps back as an odorous hand clamps over her mouth and her arms are wrenched behind her back. She tries in vain to scream, to struggle; realises too late that she's being mugged.

But suddenly there's a commotion and the pressure slackens. Taking advantage, Audrey twists out of the grip, hurls herself across the pavement, and turns to see Ralph pitching his bulk against her attacker until he has him in a chokehold.

'Don't you touch my wife!' he screams, shaking the man. 'How dare you touch my wife!'

The man locks eyes with Audrey and she watches as he struggles for air. He's well-restrained. Ralph will stop in a minute, she thinks. But her husband keeps up the pressure.

'He can't breathe!' Audrey gasps, but Ralph continues to squeeze the man's throat until his body goes limp. Only then does he let go; only then, when it's too late, does he let the man's lifeless body slump to the pavement. Ralph's eyes meet Audrey's, unflinching.

January 2013

St Ives

'Just look at that view!' I said to Mum as we came to a standstill at the top of a climb. We were on the South West Coast path and the sand of Carbis Bay arced out before us, looking as if it wouldn't be out of place in the Caribbean. It was one of those crisp, cold days for which the phrase 'biting cold' was invented, and Mum and I were bundled up in our woollies but the sun sparkled on the sea, which reflected back the blue of the sky. 'Isn't it gorgeous?'

'It makes me wish I was an artist,' said Mum, her hand shielding her eyes from the brightness of the sun.

'Why don't you try painting?'

Since John and I had met in the autumn, we'd ironed out a deal that meant each of us saw Mum once a month, our visits dovetailed so one of us saw her every fortnight. This, we felt, was both manageable for us and good for her: while John took her out for lunches with the family and concentrated on practicalities like scooping leaves out of the gutters or DIY jobs around the house, I tried to do a variety of more fun things with Mum – the spa, shopping, afternoon tea, walks.

It felt right to me to be doing something and, even though in a corner of my soul, I knew that half a day once a month was not a lot, some of the guilt I'd been carrying about not being a good daughter was being assuaged. I was now a woman who visited her mother regularly; a woman who took an active interest. I walked slightly taller for it.

Mum had never really said how she felt about our visits, though. Did she realise John and I were keeping an eye on her? I told myself she was pleased to see us but, secretly, I wondered. Mum always opened the door with a smile, but she also insisted that we really didn't need to keep coming down. She was often on her computer, researching goodness knows what when I arrived, and sometimes I got the impression she'd actually rather I hadn't turned up. She wasn't very talkative, especially today. Instead of mooching about the shops like we'd planned, I'd taken advantage of the beautiful day and insisted we take a walk along the coastal path and I wondered now if she'd rather have gone shopping. The coastal walk had been more tiring than I'd imagined, with quite a steep climb that had left Mum noticeably out of breath. I'd already decided we'd take the train back.

I nudged Mum with my elbow. 'Why don't you try painting?'

Mum's lips moved, her words snatched by the breeze.

'What was that?' I craned to hear.

'I used to paint,' she said. She held her hand up as if holding a paintbrush and made some strokes in the air.

'Really?'

'I went to art classes for a while. Less than a

year, I suppose. When you were only little.'

'Oh wow! Were you any good?'

Mum stared out at the ocean, her hand shielding her eyes from the sun. 'My teacher thought so. He said I had a talent. Do you suppose you can see the Scilly Isles from here? Or are we facing the wrong direction?'

'No idea,' I said. 'But that's amazing about the painting! Why don't you do it anymore?'

Mum looked like she was going to say something else so I waited, but she remained silent, her eyes on the sea.

'Why did you stop painting? If you were so good? Didn't you want to develop it?'

'Ohh, different reasons. Come on.' Mum started walking again and I fell into step next to her. 'I didn't have time – when you two were young,' she said after a minute or two. 'Your father liked everything at home to be "just so" and it took a lot of my time. You know, shopping, cooking, cleaning, taking care of you two...' Her voice trailed off.

'But later? When we were older? Surely you had more time then?'

Mum shook her head dismissively. 'It's just ... look, it's something I didn't pursue any further. That's all.'

'It must have been hard, having twins,' I said, thinking at the same time how I'd give anything for the chance to bring up twins of my own. 'Pa obviously wasn't very hands-on.'

'He was very traditional. He thought his role was to provide. And he did that very well. But when it came to parenting...' Mum laughed. 'I

81

don't remember him ever lifting a finger in that department.'

I fell behind Mum as we had to walk single file through a narrow bit of the path. It descended steeply towards the beach.

'He used to take John on those "boy's trips". Do you remember? You know: fishing, camping. And those days at Lords watching the cricket?'

'Oh yes.' Mum turned around and laughed again, her hair whipping her face. 'All my idea.'

I ran a few steps to catch up. 'What?'

'I thought it would do them both good to spend time together. I used to beg Ralph to take him away.'

'No!' John used to lord it over me because he'd been picked, not me. I shook my head, recalibrating the memory. I felt slightly sorry for my brother now.

'Yes,' said Mum. 'He was so desperate for your father's approval. Do you remember how he used to follow him around like a puppy? It used to break my heart. I tried to distract him but he was never interested in what we were doing.'

'Wow. He loved those trips. He used to count the days.' I fell silent, remembering. 'And then, once they were back, Pa would go back to work and it was as if the trip had never happened and John would mope about the house with a face like a wet weekend.'

'I know. Sometimes I wondered if they did more harm than good.'

I caught up with Mum once more as we emerged from the path onto the golden sand of Carbis Bay. The tide was out and the sand seemed

82

to stretch for miles.

'I don't think so,' I said. 'You know, I once suggested that I went fishing with them. I thought it would be fun. But John wouldn't even let me ask Pa. He said I wouldn't understand because it was a "man thing".' The cattiness in my laugh surprised me.

'I suppose it's only natural for a boy to look up to his dad,' Mum said.

'I guess.'

'And we did our own things, too. Didn't we?' Mum looked at me. 'You used to love learning how to do things around the house.'

'I did,' I said, and I thought about me standing next to Mum, pretend-ironing the hankies while she ironed our clothes; about me standing on a chair next to Mum in the kitchen, sneaking licks of cake batter while helping her make cakes and biscuits – we were probably even in matching aprons that Mum had sewn herself – the picture of '70s domestic bliss. Yes, she was right: I had wanted to learn everything. But, with that thought came the memory of the uneasiness that had underpinned my childhood: an unexplained sense of nervousness; a sense I'd always had that we were walking on pins; that our life was a house of cards that could topple at any minute.

Yes, I'd been desperate to please Mum – but it was driven by a need to keep the house of cards standing. Now, looking out at the sea, I shook my head. I'd never seen it before: John had tied himself in knots to get Pa's approval, while I'd tried, like a bumblebee banging itself again and again against a closed window, to reach Mum. I'd craved – but never got – her love.

'I tried with John,' Mum was saying, 'but he was never interested in that side of things – the cooking and everything.'

My realisation was too heavy to articulate. 'His loss,' I said with a smile. 'These days everyone loves a guy who can cook.'

We both laughed. Mum shook her head. 'Look at us walking down memory lane. Come on. Let's get going. Are you going to march me back or can we please take the train?'

August 1972

Bombay, India

Audrey walks into her kitchen and surveys the scene. Ralph's cook is at the epicentre of what looks like a mini-hurricane. Five of the six burners on the hob have pans bubbling on them. The oven's on and the worktops are all in use: chopping boards, knives, vegetables, and empty dishes cover every surface. The ceiling fans are whirring but, still, the air is plump with steam.

'Madam, you want taste?' the cook asks.

Audrey waves her hand. 'No. No, thank you. You make Sir's favourite?'

'*Haan*,' the cook nods.

'*Acchaa*. Lovely. Thank you.'

Audrey takes one more look around the kitchen, happy that everything's under control.

'Everything will be ready for eight o'clock?' Audrey asks. 'Send snacks and drinks out to the garden with Madhu, and then serve dinner in the house.'

The cook nods and Audrey backs out of the kitchen.

Already dressed for dinner, she drifts out of the back door and into the garden, where she stops for a second to inhale the heady scent of the night jasmine. It's rained heavily today and this magnifies the myriad fragrances rising from the flowerbeds. Audrey breathes in deeply, this smell of earth, rain, and flowers now as vital to her soul as oxygen is to her lungs. The garden's well-established and there's evidence in the riot of colour and scent that it's well taken care of by the gardener who's worked at the house for decades. Audrey walks slowly across the lawn, gently touching the leaves and petals of her favourite blooms. In the distance, under the hum of the city, she can sense the gentle shifting of the sea. She breathes in deeply. *It'll be all right,* she tells herself. *He loves you.*

It's been a tough few weeks since the attack outside the restaurant. Although the law sided with Ralph – it was clearly self-defence – he's been tense, and Audrey's barely slept; black circles hang under her eyes; there's a pallor to her skin. A distance has crept between the two of them and Audrey senses that she's fallen off the pedestal on which Ralph once placed her. Although that night has never again been alluded to, the weight of blame hangs heavy. In every breath, in every movement, Ralph lets Audrey know that he thinks what happened is her fault. If only she'd stayed in

85

the restaurant; if only she'd done as he'd said.

Tonight is Audrey's attempt to make everything right once more – to win back the respect of her husband – to apologise, because, without the pedestal, without Ralph's adoration and respect, the little emotional games he plays with her take on a darkness. They become something else: something Audrey doesn't want to think about.

The screen door opens behind her and Audrey turns to see Ralph standing in the doorway.

'What's going on?' he asks. 'We don't have guests.'

Audrey takes a deep breath and steps towards him. Gingerly, she positions her body against his and slips her arms around his waist.

'Can't I spoil my husband from time to time?'

Ralph's body doesn't soften. He returns the embrace stiffly, one arm loosely around her shoulders. Audrey leans in to kiss him and notices at once a hint of perfume on his skin. She could ask him where he's been but she knows she won't get an honest answer, and tonight is a night for apologies, not recriminations.

Ralph breaks away from her; starts to walk down the garden.

Audrey watches as he idles down the lawn, then turns and faces the house, his hands on his hips. She can't read the expression on his face; it's not one she's familiar with. Madhu appears with the drinks and snacks and sets them up on the table on the terrace. Ralph strides back up the garden, splashes some gin into a tumbler, adds ice, fresh lime and tonic, takes a sip. He picks over the snacks that the cook's prepared, picks up a

86

samosa, blows on it, and pops it in his mouth.

'Red. Sit down,' he says, his mouth still full, flecks of pastry escaping as he speaks. He nods to the table. 'I don't know what all this is for, but I have something to tell you.'

Audrey goes silently to the chair, sits down. She puts her hands neatly on the table, her fingers intertwined.

'What is it?' She cocks her head. Ralph chews. Audrey waits for him to swallow.

'Something important,' he says.

Audrey raises one shoulder in the tiniest of shrugs. It's a question: what?

Ralph looks at her levelly, steeples his hands in front of his mouth, index fingers touching his lips: 'We're moving to England.'

Audrey knows better than to say anything before Ralph's finished.

'There's no longer a role for me here in Bombay,' he says. 'My company will be relocating us.'

'Is this to do with...?' she can't say it. She can't mention the dead man. But maybe the recent court case sits uncomfortably with his company: no-one wants a killer on their payroll. Ralph holds up a hand to stop her.

'As I said, there's no longer a role for me here in Bombay.' He pauses. 'For the record, it is nothing whatsoever to do with events that may have taken place.'

They sit in silence. Audrey's shocked. She'd thought they would remain in India long-term. It's her home now. She thinks of the life she's built for herself here; the way she's fallen in love with India. She's going to miss the garden, the house – the *ayah*, the houseboy, the cook. She's going to miss the teeming mass of humanity that is Bombay; the sights, the smells, the sounds, the heat, the relief that the monsoon brings. She's going to miss Janet and her precious visits to the dusty church. England in comparison seems dreary – in her mind, it's flat, two-dimensional. For Audrey, the greyness of her home country has grown out of all proportion; she's forgotten that England has sunshine, too. In her memory, the sun never shines back home; England is a country of tragedy and of gravestones; a country in which even nature cries real tears.

'You needn't worry about a thing,' says Ralph after some time. 'I have funds to purchase a house of significant standing in London.'

'And Madhu?' asks Audrey. 'Will she come with us?'

Ralph lets out a bark of a laugh. 'You'll have to learn to look after the children yourself. You won't need to work. How difficult will it be to look after two small children? Millions of women do it.'

Audrey remains silent. The fact is, while she was happy enough to take on the twins, parenting's far harder, than she imagined. She's not a natural mother: soothing crying babies doesn't come easily to her and she's become dependent on the *ayah*, for whom these things are intuitive. 'Magic Madhu,' she says gratefully when the *ayah* eases John out of a tantrum or helps Alexandra drop off to sleep. The thought of having to get up in the night to deal with the vagaries of the children terrifies her almost more than the thought of moving back to England.

Ralph takes a sip of his drink and smacks his lips contentedly. He leans back in his chair, every inch the boss. 'If I've been quiet the last few weeks it's because I've been thinking. There's plenty to plan. The shippers are coming on Monday.' Then he raises his glass to Audrey, takes a swig: 'Cheers to that.'

February 2013

Penzance, Cornwall

The pub John had asked me to meet him in was easy to find; the Sunday afternoon parking not so. In the end, I'd left the car in the town car park and walked the riddle of streets to The Fisherman's Arms. John sat alone at a table, stooped over his mobile phone, a pint of Cornish cider on a cardboard drinks mat in front of him. He wore a tatty green sweater, jeans, hiking boots – the picture of the scruffy millionaire. He stood up to greet me.

'Hi,' he said.

'Hi.' There was an awkward pause during which I thought about giving him a little hug, but John sat straight back down and the moment was lost. I knew it was nothing personal – this was just how John was. I'd always been the more demonstrative twin. Mum used to joke about it: 'Alexandra does the emotion for both of you,' she'd say, laughing. 'And John does the bossiness,' I'd add under my breath.

'Sorry, I didn't get you a drink,' he said, nodding towards the pint. 'You're driving, right?'

'Yes. But I'll have a coffee.' I ordered at the bar, then pulled out a chair and sat across from John at the table. My knees knocked the wood when I tried to cross my legs. I uncrossed them and leaned forward on the table instead, unsure of how this conversation was going to go. John had called the meeting.

'We've both watched her for a few months now,' he'd said on the phone. 'You can't deny she's vague. You can't deny she forgets things. More than I think is normal for her age. She clean forgot I was coming down once. I think we should get together and have a think about how we're going to take this forward.'

John was right. Mum hadn't been herself. But it wasn't anything I could put my finger on specifically. Yes, she forgot stuff – but who didn't? I had the best part of three decades on her and I forgot stuff. I had 'senior moments' myself. Yes, she was always looking off into the distance and reminiscing about the past. This, I couldn't deny. But was it serious? I was for a more organic approach. I felt the decision to move had to come from Mum herself, not from John and me pushing her.

'So – what are your thoughts?' John asked me now. That's my brother: straight to the point.

'I'm fine, thanks for asking. How are you?' I said.

John rolled his eyes and I goggled mine back at him.

'She seems okay?' I said.

John sighed. 'I thought you might be like this.'

'Like what?'

'Defending her.'

'I'm not defending her.'

'Yes, you are.'

'No, I'm not. She seems okay. A little forgetful, maybe. A little vague. But she's nearly seventy. I'm sure that's normal. Physically, she's in great shape. We walked a bit of the South West Coast path last month.'

'I'm not asking whether or not it's normal,' John said. 'I'm not saying she has dementia. What I'm saying is that this is as good as it's going to get. It's only going to get worse from here in. She's not getting any younger.' He gave me a minute to absorb his words. 'I'm asking you to help me come up with a way to move forward. I have a lot on my plate. I need to get this settled in my head before we get into crisis management mode.'

'Crisis management?'

'If she starts to go downhill. I don't want to make a panicky decision when we're up against it. I'd like to take our time and make sure we pick the right solution for her. Even if she carries on in a normal ageing trajectory, it's going to get worse and we're going to need a plan.' John paused, met my eye. 'You know she locked herself out the other week?' I nodded – I did know. It turned out she'd already done it once; had used the spare key from under the plant pot out the back and forgotten to put it back. Too embarrassed to call either of us, she'd sat on the garden wall, waiting, in the hope that someone could help. A neighbour had called John and he'd driven over, had a chat with the neighbour, handed over another spare key. 'I don't want her to be a burden on her neighbours,' John said. 'I don't want them thinking badly of us, like we can't be bothered to help her.'

'But we do help her!'

'She didn't call us – remember? And don't get me started on what happens if she falls. What if she falls at home and breaks her hip – lies there for how many days? This is our future.'

I put my head in my hands. John was the worrier of the two of us. He saw danger in everything, always envisaged the worst possible outcome, and the fact that Valya had fallen down the stairs clearly hadn't helped. I knew all this about John, but it didn't make dealing with him any easier.

'I don't know what to say,' I said. 'I think you're over-thinking things.'

'I'm not. You know, the night after the car accident, she called me Mack.'

'Mack? Do we even know a Mack?'

'Exactly. She looked right at me – almost through me – when she was lying in that hospital bed, and she called me Mack. She looked like she was about to cry.'

'Strange. Did you correct her?'

'Yes.'

'And?'

'She shook her head and said "Of course. Silly me."' John did quite a good impression.

I traced the wood grain on the table. 'I don't think you can read anything into that. Really. Not given she'd just had the accident.'

'Anyway, look, let's not get sidetracked,' said John. 'We're here to think of solutions, not drag over the past.'

'So, what solutions do you have in mind?'

John picked at the skin around one of his nails. 'Well. As I said the other day: perhaps some sort of sheltered housing would be the way to go.' I recoiled as an image of frail old ladies on Zimmer frames filled my mind: Mum would shrivel up and die. But, equally, I didn't have space for her at home. 'You know,' John continued, 'something safer, where she's got people to keep an eye on her twenty-four seven.'

I turned away, shaking my head.

'Come on, Lexi. Admit it. You don't want to be constantly running after her any more than I do. We both have busy lives. Work. Family. I know you've moved down here to be closer but seeing her once a month is about all either of us can manage – right?' He looked at me and I pursed my lips. 'You don't want to be worrying about her all the time, jumping each time the phone rings, spending nights dashing down to the hospital, do you?'

I said nothing.

'Let's be honest: neither of us has time to baby-sit her every day.'

'We're not at that stage yet.'

'*But when it happens,*' John spoke through clenched teeth.

'*But it's not happened yet.*' I echoed his tone.

'I want to be prepared.'

'I hear you. I do,' I said, trying to be reasonable. 'But sheltered housing? She'll never go for it.'

'There are some nice places out there. I looked.'

'But she's still entirely self-sufficient. And happy. She loves that garden.'

John laughed: a snort that sprayed cider onto the

table. 'Happy's not a problem, Lex. She's happy as bloody Larry. She's got no idea. Floats about in a dream world.' John shook his head and laughed.

'Come, now. That's a bit harsh.'

'Really? Look at what almost happened with the painting.'

I tutted. Mum had a painting – a small piece that had always hung in the loo in Barnes. 'If anything happens to your father and me, and you need money,' she'd told John and I while we were growing up, 'that painting's worth as much as the house.' I'd found it hard to believe: although the scene of country flowers was pretty, I saw nothing special in it: the lines were blurry and the colours muted – it wasn't to my taste at all.

Still, a few months ago, John had arrived for lunch to find Mum had almost handed over the painting to a con man. John knew at once it was a scam that'd been going on in the area: the gang targeted the elderly. Under the pretence of cleaning artwork, jewellery, and antiques, they would take the originals and swap them for copies. Most of the victims never noticed the difference. Although Mum had denied she'd ever been going to get the painting cleaned, John had thought differently.

'You don't know she was going to hand it over,' I said now.

'Why else would she have had it out?' he asked. 'She was so evasive about the whole thing. Thank God I turned up when I did. She wouldn't tell me why that man had been there, nor why the painting was out. When I told her about the scam, she had to sit down with a sherry.' John shook his head as he recalled the day. 'We nearly lost our inheritance that day, Lexi.'

'You've no idea if that's our inheritance or not.'

'Oh, come on, Lexi! What else is she going to do with it?'

'Pa didn't leave anything to us. Remember he wanted us to "make our own way in the world"? Maybe she'll do the same?'

'I know, I know. "I'm a self-made man and proud of it."' John's impression of our father was also eerily good; for a moment he was right back in the pub with us. 'Anyway, this is Mum. Of course she'll leave us something, and the painting's worth a fortune.'

I shook my head. 'That's all by the by. The point is, we can't push her out of her home just because she might – or might not – have believed a con artist.' I paused. 'She'd hate it. She'd curl up and die.' I snorted. 'Maybe Valya dived head-first down the stairs rather than go into a home.'

'Valya didn't know what her name was, let alone what was about to happen to her. She had the memory of a goldfish by the time she died.'

I tutted. 'Anyway,' I leaned forward over my coffee cup, cupping it with my hands. 'Back to Mum. So you want a plan "moving forward" and you're thinking sheltered housing?'

John leaned back. 'Yes. Exactly. Somewhere where there are people – professionals – there to keep an unobtrusive eye on her. Where she's got a built-in support network to act in an emergency. Maybe she'll even make some friends.'

'Hmph.' I was trying to imagine explaining all that to Mum.

'If we go for something where she can sell her current house and invest the money in a flat of some sort, it can continue to be an investment. Rather than, say, something like a retirement home where you're paying people to look after her and there's no investment.'

I closed my eyes. My brother: always looking at the financial bottom line.

John buried his face in his hands. When he looked up again, he looked utterly defeated. 'Well, can you come up with a better idea?' he said. 'I can't think of any other solution. I mean, God, Lexi. Work is shit at the moment. I mean, really shit.' His voice caught. 'The twins just seem to need money all the time. Money and lifts and clothes and gym classes and riding lessons and music classes and school trips. It's one thing after another. I'm hard up against it and worrying about Mum is just one thing I don't need.'

I rubbed my jaw. As far as I knew, John was doing really well. He must be ploughing all his money back into the business. But, if cash flow was an issue, why didn't Anastasia get a job? Even something part-time while the twins were at school?

'All right, all right,' I said. 'But isn't this something that should come from Mum herself? She needs to believe she needs to move, otherwise it'll be a disaster. We can't force her.'

'That's where we come in. We need to plant the idea in her head. Water it.'

I laughed. 'Good luck with that!'

John narrowed his eyes and exhaled. 'We could always try to expedite things.' His voice was low and I wasn't sure I'd heard correctly.

'Expedite?'

He cocked his head. 'You know … speed things up a little.'

I shook my head.

'Do small things to make her start doubting herself.'

'What?' I stared at my brother.

John shifted awkwardly on his seat. 'You know … there are ways. It wouldn't be too difficult.'

'John! That's evil! Pure evil. How could you even *think* of such a thing?'

He closed his eyes. He had the grace to look sheepish, I'll give him that. 'But if we don't,' he said, 'how are we going to get her to agree to move?'

'How about we talk to her? Express our concerns. Good grief, John, she's our mother, not the enemy!'

John drained his pint. 'Anyway, think about it. I'm going to do some research, check out some places.'

I closed my eyes.

'I'll send you some info,' he said. 'Maybe we can see a few places together.' I didn't say anything. 'Look, I know what you're thinking,' John continued. 'But they have nice retirement villages these days.'

'Whatever,' I said. I pushed back my chair and stood up. 'Do what you want. I'm going to go and see Mum. I know it's not your turn, but why don't you come too?'

'Sure,' John sighed. 'As long as the end's in sight.'

15 July 1973

Barnes, London

Audrey walks to the front door, turns around, then walks through the entrance hall of the Barnes house and into the drawing room, trying to imagine how it will look to the dinner guests seeing her home for the first time. For London, the four-storey semi is generously sized. It's also been beautifully decorated and fitted out but, for Audrey, there's a hollowness at its heart: something is missing.

She pauses on the threshold of the ground floor drawing room, enjoying the way the light from the well-placed lamps pools in the room. She likes the elegant furniture that the interior designer has chosen; she likes the soft colours of the décor. Her eyes roam the room and everything she sees is pleasing to her but still something isn't right. Audrey breathes in the scent of the house and, in that moment, in that deep inhalation, she realises what it is that's absent from her impressive London home: India. The damp-earth smell of India; the faint stench of the city, stronger near the slums, but noticeable even in the area where she and Ralph had lived. Even though it's mid-summer, London's been grey and overcast all week, the sun steadily losing its game of hide and seek with the clouds. Outside the house, the most dominant smell on the busy street is that of exhaust fumes. Audrey has the sense that she's living on tarmac and concrete; that she's disconnected from nature. She misses the dirt, the earth, the mud and the rawness of Bombay. As she stands in her beautiful home, a sob rises in Audrey's chest; even after being in England for a year, her longing for India is still visceral.

Audrey gives herself a little shake and walks over to the gilded mirror that hangs above the fireplace. 'You're very lucky,' she tells her reflection. 'You have what so many women dream of: a beautiful home. Two children. A husband who loves you...' She pauses, rallies herself. 'You're turning thirty,' she says firmly, 'and you're very lucky.'

The priceless piece of artwork which she bought with the inheritance from her parents hangs in the downstairs cloakroom, its colours judged by the interior designer to be discordant with their home's colour scheme. It tickles Audrey just a little that the most valuable item in the house hangs in the loo; that neither Ralph nor the disapproving designer have a clue.

Audrey opens a cabinet and picks out three scented candles, which she places strategically in the entrance hall, drawing room and dining room. The scent is of her garden in Bombay: night jasmine. When she'd walked into the bijou shop in Richmond that had sold the candles, she'd been almost struck down by the fragrance. It had taken her straight back to the soft warmth of her garden and, in a daze, she'd bought the entire stock.

Happy after these minor adjustments, Audrey walks back to the front door and retraces her steps.

What impression will her guests get when they walk in? It's important to her. She's entertained many of Ralph's work associates and clients for dinner parties but, for her birthday dinner tonight, it's the first time she's hosting people she's picked herself. She's tried, all year, to make friends in London, inveigling herself into established cliques that revolve around the children. But people are not as friendly in London as the expats were in Bombay; they seem more stand-offish and, although they've slowly begun to accept her presence on the edges of their groups, she can't shake the feeling that the friendships on offer are superficial. She joins in, but she's not yet one of them. This dinner is designed to change that; to seal her friendships. It's an olive branch, an offering to the mummies from the twins' new nursery school: Come into my home. This is who I am. Please like me.

She hears footsteps padding down the stairs.

'They're asleep,' Hannah says softly.

'Thank you.' Hannah is Audrey's little secret, her baby-sitting fairy. Ralph expects not to be bothered by the children when they're entertaining and he blames Audrey if they patter down the stairs at night wanting hugs and sips of water.

'It ruins my image,' he claims. 'I'm there talking to my clients and then – ugh – to have a child attached to me at the dining table? It's not on, Red. Don't let it happen again.' Audrey's tried to tell her husband that if he came home earlier the night-time visits would stop; sometimes they're the only times the children see their father. She suspects they do it because they've missed him.

But she's also not keen for John and Alexandra to get into the habit of coming down at night so she places an ad on the newsagent window and hires Hannah, a teenager who lives down the road, to babysit upstairs while they entertain two floors below. It's another thing about which Ralph has no idea.

'What time are the guests arriving?' Hannah asks.

Audrey looks at her watch. 'In about half an hour,' she says. 'Mr Templeton will be back any minute.'

Hannah knows the drill. She nods and disappears back upstairs to her perch in the third floor study. Audrey wishes Ralph knew his own drill: be home before your guests arrive.

'I've got a job!' Audrey says. Her birthday dinner has gone down well, her birthday cake is cut and she's let herself relax in the moment. Even though Audrey's been unable to taste the feast she's spent all day preparing to Ralph's exacting specifications, her friends seem to be enjoying it and Ralph, despite arriving literally at the same moment as their first guests, has been doing what he does best: entertaining. He's been every inch the suave host, making Audrey feel a swell of pride in her husband as he's charmed the ladies at the table and impressed their husbands. Now she's a little giddy with her drinks, and she's no idea now what's prompted her to make her announcement in such a public setting. Unfortunately there's no taking her words back: they fall in a chasm between conversations and Audrey realises that the whole table has turned to face her. She raises her glass and her guests quickly follow suit.

'I hope you'll join me in raising a glass to my new job...' she pauses, imagines a drum roll, 'at the library! Bottoms up!'

'Bottoms up! To Audrey's new job,' the guests echo, then one by one, they become aware that Ralph has not joined in. Silence falls like a guillotine. Ralph is staring at his wife. Audrey smiles nervously at him. But she's drunk, and the full dining table gives her courage.

'Aren't you pleased for me?' She smiles brightly at Ralph. She'd imagined he would be: it's the public library. It's not like she'll be dancing in a cabaret. Ralph stares back. The guests feel tension in the air. Their gazes drop to the tablecloth; they sip their drinks, fiddle with their cutlery, look at each other. Ralph continues to stare at Audrey.

'We'll talk about this later.'

'What's the problem?' asks Stella, the only working mother of the group. 'I think it's terrific.'

Audrey shoots her a look. Stella has no idea that Audrey is now feeling as if she's trying to skate across the Atlantic on a layer of gossamer ice.

'It's all right, Stella,' says Audrey. 'We'll talk about it later. No need to talk work now!' She gives a little laugh. But Stella won't let it go.

'What's the problem, Ralph?' she asks. 'Don't you want your wife to work?' Her voice is defiant. Audrey realises that she, too, is a little tight. 'Don't tell me you're one of those dinosaurs who believes a woman's place is in the home!'

Audrey fingers her necklace. 'It's okay, really, Stella. Ralph's right. I should have told him first.'

102

'Well,' says Ralph, ignoring his wife and looking levelly across his glass at Stella. 'Since you ask, yes, I do believe a woman's place is in the home. I work. I provide for my family...' he sweeps his hand at the room as if to show just how well he provides for his family, 'and looking after the home is the least Audrey can do.'

'I don't believe it,' snorts Stella. 'You *are* a dinosaur. You're one of those 1950s throw-backs. Have you heard yourself? "I do believe a woman's place is in the home"!' She mimics Ralph's tone, and an icy hand clasps at Audrey's heart. She wills Stella to shut up. 'I mean, good God, Ralph, it's 1973 not 19 bloody 50!'

'Stella,' says Stella's husband. But Stella shakes her head at him, waves him off.

'No seriously,' she says. 'I'm not finished here. Audrey's got a job. She wants to go to work and she's excited about it. Why shouldn't she be? I'm sure she's more than capable of managing her time. It's not like she's going to leave the children home alone, is it?'

'Yes, Audrey. What were you going to do with the children while you're out at work? Earning a crust at the library?' Ralph spits the words and Audrey realises why he's so upset. Suddenly she realises that by taking a job – a job which she'd hoped would help her get to know the community – she's made it look as if they need her part-time salary to survive; she's made it look as if Ralph is not providing enough, and she knows how much her husband will loathe that. Ralph turns his gaze to Audrey, one eyebrow raised, and waits for her reply.

'It's okay. They go to nursery school. The job is only part-time. A couple of hours a day. It's for fun, not for anything else.'

'Seems you've got it all sorted,' says Ralph smoothly.

His voice implies otherwise. Stella still hasn't really comprehended how much trouble Audrey is in. She looks from one to the other then puts on a baby-girl voice.

'Oooh!' she giggles. 'Looks like there's going to be quite a discussion tonight *chez* Templeton.' She looks at her watch, then at her friends. 'Maybe we'd better leave them to it.'

Audrey looks around the table; looks at these people she was hoping would become her friends, her confidantes. Moving as a clique, they're all nodding and stretching their limbs, smothering yawns, and looking about for handbags. Still the outsider, she suddenly feels so very alone.

'Wouldn't anyone like coffee?' she asks, looking at the slices of birthday cake that still sit on the plates. 'Coffee and *petits fours?*'

Heads all around the table shake and Audrey sags with defeat. The evening's mood is broken and the guests start to get up from the table.

Audrey escorts them to the door with Ralph's arm around her shoulders, his hand cupping her neck in a way that makes her want to edge away from him. She takes his hand and pulls it down to her shoulder. He puts it back on her neck, his index finger and thumb pressing a fraction too tightly.

When the door closes behind the last of the guests, Ralph uses the hand on Audrey's neck to wrench her around, half-choking her in the process. An image of the dying man's face in India flashes into Audrey's mind – a year ago to the day. Her face is centimetres from Ralph's and she can smell the garlic and liquor on her husband's breath; see spittle on his lip. He stares at her face, breathing hard, then he gives her a little shake by the neck, as if to remind her of what he's capable.

'Don't you ever – *ever* – humiliate me like that again. Do you hear?'

Audrey presses her lips together and averts her eyes. 'Sorry,' she whispers.

'And, as for your so-called *job*. Don't you dare even think about it.'

Audrey's nod is barely there.

'Say it,' Ralph says. 'I want to hear it. Repeat after me: "Ralph Templeton's wife will never work."'

Audrey swallows, takes a shallow breath. Her throat feels bruised. 'Ralph Templeton's wife will never work,' she whispers.

September 1976

Barnes, London

Audrey's shoes tap on the damp pavement as she walks home from school faster than usual. She gives herself a little smile of triumph; John and Alexandra have settled well and her days are now her own. Audrey's hyper-aware of her surroundings this morning. She's taking in the scent of the fresh morning air, the dampness that hangs in the trees, and the mundane sound of the cars passing her as she hurries down the street. She's aware of the hand that's pulling her shopping trolley; aware of the rhythm that's sent from the handle up her arm as the wheels roll over the joins in the paving stones.

She's aware, too, of her heart beating, an exciting pulse. For the first time since she left India, she feels the life thrumming in her veins. Today is a big day and Audrey is as terrified as she is excited. After careful negotiations with Ralph, she's established that he has no objection to her being out in the mornings to attend adult education classes as long as they are 'edifying.' He thinks it's 'ladylike' and 'appropriate' for his wife to 'improve herself', so she's signed up for art classes at the local adult education college. Today she'll attend her first class. It's a basic introduction to art but she's hoping once she's mastered the basics she'll be able to move on to oil painting.

She's desperate to get out of the house.

Audrey feels like a schoolgirl as she pushes open the door to the adult education centre. The smell of council disinfectant is identical to the smell in the twins' school and she feels she should be looking for the headmistress's office, not a classroom for herself. She's a little early and there's no one in the foyer, but there's a poster on a board that lists where to find each of today's classes. She runs a finger down the list, squinting slightly until she finds her art class. Teacher: Dave Mac-Donald. Classroom: E16.

Turning around, Audrey realises she can smell coffee and hear, faintly, the clatter of cup and saucer. She follows her senses and finds a small canteen that consists of a self-service hatch containing pastries, cookies and croissants, and a lady in an apron pouring teas and coffees. A handful of people decorate the room: a pair talking intensely on a sofa that's seen better days, and two individuals flicking through newspapers at separate Formica tables. Audrey gives the room a vague smile.

'Hello duck, what can I get you?' asks the lady in the apron, and Audrey orders a tea for lack of anything else to say. She waits while the tea is prepared and then walks with it into the room. Sofa or table, she thinks? Sofa or table? Her feet carry her to a table and she puts the tea down, returns to a magazine rack and picks up the first magazine she sees, sits down and starts to flick through the pages. She's timed it all wrong, of course. There's only five minutes until she needs to be in the classroom and in that time her tea, in its polystyrene cup, is still too hot for even a sip.

Self-conscious, even though the other people in the room aren't looking at her at all, she closes the magazine, returns it to the rack, picks up her tea, and makes her way to room E16. The door's open, and a few people are already sitting in the crescent of plastic chairs that face the front. Audrey chooses a seat a little left of centre, and sits down, tucking her cup of tea under the seat so she doesn't kick it over.

Within seconds, a grey-haired lady walks in. Audrey gives her a polite smile, which the woman takes as an invitation to sit next to her.

'Hello,' says the woman.

'Morning,' says Audrey.

As others begin to trickle into the room, the other woman takes out a sketch pad and a pencil and balances them on her knee. Audrey reaches into her bag and pulls out the A3 pad of paper and pencil she's brought with her, then a man walks into the room and the breath is almost sucked out of Audrey's lungs.

He looks casual in jeans and a loose black sweater, but its sleeves are pushed up to reveal elegant wrists and dark hairs on olive skin. In the jeans, his legs look long; his general outline is slim. The man has a wild beard and a moustache – both of which Audrey tends to dislike – and they hide much of his face but what skin of the man's face Audrey can see – on his upper cheeks and on his forehead – is completely unlined: he could be anything from twenty-five to thirty-five. There's something about the line of his cheekbones and the shape of his eyes that resonates with her; there's an aura of strength and kindness about his face, but it's the man's dark-brown hair that she finds herself drawn to; it's his hair that pulls a silent moan from her soul. It falls to his collarbone and is a tangle of pre-Raphaelite curls. As he walks into the room, his eyes, the rich brown of dark chocolate, catch Audrey's and the shock is physical, as if she's been punched in the abdomen. Audrey can't drag her eyes away from his; a lifetime of emotion passes through her: recognition, understanding, and, somehow, a sense of inevitability. She shifts on her seat, a half-smile frozen on her face. Despite the flared trousers and polo-necked sweater she's chosen to wear today, she feels naked under the man's gaze.

'Good morning,' the man says to the room without taking his eyes from Audrey. Although there are now at least six people in the classroom, it's as if he's speaking only to her. 'Are we all here for Art 101?' Finally, the man drags his eyes away from Audrey and sweeps his gaze around the room. 'If anyone here is expecting aerobics, you're in the wrong classroom.' He waits, walks to the classroom door and taps it shut with his foot.

'Do you know him?' Audrey's neighbour whispers.

Audrey shakes her head; makes herself shrug.

'Really?'

Audrey shakes her head. She doesn't blame her new friend for thinking that; she already feels she knows this man's soul.

The man continues. 'Right. Good morning. My name's Dave MacDonald but, if we're going to get along, I'd rather you called me Mack.'

Mack. Audrey says the word to herself once, and then again: *Mack.*

March 2013

Penzance, Cornwall

A wall of coffee-scented warmth hit me as I pushed open the door to Starbucks. I held onto the handle and tried to close the door quietly but the wind snatched it from my hand, slamming it with a bang that caused everyone in the queue to jump and turn.

'Sorry,' I mouthed. 'Wind.'

I spotted my brother at once, his lanky shape familiar among the strangers. He was at a corner table, a couple of brochures and two coffees in front of him. I made my way over, wondering if Anastasia was somehow with him but out of sight.

'Morning,' I said, pulling out a chair across the table from him.

'Morning.' He pushed one of the cups towards me.

'For me?'

He nodded and I raised my eyebrows. Hospitality. 'Thanks.'

'Thought you might need it,' he said. 'Early start and all that.'

I held the cup in both hands, enjoying its warmth. 'Thanks,' I said again. 'So what's the plan?'

'Well, I've brought a couple of brochures to give you an idea of what's out there.'

I steepled my hands together and pressed them against my lips. 'Okay. How many are we viewing today?'

'Just the one.'

'Specifically?' I reached for the brochures but John snatched them out from under my hand.

'All in good time.' He picked up one. 'First the worst. We're not viewing this one but I wanted to show it to you so you have something to compare before we head out. This is what we were looking at for Valya until she deteriorated so badly she needed a specialist place.'

The picture on the front of the brochure was of a house not dissimilar in size to the old Barnes house. It was taken at dusk and the lights were blazing.

'It's what they call a "private care residence",' said John.

'It already sounds too much. She doesn't need private care. She doesn't need any care.'

'I just wanted to show you the sort of thing she might end up in if we don't get her somewhere good now; if we're forced to make a snap decision in crisis mode.'

I looked at the table. As usual, John was envisaging the worst possible outcome; fire-fighting a situation that might never arise. But I knew from a lifetime of arguing with my brother that there was no point in even trying when he had this head on. John opened the brochure and pointed to a picture of a stuffy living room. True, it was spacious and nicely decorated, but I couldn't see Mum in it. Not even when she really was old and doddery.

'Look at the communal areas,' said John. 'It's like a private home.'

'A private home full of dribbling strangers.'

'Please can you try to be constructive about this?'

'She's nowhere near anything like this.' I waved my hand at the brochure. 'I'm sure this *home* has its merits but Mum's not at this stage. She's not ill and she's not infirm. She doesn't need her meals cooked or her shopping done. There's absolutely no point in looking at anything like this. You're jumping the gun. At most – *at the very most* – all she needs is an emergency number she can call if she falls, or has some sort of problem.' I shoved the brochure, shooting it across the table towards John. 'There's no way we can sanely ask her to consider anything like this. She's in great shape. Seventy is the new fifty!' I stopped abruptly, my rant suddenly out of steam.

'Keep your hair on.' John looked taken aback. 'I said we weren't seeing it.'

I lowered my voice. 'Look. If we even bring up the idea, she'll get paranoid we're trying to push her into some sort of a home and she'll stop calling us when she needs help. Then who picks up the pieces? What we need to do is help her keep her independence. It must be awful to think that the kids you spent your life bringing up just want to shove you into a home.'

I sat back, surprised at myself. I hadn't realised I felt so strongly about this. I should have put my foot down before now. I'd thought our arrangement of monthly visits was working well, but John, I saw now, lived in fear of the middle-of-the-night call which he – being closer – would have to field. I realised now that these brochures – this visit today – weren't so much about Mum and her needs, but about John wanting to minimise his responsibilities before they started mounting.

The question was: how did I feel? Was there even a small part of me that would feel more at ease if Mum was safely ensconced in a place like this? Goodness knows, life was stressful enough as it was. Or would putting Mum in a home eat away at my conscience, negating any benefit I'd get from knowing she was well taken care of? I imagined Mark and I in the future, taking a baby into a retirement home to see his or her grandmother, and shuddered. I'd always imagined our child to have a much more active grandmother, not a shell of a person sitting in a worn velour chair. But what was the alternative? I tried to slow my breathing; regain some objectivity.

'Let's be honest,' John said quietly, 'it's not like she's had much of a life to miss. We'd just be making her world slightly smaller, and *so* much safer.'

'What do you mean "she hasn't had much of a life"? She's had a great life!'

'Lex. Come on! She never went to university, or had any idea of a career. She never had any outside interests. She was always at home doing housework and running about after Pa. She had no life to call her own.'

'How can you say that?'

'I'm not saying she was unhappy – just that that was enough for her.'

'You make her sound like such a doormat.'

113

'She *was* a doormat!'

I looked at John in disbelief. 'You really think that?'

He shrugged. 'Yes. She was a complete sap when we were growing up. Pa pushed her around and she never stood up to him.' His voice went quiet. 'I hated her for that.'

A picture of John kneeling on the floor playing fiercely with his Meccano, his face pinched and white, came to mind, and I realised that, despite living in the same house with the same parents – despite being twins – our experiences of childhood were completely different. While I'd watched everything – observing in silence – he'd looked away.

I shook my head. 'You are *so* wrong. She chose not to stand up to Pa in order to keep the peace. He was sometimes a complete git to her and she sucked it up for a quiet life. It was an active choice that she made. I could see her thinking about it sometimes. Like, she would be standing there, shaking with anger, and calculating what to do. I think she was actually really clever. She let him believe he pulled the strings but, really, she was managing him. She's a brilliant psychologist.'

John shrugged. 'Whatever.'

'Do you remember how Pa never shouted when he was really angry? He'd go quiet – you know, really quiet, with that super-controlled voice? I was more scared of that than anything else. Remember? And Mum'd stand really still and fiddle with her necklace. I always remember her doing that and, if you looked, you could see her weighing up everything and we'd all be standing there holding our breath, waiting to see what was going to happen, and then she'd say very carefully, "Your father's right," or "You're absolutely right, Ralph, forgive me," and everything would be okay. Don't you remember?'

'A bit, I guess. I do remember her saying "Your father's right." It's all she ever said. That and "Listen to your father."'

'You know it was her who made Pa take you out on those weekend trips?'

'Uh-uh.' John shook his head. 'We did those because Pa wanted to.' I saw hurt flash in John's eyes and I looked down at the table.

'Sorry.' I waited a minute before speaking again. 'She was just trying to give us a good childhood. She asked me recently if she was a good mum. I think it was really important to her to give us a stable home. After losing her own mum so young.'

'I guess so.'

'And then her dad died pretty young, too. But she turned it around: she went to India soon after that – met Pa there.' I fell silent, trying to picture what it must have been like for Mum to find herself alone, then to pick herself up and travel, alone, to India. 'I think it affected her more than we can know.'

'Well – of course.'

'I always felt she kept us a bit at arm's length while we were growing up. Did you? Actually, don't answer that: you were never that close to her. But I always wonder if it was because she lost her own parents – like she wanted us to be almost emotionally independent in case anything happened to her.'

John shook his head. 'Talk about over-thinking.'

'No, really. I think about this a lot. So, on the one hand, you've got her holding us at arm's length so we're not so terribly devastated if anything happens to her and, on the other hand, we've got her trying so hard to give us this stable home and perfect childhood but not quite getting it right.' I shook my own head. 'And, all the time, she was dealing with Pa and his moods. It can't have been easy.'

John frowned, the brochure still in his hands. 'I can't believe you think about this stuff. Haven't you got anything better to do? Like – um?' He tapped the brochure with his index finger.

'Do you realise that we're all she's got?' I said. 'Her parents are gone; her husband's gone. She's got no one.'

John held up the brochure. His face was closed. Subject over. 'God, Lexi. Please. Let's not get off the topic. So we both agree this one is too much. For now.'

'Yes,' I sighed. 'But is the one we're seeing any better? Wouldn't it be better to look for some sort of halfway house that'll let her keep her independence? Or can we just get a carer to look in on her every day in her current house? I feel we owe her that.'

John shook his head. 'That's money down the drain. Where's your return on that? At least if she buys a property, we can sell it after ... you know. Get some money back. Maybe even make a profit.'

'It always comes back to money with you, doesn't it?'

'Makes the world go round.'

116

'Yes, but ... while she's alive, shouldn't she be able to use her own money?'

'It's all we have as our inheritance.'

I placed my hands palm down on the table and looked John in the eye. 'Can you please not talk our inheritance? It's really morbid.'

I felt sorry for him; as far as inheritances went, he hadn't done well to date. Anastasia had persuaded him to spend a fair amount converting their downstairs room into a bedroom for Valya on the understanding that they'd one day recoup it from Valya's life insurance. But the life insurance hadn't been worth a lot and what there had been had gone entirely to Anastasia's brother. The news, after Valya's death, had come as a bitter blow. But still, I found his constant harping on about Mum's money disturbing.

'I don't know what Mum's planning to do with her money,' I said. 'It's not something I lie awake thinking about.' I heard myself say the words, but it was a lie. There was a part of me that, in the wee hours, hoped that Mum would at least leave us something. How could she not? With my drop in salary, Mark's unemployment had eaten into what little savings we had and I didn't even want to think about the possibility that we might have to go the private IVF route if I didn't get pregnant soon. I was too old for NHS treatment. 'You can't have it both ways,' I said. 'Either we look after her ourselves and save her money, or we have to accept that it's going to cost money for her to be looked after.'

John pushed a brochure towards me. 'Anyway. That's all by the by. This is the one we're seeing today. I think you'll like it.'

The picture on the cover was of an attractive residential development: Harbourside. I liked the look of it at once. Slowly, I leafed through the pages, taking in the fully serviced houses and apartments that could be bought; the gardens, the restaurants, the swimming pool, the residents' diary of activities, the pictures of young-looking, active people not sitting about in chairs staring at television screens, but *doing* stuff. People who looked like Mum, carrying golf clubs, having dancing lessons, eating on the terraces. It helped that the property had been shot on a sunny day – it looked so nice I wanted to live there myself.

I looked up at John and saw he was smiling. 'See? Nice, isn't it? It's for the over fifty-fives. She can't possibly deny that she's that. She could move in at once.'

'Fine,' I said, closing the brochure. 'This one and this one only.' Even so, a doubt crept into my mind. Mum was so fiercely independent. She always had been. Could I really see her taking dinner in the development's restaurant, joining in the *boules* on the lawn?

'There's absolutely no harm in looking at it. So we know what's out there. No one ever died of too much information.' John gathered the brochures and stood up. 'Right. Grab your coffee. Let's go and look.'

December 1976

Barnes, London

Audrey's senses are on full alert as she walks down the High Street. She's checking not for potential muggers but for the gossipy wives and mothers of Barnes. Consequently she's dressed in a beige raincoat and a headscarf, with not a single detail of her attire – not bag nor shoe – in any way memorable. Before she walks into the backstreet that houses the quiet coffee shop, Audrey takes one last glance at the High Street – she can't be sure who might be passing by car but, on the pavement, there's no one who knows her and it's with a sense of relief that she slips out of view of the main thoroughfare.

Oh, my word, if Ralph finds out, she thinks, and she tuts out loud to herself as she walks. *What are you doing: are you crazy?* Audrey knows how possessive Ralph is. She's very well aware she's playing a dangerous game but it's one she can't resist. In the months since she started her art class, she and Mack have struck up a friendship of sorts. After class, she packs her things more slowly than the other students; goes to the toilet so she'll be last to leave; does anything to ensure that she has a few moments alone with her teacher. And then, when everyone has gone, she and Mack talk, sitting on the desks, legs swinging, with the smell of paint hanging in the air. At first it's mundane things that occupy them – her art, her technique; his background; how he came to teach – and then it's deeper things: his failed marriage, her life in India. Mack, too, has lived abroad. He understands the longing in her soul for the heat, the colour, and the scent of foreign, soil. Audrey lives for these chats; she feels herself unfurling like a flower in the spring sunshine when she's with him. He is, it strikes her, the polar opposite of Ralph.

And, while nothing happens, her chats with Mack are laced with the *frisson* that there could be more. They dance around each other in a complex ballet, both aware of the possibilities that hang heavy between them, but Mack is a gentleman. He knows Audrey's married. It was she, not he, who suggested this meeting in the coffee shop.

Approaching the café now, Audrey sees Mack through the window before she goes in, and heat rushes to her face. He's dressed in the black polo neck sweater that she loves so much, his hair wild above it. A bell on the café door rings as she pushes through it. Mack looks up and, in that unguarded moment, she sees how pleased he is to see her. The realisation that he's there for her if she wants him makes her breathless. Mack pushes his chair back and stands to greet her.

'Mrs Templeton,' he says, and he leans in to her and kisses her cheek so close to the corner of her mouth that his lips brush hers. It sends jolt of electricity through Audrey's body and she senses that he feels it too. Audrey drags out the moment for as long as she can, leaning slightly in to him and inhaling the clean scent of his skin, imagining herself waking up next to this skin, these lips. After a rudely long moment they pull apart.

'Mr MacDonald,' she says. 'What a lovely surprise.'

June 1976

Barnes, London

Audrey sits at her dressing table and examines her face in the mirror. There are a few light wrinkles and the ghost of a shadow under her eyes but, at thirty-three, she's not looking older than any of her peers. Her skin is fair, almost translucent, and, while her lips are starting to lose the plumpness they had when she was in her twenties, their cupid's bow is still well defined. A splatter of freckles runs across her nose and cheekbones, as if she'd run past a pebble-dashing machine, and her eyes, which have in the past tended to show something of the sadness she's carried with her since the death of her parents, seem alive today. She runs a hand through her hair, examining the roots for greys, and is pleased to find not a single one diluting the auburn.

Quickly, she dusts some loose powder over her cheeks, adds mascara, a smudge of eyeliner and a flick of blusher. She sprays perfume at her throat then, with a sigh, she stands up and walks to the full-length mirror. Feeling nauseous now the day is here, Audrey steps out of her dress, out of her slip, her bra, and her panties, and looks at her naked body in the mirror. She has good muscle tone; her legs are shapely. She turns so she can't see the V between her legs. *That's okay,* she thinks. *I'll stand like that.*

Audrey examines the backs of her thighs and her bottom, checking for obvious dimples. The art class is progressing well. Three students dropped out after the first term but the remaining seven appear to have some talent and today they're taking their first life-drawing class. In front of the mirror, Audrey turns this way and that, experimenting with poses for the hundredth time that week. Mack said she can choose how she models. She drags over a stool. Would sitting be better? She's nervous, but not so much of the art class as of being naked near Mack. Since that first meeting in the coffee shop, they've continued seeing each other outside the classroom: grabbing coffees, lunches, and taking in the occasional art exhibition if Ralph's away. Audrey loves seeing art with Mack; loves watching the way he looks at the pieces. His knowledge seduces her. Unlike Ralph he's a renaissance man.

But nothing's happened; they're not lovers – not yet – although Audrey knows the descent into adultery is inevitable. She knows that, when the time comes, her acquiescence will be as natural as the changing of the seasons and she's looking forward to it in the same way you might anticipate the start of summer: all warmth and golden light. But, for now, she's savouring the delicious torture of wanting but not having. She knows deep inside herself that, somehow, today will be a watershed.

While the class draws her, Audrey sits very still and thinks about Mack. She can't understand why every woman in the world isn't throwing themselves at this beautiful man. It's not just his looks; it's his soul. Mack's an old soul, a wise soul with a kind heart, and it's this as much as his hair, his eyes and his physical presence that's drawing Audrey to him. She's not felt like this about a man since those heady days when she first met Ralph – those days of kissing on the back seat of the Daimler, unaware of anything but Ralph's touch.

And now Audrey lets herself imagine, as she looks at Mack pacing the studio, that he's her husband; that to go home with this incredible human being would be legitimate, above board, and a part of her daily life; that every night he would make love to her – and her belly shivers with excitement. She gives herself an imperceptible shake. *You're getting ahead of yourself Audrey. You'll never leave Ralph.* And then she hears a smaller voice in her head: *But you're in love with Mack.*

Audrey exhales, trying not to move. *Focus,* she tells herself. *You're not leaving Ralph Templeton.* There are many reasons why she won't leave her husband but more important than any of them – more important than her marriage vows, more important than the highs and lows she weathers with Ralph, and far more important than the man currently pacing the art room – is the commitment she's made to John and Alexandra.

The twins are closer to her than they are to Ralph and, even then, she feels guilty because she knows she doesn't love them in quite the same way as their birth mother would. She's spent enough mornings in the library, lost in psychology text books, to know that the death of her parents has damaged her. She understands now that the sudden loss has caused her to live her life with a sense of ephemerality – a sense that everything can be lost in a moment – and to know that it's this that's stopped her from becoming too close to the twins. But, even so, even with that distance, she's the best they've got and she can't bear to think of what would happen to them if she left them without the love of the woman they know as their mother. Ralph might marry again; far more likely he'd just hire a nanny and carry on ignoring them.

Audrey brings her mind back to the classroom. She's now been sitting still with twelve pairs of eyes on her for forty-five minutes but Mack hasn't looked at her once. He's working intensely with his students, checking their easels as he moves about the room. It's another day in the office for him; he looks everywhere but at Audrey and his apparent disinterest leaves her feeling strangely deflated. She's steeled herself for him to see her naked; for the feel of his eyes moving over her bare skin, and now she feels a breath of disappointment. What had she hoped for? That he would compliment her on her naked body in front of the class? Gaze longingly at her breasts? Let his hand fall onto her bare bottom? She feels a flush rise in her cheeks. Is that why she'd volunteered to pose nude? Was that her motivation?

'Right, now,' says Mack, rubbing his hands together. 'Time to start wrapping it up. You have just five more minutes. Five minutes, people.'

As the last student leaves, Audrey, now in her dressing gown, moves to the back room to find her clothes. From the classroom she hears the door close and then Mack is suddenly behind her, his hands on her shoulders, his lips at her ear. She smells the essence of him – no cologne, just clean skin and the fresh-air scent of that ridiculously curly hair – feels the firmness of him behind her.

'Thank you, Mrs Templeton. You're a natural,' he says in her ear and, as he says it, his hand slides down her body, his fingers grazing her breast through the thin satin as he looks for, finds, and fingers the sash of her gown. He pauses long enough for her to know he's asking permission. Her silence is her reply. She realises now that he's worked hard to ignore her this morning; that he wants this as much as she does. The moment has been months coming and Audrey is more than ready. Mack pulls the sash, lets the gown fall open. Audrey doesn't move. Mack's hands slide up her body once more, his hand brushing the bare skin of her breast before settling on her waist.

Audrey keeps very still, savouring the moment, waiting to see what he'll do next. Mack holds Audrey like this and she feels the tickle of his beard as his lips graze her neck. 'I adore you, Mrs Templeton,' he breathes, and he kisses her neck again. Audrey turns around and lets the gown drop.

April 2013

St Ives, Cornwall

As soon as I pulled into the narrow lane were Mum lived, I saw that John had beaten me there. His car was parked in the road with the kind of military precision not many people achieve. I tucked mine in behind it as best I could, trying not to scratch the paintwork on the hedge while leaving enough space for other cars to squeeze past. John was standing outside the front door. He turned when he heard my footsteps on the driveway.

'She's not here.'

'What do you mean "she's not here"? I spoke to her last night. She knows we're coming.'

After weeks of to-ing and fro-ing, John and I had hatched a plan to come down together, have lunch at Mum's, and gently introduce the idea of her moving to Harbourside. A two-bedroom house had just come up for sale at a price that would leave Mum change after she sold the bungalow. It looked perfect. I'd psyched myself up for the meeting today.

'What do you think I mean?' John said. 'She's not here. I've been ringing for ages.' I could tell by the tone of his voice that he was already in one of his moods and I sighed to myself. When John was like this, there was no reasoning with him: he

126

saw the worst in everything.

'Let me try,' I said, hoping I'd have the magic touch that would bring Mum skipping to the door.

'I'm telling you, she's not here,' John said. 'She comes to the door really quickly. It's not a big house.'

'Maybe she's in the loo. Or getting changed, or something. Give her a minute.'

We stood impatiently for a minute.

'Have you got the brochure?' I asked.

'In the car.' John looked at his watch, then rang Big Ben twice in succession. Nothing.

I banged on the door with my fist; I opened the letter box, bent down, and shouted through it, 'Muuum!'

'I'm telling you: she's forgotten.' John looked almost pleased. He marched over to the garage, tested the door, then put his face to a crack. 'Car's gone. She's out.'

I sighed. 'Now what? Do we wait?'

I got down on my knees and looked through the letterbox. There was no sign of movement, certainly no smell of cooking.

'Pub? We could have a quick drink and come back? She might have got the time wrong.'

John raised an eyebrow. I chewed my lip in reply; we'd been brought up in a house where lunch was on the table at one come hell or high water.

'We could call her,' I suggested. 'On her mobile?'

John laughed. 'Try if you like,' he said. 'She never turns it on "unless it's an emergency".' He used his high-pitched granny voice. 'Like us trying to track her down when she goes AWOL isn't an emergency.'

'Well, there's no point in us standing here. There's nowhere we can walk to, is there?'

'Not really.'

'Well, come on then. I'll drive.'

John followed me to my car and we both climbed in. I eased the car carefully into a tight three-point turn, then jammed on the brakes as Mum's Mini turned into the lane, missing us by a cat's whisker.

'Oh, finally.' I glanced at the dashboard clock. Mum was twenty minutes late.

'Look, just don't give her a hard time. Okay?' I reversed the car back into its parking space, giving Mum room to inch past us and into her garage. 'Maybe she was picking up something she needed for lunch.'

John and I got out, and walked down the driveway again. Mum emerged from the garage smiling brightly as she fumbled for her keys.

'Hello Alexandra, John. To what do I owe the pleasure?'

John looked at me. I stepped forward and gave her a hug.

'Hello,' I said. 'You look great!' And I wasn't lying – Mum did look great. There was a bloom in her cheeks and a light in her eyes. Today she was wearing a periwinkle coat that brought out the colour of her eyes.

'Is everything okay?' she asked, looking from John to me and back. 'Weren't you coming next week? I was going to cook sea bass with sherry.'

John opened his mouth to speak but I cut him off.

'We spoke last night,' I said gently. 'Do you remember?'

Mum frowned. 'Yes. Yes, of course I remember. But I thought we were talking about next week.'

I laughed. 'A misunderstanding. That's funny! We must have been talking at cross purposes the whole time. Ha ha!' I saw that John was glowering at me. 'But we're here now,' I said. 'Are you free?'

She shrugged. 'Well, I'm rather busy. But I could make a macaroni cheese or something now you're here?' Her smile didn't reach her eyes.

'Okay,' said John. 'Sounds good.' He walked towards the front door.

'That's very kind of you but utterly unnecessary,' I said, glowering at John. 'Let's go to the pub.' I turned to Mum. 'What time does The Ship stop serving?'

She looked at her watch. 'Two thirty, I think. Just give me a minute.'

Inside the house, Mum disappeared off upstairs to get ready for lunch.

I turned to face John. 'Couldn't you see she didn't want to cook?'

He tutted. 'I just thought the conversation would be better had at home than in a noisy pub. Anyway,' he said dismissively, 'the point is, she forgot today, even after you spoke to her last night.'

I shook my head. 'Don't read anything into it. She thought we were talking about next week. I honestly don't remember if I mentioned specifically that it was today. Maybe I just assumed that she knew. I should have made it more clear. It was probably my fault.'

I walked over to the dresser while John flopped down on Mum's sofa. We were waiting in the long space that served as living and dining room. The majority of the furniture was new – smaller and more modern than the stuff we'd had in Barnes. Although not grand, it suited the house. I touched my finger to the surface of the dresser, leaving a mark in the fine layer of dust that covered it. I looked around at John to see if he'd noticed and he raised an eyebrow at me. It was obvious that Mum hadn't been expecting us. The dining-table was set up as a workspace; Mum's laptop was open, surrounded by books.

'That's another thing to worry about.' John nodded towards the computer. 'She's on it all the time. Do you even know what she's doing?' I shook my head. John continued. 'Do we need to talk to her about internet safety? I've just been through it all with the twins: "Don't give out your personal details," "People might not be who they seem," etcetera, etcetera.'

'I'm sure she'll be fine. She wasn't born yesterday.'

'I've got loads of antiques!' John put on his granny voice. 'Come and help yourselves ... here's my address!'

'God, John. You're such a worry-wart! I don't know how Anastasia puts up with you sometimes.'

'Because I'm her meal ticket,' he said flatly.

'Trouble in paradise?'

He sighed. 'No.'

'Regrets?'

John snorted. Mum clattered down the stairs

and burst into the room.

'I was just looking at your books,' I said. 'Looks like you've got quite into the internet.'

'Oh yes,' she said. 'Have been for a while now.' She went over to the laptop and tapped the space bar. I saw a flash of Mediterranean colour, then it was gone as Mum closed down the computer. 'It's amazing what those things can do. I haven't learned the half of it yet but I'm getting there. I'm doing an online course as well. But first I had to use the books to learn how to get online.'

'Good for you.' I picked up a picture she'd printed out. It was of a piece of artwork; a family picnicking under an olive tree. The picture had a warmth to it that made me think of holidays. 'Nice,' I said.

Mum nodded, her eyes lingering on the picture. 'Right, come on, let's go.'

December 1976

Barnes, London

Ready for the dinner that was originally booked for eight o'clock, Audrey can't settle. She's been up and down the stairs, in and out of the drawing room, trying to kill time with little tasks. *By the time he gets here,* she thinks, *I'll have walked two miles just around the house.* She forces herself to sit down on the edge of an armchair and picks up a magazine, flicks idly through it. She's already telephoned the restaurant and moved the booking to eight thirty, but Ralph really ought to be here by now if they're going to make even that. She slaps the magazine back onto the coffee table and sighs, then she stands up and walks over to the bay window, easing herself behind the pair of chairs that frame the space and pulling open a chink in the curtain. It's dark outside and Audrey can't see anything beyond the pools of light illuminated by the street lights but, somehow, looking helps, even when there's nothing to see.

She pulls the heavy curtain back into place and wanders over to the bookshelf, turns her head sideways and peruses Ralph's book collection. He hasn't read half of them, she'd bet, and why would he want to, she wonders, looking at some of the titles. They're books picked by the interior designer, not for content, but for the beauty of their spines. She turns away in disinterest and lets her gaze drift around the elegant drawing room. The classic décor is brightened by the blues, greys, and golds of the large silk rug that graces the stripped wooden floorboards in the centre of the room. Audrey half-closes her eyes and tries to picture the rug back in the Bombay house, where it had lauded over the upstairs landing.

The sound of the key stabbing at the lock jolts Audrey back to Barnes. She smooths her dress over her thighs and takes a quick look at her face in the mirror that hangs over the fireplace. Yes, she looks fine. It takes Ralph three attempts to get the key into the keyhole before the lock turns and the door pushes open.

'Hello, darling,' Audrey says, moving out to the

entrance hall to greet her husband. 'I moved the booking back half an hour. We should still make it if we get a move on.' She looks up and sees that Ralph has closed the door behind him and is standing motionless in the entrance hall. She can smell cigarettes and alcohol. His face looks disconnected somehow; there's something in his eyes that makes her cower back towards the drawing room, a kitten to his Rottweiler.

'Send the babysitter home,' says Ralph.

'But...'

'We're not going.'

'What? How come? We can still make it.'

'I said: we're not going.' Ralph's voice is ominously quiet. 'Go on. Up you go, and tell her to go home.'

Audrey knows better than to argue. Slipping off her heels, she hurries up the stairs to the third floor study, where Hannah is ensconced for the evening. Audrey's breathing hard when she gets there, and it's not entirely from the exertion.

'I'm so sorry,' she says to Hannah. 'We're not going out after all. Something's come up. I'll pay you for the evening, of course.'

Hannah shrugs and gathers her things, and Audrey follows her back down the stairs. Ralph hasn't moved. He's still standing by the door.

'Goodnight,' he says to Hannah as she passes him. She gives him a nervous smile and Audrey wonders if she, too, smells the alcohol on Ralph's breath. The door clicks closed behind her.

'So,' begins Audrey. 'What...'

'Upstairs. Now.' Although Ralph's voice leaves no room for questions, he gives Audrey a little

133

shove as if to underline what he's said. Audrey looks at him out of the corner of her eye, trying to assess what's going on, but still she walks obediently to the staircase. Ralph shoves her again, making her stumble and throw out her hands to break her fall.

'Move it,' he says, and Audrey recovers herself and scampers up the stairs to their bedroom. Ralph follows her into the room, closes the door behind them and turns the key in the lock. He walks over to the window and yanks the curtains shut with a violence that's not entirely usual, then he turns to face her. He's very drunk, Audrey suddenly realises. This is more than a couple of drinks after work – this is the work of a whole afternoon in the pub. Ralph's face is distorted with anger. It's not the first time Audrey has been afraid of her husband but it is the first time that she realises she might be in some sort of danger. She backs towards the door, her breathing shallow.

'Don't even try,' says Ralph. 'It's locked.' He dangles the key to show her that she won't even be able to unlock the door, then puts it into his trouser pocket.

Audrey says nothing. She knows better than to ask what this is about. Ralph will tell her when he's ready. He starts to pace up and down the room, his steps carrying him between the wardrobe doors and the door to the *en suite*. Audrey's gaze follows him: left, right, left, right.

'So,' Ralph says eventually. 'How's your art class going?'

Audrey stiffens. Ralph walks over to her, pushes her chin up with his thumb, and holds her face by the jaw. She stares at his nose, noticing with revulsion something clinging to the hairs inside his nostrils.

'Maybe you didn't hear me. I said: how's your art class going?'

'Fine,' says Audrey. It's difficult for her to speak because Ralph is still holding her jaw. Her words push her jawbone against the tendons of his cold fingers.

'Are you enjoying it?'

'Mmm-hmm.'

'What are you enjoying the most?'

Audrey swallows. 'Still life,' she says through clenched teeth. It's the first thing that comes into her head. She knows where this is going – but how? How did he find out?

'Still life?' says Ralph. He drops her jaw suddenly, causing her to stumble backwards, and he walks away from her, towards the curtains. He lifts the edge, peers out at the street, then replaces the curtain, fussing with the fabric, making sure that there's absolutely no gap between the two curtains. He shrugs off his jacket, opens the wardrobe door, pulls out a hanger and places his jacket carefully on it. Then he turns back to Audrey. 'Still life, eh?' he strokes his chin. 'How many students are there?'

'Seven,' says Audrey. 'There were ten, but three left.' She's blathering, struggling to keep the conversation on an even keel, but she knows, even as she says it, that she's losing. She's a mouse; Ralph the cat, and he's playing with her. A part of her wants him just to come out and say it. Maybe he'll be so angry he'll strangle her, push her down the stairs, or bash her brains out with the Templeton family clock, and it'll all be over. In this moment Audrey would almost rather that than face what she suspects she's about to hear.

'Your teacher. Is he good?'

Audrey's head moves marginally up and down.

'He's good, but three students left? Hmm. I wonder why.'

Audrey shrugs.

'Why do you think they left, Audrey?'

Audrey swallows again. *Just get it over with,* she thinks.

'Maybe art wasn't their thing?'

'Or maybe they didn't like him. Tell me about him.'

'Who?'

'The teacher.'

'What do you want to know?' Audrey's voice is reed-thin.

'What's his name? What are his qualifications?' Ralph undoes his tie, holds it in his right hand, and lashes it against his left hand like a riding whip, takes a step closer to Audrey. 'What does he have that I don't have?'

Audrey moves towards the door to the *en suite*.

'Not so fast, my precious,' says Ralph, grabbing her by her clothes. 'Hit a nerve, did I? It's true that you're going out with your art teacher? Having coffees with him? Private art classes? *Fucking* him?' Ralph's eyes close in disgust as he says the word. 'I didn't want to believe it. I didn't want to believe that you could betray me like that.' His voice breaks but he recovers quickly. 'Why, Red? Why?' He shoves her against the wall as he's speaking, causing her head to bash against the solid brick. He holds her there by the shoulders. Spittle from his lips sprays her face as he shouts, 'Aren't I enough for you? Don't I give it to you enough? Aren't I good enough?'

Audrey's crying now, silent tears slipping down her face.

'Answer me!' yells Ralph. He shoves her against the wall again, then grabs her shoulders and flings her towards the bed, where she lands sprawled on her back. She starts to sit up but Ralph is on her, crouching over her, pushing her back down as he hikes up her skirt and rips her tights down her legs. She lifts her hips a fraction to allow him to pull down her knickers. She knows what's coming; she knows that to resist will make it worse.

With one knee still holding her down, Ralph rips open his belt and unzips his trousers. Then he rolls her over onto her belly, pulls her hips up and slams himself into her. The pain is blinding white; Audrey clamps her mouth shut to stop herself from crying out. He grips her hips hard, his fingers digging into her flesh and she clutches the edge of the pillow, squeezing tighter each time he rams into her. She turns her face into the pillow, her mouth open, gasping for air, trying not to make a sound.

Eventually Ralph shudders and pulls out. Audrey hears him grab a tissue from the bedside table and wipe himself, then the sound of him doing up his zip and belt. Ralph comes over to where Audrey is still lying face down on the pillow and rolls her over. She moves to pull her skirt down but he stops her, slapping her hands away from her legs, leaving her splayed and bare.

'You seem to have forgotten something, dear wife,' he says. He leans down and traces his finger over and around her face. Audrey lies stock-still, petrified. 'You seem to have forgotten that you're mine. Mine!' He laughs and shakes his head. 'Oh, you've no idea. No idea! No one leaves Ralph Templeton.' He pauses, breathing hard as stares at Audrey's body. 'You'll never see that man again. *Never!* No more *art class,* no more *coffee mornings,* no more out-of-the-house at all. Do you hear me? You will not humiliate me. *You will not!*' Ralph pauses again and the silence is almost as loud as his words had been. Then he jumps up and walks to the door, taking the key out of his pocket and smoothing his hair as he goes. Audrey hears him clatter down the stairs; hears the chink of his keys and the slam of the front door behind him.

Audrey uses the adrenalin that's still pumping through her body to heave herself up from the bed. Hunched over, she shuffles into the bathroom, where she cleans herself, gently washing the parts of her that are torn and swollen. She'd like a bath but she's not sure how long she has. She still believes in her marriage but there's a limit. Ralph's brutality tonight has pushed the blinkers away from her eyes. She can't put up with this. All she can think of is Mack. She'll run to Mack and he'll know what to do. Maybe they'll leave – leave London, maybe even leave England – they'll find somewhere to live. In her imagination, she sees a glimpse of India – of palm trees, exotic birds, noise, chaos, flowers, and sunshine, and some-

138

thing inside her softens. When the divorce goes through, she'll fight through the courts for the children. For now, she knows they're safe – Ralph has never lifted a hand to either of them – for now, all that matters is that she gets herself to Mack. Audrey half expects that Ralph's only pretended to go out; that he'll be waiting for her downstairs, ready to degrade her again.

Back in the bedroom Audrey climbs on a chair and pulls her suitcase down from on top of the wardrobe. She throws it onto the bed, opens it, opens her cupboards, and starts putting clothes, shoes, underwear, and cosmetics higgledy-piggledy into the bag. All the while, she has half an eye on the door. She's still expecting Ralph to reappear.

She's half expecting him to attack her again.

With the suitcase full, Audrey has just one more thing to do. She puts her hands to her ears, feeling the emerald earrings she'd put on for the dinner she and Ralph were supposed to attend that night. She removes them, takes them over to her leather jewellery box, and puts them neatly back in their place. Ignoring the pieces that Ralph has bought her, she takes only the simple silver bangle her father bought her when she turned eighteen. As Audrey slides it into her bag, she hears a fine click, the air pressure in the room changes, and she knows, before she turns, that the bedroom door has opened. She freezes; steels herself for the physical blow that she's sure will come but, instead, there's a voice:

'Mummy!'

Audrey spins around and sees two little faces

peering around the bedroom door, looking for signs of the father who never allows them into the room. Audrey rushes to the door, arms outstretched, hoping to prevent the twins from seeing the open suitcase on the bed.

'What is it?' she asks, gathering them in a hug. 'Can't you sleep?' She tries to usher them out of the room, back onto the landing, but John wriggles free and pushes past her, Alexandra close behind her.

'Lexi had a bad dream,' John starts, but then he sees the suitcase. He walks over to it, notes that it's almost full, looks accusingly at Audrey. 'Are you going somewhere?'

Alexandra is right behind him.

'Mummy,' she wails. Her face is tear-stained; she's clutching her teddy bear in her hands. 'Where are you going?'

Audrey takes their hands in hers, strokes the peachy-soft skin.

'Nowhere ... nowhere at all. Now, back to bed.'

'Why are you packing?' Alexandra is still crying.

Audrey looks from Alexandra to John: two small children in their nightwear; two small children with terrified faces, scared that their mother's going somewhere. They have no idea what she's planning. A galaxy of emotion passes through Audrey and she throws out an arm to steady herself on the wall. She knows Ralph won't harm the children, but what he will do is ignore them. Audrey is the first to admit she's not a natural mum – she's never been one of those Earth Mother types – but she's all John and Alexandra have.

The moment stretches. Alexandra steps towards Audrey, puts her hand on her knee;

'Can we come too, Mummy?'

Audrey gathers the girl into her arms and nuzzles the sweet, biscuit smell of her neck, smooths her shiny locks of hair, still damp with sweat from her dreams. Then Audrey takes a deep breath. She hears herself speak as if she's at the bottom of the ocean, the words distorted, coming from somewhere else.

'You sillies! Mummy's not going anywhere,' she says. 'Mummy was just testing to see if she needed a new suitcase. Ready for our next holiday.' She holds out an arm to John and he steps forward, allows himself, stiffly, to be embraced.

'Really?' he asks. 'You're not packing?'

'No, silly billy!' She ruffles his hair and releases the children. 'I know how many dresses I can fit in now. I was just starting to put everything back. Right, come on. Back to bed.'

Audrey walks the children back up the stairs to their rooms, tucks each child back into their bed, administers sips of water and strokes soft foreheads until the twins' features relax into sleep. Then she goes back down to her bedroom and, piece by piece, her face wet with tears, she takes her clothes back out of the case.

April 2013

St Ives, Cornwall

The Ship was a modern pub, the decor bright and modern, the floor wooden. As Mum pushed open the door, we were met with the smell of cooking and almost all of the tables were occupied with people tucking into roast lunches.

'That's a good sign.' I waved my hand around the room taking in all the people.

'Yes, it's very popular.' Mum's eyes rolled over the room. 'I hope we get a table.'

'There's one,' said John, indicating a small table in the corner. He forced his way through the maze of tables and threw himself onto a chair.

'Right. Drinks,' he said once we'd all settled. 'I'll go. What does everyone want?'

'A gin and orange, please,' said Mum.

'I'll have a Perrier. Driving.'

John nodded and headed over to the bar.

'Nice of him to go,' I said. 'I wasn't expecting that.'

Mum pulled a face. 'Me neither.'

I looked at the menu scrawled on the blackboard next to the bar. 'What do you recommend?'

'I hear the veggie lasagne's good. Not too heavy. It comes with a salad. Mmm. I think I'll have that.'

'Sounds lovely.'

Mum rubbed her belly. 'I don't eat much meat these days. It takes me days to digest it. I really can't stand great hunks of meat anymore.'

John reappeared with three glasses balanced in his hands.

'We were thinking of having the veggie lasagne,' said Mum. 'It's really good.'

'Well, you're getting the roast beef. I've ordered it for all of us.'

'Oh, lovely,' said Mum. 'I'm sure it's very nice.' She smiled at me and the brittleness of it reminded me of the old days back in Barnes when my father had been alive. I realised now that it was a wallpaper smile; a smile designed to smooth over the cracks. I'd seen it a lot when I was growing up; when Pa was shouting or in one of his funks. I stared at Mum for a minute, seeing for the first time the adult dynamic between John and her. My brother bullied her, and she took it.

John pulled a receipt out of his pocket and studied it. 'Twenty-two pounds a head. So ... shall we call it twenty each?' He looked at Mum and I expectantly. Neither of us moved. 'What?' he asked. 'We're all adults. Why should I pay?'

Mum reached for her handbag.

'No, Mum. I'll get this.' I put two twenty pound notes on the table.

'Thank you, dear,' said Mum. She picked up her drink. 'Cheers!'

John and I raised our glasses. 'To pleasant surprises,' Mum said.

'To family,' I said. We sipped our drinks. I looked at John out of the corner of my eye, wondering if now was as good a time as any to broach

143

the topic of Harbourside. He stared into his pint, as if the answers to everything lay there. Mum looked from John to me, a bemused smile on her face.

'So, will you come down next week as well?' she asked. 'Or no need now?'

'Oh...' I stalled, wondering how to be tactful. 'If you want us to.' John gave me a look. 'But we don't really need to, do we? Now we're here.'

'It's up to you,' said Mum. 'It's always nice to see you but I never want you to feel beholden. You have your own lives to get on with.'

'Well – maybe let's leave it for another time. I do have a lot on at the moment. Exam marking and ... you know.'

'No problem. I'll do you the fish next time,' said Mum. 'It's lovely. It's a Nigella recipe. I got it off the worldwide web.'

'Amazing, isn't it, that web thing?' said John. Again, I kicked him under the table. 'Anyway, Mum,' he paused for a fraction, and I watched his Adam's apple rise and fall as he swallowed. 'There's a reason we wanted to see you today.'

'Oh?' said Mum.

The bench seat that she was on was slightly lower than the chairs John and I were on and she looked up at us, trustingly, like a child. I felt as if we were about to start walking down a path from which there would be no return. Suddenly I felt the need to rummage in my handbag for something.

'Lexi and I wanted to talk to you,' John said.

'Go on,' said Mum.

'It's about your living arrangements,' said John.

'We're worried about you living alone.' He bit his lip. 'We're not saying you need to move right now or anything but, looking ahead, we think it's probably time to start looking for some sort of, umm, sheltered housing type thing. You know – where care's available. If you need it.'

There was a silence. I focused on my bag. Now John was saying the words out loud, it sounded all wrong.

'We're not talking about an old peoples' home. More of a really nice residential development where there'll be support,' he said. There was a silence. 'Lexi and I have had a talk. You know, after the accident and whatnot. We think you need to have someone on hand for if you fall over at home, or lock yourself out. You know – just the kinds of things that start to happen to people as they get older. You'll be seventy this year.'

Still Mum didn't say anything. Finally I looked up from my bag. Mum was staring at us. I noticed again how blue her eyes were; how smooth and unlined her cheeks were.

'A house is a big responsibility,' said John. 'We don't think you living on your own is going to continue working. Moving into the future. There are some really nice developments around the area.' Mum opened her mouth but John carried on. 'There's a place where you can own your own home and have your independence, but there's care available if you need it. A bit like a holiday home for the older generation. Have you heard of Harbourside?'

Silence.

'Lexi and I had a look. Got the brochure. It

145

looks nice. We think you'd like it – and guess what? There's a two-bedroom house for sale at the moment.' He beamed at Mum but she didn't return the smile. She looked slowly from John to me and back again as if she were having trouble processing what was being said. I pressed my lips together, wishing, wishing, wishing I wasn't there.

'I see,' said Mum. She looked from John to me. Her fingers worried the grain of the wooden table. 'Is this true, Alexandra? You two went house hunting for me?'

I bit my lip and nodded.

'You think I should sell my house and move into some sort of old people's development?' John gave the smallest of nods and Mum laughed. 'You think that, too, Alexandra?'

'No,' I said. 'It's not like that. Please don't think that! We just thought that you might have a ... better quality of life...' I cringed as I said it, 'if you had access to some sort of warden or emergency call-out. You know, someone who could be there in a flash. Rather than you having to call one of us and wait while we drive down.'

'Better quality of life?' Mum echoed. She raised her eyebrows. 'Better quality of life?'

'Mum, please.' I leaned towards her, my words fast and earnest. 'Harbourside looked really nice. I wouldn't mind living there myself. The architecture was beautiful – it looked like a high-end holiday resort. Really nice architecture, lovely houses and apartments. And so much to do! Dancing, fishing, outings. It's for the over fifty-fives so it's not like it's stuffed with oldies.' Finally I made eye contact with Mum. 'Look, it's not like

146

we're trying to put you in a home. We're just trying to find somewhere safe for you to live, where you'll have access to everything that you need as you get older. Going forward. Because we can't always be there, and we love you.'

Mum closed her eyes for a moment before she spoke. 'Well,' she said. 'When the time comes, we'll consider options. But that time is not now. As far as I'm aware there isn't a problem with my quality of life.' Again she laughed, a joyless snort of a sound.

'But Mum,' John said, and I kicked out under the table, searching in vain for his ankle, willing him to shut up now. 'Remember when you had the car accident?' he said. 'Lexi and I tied ourselves in knots trying to sort everything out for you: the hospital, the car, the insurance, looking after you, shopping... And we have other responsibilities. There are only so many hours in the day.'

Mum looked at him with so much hurt in her eyes that I had to look away. To be fair, that hadn't been her fault.

'Is this why you wanted to see me today?' she asked. 'Is that why I've been honoured with a visit from the pair of you together, instead of the solo fortnightly visits? You came down here to tell me to sell my home?'

'Lexi and I are just worried about you,' said John. 'You can't deny you're losing your memory. Lunch was always this week, not next week.'

'Okay fine,' said Mum rolling her eyes. 'A clerical error. It's hardly Alzheimer's.'

John shook his head. 'It's not just that, Mum. You're not as sharp as you used to be.'

147

'You try being sixty-nine,' Mum said. 'I'd like to see you do what I do at my age.'

John refused to be drawn. 'You've had quite a serious accident *and* locked yourself out. And what if you fall down the stairs next time? Like Valya. Hit your head and lie there with a broken leg for days. At least I was around to find Valya. Not that it helped.'

A shadow passed across Mum's face. 'Don't bring Valya into this. What happened to Valya doesn't do you any favours ... any favours at all.'

I looked at Mum sharply. Her face looked pinched.

John continued, his expression impassive. 'We just want to make sure there's help available – quickly – if you need it. Lexi and I can't always drop everything and come.'

'You really don't need to worry about me. Okay? I absolve you of any responsibility. Get on with your own lives and don't worry about me. It's nice to see you, but I don't *need* your visits.'

'Table eighteen?' asked a voice behind me. 'Three roasts? Super. Here you go.' The waitress balanced her tray on the edge of the table and unloaded the plates of food. 'You've got cutlery?' she asked. John unfolded his napkin and spread it on his lap, cut open his roast potatoes and sprinkled salt liberally over them. He poured gravy over his beef, then took a forkful.

'Lovely,' he said, chewing. 'Really good. Good choice.'

Mum stared at the pile of meat and vegetables on her plate. She made no move to pick up her cutlery.

148

'We just want what's best for you,' I said, reaching for her hand. She pulled it away.

'Best for who?' she asked. 'No. On second thoughts, don't answer that.' She sat back and shook her head. 'After all I've done for you.' She shook her head again. 'After *all* I've done for you.' She pushed her plate away and stood up. 'Enjoy your lunch,' she said, and marched out of the pub.

April 2013

St Ives, Cornwall

'Now look what you've done!' I shouted at John. 'Happy now?' I threw my cutlery back onto the plate with a clatter, jumped up and ran out of the pub after Mum, pushing my way through the tables without caring that everyone was staring. I banged through the door and out onto the street, looking left and right to see which way Mum had gone.

'Wait, Mum! Wait!'

I saw her hurrying down the road towards the harbour. It was a steep descent and I ran to catch up with her, terrified that she'd stumble or slip.

'Mum!' I grabbed her arm and pulled her around to face me. 'I'm sorry about what John said. I don't know how I let myself get dragged into that. He's just worried, that's all. Please don't listen to him. We won't make you do anything you don't want to do. Please, Mum. It was just him

149

thinking aloud. Please come back. Come back for your lunch?'

Mum shook her head and I noticed two spots of colour still high on her cheeks. 'No,' she said. She jerked her arm away and continued to walk. I hurried after her.

'Okay, then let me take you home. Come on, it's the least I can do.' I took Mum's arm and turned her back towards the car park. She shook my hand off her but walked stiffly alongside me. I started sentences in my head but nothing reached my mouth. I didn't know what to say to her. When we got to the car I opened her door and held it for her, as if she'd try to run away if I left her. When she'd got in I slammed the door, then quickly dialled John as I went around to the driver's side.

'I'm just dropping Mum home. She doesn't want to come back,' I said. In the background I heard the noises of the pub.

'Okay.' John sounded as if he was speaking with his mouth full.

I sneaked a look at Mum every now and then as we drove. Her whole body was angled away from me as if she couldn't get far enough away. She stared out of her window and I tried to draw her in with small talk, pointing out a new shop or commenting on a nice car going the other way, but she responded only with the smallest nod or shake of her head, as if I was interrupting her thoughts. Sadness washed over me. I had the sense, as always, that I didn't know my mother at all; that I didn't know how to break through to her. I clenched my jaw. It was so frustrating. I put on Classic FM and let the sound of a piano concerto fill the car until I finally pulled into Mum's road.

'Here we are then,' I said. I took a deep breath. 'Look – about what John said...'

Mum didn't even look at me as she got out of the car.

'Don't stress about it,' she said, and disappeared into her house, leaving me with the sense that I'd once again failed to connect.

December 1976

Barnes, London

Audrey stands on the doorstep of the Barnes house and waves until her arm aches; she waves at the white car that's taking her husband to the airport until it disappears from sight. To her neighbours and to passers-by she looks every inch the dutiful wife. Feeling as if she's on a stage, Audrey smiles to her next-door neighbour, who's bringing in the milk.

'Good morning!'

'Morning,' replies the neighbour, a woman who, despite having four children under five and a dog the size of a small horse, is always immaculately turned out. Even now she's in full make-up and looks as if she's had her hair set.

'Off anywhere nice?' asks the neighbour, nodding her head in the direction the chauffeur-driven car's just gone.

'He's off to India. Business,' says Audrey.

'Won't be here for Christmas then?' asks the neighbour.

'No. He won't.'

The neighbour pulls a sad face. 'Aw. The poor children. Will they miss their daddy?'

'Of course,' says Audrey, 'but, you know … we'll make it fun.' She shrugs as if to show she's making do with a bad lot but, in reality, she's overjoyed to have some respite from the oppressive atmosphere that's choked the house since the night of the rape. Anyway, today Audrey has an agenda. Back inside the house, she closes the front door gently, listening to the latch click into place, then she leans against it, breathes deeply in and out, and listens to the silence: no children, no husband – the house to herself. She feels the first kick of adrenalin as she thinks about what she's going to do with Ralph safely out of the way; about what's been consuming her for the past nine days – although she still has to wait a little longer.

Audrey walks into the kitchen and sets about preparing herself a coffee. When it's done, she picks up the phone and brings it over to the kitchen table, where she sits with the day's newspaper. Audrey tries to focus on the headline story as she blows gently across the surface of the coffee but she's taking nothing in. She looks at the phone, picks up the handset, listens to the dial tone, then replaces it carefully. She's told herself that she must wait for Ralph at least to have reached the airport and checked in: another hour. There could be any number of reasons why he might turn back: forgotten passport, documents –

anything. She stares at the paper, sips her coffee.

When she's turned all the pages of the paper and sipped down to the dregs of her coffee, Audrey stands up, takes her cup to the sink and washes it. She looks at the kitchen clock. The second hand clunks stubbornly around the dial, each tick a monumental effort. Twenty minutes to go. But he's not back. If he comes back now, he'll surely miss his flight. Audrey dithers in the kitchen, arguing with herself. Is she safe now?

'Oh, for goodness' sake,' she tells herself. Her voice, competing only with the ticking of the clock, sounds loud in the silent house. She goes over to the kitchen table and sits down. She clears her throat, picks up the handset and starts to dial the number she's committed to memory. When the line connects and she hears the ringing sound, she clears her throat once more, gives a little cough, and waits, her blood thrumming in her veins. She waits and waits, but the number rings on: no answer. She places the receiver carefully back into the cradle.

Audrey hasn't thought about what she'd do if Mack doesn't pick up. She's assumed he would; of course he would. In her mind's eye, Mack has been waiting desperately to hear from her since the first day she'd failed to turn up to art school, if not before. It's inconceivable that he's out. Emboldened, she dials again – no reply. Audrey slams the receiver down harder this time, causing the phone's bell to give one startled tring.

'Hmm,' she says out loud. She stands up, the legs of her chair scraping across the kitchen floor tiles. She marches out to the hall and, before she

153

gives herself a chance to think twice, she grabs her coat, picks up her handbag from the hall table, scoops up her keys, and dashes out into the street.

Audrey is unaware of the traffic, of the pedestrians, of the cold, clammy air that encircles her, frizzing her hair and dampening her coat as her shoes click along the pavement. She reaches the familiar college, walks across the car park, pushes open the door and enters the foyer with its ever-present smell of disinfectant. Her eyes are drawn at once to the noticeboard with the class lists and she sees immediately that something's different; even from this distance, she sees handwriting, some sort of amendment. She walks over to the board and takes in the news: her art class has a new teacher. A felt-tip line runs through her lover's name. Over the top is handwritten a different name. Audrey spins around, looking for someone to ask. The reception desk is empty but there's a sign next to a phone, asking people to call the office with any queries.

Audrey dials the number.

'Hello?' she says. 'I'm calling about the introduction to art class. Taught by, um, Dave Mac-Donald?'

'Yes?' says a woman's voice on the other end of the phone. 'How can I help you?'

'Well, I'm just in the foyer and I just wanted to ask why Mr, um, MacDonald isn't taking the art class anymore?'

Audrey hears a rustling of papers. 'Ah, yes, yes,' says the woman's voice. 'The class is now being taken by Mr Steven Roach.'

'Why?' asks Audrey. 'What happened to Mr MacDonald? Why isn't he taking the class any more?'

'Mr MacDonald, I believe, erm ... hold on a sec...' Audrey hears as the woman turns to speak to someone in the room with her. 'Susan? Why isn't Mack taking the adult art class anymore? Just got someone on the phone ... ah ... okay. Oh, that was it, was it? Is that all we know? Okay ... okay. Thanks.' The woman's voice comes back to the phone line. 'Oh, he resigned,' she says casually, as if the news she's delivering is of no consequence at all. Audrey grips the edge of the reception desk, steeling herself. 'With immediate effect. I think he was moving away. He left, what, a week ago?'

Audrey sways a little as she listens. The voice sounds like it's coming from the moon. She hears herself reply; hears herself thank the woman, end the call. With her coat flapping open around her, she walks like a zombie out of the college, aware only of the contact her feet have with the pavement. Eventually she spots green grass, recognises Barnes Green, crosses roads to get herself there, finds a wet bench and collapses onto it, her head in her hands. Why did he leave just like that? Without telling her, leaving no forwarding address, nothing? How can she find Mack now? Audrey needs to explain to him what happened. She needs to tell him that Ralph found out; explain that she had no choice; that she couldn't leave the children.

Audrey has never spoken to Mack about Ralph. She'd been almost religious about keeping the

155

two sides of her life completely separate. It's funny, she often thought as she lay entangled with Mack, how making love with him didn't seem as much of a betrayal as talking to him about her husband; giving away details of their life together. And now she realises that Mack had no idea what Ralph was like; no idea of how Mrs Templeton tiptoes around her husband. Mack probably thought she'd just got bored of him: lost interest in the class and dumped him. She thinks about the injustice of it all and moans.

As Audrey sits on the bench, tormenting herself with what Mack must have thought of her, she suddenly remembers that his phone had rung: it hadn't been disconnected. She jumps up and turns towards the road that will lead her to Mack's apartment. As she walks, this time with a purpose in her step, Audrey feels the thrill of the illicit in her bones. Her body remembers taking this walk on the days when she was stealing an hour or two to meet Mack at his home and she tells herself, as she walks along, that this is not the case now; that her body must not anticipate her arrival at his house in such a way.

She passes under the railway bridge and then the red-brick mansion block with its glorious river views comes into view. Audrey steps up to the front door and buzzes the number to Mack's flat. She repeats this three times, waiting a minute in between each buzz. She hears steps behind her and turns to see a woman whose face is familiar from her previous visits. The woman appears to be some kind of professional – a consultant of some sort, maybe. Despite being home in the middle of the day, she's dressed in a sharp business suit and heels, and carries a smart leather handbag. Audrey can see the top of a bulging desk diary at its opening. Even though Audrey had pretended she was having art lessons with Mack in his home and had spoken several times at unnecessary length to the woman about the quality of the light over the river, she's pretty sure that the woman guessed the real reason for her visits. Now, as the woman rummages in her handbag for her key, Audrey takes her chance.

'Hello,' she says. 'I was supposed to be meeting Mr MacDonald for an art lesson. But he doesn't seem to be home. Have you seen him recently?'

The woman stops rummaging and examines at Audrey, as if wondering what to say. 'Mmm,' she says finally. 'I saw him last week. He was moving out.'

Audrey's insides freeze. 'Are you sure?'

'Positive,' says the woman. 'He'd hired a van. Double-parked while he loaded it.'

Audrey presses her lips together and tries to look thoughtful. She wants to ask if he left a forwarding address but, equally, she doesn't want to admit that she has no idea where Mack has gone. She slaps her forehead.

'Oh, yes!' she exclaims. 'Silly me. I remember now he'd told me he was moving. Oh, how silly I can be. Mind like a sieve.' Her laugh is brittle. 'Anyway – thank you. Take care!' She turns to go, but the woman continues to speak.

'I don't know what happened to him,' she says. 'He looked as if he were in some kind of trouble.'

Audrey spins around. 'What? What sort of trouble?'

The woman looks at the ground then back up at Audrey. She chooses her words carefully. 'It looked like he'd been in a fight.' She pauses, looks appraisingly – challengingly – at Audrey. It strikes Audrey that she knows how upsetting this will be for her to hear; that she's being deliberately cruel. 'His face was quite bashed up.'

Audrey's hand flies to her mouth. 'Really? What do you mean "bashed up"?'

'Two black eyes, cuts, bruising.' She peers at Audrey. 'You want me to carry on?'

Audrey can barely breathe.

The woman seems to be enjoying cataloguing Mack's injuries. She continues even though Audrey doesn't reply. 'I don't know how he managed the move, to be honest. He must have been in a lot of pain. One eye was so swollen it barely opened and his nose was clearly broken, as were – I'd say – a couple of his fingers. He'd bandaged them together but I could see they were very swollen.' She pauses thoughtfully. 'You know. Kind of black and disfigured?'

Audrey thinks of Mack's long, elegant fingers – the tools of his trade. However painful the injuries were, it wouldn't come close to the pain of not being able to paint.

'Did he say what happened?' she asks. 'A car accident – or ...?'

The woman sighs. 'Maybe. But my money's on a fight.'

'But he's not the fighting sort – he's just not!'

'Look. I'm just telling you what I saw.' The

158

woman slots her key into the lock. 'Anyway, I have to go. Hope you find him. See you around, maybe.'

Audrey nods to the woman and turns away. She crosses the road and leans her elbows on the wall as she stares at the river Mack had loved so much. Its waters slide by, as they always have done; as they always will do. She thinks about her lover's injuries. She knows now where her husband went after he raped her; what he did next.

'Oh, Mack,' she says to the river. 'I'm so sorry.'

December 1976

Barnes, London

'Hello?' The line is crackly, echoing. There's a lot of background noise. Standing in the hall of the Barnes house, Audrey presses the receiver against her ear better to hear.

'Audrey.'

'Mack?'

'I'm in a phone box. I only have one coin. Don't say anything, just listen. I'm okay. But I'm leaving. Don't follow me. Your husband...' His voice breaks. 'Please don't follow me, Audrey. For your own safety, don't try to find me.'

'But...'

'But nothing. Please Audrey. If you love me, forget me. Please. I love you. I love you with all my heart. I always will. Stay safe.

'I love you, too. I love you, Mack.' It's the first time she's said the words.

The line beeps and goes dead.

Audrey sinks to the floor.

April 2013

Truro, Cornwall

I was sitting at the kitchen table when the invitation arrived. It was one of those beautiful early summer mornings and I was eating scrambled eggs on toast while flicking through the news on the iPad. I heard the letterbox rattle and the post land on the doormat with a thwump that was heavier than the usual pile of flimsy bills. I looked up from the iPad, wondering whether it was worth getting up to see what had caused the thwump. I heard Mark clattering down the wooden stairs.

'Can you bring the post?' I shouted. The steps paused, then Mark appeared in the kitchen, a cream envelope in his hand, his coffee-cup in the other.

'Fancy,' he said, dropping a thick, cream envelope onto the table.

I picked it up and weighed it in my hand. The postmark was from Cornwall but I didn't recognise the writing: thick, black calligraphy addressed only to me: Mrs Alexandra Scrivener. Raising my eyebrows at Mark, I picked up a knife, slid it neatly across the top and pulled out a card.

'Wedding?' Mark sat down with his cereal.

'No,' I said slowly, still digesting the news. 'It's from Mum. She's asking me to go on a cruise.'

As I said it I widened my eyes at Mark across the table and he echoed the expression with a shrug. Aside from a few stilted phone calls initiated by me and ended prematurely by Mum, I hadn't heard from Mum since the disastrous lunch. Nothing more had been said about her living arrangements. It was now the white elephant between us, and I suspected she'd been avoiding calling John and me, perhaps even when she needed to. The whole thing sat so badly with me I'd been guilty of sweeping it under the carpet – which made me feel even worse. I wondered, with a leap of hope, if this was an olive branch.

'Wow,' said Mark. 'When?'

'July.'

'Where?'

'Greek islands.' I held up the invitation and read out loud. '"Dear Mrs Scrivener, Mrs Audrey Templeton requests the pleasure of your company" blab blah, "sailing out of Venice for seven nights, calling at Corfu, Mykonos, Santorini, and Katakolon." Oh my God.' I looked at Mark. I'd always wanted to go to Venice. 'What do you think?'

'Well,' he said carefully, 'in theory, I have no objection...'

'But, in practice?' I looked at Mark and he raised an eyebrow and patted his tummy. He worried that I might be pregnant. The thought made me catch my breath.

'I doubt it,' I said. As fruitless month had passed

after fruitless month, I'd slowly let go of the hope that I was going to conceive naturally. 'The baby' had become a topic we no longer talked about, and I'd assumed that Mark, too, had given up hope. After the summer, I'd been planning to open a conversation about it; to look at fertility treatments; see if Mark was prepared to go ahead with IVF. But, as far as being pregnant by July was concerned, hell had more chance of freezing over, and, now the idea of a sunshine holiday had been dangled in front of me, I realised how badly I wanted it. Even though Mark had work now, the last year had been incredibly draining.

'Baby's not going to happen given our track record.' I looked at the invitation. 'I wonder why it's just me. I couldn't justify it.'

'Well,' said Mark. 'Maybe she's got a family-only agenda? And, given she's sent such a fancy invitation, I'd say she's offering to pay, wouldn't you?'

'Maybe.' My stomach fizzed with excitement. 'Maybe she is. If she is, can I go? What do you think? Would you mind?'

'Silly question.'

I shoved my chair back and ran to Mark's side of the table, hugged him awkwardly from behind and kissed the top of his head. 'Thank you, thank you! You're the best husband ever.'

'She only just notices,' he deadpanned, catching my hand and giving it a squeeze. I grabbed the card and showed it to him, reading it through again. 'Oh my life! Venice, Corfu, Mykonos, Santorini!'

'Look, Lexi, before you get too excited, why don't you call your mum and just clarify what the

162

arrangements are.'

The phone rang.

'It's her,' I squealed. 'Talk about serendipity.' I picked up the phone. 'Mum!'

'It's me,' said John. 'Sorry to call so early but I just wanted to ask if you got anything from Mum today?'

'Yes, I did! The cruise?'

'Yes.'

'Was it just you? Or Anastasia and the kids as well?'

'Just me.'

'Just him,' I mouthed at Mark. 'So are you going to go?' I asked John. 'I can't wait!'

'You're actually considering going?' he asked.

'Well ... yes ... aren't you?'

'Don't you think it's just a little odd, Lexi? A cruise? Out of the blue. Mum's never been on a cruise in her life.'

'What do you mean? I thought it sounded lovely. It's over her birthday, if you noticed, and she loves the sea. That's why she moved to Cornwall. Remember?'

'Anyway,' John's voice was dismissive; I could hear him shaking his head. 'I can't possibly go.'

'Why not?'

'Umm, it's a cruise?' John said the word as if the very feel of it in his mouth made him want to throw up. 'Substitute a "floating twenty-four-hour buffet packed with people so unimaginative they can't plan their own holiday" for that, and you might get my feelings on the subject.'

'Oh, John! Come on, seriously?'

'Besides, I can't justify spending that kind of

163

money on something like this.'

'Mark thinks Mum's paying.'

'Even if she is, we still need to get to Venice.'

'It'll only be a couple of hundred quid. Maybe less on a budget airline.'

'A couple of hundred quid? Forget it. If the cash cow came to stay – even if it moved into my house and slept in my bed – even then a ticket to Venice would be the last thing on my wish list.'

I shook my head and mimed winding up a machine at Mark: *he's going off on one.* Mark nodded sympathetically and resumed reading the news.

'And then there's drinks, expenses,' John was saying. 'Excursions. Presumably we'll have to *do* stuff when we get off the ship. You can't expect Mum to pick up the tab for everything. And those excursions cost an arm and a leg. Anastasia has a friend who went on a cruise and she said it was daylight robbery.'

To be fair, I hadn't thought about that. But it's not as if John was short of a penny; he just didn't like spending it.

'Besides,' John continued. 'It's completely un-fair for me to leave Anastasia alone with the children for a week. I don't know what Mum was thinking not inviting them. Anastasia couldn't cope for a week without me.'

'Heaven forfend your wife spends a week alone with her kids.' It slipped out before I could stop it, so I rushed on, regretting the words even as they tumbled out of my mouth. 'Why don't you ask Mum if you can bring them too?'

'Are you out of your mind?' John snorted.

'Children? On a cruise ship? What if they fall overboard?'

'Loads of kids go on cruises. Don't they even have those Disney ones especially *for* kids?'

'Lexi. Whatever way you look at it, it's out of the question. All right? Sorry.'

I hung up the phone. If John refused to go, would Mum cancel the cruise? Was it a case of both of us or none of us? Or could she and I go alone?

'Let me guess,' said Mark. 'John won't go?'

'Yeah. He said he can't afford the flights and excursions, and that "it's not fair on Anastasia" to leave her with her own kids.'

'Look, Lex, I've got to go,' said Mark, getting up. 'Can we talk about this tonight?' I picked up the invitation and looked at it, now feeling more regret than excitement. Mark kissed me. 'He'll come round, promise. If there's a free holiday involved, trust me, your brother will go. Bye.'

I waited till lunchtime to call Mum: I was out of the habit of calling her, which made the call feel more momentous than it should do. Morning break wasn't long enough, and I didn't have any free periods in the morning. Sparked by my nerves, I taught my classes with far more energy than usual, noticing with detachment how well the students responded to the higher-octane lessons. At twelve thirty I took my mobile phone to a sofa in a quiet corner of the staff room and, breathing slightly harder than usual, dialled her number.

'Hello?' came Mum's voice.

165

'Hello, Mum.'

'Alexandra,' she said. 'What's up?' And I felt a wave of guilt for not calling more often, for letting things slide since the lunch. Suddenly I didn't know what to say.

'How are you?' I hedged.

'Fine, thank you.' A pause. 'And you?'

'Good thanks. All good.' Another pause.

'Was there something? It's just I'm in the middle of something...'

I took a deep breath. 'I was just wondering. Did you, um, send me something in the post?'

'Oh, it's arrived!' I could feel Mum's smile. 'That was quick. I only posted it yesterday. First class, mind.'

I relaxed back on the sofa. 'Yes. Thank you. It ... um. Wow. I don't know what to say. It sounds fantastic. Wonderful. A trip of a lifetime.' How could I ask if she would be paying?

'Well, I did do a lot of research into the itinerary. So, do you think you'll be able to come? It's over the school holidays. I timed it deliberately.'

'Mmm, well, I'd like to, but I just need to go through the finances tonight with Mark. You know ... things are...' I took a sharp in-breath to quell a sob that came from nowhere. Even though Mark was now earning, I was mentally earmarking every spare penny we had for IVF. My worries about that were buried in a crevasse inside my soul; I plastered over the top on a daily basis but every now and then a tiny crack appeared and raw emotion exploded out, catching me by surprise.

'Don't worry about the cost,' Mum said. 'It's my treat. It's something I'd really like to do with

166

you and John.' She paused and the line crackled. 'I've been thinking about what you both said. About moving.'

'Oh, Mum. About that...'

'No, listen. You're right. I can see that now. I'm a liability.' Mum's voice wobbled. She sounded odd, not quite herself. 'This cruise will be my "last hurrah". We'll have a blast and, when we get back, I'll look at that development you mentioned. Okay? That place with the dancing and the golf where you can buy your own house.'

'Oh, Mum.' The victory felt like defeat. 'There's no rush. Really. Maybe we were being too hasty.'

'No, you're right. I'll turn seventy this summer. Eighty's just around the corner. I'd rather choose my next home than have you do it when I'm incapacitated and put me in some god-awful box of a place.' Mum gave a little laugh. 'Anyway, the point is, I'm inviting you on the cruise, so I'll be paying for it.'

'Really? Thank you so much.'

'Flights, too. They won't be anything fancy, I'm not sending you first class, but I'll get you there. I don't want you to worry about a thing financially. I know what it's like.'

'Oh, Mum. Thank you.'

'So you'll come?'

'I wouldn't miss it for the world. Such a nice idea. Thank you.'

'You're welcome. I know you always wanted to go to Venice – me too – but your father...' I knew exactly what she meant. My father had not been one to waste money on frivolities such as sunshine holidays, let alone cruises. 'Do you think your brother will come?'

'I suspect so,' I said, thinking that all his financial reasons for not coming had been removed. 'If he can persuade Anastasia to let him out of her sight...'

Mum chuckled. 'I should imagine he would be grateful to get away for a bit. Right, I'll call him now.'

15 July 1978

Barnes, London

'Happy birthday to you! Happy birthday to you! Happy birthday dear Audrey, happy birthday to you!'

Someone raises three cheers for Audrey and she raises her wine glass at the people sitting around her dining table, their faces flush with alcohol.

'Thank you very much,' she says. 'Now, I think it's high time I brought dessert.'

'A birthday cake, I hope?' calls one of Ralph's business associates.

Audrey looks at her husband.

'Yes ... of course there's birthday cake,' says Ralph with a smile as sweet as the cake Audrey's about to bring. 'Black Forest gateau. My wife's favourite.'

The implication is that Ralph has ordered the cake and there's a chorus of ahhs from the women around the table; a few admiring looks from the men: Audrey's looking fantastic tonight in a red dress that brings out the fire in her hair. Ralph sees the way the men appraise her; he stands up and moves behind his wife's chair, his hands proprietorial on her bare shoulders.

Audrey raises a hand to Ralph's and gives it a squeeze. He drops his head down and kisses the top of her collar bone.

'You two are just so sweet,' says one of the wives. 'Just look at you with your perfect marriage and your perfect children. You're an example to us all.'

Audrey smiles, then pushes her chair back gently and walks around the table gathering up everyone's plates while Ralph looks on proudly.

Audrey carries the plates out to the kitchen and places them in the sink. She stares for a minute out at the inky blackness of the garden, its features invisible thanks to the light inside, and she gathers her thoughts. It amuses her that the dinner guests think she and Ralph have a perfect marriage. She couldn't explain the complexities of her marriage to anyone – even she finds it hard to fathom.

It's been two years since the business with Mack, and the pain of missing him has slowly subsided. True, there are still mornings when Audrey wakes with the feeling of her lover's hands on her bare skin, and carries with her all day the feel of his touch on her heart, but, in her head, Audrey knows that the decision to stay with the children – with her husband – was the right one. She imagines that, one day, her heart will catch up with her head. *Did I do the right thing, Daddy? Was I right to stay?* She looks at her reflection in the dark window and nods to herself.

Audrey's thoughts turn to Ralph and she shakes her head as she thinks about the convoluted reasons why the two of them are still together. No outsider would understand it. Yes, Ralph may be controlling and autocratic but Audrey's learned over the years how to manage him – she's learned how not to incense him; how to defuse his funks. Maybe he's even softened a little and, under the veneer of perfection, Mr and Mrs Templeton rub along all right. She takes a deep breath, lifts the cake carefully out of the fridge, and gazes at what is perhaps her most impressive cake ever.

The Black Forest gateau is a work of art. Audrey's spent the best part of a week perfecting it; this concoction of black cherries and cream is her fourth attempt and she knows she's nailed it.

'Right. Showtime,' she says.

She gathers up eight dessert plates and eight cake forks, and carries them into the dining room. It's Ralph's cue to go and get the cake, to bring it in in a blaze of candles but, as Audrey fiddles with the plates, she realises Ralph isn't going to go. He's having far too much fun playing the role of the genial dinner party host. He's just said something and the guests have fallen suddenly quiet, as if they were talking about her.

Audrey heads back to the kitchen, lights her own birthday candles, and carries the cake she's made back to the dining room, kicking the door open with her foot as she enters. Only when she places the cake on the dining table do the guests actually notice. There's a chorus of exclamations: the cake is stunning.

'Wow, Ralph! Where did you find that? You dark horse,' says one of Ralph's work associates.

Ralph looks modest. He must practise that, thinks Audrey, as she watches him, curious as to what he's going to say.

'I had it made,' says Ralph. 'I commissioned it myself.' He looks at Audrey with a glint in his eye and she lowers her gaze. It's not technically a lie, she thinks. Not when you think about the way Ralph had brought home a cookery book, pointed to the cake he wanted to serve on her birthday, and asked her to make it. One of the women catches Audrey's eye. She's trying to get her to look at something but Audrey doesn't understand what. It's only when she looks down to pick up the knife that she sees the distinctive blue of a Tiffany's box on her placemat, its signature white bow almost asking to be untied. She looks at Ralph.

'For me?'

Ralph nods, a smile playing on his lips.

'Open it!' calls one of the women.

Audrey looks hesitantly at Ralph, still remembering the *faux pas* she made on her birthday five years ago. She's careful these days never to wrong-foot her husband in company.

He nods. 'Open it.'

The guests take up the chant. 'Open it, open it, open it!'

Audrey feels the slide of the ribbon as she gently pulls one end. She opens the box and gasps: diamond stud earrings. Huge diamond studs. With her hand over her mouth she turns the box to show her guests. The women gasp; the box is passed around.

'You're so lucky!'

'They're beautiful!'

'I'm lucky if my hubbie even remembers my birthday!'

One of the men stands up and slaps Ralph on the back. 'Cheers, mate,' he says. 'Nothing like setting a precedent!'

'And don't you forget it,' laughs his wife.

Ralph steps forward. 'Let's all wish my wife a happy birthday. One, two, three...'

The guests join in singing *Happy Birthday*, and Audrey blows out her candles.

'Make a wish, make a wish!' call the guests.

'As if Audrey needs to wish for anything!'

'What do you wish for when you've got every-thing?'

Everything? thinks Audrey. Has she got every-thing? Perhaps she does. The thought pleases her. And then, as Audrey prepares to make the first cut, she thinks of the one thing she wants that money can't buy: Mack. The knife slices through the sponge.

PART II

During

12 July 2013, 8 a.m.

'We've spent longer getting to the airport than we'll spend actually flying to Venice,' John said as I hauled my suitcase onto a baggage trolley at Gatwick Airport. 'Logistically speaking, I don't like that we've spent all that time working our way north-east on the train when we're going to get on a plane fly south again.' He shook his head, disapproval oozing out of him, while I scanned the departure hall, looking for the check-in desk. My brother was in one of his moods, and I'd borne the brunt of it since we'd left Cornwall on the 5 a.m. train.

'This way,' I said, and started to walk, leaving John to drag his own case.

'I mean, why we couldn't have flown from Bristol or Exeter or Bournemouth is beyond me. Any of those would have been easier than coming all the way into London.' John strode beside me.

'Because there were no direct flights,' I said, my patience by now as fragile as the crispbreads he kept pulling out of his pocket and nibbling in a way I'd come to think of as distinctly rat-like. Mum had given us the option of taking a non-direct flight from Bristol or of taking the train to London and getting a direct flight. Despite the long journey up from Cornwall, John had insisted on the latter on the basis that there was less of a chance of our luggage getting lost in transit. I'd tried to argue but he, as usual, knew best.

'But *why* aren't there any direct flights?' he said. 'I mean, we can't be the only people living in Cornwall who want to fly to Europe in July – am I right or am I right?'

'You're right,' I said. 'Right, this is us.' I positioned the trolley adjacent to a pleasingly empty check-in desk and fixed John with the look I give my class when they're misbehaving. 'Okay. We all know where you stand on local flights to Europe. But now we're here can you please drop it? We're checking in for a flight to Venice. I'm very excited, and I'd like to enjoy the moment.' I softened my voice. 'Please?'

'Next please!' called the woman behind the check-in desk and I pushed the trolley forward, wondering if John would check in with me or separately. It was odd to be going on holiday with him instead of Mark and I felt strangely self-conscious as I approached the counter: my brother and I hadn't been on holiday together since our early teenage years. Mum had flown to Venice a couple of days before, saying she wanted to spend more time there. While that was undoubtedly true, I also suspected she was tickled by the idea of John and I travelling together. It had always bothered her that we weren't as close as twins should be.

'After your father and I've gone, all you'll have is each other,' she used to say when we were teenagers. 'Nurture that relationship. It's special. Look after each other.'

That's all very well, I used to think, if you had a normal brother. But John somehow seemed to be missing something; the gene that enabled him to relate properly to people, perhaps. He and Mum were similar in that respect. Both kept their distance. Or, I suddenly thought, maybe the problem was me.

I handed my ticket and passport to the woman behind the desk and John reached over and plonked his on top. Was he, too, thinking about holidays of the past at this moment? About long car trips, vomiting into hedgerows on the side of winding A-roads, flapping windbreaks, the cold, brown, British sea in which our father had forced us to swim, teeth chattering?

'Where are you flying to this morning?' asked the woman. Her make-up was immaculate and I realised how I – having been up since before dawn – must have looked in contrast. John stood behind me, a shambles in crumpled combat trousers, a polo shirt, and a fleece. He stooped down and checked the name tag on his bag.

'Venice.' I couldn't keep the smile out of my voice. 'Very early start, though. We've come up from Cornwall.' I beamed at the lady but she didn't look up.

'How many bags?'

'Two.'

'Have you packed them yourselves?'

'I have. Can't answer for him. John?' I said.

'Yep.'

The woman went through the rest of the questions then started tapping at her keyboard. Behind me I heard the slightly soggy crunch of John biting into another crispbread.

'We don't have to sit together,' I said suddenly. 'I mean. He's not my husband. If you have any spare single seats you need to use, that's perfectly fine.'

'No. You're all right,' said the lady giving me a megawatt smile. 'I've got you two together. Here you go – 24A and B. Boarding at Gate 18 about nine fifteen.' She handed over the boarding passes. 'Enjoy your flight.'

Until the very moment I laid eyes on the gargantuan cruise ships berthed at Venice's cruise terminal, I'd never understood why people chose to go on a cruise. For me, it was something that 'other people' did: older people, less independent people, maybe; people who wanted a structured holiday. I'd always seen the ads in the Sunday supplements and moved swiftly on; not interested, never tempted, and perhaps even slightly repulsed by the thought of – as John so succinctly put it – 'being herded around Europe like seaborne cattle.'

In fact, if Mum hadn't organised this trip, I suspect I may have got through my entire life without ever having set foot on a cruise ship but now, as our glossy wooden water taxi rounded a corner in the canal and I saw the ships lined up their berths for the first time, I gasped and scrabbled reflexively for my phone to take pictures. The cabin door of the *motoscafi* opened and John, presumably having felt the engine slow, emerged from where he'd been hiding from the sun, the wind, the humidity and, I suspected, perhaps even life itself.

There was a moment as he took in the ships and the crowds of people snaking their way around the quay, then, 'Crikey. They're massive.'

'Floating hotels,' I said, trying to get a whole

ship into one camera frame. 'But I don't think ours is one of those really huge ones.'

'One, two, three, four, five, six, seven, eight nine, ten,' said John, his finger waving in the air as he tried to count the decks. 'That one must have sixteen decks. Look at it! It doesn't look like a ship at all – it's like a block of flats with a point at the front.' He gave a hard laugh. 'I mean: give me a yacht any day.'

'I think ours is only ten or twelve decks,' I said. 'Certainly not sixteen.' I squinted at the funnels, identifying our cruise line, and then our ship by name. I pointed. 'Look, there it is! There's our ship. That one!'

John's gaze followed my finger and he looked down at a paper in his hand and back up at the ship.

'Yep. That's it.' He pursed his lips, taking in the lines. 'At least it looks like a ship.'

I had to agree: ours had an elegant line to it. I bit my lips to stop myself from smiling; despite myself, there was something undeniably glamorous about embarking for a sea voyage and a shiver of excitement ran through me.

John nodded. 'Well,' he said. 'Let's see what it's like inside.'

'Pleased you came now?'

He huffed. 'There's not a fibre of my being that's looking forward to being trapped on this monstrosity for a week but if it's what it takes to get Mum to consider moving into Harbourside, then I'll do it.' He crossed his arms over his chest.

'There's not a part of you – not even a tiny part – that's looking forward to this?'

He shook his head.

'Really? Not seeing Mykonos? Or Santorini? I've always wanted to see those places. They look so beautiful, so vibrant in the brochures.'

John sighed. 'Okay, yes. I'm looking forward to seeing the islands. As long as I can get away from the crowds. And I've no intention of spending every day at sea gorging myself.'

'I'm sure they'll have crispbreads,' I said.

'*Per favore,*' said the driver, holding his hand out to me. '*Arrivati.*'

'*Grazie.*' I took his hand and stepped onto the quay. Behind me, I just knew John was shaking his head.

12 July 2013, 4 p.m.

'I hope you're not claustrophobic,' John said as he followed me along the corridor of Deck 8. 'I can't think of anything worse than being stuck in a tiny room on a rough sea.'

'Fifty-four, fifty-six, fifty-eight and, here we are: zero eight sixty.' I looked at my key card to check I'd got it right. 'And I presume that's yours next door. Look – yes it is. Right – ready?' I swiped the key card and pushed open the door. 'Let's see.'

If I'd thought we'd be sleeping in the maritime version of shoeboxes, I was mistaken. The cabin was by no means large, but neither was it unpleasant. In front of me I saw a bed, a dressing table and chair, a small sofa, and a coffee table.

Right by the door was a compact wardrobe area, and I noted with surprise that my suitcase was already there. There was a door, presumably leading to the bathroom, and, at the far end of the room, double doors opened to a balcony. Outside I could see two wooden lounge chairs and a table. Decorated in fresh, sea colours, the room was bright and breezy. I held the door open with my foot and turned to John.

'You coming in?'

'I'll look at mine.'

'All right – see you in a bit.'

The door sprang shut when I let it go and I took a deep breath, revelling in the peace and quiet after so many hours travelling. I checked out the bathroom – now that was definitely compact – then opened the balcony doors, letting the breeze rush into the cabin and sweep away the sterile smell of the air-conditioning.

It didn't take long for me to unpack. When I was done, I slid my suitcase under the bed and stepped out onto the balcony. Alongside us an even bigger ship drew up its gangplanks, its horn reverberating across the port. The water between our two ships churned as the huge propellers moved the other liner backwards out of the berth as if it were no larger than a Mini. People lined the decks; they were waving and cheering; some held glasses in their hands; music pulsed from the decks; every now and then I caught a snatch of an announcer encouraging the party atmosphere in any number of European languages. I smiled at their excitement and waved at the people on their balconies: soon it would be our turn to leave. Inside the cabin, my phone rang. I turned my back on the frivolities and stepped back inside.

'Hello?'

'Alexandra,' said Mum. 'Good. You're here. How was your journey?'

'All good. Did you have a good time in Venice?'

'Oh, it was lovely, thank you. Really lovely.' Mum's voice was wistful. 'Wish I'd done it years ago.'

I made a noncommittal sound.

'Anyway. John came with you, presumably?'

'Yes.'

'He didn't do a runner halfway here?'

'No. He's here. He's in his cabin.'

'Good. How are your rooms? Not too small, I hope?'

'They're perfect. Thank you. I love the balcony – it really makes the room.'

'I'm glad. I thought you'd like that.'

'It's lovely. I've just been on it,' I said, thinking at the same time how much more I would have liked it had Mark been with me. Still ... I'd sailed down the Grand Canal in a *motoscafi* like George Clooney arriving at the Venice Film Festival, and I'd seen some of the sights of Venice. Now I was about to spend the week sailing around the Greek islands on a luxurious cruise ship. Life could be worse.

'Why don't you come to my cabin for the sail-away?' Mum said. 'I'm at the front. We should get a good view of Venice as we go through. Will you tell John?'

'Sure. I'll get him. We'll be there in – what time are we leaving? Half an hour?'

'Perfect.' She told me her cabin number and hung up.

I rapped my knuckles on John's door. There was a rustling sound, the lock turned, the door opened a crack, and John's face peered out.

'Only me,' I said, and he opened the door wider, blocking the entrance to the room with his body as if to stop me stepping inside. 'All unpacked?'

'I didn't bring much.'

'Anyway, look. Mum called. She said we should go up to her cabin for the sail-away, which is in about,' I looked at my watch, 'quarter of an hour now. She's at the front.'

'I was going to sit on my balcony for it,' said John. 'I'm on the right side for San Marco, I think.'

'Suit yourself. But I kind of got the impression Mum would like to be with us. And the view from the front will be a lot better.'

John sighed. 'Okay. All right. But I hope we're not going to spend the whole trip doing what Mum wants. There are things *I* want to do, too. And, if she thinks I'm joining in with any cruise ship "happy campers" stuff, she can forget it. Did you see the activity sheet? Line-dancing? Bingo? Jesus, Lex. No way am I doing any of that.' With his foot wedged in the door, he leaned back towards the wardrobe and grabbed his camera and room key, then he followed me out, watching carefully until the door had swung to a hard close.

'I hear you, but please be reasonable,' I said as we walked towards the front of the ship, our footsteps muffled on the bright blue constellation

183

carpet that swallowed the entire floor of Deck 8. I hurried to keep up with John as he strode ahead, his thin, white legs, bare from the knees down, eating up the corridor, the old-fashioned camera bag he carried banging on his hip with every step. 'This is Mum's cruise, not ours. Essentially, we're here for her. There's a reason why she invited us, and I'm guessing it was for company.'

'No such thing as a free lunch.' John looked ruefully over his shoulder at me as he said it and, for a moment, I saw not him but our father.

'Exactly. No such thing as a free cruise. And don't you forget it. Stairs!'

We turned a hard right to the lift lobby, and took the stairs the two floors up to Deck 10, where we continued our walk to the front of the ship and rang the doorbell for Mum's cabin.

'Maybe we could do split shifts,' I whispered as we waited for her to answer the door. 'You stick with her in, say, Corfu. I'll go with her in Mykonos, and we can split Santorini and Katakolon. Fair?'

'I'm planning some hard walks – especially in Corfu – and it'll be hot,' John said. 'She might enjoy pottering about with you more? Please?'

I was still in debt to John for the years he'd been there for Mum while Mark and I had lived in London and he knew it. I sighed.

'I suppose so. We can mooch about the ports, I guess. Do a bit of shopping...'

Footsteps padded up to the other side of the door and Mum opened it wide and bowed with a flourish, a glass of champagne in her hand.

'Welcome to my humble abode.'

Mum indicated for us to walk past her into a room that bore no resemblance at all to mine and John's.

'Wow,' I breathed. 'Can I look around?'

'Help yourself,' said Mum. She'd clearly spared no expense: the door opened into a large living room with a dining alcove and a long, side balcony furnished with teak loungers and an outdoor dining set. Beyond that was a bedroom with one of the biggest beds I'd ever seen. The surroundings were luxurious, at odds with Mum's humble home, but already the room smelled of her – more specifically, of night jasmine – Mum's signature scent. She never travelled without a fragranced candle and I knew I'd find it in the bathroom.

I padded across the carpet, shaking my head in wonder, and stepped into the bathroom to find a full bath with its own porthole, a full-sized shower, double sinks, and a walk-in wardrobe I'd be proud to own in my own house. I picked up one of the bottles of complimentary toiletries: Bvlgari. I stepped back out of the bathroom

'Look, Mum,' I said as she beamed at me. 'I'm a little worried: are you sure your bathroom's big enough? Shall I call Guest Services and see if they've anything better? It *is* your birthday and I don't want you slumming it.'

Mum tittered. 'Lovely, isn't it? It's an Owner's Suite. I suppose it's a bit extravagant to have all this space just for me but I thought, well, as it *was* my last hurrah...'

John, who'd been examining the contents of the free-standing walnut bar, turned and opened his mouth. I saw the expression on his face and cut him off.

'Good on you, Mum,' I said. 'It's gorgeous. A real home from home!'

She smiled. 'You haven't seen the best bit yet. John? I'll need you for this. Come. Alexandra, bring the champagne.' I picked up the ice bucket and two empty flutes and followed as Mum lead us past the enormous bed to a heavy metal door with a huge metal lever on it.

'I'll need you to open this,' she said to John. 'The butler,' – another titter – 'opened it to show me but then shut it again. It's too heavy for me. Has to be heavy, for the winds.'

John grabbed the lever and grunted as he struggled with it before succeeding. Mum shoved the thick door open and secured it with a chain.

'Come,' she said.

We followed her out onto a forward-facing balcony. Sunshine pooled on the wooden decking, giving it the feel of a poolside terrace, but it was the panoramic view forward that took my breath away.

'Wow,' I breathed, leaning on the railing. 'I want to spend the whole week here. It's like that moment in *Titanic*, the movie. You know, Kate and Leo at the front.' Realising the fate of that ship, I searched for a better metaphor. 'It's like you're the captain.'

'Speaking of which: look,' said. Mum, pointing above and behind me. 'The bridge is right behind us. The captain waved to me earlier.' She chuckled.

I looked up and saw through the smoky glass

186

the silhouettes of a group of officers. Not wanting to be caught staring, I turned back and nodded towards the small swimming pool in the bow of the ship. 'Is that the spa pool, do you know?'

'No, it's the crew pool, I think,' said Mum.

'Nice,' conceded John, who by now had examined the view from every possible angle. He held a pair of binoculars. 'It's nice and private. And they even give you binos. We'll have a great view from here.'

'I know,' said Mum. 'I booked this suite deliberately. The travel agent advised me. I asked her which cabin to take for the best view of Venice as we left. I doubt I'll ever get to do this again, so I wanted to do it in style.'

'Well, you certainly did that.'

The ship's horn sounded: a deep note that reverberated in my chest.

'We're moving!' I ran to the front of the balcony and looked at the dock as we slid away from it. I waved both arms at the people on the adjacent ship.

'Oh my goodness, it's so exciting!' There was a silence. I looked at Mum. She was staring at the dock, transfixed, then she raised her hand in a static wave and mouthed something I couldn't catch.

'What?'

Mum's eyes snapped back to me and she smiled brightly. 'Nothing.' She reached in her pocket and took out a handkerchief. I saw that her eyes were shining. 'It's just ... departures. All those people. So many emotions...' She shook herself again. 'Anyway. Quick, get your glasses.'

187

I topped up Mum's flute and poured for John and me. When we all had our glasses in our hands, I raised mine and tapped it with a finger.

'Ting! Ting! Ting!' I said. 'I propose a toast. To Mum. Thank you for inviting us to be a part of this trip. I hope you have the best birthday ever. And may you have many more happy and healthy years. Cheers!' The wind whipped my hair around my face and I pushed it back to take a sip.

'Cheers,' said Mum.

'Cheers,' echoed John, taking a swig of his champagne. We all turned to face the front as the ship made its way slowly through Venice and out to the open sea beyond.

14 July 2013, 9 a.m.

After a day and two nights at sea, Mum, John, and I fell into the rhythm of ship life, quickly finding out favourite places. John holed up in the library, examining books, charts, and maps, and bluntly refusing to join in any activity, while Mum and I discovered we both loved nothing more than promenading around the decks, gazing out to sea and lounging in deck chairs, people-watching with endless cups of tea.

Shunning the formal dining room, we took our meals in Ocean Breeze restaurant – a large circular buffet, which, at breakfast, was stuffed with every type of food anyone could possibly want, from full English breakfasts to Chinese dumplings and Indian *dosas*.

On our second morning, I'd just sat down with a plate of fresh fruit when I saw Mum walking slowly down the length of the restaurant, a plate of food held carefully out in front of her. She was wearing a simple blue dress and flat shoes but it was taking all her concentration to walk steadily as the other, younger passengers weaved around her, their plates piled high with doughnuts, pastries, toast, and hot breakfasts. I waved.

'Mum, Mum! Over here!'

She didn't hear me over the din. The restaurant was full and Mum was looking carefully around for somewhere to sit. In that split second she looked old – like a grandmother – and my insides contracted with the thought that she might never know the joy of having grandchildren to call her own. Not for the first time, I felt like a failure.

Pushing my chair back with my legs, I jumped up. 'Mum, Mum! Over here!'

This time she stopped and turned, having heard my voice but not knowing where to look. I started walking towards her. 'Here, Mum. I've got a table.'

A smile broke over her face and she made her way towards me. 'Thank goodness for that, Alexandra. There's no space anywhere. I've been around the restaurant several times looking.'

'Oh, Mum. It's only this busy because we're at sea. When the ship docks, everyone will rush off and the restaurants will be much quieter.'

'I hope you're right. I can't go through this hoopla every day, just to get my breakfast.'

'You won't have to. I'm sure.'

We ate in silence for a bit, both of us keenly observing the people swarming around the restaurant.

'So, we arrive in Corfu just before lunch,' I said by means of conversation as our eyes followed a twenty-something man in the shortest denim cut-offs I'd ever seen. 'What are you going to do between now and then?'

'I'm going to the spa,' Mum said, dragging her gaze back to me. 'Facial and foot massage. At the same time.' She wiggled her shoulders a little.

'Nice.'

'I deserve it. I've been to the Early Bird Step and Tone class yesterday and today.'

'What? Before breakfast?'

'Yes. First thing in the morning. Helps me get the old muscles going. You should try it.'

'There are classes like that at Harbourside,' said John, appearing behind me with a plate of chocolate croissants and a coffee. 'Just think, you could do them every day. In fact,' he said, clearly pleased with himself, 'I should imagine that life there wouldn't be so dissimilar to life on board a cruise ship. There's something on offer every day, and a lovely little restaurant. You'd never have to cook again, if you didn't want to.'

He plonked himself down at the table, an act that surprised me given how little Mum and I had seen of him in the last twenty-four hours.

Mum squinted at her watch. 'Speaking of which, it's time for me to go. So, will we go ashore together later? It would be nice to spend some time together. Or do you want to do your own thing? Do you have plans?'

John opened his mouth to speak.

'I'm happy to potter about with you,' I said, cutting him off before he started. 'I don't have an agenda, really. Just want to soak up a bit of the atmosphere, see some of the old town.'

'Sounds good to me,' said Mum. 'Oh, and before I forget, we've got a dinner reservation in the Italian restaurant tonight. Valentino's. At eight. I believe the ship sails early evening and I'd like you both to be there.'

I looked at John. He sucked in his cheeks.

'Sure. I'll be there,' I said pointedly. 'John?'

'Yes,' he said.

'Great,' said Mum. 'There's something I'd like to talk to you about.' She pushed her chair out and stood up. 'Right. See you later.'

I waited for her to move out of earshot then tutted at John. 'Did you have to bring up Harbourside? Let her enjoy her holiday. Please! She's said she'll look at it after the cruise. She doesn't need you banging on about it all the time.'

'I was just trying to get her used to the idea. Immerse her in it until she's not scared of it anymore. Flooding, I think psychologists call it.' He was chewing a croissant while he spoke and flakes of pastry stuck to his lips. My brother consumed food as if it were alive; as if he had to shovel it into his mouth before it ran away. For him there was no pleasure in savouring taste; the act of eating was merely a means to an end. The word 'mastication' sprang to mind.

'Thanks, Dr John,' I said.

'You're welcome.' He gave me a big smile that revealed chocolate smeared on his teeth.

'Right,' I said, 'I'm going to catch some sun by the pool. Enjoy Corfu, if I don't see you first.'

'Cheers. You too.'

14 July 2013, 11 a.m.

Mum had left her cabin door on the latch so I could let myself in. I found her on the front balcony, the binoculars pressed to her eyes. Although the sun was hot, the wind from the ship's motion was bracing and I had to steady myself for a second.

'Land ahoy!' Mum called as I stepped past the loungers.

'Corfu?'

'Expect so. Here. Take a look.'

Up at the front railing, I put the binoculars to my eyes. It was strangely emotional to see land after a day or two at sea. There was a large part of me that didn't want to disembark; I'd got used to the rhythm of the ship, to the rumble of its engines and the gentle lull of the waves as I lay in bed at night. I'd come to love, too, the hypnotic sight of the waves breaking on the bow when I looked down from the promenade deck, and I liked the feeling of being in constant motion. Deep down, the thought of being on land once more, of walking slowly around a hot, Greek town thronging with tourists didn't appeal in the slightest.

I handed the binoculars back to Mum. 'You don't really need them anymore. We're quite close.' I paused. 'I almost don't want to arrive. I'm quite enjoying being on the ship.'

'Me too.'

'I wish we could ask the captain if we can go around for a bit longer. Do you know what I mean?'

Mum nodded. 'I always get a bit nervous as we approach land.'

'As you do every day?'

Mum gave me a sharp look and I regretted my sarcasm.

'How do you think I got to India?' She paused. 'I sailed. On the *SS Oriana*. Beautiful, she was. Nothing like these cruise ships. A real liner.' Mum smiled.

'I never really thought about how you got there. I guess I just assumed you flew.' I was silent for a minute, imagining what it must have been like. 'How old were you?'

'Twenty-seven. It was scary – of course it was – but I had to get away.' She took a deep breath, then spoke again. 'I loved the journey, the voyage. It's one of the reasons I wanted to come on a cruise. Although my reasons for leaving England were sad, I've always hankered after those days I spent at sea. I'll never forget as the ship neared Africa and the weather grew warmer and warmer. We went from wrapping up on deck to sipping iced drinks and seeking out the sea breeze. The journey was cathartic.' Mum stared at the land mass in the distance. 'I always have this sense that the sea washes away the past. It's always there ... the waves are always rolling in, no matter what happens in life. It makes me realise how insigni-

193

ficant my problems are.'

I hadn't questioned why Mum had picked a cruise over any other type of holiday we could have done. Standing there on the balcony, I realised I never really thought about her as a person; I never thought about what her hopes, her fears and dreams might be. She was always just 'Mum'; more often just a problem that needed solving.

Mum gave herself a little shake. 'Anyway, no point dwelling on the past. You're lucky to have a husband like Mark. I'm so glad you got a good one the second time around.'

She looked back out at the sea, avoiding making eye contact with me. These days, we never spoke about Richard, my first husband. He'd been controlling and cruel. I'd been the last person to see it. Swept along with the romance of the relationship, I'd ignored the fact that he'd eroded my confidence until I was a shell of a person. It'd been Mum who'd helped me see what was really going on; Mum who'd helped me get out of the marriage.

'Me too,' I said. 'If only I'd met Mark earlier.' It was a thought I had a hundred times a day. I'd wasted the best of my child-rearing years in a joyless marriage with a man who never wanted children, and only met Mark when it was almost too late.

'You can't say that,' Mum said. 'You might not have been right for each other earlier. These things – they happen when the time's right. I really believe that.'

'But...' I took a deep breath. There was something about looking at the ocean that gave me confidence. I gripped the railing. 'But ... if I'd met Mark sooner, you might have grandchildren by now.'

Mum swung around to look at me. She knew a little about the struggles Mark and I had been having to conceive – the trail of almosts, not-quites, and a miscarriage – but we never really spoke about it.

'Grandchildren? Is that what worries you? Giving me grandchildren?'

'Well – obviously I want a baby. But yes. I want you to have a grandchild. Grandchildren – not adopted like John's. Real ones that are biologically yours.' I bit my lips together, willing myself not to cry. 'I feel like such a failure. You had us by the time you were thirty, and look at me: I'm forty-two and it looks like it's never going to happen.'

'Oh, Alexandra.' Mum put her hand over mine on the railing. She opened her mouth as if she was going to say something then closed her eyes and squeezed my hand. 'Don't do it for me,' she said. 'Do it for you. I can tell you, there's not a single day that I've sat and wished for you to give me grandchildren. I promise you that.'

'Really?'

'Yes. Really.'

'But I thought you'd love to have grandchildren of your own.'

Mum laughed. 'This is your life. Don't have children for me!'

I stared into the distance. I could make out buildings on Corfu now. A tangle of emotions swept through me. Mum wasn't expecting grandchildren from me? All I could do was nod into the wind.

'How does Mark feel?' Mum asked.

'He's happy to look at fertility treatments if it's what I want. But I don't think he wants to keep trying if it doesn't work,' I said. 'Anyway, it's not like we can afford to do something like IVF more than once. If that.'

'I'm a great believer in fate,' Mum said. 'Try not to worry about it. Maybe things will work out. And if they don't … well, just accept some things just aren't meant to be.' Mum paused. 'The world works in mysterious ways.'

'I guess.'

'And, Alexandra, if it doesn't work out you can still have a very fulfilling life without children. Don't beat yourself up about it. I know how hard you can be on yourself.'

I turned away, pulling my hand out from under Mum's, and wiped my cheek. That was easy for her to say. She wasn't the one with no child to call her own.

'Sea spray,' I said. 'I'm going inside. Can I get you anything?'

14 July 2013, 11 a.m.

Corfu was hot. I understood that before we'd even left the port. It was a quiet, stealthy heat, the type of all-encompassing dryness that hits you from every angle, toasting your skin, filling your lungs, and making the inside of your head buzz. A shuttle bus, its plastic-covered seats burning hot despite the air-conditioning, had driven Mum and I, fanning ourselves with our port notes, the short distance down the terminal pier past those passengers too impatient to wait and now, as we exited the terminal, the heat radiated up from the concrete making me feel as if the rubber soles of my shoes would surely melt. The air smelled of the sea and of wilting vegetation with an undertone of fish. I felt an overwhelming urge to turn around and head back to the quiet coolness of the ship.

'I'd like to take a look around Corfu Town,' Mum said as we stood on the roadside wondering in which direction to walk. She looked cool in a straw sunhat and sunglasses. My own hair was already hot to the touch; already I regretted my bare shoulders. 'I've heard it's very pretty. Do you think there's a bus we can take?'

Masking a sigh, I looked at a leaflet I'd picked up in the terminal building. 'Apparently it's a UNESCO World Heritage site,' I said. 'It's a "delightful medieval enclave..." Hmm ... and Spianada Square sounds nice: shops, restaurants, statues, fountains and, if you've the energy for it in this heat, "intriguing alleyways". Shall we try and go there?' I wondered what John's plans had been.

'Let's do it. YOLO,' said Mum.

'What?'

'Need any help, ladies?'

'Stavros,' said Mum, holding out a hand, which the man picked up and kissed. 'This is my daughter.' Stavros bobbed his head towards me. 'Alexandra,' Mum said, 'Stavros is on the Ents team. He teaches Step and Tone. Good timing. We were just wondering how to get into the town.'

'Taxi is best,' Stavros said. 'Allow me, please, to help you.'

He whistled and, within seconds, a dusty black Mercedes broke from the rank of parked cars and drew up next to us. A young man jumped out, slapped Stavros on the back and, after a torrent of rapid Greek, Stavros motioned that we should get into the car.

'All sorted,' he said. 'He's my friend. Ten euros there. Ten euros back. He'll wait for you.'

Mum and I sank gratefully into the air-conditioned interior.

'Hot,' she said to the driver, flapping her hand up and down.

'Yes, hot,' he said. 'I take you through old town. Very pretty. You sit cool through old town.'

'Lovely,' said Mum. 'Thank you.' She turned to me. 'I wonder where John is.'

'It'd be funny if we passed him,' I said, imagining him hiking through the old town with his guide and his backpack.

'We could wind down the windows and wave. Waft a little cool air towards him.' Mum looked so much younger when she laughed.

The taxi dropped us off on a pretty street lined with shady trees. 'That way,' said the driver, waving towards a line of cafés and restaurants. 'I wait here.' I took Mum's elbow as we crossed the street, unsure on the uneven cobble stones and unfamiliar with the way the traffic came, and we followed the crowds into the end of a narrow street lined with shops. But what was presumably usually a relatively quiet town was thronging with tourists. Wares were piled up outside kooky little shops. Signs, scrawled in English, fought for attention.

'This is the disadvantage of a cruise,' said Mum twenty minutes later, as we stood three-deep in a leather goods shop, trying in vain to view a handbag she liked. 'Thousands of people in a tiny town at the same time.' She sighed. 'Come on, let's go.'

'Don't you want to see the bag? It's nice.'

'I can't stand up anymore.' Mum fanned herself with a lace fan she'd bought in the previous shop. Her face was flushed: the effort of walking in the heat on the higgledy-piggledy cobbled streets, which appeared to run randomly up and down hill, had clearly taken its toll. She took a cotton hankie out of her bag and patted her forehead. 'Let's go and find somewhere to sit down. I could do with something cold.'

I took her arm again and slowly we unwound the twists and turns we'd made in the rabbit warren of back streets, trying to remember how to get back to Spianada Square and its rows of shaded cafés. Mum was breathing hard, her weight heavy on my arm. We sank gratefully onto the chairs at an empty table in the first café we came to and ordered two local beers.

'Medicinal,' said Mum taking a big drag of hers. 'Goodness, that's good.'

'Cheers, birthday-girl-to-be.'

Mum chinked her glass against mine and we both drank.

'Speaking of which,' I said, licking beer froth off my top lip. 'Do you have any idea what you'd like to do on your birthday?'

'I thought we could all have dinner together.'

'Is that all? We have dinner tonight as well, right?' I wondered how John was going to take the thought of two dinners in a row.

'Yes. Valentino's at eight tonight. For tomorrow I saw that there's a White Night party by the pool that starts at ten. I know it's late but, if we're up for it after dinner, maybe we could have a dance as well.'

I laughed. 'Seriously? You want to go to the White Night party?'

'Why not? YOLO and all that.'

'What's with this "YOLO"? I've no idea what you're talking about.'

Mum shook her head at me. 'For a youngster, you're not very with-it, are you? You Only Live Once. We said *carpe diem* in my day but YOLO's more fun. I saw it on the worldwide web.'

I snorted. 'It reminds me of Rolos.'

'You can have my last YOLO,' said Mum.

I laughed. 'Very good. Well. If that's what you want … why not? But I can't see John agreeing to go dancing. Can you?'

'Miracles happen.'

'Pigs don't fly.'

We fell into silence. Mum looked at her beer. I wanted to say something about John; about how Harbourside had been his idea, not mine; about how we both just wanted her to be safe. As I struggled to find the right words, I stared vacantly at the square, letting the unfamiliar heat and bustle permeate my skin as if I could absorb the essence of Corfu by osmosis. Mum also appeared to be lost in thought.

'Were you happy?' she asked apropos of nothing. 'You and John. As kids. Are your memories happy?'

'Largely yes,' I said. I looked at her and she met my gaze with honesty: *what do you mean by 'largely'?* she was asking. *It's okay to tell me.* I'd the sense that layers were peeling back; that, for the first time ever, I might get a chance to see something of Mum's hidden core. I took a deep breath. 'But sometimes – and I hope you don't mind me saying this – sometimes, I felt as if you were somehow holding back from me. From us. Were you?'

Mum closed her eyes and exhaled. Without her having to say anything, I knew it was an admission. Her lips moved as she worked out how to put her reply into words.

'Losing my mum changed me,' she said eventually. 'I often wonder how I'd have turned out had she – and then Dad – not died so young. But what happened was it taught me that people aren't necessarily in your life forever. That, overnight, they can disappear. So I suppose that, yes, I did hold myself back a little. Part of it was subconscious – but partly I also felt I was protecting you. Yes. Protecting you...' her voice trailed off.

'From what?'

'Oh...' She waved her hand vaguely. 'Just, protecting you.'

It was as if a veil had come down over her eyes. I changed tack. 'Were *you* happy?'

Mum exhaled. 'Yes. Yes, I was happy. Largely.' She smiled.

'It's just...' I ran my hands through my hair. 'I always felt there was some sort of undercurrent in our house. Fear, maybe? An invisible monster in the corner – something that was ready to spring out at us at any given moment. I used to think it hid behind those big curtains in the living room.' I gave a little laugh. 'I don't know what it was – or if I even imagined it. Obviously it didn't live behind the curtains. Did I imagine it?'

Mum closed her eyes and opened them slowly. 'An undercurrent of fear? Of your father? I suppose there might have been.' She paused. 'I'm so sorry. I tried to shield you.'

Mum fell silent again but I could see her face working as she struggled to say something. Emotions flickered across her face, then she said: 'Do you remember the night I was packing? You must have been quite young. Five or six?'

I closed my eyes. A snatch of half-formed memory played in my mind. A door slamming. The sound of arguing. My father's voice, rough and harsh. Footsteps thundering down the stairs. John and I peering into our parents' room. Mum's face, pale, pinched, and stained with tears. Something about a suitcase.

'Did we come to your bedroom?' I asked. 'And your suitcase was on the bed?'

'Yes. That night.'

I had the sense suddenly of the penny dropping. I'd never believed what Mum had told us that night – something about seeing what fitted in the case – but I hadn't let myself question it further. 'You were going to leave, weren't you?'

Mum nodded. 'I was. But I couldn't. I couldn't leave you.'

I stared at my beer glass, as this new information sunk in. 'You could have taken us with you.'

Mum shook her head. 'Your father would never have let me.'

'But you wanted to leave? Were things that bad?' And then another thought: 'Was he violent?' I didn't remember being hit. 'Is that what we were scared of?'

Mum inhaled, her hand on her chest. 'No. He never laid a hand on you. We were all slightly afraid of his moods, I suppose. He could be very difficult.'

'I know. But was he ever violent towards you? Like, when John and I weren't around?'

'He didn't hit me or anything like that.' A micro-pause. 'Did you ever hear anything?'

I shook my head. 'It was more the silence.'

Mum gave a little laugh. 'I know what you mean.'

'John doesn't remember any of this. I think he blocked it out.'

'Do you two talk about it?'

'No. Not really. Maybe a bit lately. But no.'

'Tell me what you do remember. The good bits.'

I sat back and exhaled; thought for a second; pushed the memory of fear from my head. 'Pretend-ironing,' I said. Mum smiled. *Listen with Mother* on the radio. Sewing. You being so patient when I had to do that awful embroidery for school – do you remember it? I just couldn't get the stitch right, and I kept expecting you to shout at me but you were so patient. I think you even finished it for me in the end.'

Mum's eyes crinkled with her smile. 'I'm sure I'd never have done that! What else?

203

'Cake-making. Blowing bubbles in the summer. Roller-skating down the hall. Hide and seek. Those afternoon picnics in the park. Bedtime stories. The way you slammed the book shut at the end.'

Mum chuckled. 'Probably shouldn't have done that. Happy memories then?'

I nodded. 'Yes.' A pause. 'Do you regret staying?'

Mum put her hand on mine. 'No. No matter how hard things sometimes were, I was always sure I'd done the right thing.'

'Okay. Good.'

'What about John? What do you think he remembers?'

I pursed my lips. 'I don't know. He was different, wasn't he? You'd send us upstairs to play – I think you thought we played together – but I'd read, and he'd be playing Meccano or one of his card games or something. Solitaire, wasn't it?'

Mum nodded and took another sip of her beer. 'This hits the spot, doesn't it?' She turned the bottle so she could read the label. 'John's become very like your father, hasn't he?'

'Yeah. I guess. Sometimes he looks like the spit of Pa.'

Mum's finger traced a pattern in the condensation on the side of her glass. She looked at it intently then back up at me, her face troubled. 'It's more than looks. There's something else.'

She was talking, I was sure, about him trying to get her to move. I took a deep breath. 'Mum. About Harbourside. I know you worry that he's trying to do to you what he did to Valya, but...'

Mum looked sharply at me. 'What did he do to

Valya? Did he tell you?'

'Tell me what?'

Mum stared at me, her eyes searching my face, and I looked back at her, confused.

'What did you mean by "what he did to Valya"?' she said.

'Well, you know – how he pushed to have her put into that care home.'

Mum sat back in her chair. 'Oh.'

'What did you think I meant?'

'Oh... nothing, dear. Nothing.' She squinted up into the canopy of trees that shaded us from the sun. 'Pretty birds,' she said. 'Swallows.' There was a silence, then Mum spoke quietly: 'Your father once killed a man.'

'What?'

'Your father once killed a man.' Stronger this time. A look that was almost defiant.

'What?'

'It happened in India. It's no secret.'

'How come I didn't know about this?'

'It's not the kind of thing you talk about, is it?'

'But what happened? Were the police involved?' I imagined my father on the run; a fugitive. 'He *murdered* someone?'

Mum sighed. 'It was so long ago. We'd gone out for dinner. Someone tried to mug me. It wasn't murder. It was self-defence.'

'But how? How did he kill him?'

'Your father had him around the neck. I don't think he realised how strong he was.'

I listened with my hand pressed to my throat. My father had been a big man; strong. I could imagine the unintentional force he'd put behind a chokehold, especially if he was angry.

'Were John and I born then?'

'Yes. Yes, you were. You were at home with the *ayah* that night.' Mum was staring into the distance. 'We left India soon after.'

'We ran away?'

Mum tutted. 'No. We just decided it was time to leave.' Mum's eyes misted over. 'There was nothing to be ashamed of, but Ralph felt that everyone knew. I suppose he just wanted a fresh start.'

'I had no idea.'

'Well – you wouldn't.'

There was a silence as I assimilated this new fact about my father.

'So ... you think John is like Pa?' The words now had a new weight to them. I was testing; how far was Mum going to take this? An ugly thought tried to surface in my mind and I pushed it back down and sat on it.

Mum nodded. 'Yes. Yes, he has. There's a side to him that sometimes ... oh, I don't know ... mothers are supposed to have a special bond with their sons. You know, the whole mother–son thing? But I never felt it with John. I wanted to feel it, but it was never there.'

I thought back to my childhood; tried to picture how John and Mum had been together. John had always been a bit of a loner. Even I wasn't that close to him, despite the twin connection, but I'd never really thought about it from Mum's perspective. It was just how John was.

'He is quite like Pa,' I said. 'Like when he orders for you in a restaurant. I think it's just his way of showing he cares.'

206

'Huh! Controlling, more like.' Mum took a sip of her beer. 'If he were here, do you think he'd let me sit here drinking beer at this time of day? I don't think so.' She chuckled, then continued. 'It's you I felt sorry for growing up. You're not very close to John, and you hardly saw your father. All you had was me.' Mum was staring intently at the napkin ring, her lips pressed together. 'I used to worry what would happen to you – who would look after you – if I ... well, you know...'

'Well, you don't need to worry about that any-more.'

Mum smiled. 'I know.'

I took a big swig of my beer, then swirled the liquid around the glass to capture the froth tide-mark. 'By the way, while we're at it, can I ask you something else?' Mum nodded. 'Why didn't you and Pa have any more children? I'd have thought that you might have liked at least one more.'

'Oof,' she said. 'You two were the perfect pack-age. I didn't feel the need for any more. Nothing more, nothing less.' Mum picked up the menu. 'You know what? I fancy trying some of those stuffed vine leaves. Shall we order some nibbles?'

14 July 2013, 8 p.m.

I slipped my feet into the only pair of strappy sandals I'd brought and looked at myself in the mirror. I'd chosen a strappy dress and a velvet wrap for dinner. With no phone reception on the ship and no need to carry any money, I didn't even have a bag: all I would carry would be the plastic key card that doubled up as an on-board credit card. I swished a little to the right and left and took in my dress from different angles. It wasn't eveningwear by any means, and I hoped it would pass muster at Valentino's – a speciality restaurant that had a smart dress code.

I flicked my hair and added a slick of lipstick. 'You'll do,' I said to myself in the mirror. I picked up my key card, stepped out into the corridor and rapped my knuckles on John's door.

'Oh, hello,' he said, poking his head out around the door. I caught a glimpse of guide books piled up on his dresser. He wore dark trousers and a white shirt, above which his face, red from the sun, glowed like a beacon. 'Will I need a tie?'

'Doubt it.'

'Jacket?'

'Uh. Maybe. Come on, we don't want to be late.'

'It's a holiday. It should be relaxing,' John said, pulling on his jacket and letting his cabin door close behind him. 'That locks automatically, doesn't it? I wonder what she wants to talk about. Maybe she has plans for the other shore visits.'

'I doubt it,' I said. 'She seemed happy just to potter about in town and soak up the atmosphere today but I'm glad I was with her. She got a bit hot and flustered. How was your day anyway?'

'Great. I climbed to the top of the Old Fort. Thanks for taking Mum. She'd never have managed that walk.' John rubbed his hands together. 'What we need is for her to eat some dodgy seafood tonight, get food poisoning, and be confined to her cabin.' He laughed.

'John!'

We turned right for the lifts and waited for one that was going up.

'Did you go to Spianada Square?' John asked.

'Yeah. We took a cab and walked about a bit until it became too much for her, then we sat in a café and had a beer.'

'Sounds all right,' said John.

There was a silence during which I stared at the lift buttons. 'She was thinking about the past,' I said. 'You know, talking about Pa and stuff. I felt there was something on her mind.'

'Like what?'

'I don't know. I couldn't put my finger on it.' As I said the words, the feeling of unease I'd had during the conversation with Mum returned to me and the hairs on the back of my neck prickled. I shook my head a little, trying to banish the feeling. A gilded glass lift swished up past our floor without stopping. People were packed inside like sardines.

'Do you think she wants to talk about Harbourside tonight?' said John. 'Maybe she's going to surprise us and say she's already bought a property there.'

I sucked air in though my teeth. 'Please don't bring that up again.'

At last a lift stopped. It was almost full and John and I squashed into spaces a few people apart, the conversation closed. The button for the restaurant deck was already pressed; a lift full of locusts ready to swarm.

I had to do a double-take when John and I arrived at the door to Valentino's. Given its much-lauded status as a speciality restaurant and the plush nature of the ship's interior – or perhaps because of the word association with 'Valentino' – I'd been expecting a lush interior of red and gold; swags of rich velvet and gilded chairs. However, the look the ship's interior designers had gone for could most accurately be described as 'rustic Italian village.'

The walls were painted with murals of the Tuscan countryside, fake vines wound their way around the pillars, brick recesses in the walls housed collections of copper pans, and the wooden chairs all had straw seats. There was even a fake horse and cart. I had to pinch myself to remember we were on a ship in the middle of the ocean. Mum, sitting alone in her cruise ship evening finery, looked completely out of place. I could almost hear the static crackle of John's disapproval.

The waitress led us over to Mum's table.

'It's not what I expected,' Mum whispered once we'd sat and ordered our drinks, 'but the food's supposed to be excellent.'

'That's all that matters,' I said.

There was a pause while we all looked at the menu. John spoke first. 'So what's tonight about?'

Mum looked up. 'Well,' she said with an air of mystery, 'I have something important to tell you.'

John raised an eyebrow. 'Did you have a look at Harbourside?'

'Yes, I did, and very pleasant it is, too. But it's

not about that.' Mum paused. 'It's about your father's will.'

'Oh!' A nervous laugh popped out of my mouth. 'Wasn't that all sorted out when he died?'

'Well, yes and no,' said Mum. 'There's something that I'd like to make you both aware of.'

'Okaaay,' said John slowly. He passed his hand through his hair. The cutlery on the table started to vibrate. I realised my foot had started jiggling under the table and I uncrossed my legs to stop it, placing both feet firmly on the floor.

'Is it good news?' I asked.

'Let's order, then I'll explain.'

'I thought Pa's will was all finalised,' John said. 'He left us nothing. "I'm a self-made man and proud of it. You'll make our own way in the world, too." And all that. End of.'

Mum held up a hand, palm facing John. 'Let's order and then we'll talk about it.'

I looked sideways at John and saw with surprise that his jaw was clenched and that he was trying to breathe slowly through his nose. He'd mentioned our inheritance once before and I couldn't understand why it would be so important to him. Yes, he had two children to look after and quite a high-maintenance wife but his company, as far as I knew, was worth a fortune. Yet now, looking at him, I could see how much effort it was taking him not to push Mum further. He stared intently at the menu and rubbed the back of his neck as he did so. His face contorted with the effort of staying quiet.

'Everyone ready?' John said after a minute or two, then without waiting for our replies, he waved over a waitress.

'I'm getting used to the décor now,' said Mum when our orders had been taken. She intertwined her hands on the table and looked around the restaurant. 'It's quite quaint. Much nicer than the buffet.'

'Very atmospheric,' I said.

'And you don't have to search for a table.'

'Exactly!'

John's fingers drummed on the table.

'What do you think, John?' I asked.

'Very nice.'

'I believe the chef is Italian,' Mum said.

'That's a good sign.'

'So ... you were saying...?' John said to Mum.

A waiter arrived with the wine. 'Would sir like to taste?'

John shook his head impatiently. 'I'm sure it's fine. Just pour it.'

'I would,' said Mum. 'Don't want a duff one!' She pushed her glass towards the waiter, who opened the bottle with ceremony, then poured a splash. Mum raised the glass and, looking at John and me over the brim, she swirled the ruby liquid around, then held it up to the light.

'Good colour,' she said. 'What year did you say?'

'2012.'

'And that was a good year?'

The waiter nodded. John fiddled with his napkin.

Mum pushed her nose into the glass and inhaled deeply, closing her eyes and nodding as if to savour the bouquet of the wine. Finally, when I imagined John was literally about to swipe the glass out of Mum's hand, she tipped it up and took the wine in her mouth, where she swilled it around while staring thoughtfully into the middle distance. At last she swallowed, brought her eyes back to the table and smiled at the waiter.

'It's fine,' she said. 'Thank you.'

The waiter moved around the table, pouring a glass for each of us with a flourish. Finally, he placed the bottle in a wine holder and retreated. John placed his arms on the table and leaned towards Mum.

'So ... what's this all about?'

Mum put her hands on the table and studied them. Then she took a deep breath.

'Well,' she said. 'As you know, when your father died, he didn't leave you anything.' Mum looked at us each in turn, forcing us to make eye contact with her. 'I know it seemed cruel but he had his reasons, as you both know. He valued hard work.' She looked down, struggling to find words. 'Let me start again. Your father was a very wealthy man. *Very* wealthy. And he didn't want to ruin your lives by handing you that wealth on a plate. He wanted you to work for your money – to find your niche in life and understand the value of money, rather than sit back on your laurels and fritter away the money he'd earned.'

As Mum spoke, I could hear Pa's voice saying the words. *Fritter*. It was exactly what he would have said. John was rubbing his chin as he listened, his expression inscrutable. Did he still think Mum had lost her marbles, I wondered? She sounded quite lucid to me. But then Mum's gaze drifted into the middle distance and it was almost as if she was no longer at the table with us.

'Your father was a man who stood by his principles,' she said softly. 'Whether or not they were right, he stood by his principles. I admired that ... I did ... but he could be cruel.' I had to strain to hear over the general noise of the restaurant. 'It wasn't necessary to be so cruel.'

'It's okay, Mum,' I put my hand on hers. 'What's done's done. We don't have to go over this. We're fine with it.'

Mum gave herself a little shake. 'Well, there's the thing. You don't know the half of it. Your father put it in his last wishes that you weren't to be told.'

'Told what?' said John, his tone rising in frustration as Mum stopped talking and stared again across the restaurant. If he could have reached inside her body and pulled the words out with his hands, I think he probably would have.

'Well. I've thought long and hard about this. It's not a decision I've taken lightly,' Mum said, 'but I've decided you need to know.'

'Know what?' John wasn't even hiding his impatience now. 'You're talking in riddles!'

'Let me finish!' Mum snapped, then she took a breath and spoke slowly once more, as if this was something she'd said many times in her head, or even rehearsed out loud. 'It's all very well your father wanting you to be self-made but I know life's not as easy these days. I know it isn't. Property prices are, just, ugh. You're both struggling.' I opened my mouth to stop her but she raised a hand to silence me. 'I'm not blind, Alexandra. I see that. I see you both making sacrifices, battling to make ends meet, and I sit there, eating caviar in my little house, and worrying about you two.' She paused, took a sip of wine, then carried on. 'So, even though your father didn't want me to tell you this, I'm going to.' She gripped the edge of the table with both hands and looked at John and then at me. 'Apart from the Barnes house, he actually left you each half of his estate.'

'What?' John shoved his chair back, his mouth hanging open.

'I thought he left it all to you?' I stared at Mum, unable to understand what she was telling us.

Mum shook her head. 'No. I got the house. The Barnes house and the furniture in it. It was worth an awful lot – as you know, well over a million. I didn't need anything more. I have my own means.' She shrugged.

'The painting, you mean.'

'Yes. The painting.' Mum gave a little laugh. 'The famous painting.'

I rubbed my forehead, still struggling to understand. 'So ... did you sell the Barnes house because you wanted to, or because you had to?' I went back in my mind to the time after Pa's death; tried to remember if Mum had given me any clue that he'd left her nothing besides the house. When we were told that he'd left John and me nothing, we'd just assumed that Mum had got it all.

'I had to sell the house,' Mum said. 'Well, I suppose I probably could have stayed and made ends meet – or I could have sold the painting – but I'm quite fond of the painting, and I didn't want to be struggling to rub two pennies together in my old age. The house was way too big for me on my own, so I sold it to release the capital.'

I felt the blood drain from my face. 'And bought somewhere cheaper ... I had no idea. You should have said.'

'No, no. I wanted to move, too. I was ready to leave Barnes; that house. It was always your father's house, not mine. And I wanted to be closer to the sea.'

All the while Mum and I were talking John was shaking his head. I could see a tic at the corner of his mouth and his lips were pressed together; he was struggling to stop a smile from creeping across his face.

'So...' he said slowly. 'He left it all to us ... when? How?'

'Well, that's the catch,' said Mum. 'The agreement he had the Trustees draw up is that you'll get the money only when I die. Pa's theory was that, by then, you'd have made your own money, become established in your careers and have got a good work ethic. He didn't want you to know about it before I died because he thought you'd rest on your laurels. But I don't see you doing that. I see two very hard-working adults who I think deserve to know that they're one day due a significant windfall from their father. I wanted to give you that gift.' She gave a little laugh. 'I don't like to disobey Ralph's wishes, but it's not like he can tell me off, is it? He's hardly going to come back from the grave and strangle me.' Mum's eyes were bright and she held on to the stem of her wine glass. I thought of her watching Pa choke that man to death.

'How much are we talking about?' asked John.

'A lot,' said Mum.

'Thank you,' I said. I reached out and touched Mum's hand. 'It's really nice to know that.' Already my mind was racing forward. Mark and I could take a loan for IVF, knowing that one day we'd be able to pay it back. But one day, when? My thoughts stopped in their tracks when I realised we'd only get the money when Mum died. I didn't want to wish her life away.

'How much is a lot?' asked John. 'What are we talking about here? Enough to pay off the mortgage? Buy a bigger house? Are we talking tens of thousands? Hundreds of thousands?' The timbre of his voice left space for 'millions?' I was torn; curious myself, but hating John for asking.

Mum gave John a look. 'Your father had assets even I didn't know about. He was very shrewd financially, a very good businessman. You won't have any financial worries, let's put it that way.'

'Have you met my wife?' John's joke broke the mood and we all laughed.

'Even so,' said Mum. 'Look. I'm not going to say how much it is. I don't want you to start counting on it.'

'Wow, Mum.' I was shaking my head. I couldn't wait to tell Mark. 'Thank you so much for telling us. It really eases things. I feel like you've opened a huge safety net under me. You know, we've had a tough year with Mark being out of work, and...' I trailed off not wanting to bring up the baby thing.

Mum smiled. 'You're welcome, Alexandra. I thought it might help to know.'

I squeezed Mum's hand, then picked up my glass. 'To Mum!'

'To Mum,' echoed John, taking a sip. 'For she's a jolly good fellow!' We all clinked glasses and sipped.

'So what about Harbourside?' John asked when we were all quiet again. 'There's probably even more reason to do it now – it'll free up a little more of the cash you have in the house – and give you a far better quality of life.'

'I said I'd consider it after the cruise,' Mum said.

'But that means you've decided to do it – right?'

I tried to kick John's ankle under the table. Why did he always have to ruin things?

'Well, let's see,' Mum said. 'If I'm going to go doolally, as you two seem to think I will, there'll come a point where I won't know where I am and you can book me into any old hell-hole you like.'

'True,' said John. 'I'd never thought of that.' They laughed. Mum ruefully, John not so.

14 July 2013, 10.15 p.m.

After dinner, it was John who didn't want to go to bed.

'Come on, let's go for a drink,' he said as we stood outside Valentino's, hmm-ing and ha-ing about whether to call it a night. 'My treat.'

'I couldn't,' said Mum. She patted her tummy. 'I've done well and I know when to stop.'

'And it's a big day tomorrow,' I said.

'Mykonos,' said Mum.

218

'Your birthday!'

'Oh, yes.'

'You'll come for a drink, won't you Lex?' asked John, bobbing his head up and down emphatically behind Mum. I'd not seen him drunk for years. If ever.

'Sure.' I turned to Mum. 'Are you okay? Would you like me to walk you back to your cabin?'

'No need for that, dear. I won't get lost. Just point me in the right direction and I'll walk till I reach my door. Another advantage of being at the front.'

'If you're sure.'

We said our goodnights and waited until Mum was in the lift with the button for the tenth floor pressed. 'Turn right out of the lifts,' I mouthed, pointing towards the front of the ship as the glass doors closed. Mum rolled her eyes and disappeared feet-first from view.

'Right,' said John, rubbing his hands together. 'Didn't want to say it in front of Mum, but I was thinking the Buzz Bar. Champagne? Whaddya reckon?'

'Spending the money before you've got it? She may have years left. Two decades – and you don't know how much it'll be.' Despite myself, I felt a thrill at the thought of the inheritance.

'I just feel like champagne tonight,' said John. 'And don't we have on-board credit anyway? I checked my bill. Each room came with a couple of hundred quid. We may as well spend it.'

I was grateful, as we stood on the threshold of the Buzz Bar, that John was dressed semi-formally

219

and not wearing one of his cringe-worthy tourist outfits made from crease-resistant poly-cotton. The place was smart: all cream leather, low lights and discreet tables; the sound of expensive chat filled the air. It didn't feel that busy, yet every table and alcove except for a high table with two stools over by a small porthole was taken. We made our way over to it and John, magnanimous for once, fell into a conversation with the waitress about which champagne to order. Shielding my eyes from the light, I pressed my face against the port-hole. We were near the front of the ship and I could see the white of the bow wave spreading out into the blackness of the ocean. I smiled down at the water, loving the romance of travelling through the night.

John's voice pulled me back into the room.

'Here you go, Lex. Cheers!' he said, handing me a flute of champagne. 'Don't gulp it down. It's a good one.'

'I won't,' I said, the novelty of him actually paying for something not lost on me. 'Cheers. To Mum.'

'To Mum. Indeed!'

John put his glass down and leaned back on the bar stool, his hands clasped behind his head. He shook his head and chuckled to himself. 'I can't believe it. I can't believe we're going to be rich.' He banged the table with a fist. 'Unbelievable. Cheers!' He grabbed his glass and took another swig.

'Don't get carried away,' I said, but, despite my-self, a little worm of excitement wriggled inside me. Even being modest, the kind of money we potentially stood to inherit was life-changing.

'What are you thinking?' John asked. 'You're smiling. You're spending the money in your head. Am I right?'

I nodded, sheepish. The wine at dinner had loosened my inhibitions. 'It would mean so much to us. We've been trying for a baby but nothing's happening. We don't qualify for IVF on the NHS and we were about to give up. This would mean we could to give it a go.'

'Do you want my kids?' He laughed. 'They aren't all they're cracked up to be, you know!'

I shot him a look. 'And, if it worked,' I said. 'Oh my God, if it worked, can you imagine? We'd have a baby! I could give up work. We could buy a house with a couple more bedrooms...'

'I know.' John's eyes shone. 'Tell me about it. We're squashed into our house. The twins could have a bedroom each and we could have a spare room. You could come and stay.'

I snorted mid-sip pushing champagne bubbles up my nose. When Mum and I had still lived in London, not once had John ever asked either of us to stay with him. Even when Mum had been house-hunting in Cornwall, she'd stayed in a hotel.

'Look at you,' I teased. 'Host with the most now you've got a few quid.'

John laughed. 'Well, we don't have it yet, of course. But the thought that it's coming...' He banged the table again. 'God, I feel like a new person. It changes everything. Everything!' He took the champagne bottle out of its silver ice bucket, turned it to look at the label appreciatively and topped up our glasses. 'I could get used to this...'

'You're not so badly off, though, are you?' I asked. 'I mean, I know you have the twins ... Anastasia ... but business is going well, isn't it?'

John shook his head and let a big sigh escape through his teeth. 'Yeah. Business is going well. It was going *very* well. I made a fortune.' He laughed bitterly.

'What then? Anastasia's spent it?'

John looked down at the table then he squeezed his hands together and looked up at me. 'Oh God, Lexi. I don't know where to start. I've not told anyone this, but...'

'What?'

'I lost it. Nearly half a million quid. Gone.'

'How did you lose it? What do you mean?'

'I got conned.' Shifting his weight forward, he looked down at the table. When he spoke again, his voice was small. 'I feel so stupid. I should have known.'

'What happened?' In my head a film played of John handing over wads of cash to a beggar in the High Street.

'Share fraud. It all sounded legit.'

I shrugged. It was all gobbledegook to me.

'Guy calls me,' said John. 'Offers me a great investment opportunity. I meet him. He has a brochure about the company. It's the next big thing, everyone's investing in it. I did a bit of due diligence – clearly not enough – anyway, it offered a great return and Anastasia had been on my back about private schooling for the twins, she wants a bigger house, blah blah, blah. I thought it would be a quick way to make a bit of extra cash, you know, without eating into the capital. The plan was I'd get the capital back within a year, plus profits.'

'Oh, please tell me you didn't do it?'

John shook his head. 'The guy presented well. The story sounded legit. I thought I was going to get my capital back, Lex, with a bit – quite a bit – extra. Who wouldn't be tempted?'

'Oh God. What happened?'

'Shares were worthless. Worth less than the paper the certificate was printed on. I lost the lot.' He bowed his head and, for a second, he looked like he was going to cry.

'Oh, John. I had no idea. What did Anastasia say?'

'She doesn't know. But wait. It gets worse. I was embarrassed. As you can imagine. I didn't know what to do. Then I get a call from another dealer. You'd think I'd have learned my lesson, right? Huh.'

I clapped my hand over my mouth, shaking my head slowly.

'Exactly. But, Lex, I was in so deep. I'd lost so much I didn't know what to do. I couldn't tell Anastasia. How could I tell Anastasia? Look at me. I'm not an idiot.' He laughed ruefully. 'I'm under no illusions as to why Anastasia's with me and, trust me, it's not for my looks.'

I opened my mouth to reply but John held up a hand. 'I'm under no illusions, Lex. I love her but I don't kid myself it works both ways. She wanted a British education for the twins. I got her, her kids, and her mother out of Estonia and I gave them a home, became a father to the kids. Gave Anastasia respectability. Status. She was a single mother on the breadline back home. She gives me what I need. I wish it were more romantic, but it's not. For her, it's business.'

'But you had enough money? You were doing really well.'

'I thought if I could stretch a bit further, give her the extras she wanted – the ponies, the private school, the bigger house – she'd be happier. I thought she'd respect me more. Start to love me. I don't know...'

I pressed my lips together; a lump had formed in my throat. 'I had no idea.' There was a silence while John stared at his champagne glass, a mixture of emotions crossing his face. When he looked up, he'd composed himself again.

'Anyway – where was I? The other dealer?'

'Don't tell me you fell for it again.'

John shook his head. 'They must have been in it together. How could I have known? The second guy calls me up, asks if I've got shares in this particular company – the ones I'd just bought. He knew I had. Obviously. To me, it was like a call from heaven, the answer to my prayers. I didn't question it. The second guy slags off the first guy and says he's come across a few people who've been conned like that but he might just have something that'll interest me. "I've got this client," he says, "who needs to buy up all those shares for personal reasons ... I've told him they're worthless but he's adamant and – well, I don't suppose you'd be willing to sell?" and he names a price a little under what I'd paid in the first place. I didn't even stop to consider who would really want these shares, what the personal reasons could be. I leapt at the chance. I was going to get almost all my money back.'

'But then what happened? It all sounds good so far.'

'It does, doesn't it? So you're as gullible as I am. Well ... just as I'd got used to the idea that I was going to sell, the guy calls me back and says he's spoken to his boss and I need to put ten per cent of the shares' value up-front as security. If the sale doesn't go through, I'll get the security deposit back, so I agree to it. It's to be held in an account until the sale goes through.'

'You paid it? How much?'

'Forty thousand pounds.'

'What?'

'Exactly.'

'And ... then what?'

'Nothing. Never heard from him again. Couldn't trace him. Gone. The pair of them, with my savings. Nearly half a million quid.'

'I had no idea.'

'No one did. You're the only person I've told.'

'No wonder you're so uptight about money.'

'Uptight? I'm paranoid. We have nothing. It's hand-to-mouth at the moment while I claw it back. Anastasia has no idea. No idea! She's still spending faster than I'm earning and there's no backup. The inheritance ... oh my God, Lex. I can't even begin to say what it means to me. Even if we have to wait years, the thought that it's coming. I can take a loan. We can get by. I don't need to tell Anastasia anything.'

All I could do was repeat myself. 'I had no idea.'

'How long...' John looked down at the table.

His words were so quiet I strained to hear. 'How long do you think...?'

I did a double-take. 'What? You mean Mum?'

He nodded. 'I mean, she's seventy tomorrow...'

'Oh my God. John. No. Don't talk like that! She's got ages yet.'

My brother shrugged. 'She doesn't have to die of old age, you know. It can be sudden. Look what happened with Valya. One day there, gone by lunchtime. You never know.'

The hairs on the back of my neck – they prickled again.

15 July 2013, 7.30 a.m.

I woke early the next morning, still rattled by a dream in which I'd been chasing Mum through the maze of streets in Corfu's old town and slightly anxious at what the day would bring. Without Mum's knowledge I'd arranged for her suite butler to bring a champagne breakfast for all of us to her room. But now, as I lay in bed, I wondered what I'd been thinking offering her alcohol at eight in the morning. She was going to have to negotiate the twists and turns of Mykonos's cobbled streets slightly inebriated. On top of that, we had her birthday dinner and then the White Night party that didn't even start till ten.

I could hear water running in the cabin next door: John was up. At least he hadn't forgotten our breakfast date with Mum. I thought about him and Anastasia. I'd always been cynical about her reasons for picking my brother as a husband but now he'd spelt out the essence of their marriage, I felt cheated. I'd enjoyed speculating with Mark about the status of their relationship, but I saw now that I'd wanted to believe deep down that there was some magic; that, beyond all odds, Anastasia loved my brother; saw him as something more than a means to an end. I felt devastated for John that his feelings were largely unrequited. Would it have unravelled something inside him if she'd genuinely loved him? Would the right woman have been able to unlock his emotions?

I knocked on John's door. 'Ready?

'Yep,' he said. His face was shadowed with tiredness and his eyes cushioned with grey; he looked like he hadn't slept at all. His dark hair, still wet, was combed into that centre-parted style that he'd worn since he was at primary school.

'Sleep well?' I asked, but his monosyllabic grunt of a reply didn't encourage further chat. We walked to Mum's room in silence and I realised then that the confidences exchanged the previous night would never again be mentioned. My childlessness, John's financial worries, and the question of Anastasia's love were relegated back to the box from which they'd come. The closeness that we'd experienced in the Buzz Bar had been nothing more than a fleeting moment, not the dawn of something new. I wondered if John felt embarrassed at all that he'd told me.

'Do you think she'll be up?' I said as we knocked on Mum's door but I needn't have worried. When she opened it, she was fully dressed and made up.

It was clear she'd been up for some time, though she seemed flustered to see us.

'What's wrong?' she asked, holding onto the door. 'What's happened?'

'Nothing,' I said. 'Happy birthday! We've come to have breakfast with you.' I waited but she didn't move to invite us in. 'Are you going to make us sing out here in the corridor?'

'Well, let me get my key and we'll go,' she said, reaching to take her key card out of the light switch.

'No, you're having breakfast in your suite today. We're joining you. If you don't mind!'

'What?' Mum shook her head and still didn't let us in.

'Here, in your suite! Your butler should be along,' I looked at my watch, 'any minute to set it all up. I thought we'd start the day in style. Since you hate how crowded the Ocean Breeze place gets at breakfast.'

'Oh ... okay then. You'd better come in, then. But just give me a second to tidy up.' Mum started to close the door but I caught it.

'What do you mean? Tidy up what?'

Mum was halfway across her living room. 'Oh, just papers. I have papers all over the table,' she said over her shoulder. 'Won't take a sec.'

I pushed open the door and followed her into the room. Mum's dining table was indeed covered in papers; her reading glasses lay on top. She stacked the papers, bundled them into a plastic folder, and took that into her dressing room, from where I heard the safe clunk shut. John and I stood awkwardly in the living area, not

228

knowing what to do. Mum bustled back out.

'Right. Why didn't you warn me you were coming?' she asked. 'Oh, I see. It was a surprise. Well, thank you very much.'

I gave Mum a hug. 'Happy birthday.' I handed her a small box. 'This is from both of us.'

John wandered about the room, picking things up while Mum carefully unwrapped the box and opened it to see the delicate silver locket I'd chosen for her in Cornwall.

'Thank you! It's lovely,' she said.

'It opens. Look inside.' I helped Mum crack open the locket. Inside I'd put tiny pictures of John and me. 'It's bit cheesy, but it means we'll always be with you.'

'Thank you, both of you. I shall treasure it always,' Mum said, and I helped her fasten it around her neck.

I looked at John. He was standing with his hands on his hips, looking through the picture window to the side terrace. 'Right. One, two, three,' I said pointedly, and started to sing. 'Happy birthday to you ... come on John... Happy birthday to you ... John... Happy birthday dear Mu-um, happy birthday to you! Hip-hip hurray! Hip-hip hurray! Hip-hip hurray!' I gave myself a self-conscious round of applause. John hadn't sung a word. The doorbell rang; an electronic note that made us all jump.

'That'll be breakfast,' I said.

Mum made for the door.

'Well. That was awkward,' said John, his back still to the room.

'At least I made an effort,' I hissed. 'I can't

believe you didn't sing.'

The butler rolled a trolley over to the dining table. 'Good morning, good morning, how are we all today? Special occasion?' He started to set out the breakfast. A bowl of baked goods, a steel flask of coffee, a bottle of champagne, three glasses of orange juice and then, from the hot box, three plates of bacon, sausages, and eggs.

'It's my mother's birthday,' I said.

The butler stopped what he was doing and turned to face Mum. 'Many happy returns,' he said. 'Special day for a special lady.' His smile was warm.

'I'm too old for all this.' Mum sank onto the arm chair, a flush rising in her cheeks.

The butler turned back to his work. 'Mykonos today. Have you been before?'

John slid open the terrace door and slipped out onto the balcony, pulling the door closed after him. He stood, hands on the railing, looking out to sea.

'Er, no. None of us has,' I said. 'Got any recommendations?'

'I don't tend to get there much myself, but most of the guests, they see the windmills or they go to the beaches.'

'Beaches aren't really for us,' I said, nodding in the direction of Mum. 'Bit hot for...'

'Then windmills. You walk through town, take some photos, you put them on your Facebook, make everybody at home jealous ... you are from England?' I nodded. 'You take picture of white houses, blue sky, you make them jealous. It's always raining in England.'

I laughed. 'Is it far? To walk?'

'You walk as far as you like,' he said. 'Then you stop in a *taverna*, have some lunch, drink some *ouzo*, and you come back.' He folded the last napkin and placed it carefully on the table. 'Would you like me to open this?' he asked, pointing to the bottle of champagne. 'Or leave it?'

'Leave it, please. We'll do it. Thank you.'

The butler left and I banged on the window to summon John. He didn't move so I opened the balcony door and shouted. He started, as if I'd shaken him out of a trance.

'Breakfast,' I called. 'Come on! Stay with the programme.'

We took our places at the table and I picked up the champagne. 'Anyone interested? I'm sure the sun's over the yard-arm somewhere...'

'Why not?' said Mum, so I popped the cork and filled the three glasses.

'Happy birthday,' said John.

'Happy seventieth,' I said. 'May there be seventy more!'

'Oh, please,' said Mum.

15 July 2013, 10 a.m.

After our champagne breakfast, Mum and I took our time getting ready then reconvened by the lifts ready to catch the shuttle bus from the pier into Mykonos Town. We had no plans bar what the butler had recommended: to potter about, taking in the beauty of the Byzantine alleyways, to nose in a few shops, to take some photos and maybe enjoy a bit of refreshment in one of the *tavernas* but, when we emerged from the air-conditioned bus into the dazzling glare of the sunshine, Mum squinted her eyes towards a bay in the distance, craning her neck forward to see better. We stood next to a harbour, the ridiculously blue sea studded with luxury yachts, sailing boats, and motor launches. Ahead of us, a few minutes' walk away, a neat little bay curved around. I saw a beach, cafés, and restaurants, rows of white-washed buildings rising up the hill behind the sea.

'Oh, look! Is that one of those little seaside trains?' Mum asked, pointing towards the bay. 'Look, going along the front there. It is!'

I saw what she meant: in the distance, a colourful little caterpillar was weaving its way through crowds of pedestrians and mopeds.

'Oh, we must go on it. Birthday treat?' Mum said. 'I love those trains. We used to go on one on holiday down on the south coast when I was a child. I haven't seen one for years. Come on!'

We made our way carefully to the harbour, walking past restaurants, cafés full of people sitting back and drinking in the picture-postcard views, their chairs almost overhanging the edge of the harbour.

'It's so pretty,' I sighed.

Mum didn't reply and I looked back to see her shielding her eyes from the glare of the sun as she picked her way carefully along the uneven path. I took her arm.

'Here,' I said. 'Let's find somewhere shaded to

232

have a sit down and plan what we're going to do.'

'No, no. Don't fuss.' She patted my hand. 'I want to go on that train. I'm going on that train if it kills me! It'll be fun. Show us the lay of the land, so to speak, then we can plan what we're going to do.'

The crowds got denser as we approached the seafront; masses of tourists and cruise ship passengers thronged the narrow streets, all with the same goal in mind: get some nice photos, have a look for some souvenirs, sit down and have a drink. Bar owners called to us; waitresses approached with smiles and open menus. The smells of a hundred different dishes tickled our noses. Mum and I edged slowly through the chaos, searching for the point where the tourist train began.

'It's going to be down there by the seafront,' I said.

'I wonder what John's making of all this. Not really his scene, is it?'

'He'll have got on a bus to some remote town or something. Ooh, look!' she turned abruptly into an art gallery we'd been passing and I followed her inside, where canvases of Greek scenes lined the walls. Some seemed clunky, done with an amateurish hand, but others truly captured the warmth and light that I'd noticed both in Corfu and here in Mykonos. Mum was staring at a picture of a hillside of white-washed houses. The artist had captured the view from above, the canvas a cascade of blue-domed homes leading down a steep cliff to the sparkling sea below. Just looking at the picture, I could smell the heavy scent of oleander; hear the song of the birds brought to me on the hot wind.

'It's lovely,' I said, joining Mum. 'I wonder if it's Mykonos.'

'Santorini,' said the sales assistant, materialising behind us. 'Done by a local artist. Originally British, I think.'

'Oh, lovely. We're going to Santorini tomorrow.' I immediately regretted identifying myself as a cruise ship passenger lest it add fifty euros to the price, but Mum was oblivious, lost in the painting. Very gently, almost without touching, she put her fingertips to the canvas.

'It's lovely,' I said. 'Would you like it? It could be a birthday present?'

'It's your birthday?' the sales assistant asked.

'Yes.' I turned to her. 'Today.'

'Then I do very special price for you. One-time only, birthday price.'

'Mum?'

She pulled her hand back from the canvas and looked up at me as if noticing me for the first time. 'What?'

'Would you like the painting? As a birthday present?'

She shook her head. 'Oh, no. No. Thank you but no. How could I carry this around with us? No, thank you dear. No need.'

She looked briefly around the shop at the other paintings, none catching her eye in quite the same way, and we made our way back out into the sunshine.

'I could have bought it for you. I was happy to,' I said. 'A reminder of this trip.'

'Really, dear. It's enough for me that you're both here with me,' said Mum. 'No need for any more gifts.'

In a way, I could see why Mum had been so keen on the tourist train but, once we'd found the stop and seen the crowds of people waiting, I hesitated, drawn more towards a seafront café where we could sit back and people-watch. Mum, however, was adamant. Along with the rest of the tourists, we bundled into the open carriages as soon as the train had pulled up to its stop and bagged a couple of seats. I was relieved to see the carriages had a roof to shield us from the midday sun but, even so, Mum fanned herself with the fan she'd picked up in Corfu.

'Your father would never have entertained something like this,' she said. 'I used to look at these trains and wish I could go on one, just one more time, but he would never have let me.' She played with the chain that crossed the open door, clicking it open and shut. Her voice was quiet. 'Sometimes I think Ralph would work out what it was that I wanted in life and then prevent me from doing it just for his own amusement.' She sighed. 'My ride on that train when I was little was the highlight of that summer. How difficult would it have been for him to let me do it again?'

'What would have happened if you'd stood up to him?'

Mum snorted. 'I wasn't willing to find out.'

'I used to watch how dealt with him and wonder how you had the patience.'

Mum patted my hand. 'It was all about crisis

aversion, dear. I may not have gone to university, but I majored in crisis aversion.' She gave a little laugh and turned her head towards the harbour. Before I could think of anything to say, the train started with a jerk and we both lurched forward, grabbing the handrails to stop ourselves from falling onto the people opposite. With a toot and a whistle, we started to edge forward through the crowds of people.

'Happy birthday again,' I said.

Mum grinned at me. 'Thank you.'

'I can't help but feel a taxi might have been more efficient,' I said as we crawled down the road thronging with pedestrians, most of whom were walking faster than us.

'More efficient, maybe, but nowhere near as much fun.'

Climbing up the steps of the bus that was to take us back to the ship, I felt a hand on my shoulder and spun around: John. His top was wet with sweat; his face red and shiny. My nose wrinkled involuntarily.

'Hello.' I plonked myself down next to Mum and John took a spare seat across the aisle.

'Enjoy Mykonos?' he asked. 'What did you two do?'

'It was great. We took the tourist train, then had a glass of wine in one of the cafés. What about you? Hitchhike to a ruined village and climb a pile of rubble?'

'Something like that. The town was a nightmare, wasn't it? All those scooters. I got away from all of that; found some authenticity. That's the problem with cruises: even when you get off the ship you can't get away from the passengers.' He paused and I didn't reply; we were, after all, two of those passengers. 'And all those people in town selling that tourist tit-tat. They see us coming. We're like cash cows getting off these ships. And people buy it! Think what they're seeing is real. That's the saddest part.' John shook his head.

We fell into silence. I pulled out my phone and started scrolling through my photos. Yes, it had been crowded – and yes, the blasts of the scooters had irritated me – but I'd seen beauty in the colours of Mykonos: in the white of the build-ings, the blue of the sea, the narrow lanes and the pink of the bougainvillea. How was it possible, I wondered, to have so little in common with your sibling? There were times when I wondered how John and I could be related at all, let alone twins.

John poked my leg across the aisle. I looked at him and he nodded towards Mum.

'Look.'

She was asleep, her head resting on the glass window, her mouth hanging open, her port guide open on her lap. She looked old and exhausted, and her skin, under the flush from the heat, looked brittle.

'You finished her off?' John whispered.

'John!'

'God, Lexi, I was only joking.'

'Please have some respect. It's her birthday,' I whispered. 'It was hot, all right? And we walked a fair bit. Even I'm exhausted.'

'I wonder,' John stroked his chin, 'what pro-visions were made for if one of us dies before

Mum does. When she died, would the other one get the lot?' He looked at me sideways. I looked away.

15 July 2013, 11 p.m.

Mum patted her lips with her napkin, folded it, and placed it neatly on the table, then she looked at us expectantly.

'So who's up for a dance with an old lady?' she asked.

We'd had her birthday dinner, birthday cake complete with singing waiters which I'd requested just to annoy John, coffee, and even liqueurs. Now Mum was keen to get to the White Night party. She leaned back in her chair and stretched her arms around behind her. 'If we don't get going now, I don't think we'll ever make it.'

'Do you really feel up to it?' I asked. 'After Mykonos? Because we don't have to. We've had a lovely evening...'

'Of course! There's life in the old bird yet.'

'Just don't feel you have to go through with it just because you said it. We don't mind.'

'Alexandra! Enough.'

'I might retire early, if you don't mind,' said John. He spoke through an exaggerated yawn. 'Suddenly very tired.'

'I do mind, actually,' Mum said, looking squarely at him. 'If I can do it, you can do it. Come for just a bit. You don't have to dance, but come along, it'll be fun.'

'I haven't got anything white.'

'You're wearing a white shirt!' I said.

'Trousers,' he said. 'Haven't got any white ones. Or shoes.'

'You don't need to be all white. As long as you've got a bit on, I doubt they'll throw you out. Next excuse?'

'You're actually going?' he countered.

'Yep.' I pushed my chair back and stood up. 'Come on, ye who dare to dance.'

John ran his hand through his hair and sighed. 'All right. Just for a bit. But I'm not dancing.'

'Great,' said Mum. 'Children: I know a cruise with your old mum was maybe not your best idea of a summer holiday but thank you. Thank you for coming, and thank you for humouring me. It means a lot to me.' She touched the locket we'd given her. 'Thank you both for this and, Alexandra, thank you again for the train ride. Best birthday ever.'

I looked to check she wasn't teasing me, but she was smiling.

'You're welcome,' I said, and I felt a blush creep up my cheeks. It made me ridiculously happy to think I'd been able to give her something so simple that had brought her so much joy. I thought back to the beautiful painting we'd seen in Mykonos – I'd been prepared to buy it for her, too, but maybe she'd been right: there really was no need.

The White Night party took place on the pool deck. We could hear the music thumping even before we pushed through the door that led out to the deck above. There, we paused at the railings and looked down at the party. Although the deck was busy, the loungers had been pushed back to create as much dancing space as possible and it wasn't as densely packed as I'd imagined it might be. We stood for a minute and took in the scene around the floodlit pool; everyone there wore at least something that was white, if only a borrowed hat, but many had gone the whole hog and dressed head-to-toe in white, which glowed under the fluorescent lights that had been set up around the bar and dance floor. There were women in shorts and halter neck tops, women in floaty white dresses, and some in nothing but white bikinis, white captain's hats, and sky-high stilettos. A few of the men wore white suits, shoes, and captain's hats, too.

At the front of the dance floor, on a raised deck, a selection of the Entertainments team's female dancers, in white hot-pants, cropped tops, and knee-high socks, performed an energetic routine to a Britney Spears song. Two male dancers, dressed in tight white trousers, long white jackets, and white trilby hats accompanied them. As we watched, the men ripped off the jackets to reveal white vests that barely covered their rippling muscles. I could almost smell the testosterone.

'Oh look! There's Stavros,' said Mum. 'Come on.' Clicking her fingers, she jived towards the steep metal stairs that would take us down to the pool deck.

'Careful on the steps,' I called after her. 'Hold on!'

'Seriously?' John muttered. He looked at the

dance floor and exhaled. 'Shoot me now. This. Is. Hell. On. Earth.'

'Do you ever loosen up?'

'Um, let me think.' He tilted his head, placed his index finger on his lip and pretended to think. 'For things like this? No.'

A deck below, Mum headed straight for the dance floor while I went to the bar to get drinks. John arranged himself on a lounger in the shadows as far away from the dance floor as possible. The cocktails came with sparklers – gingerly, I carried a couple over to John, trying not to catch my hair with them.

'One White Hot Lady for you,' I said, enjoying the joke as I handed him a glass. 'I won't tell Anastasia if you don't. Cheers.' I clinked our glasses and turned to watch the dance floor. Now and then I caught sight of Mum in among the whirling dancers. She may not have been as expressive as some of the younger people, but she had great rhythm and I enjoyed watching her dancing salsa steps to the beat.

'She's having a great time, isn't she?' I said. 'Look at her face! She can't stop smiling.'

'Huh,' said John. I took it to mean yes. I drained my glass and stood up.

'Right. See you in a bit.' I shimmied my way onto the dance floor.

'I'm taking a breather!' I shouted to Mum over the music. We'd been dancing non-stop for ages, and I was hot. Sweaty bodies writhed all around me; I was being bumped and jostled from every angle. I didn't know how Mum could stand it.

'Okay, me too,' she shouted, the dance suddenly going out of her, and we threaded our way through the dancers to the nearby table. I flopped onto a chair, my feet suddenly aching. Mum fanned herself as she got her breath back.

John appeared, wending his way through the tables. He put a bottle of water and two plastic cups on the table.

'Thought you might need this. My contribution to victory. And on that note, I'm retiring.' He raised both palms in the air and took a few steps backwards away from us. 'No arguments. Good-night.'

He turned to go.

'Bye John,' Mum said. 'Thanks for coming on the cruise. I appreciate it.' She stood up, her arms open as if to accept a hug.

'Sore heads tomorrow,' said John. 'Anyway, have a good night.' He turned and walked away.

Mum looked at me and shrugged. Then she kissed her hand and blew the kiss at his retreating back. She watched him for a second, her hand over her lips, then she looked at me, raised her eyebrows and pulled a funny face. We both burst out laughing.

'Now let the fun really begin,' she said.

'How late are you planning to stay?'

'As long as there's any dance left in me.'

'It finishes at two.'

'Then two.'

'Mum, I won't manage that.' I shook my head apologetically. 'I'm really tired.'

'I'll be fine without you. I'm a big girl.'

'I know.'

We sat and watched the dance floor, my head nodding in time with the music. It was a song Mum knew and she sang a bar or two until the song ended.

'But seriously, Alexandra, thank you for today. For coming on this cruise. It means a lot to me. And I had the best day ever, today.' She reached for my hand and squeezed it. 'Thank you.'

'It's a pleasure, Mum. Really.'

Stavros danced up to us. 'What you doing hiding here, my favourite lady?' he said, reaching out his hand. 'You'll come and dance with me?'

Mum stood up. 'Just give me a minute. Are you off now?' she asked me.

I finished my water and stood up, too. 'Yes, I think so. You're in good hands.'

'Audrey is amazing,' Stavros said. He pronounced her name Ord-a-ree, with a long roll on the 'r'.

'It's her birthday today. She turned seventy.'

'No!' Stavros looked genuinely surprised. 'Then you must dance all night with me.'

'Come here.' Mum lunged towards me with her arms outstretched and grasped me into a hug. This was something we never did but I found my arms winding around her, too, and we stood locked in the hug for a few seconds as I breathed in the familiar scent of her perfume. Then she patted me on the back, kissed my hair, and pulled away.

'Bye darling,' she said. 'Look after yourself.'

'I'm only going to my cabin. You look after yourself!' I goggled my eyes at Stavros.

'Don't wait for me tomorrow,' she said. 'Explore

Santorini – maybe I'll see you there. I'll need a lie-in after this.' She took Stavros's hand and together they bopped towards the dance floor.

'I'm glad you had such a good birthday,' I shouted after her. Mum turned and blew me a kiss, then stepped onto the dance floor.

16 July 2013, 9 a.m.

Consciousness came slowly to me the morning after the White Night party; it was as if I hoped that lying motionless with my eyes closed might fool my body into thinking it was still asleep and do away with the headache that was threatening to rip my skull open. As I lay there, face down, cheek on a wet patch of dribble, I heard John moving about in his cabin. I heard the scrabble of the chain being unhitched, then the door opened and clunked shut again. I moved and a wave of pain rolled through my head but the ship was un-naturally still. We must have dropped anchor: San-torini. I groaned in frustration. I'd always wanted to go to Santorini. Why did I ruin this chance with a hangover?

Rolling onto my back I pressed my palms to my temples to try and hold in the pain while I thought about where I'd put my paracetamol. Easing myself out of bed, I shuffled across the cabin, banged my shin on the edge of the bed, rootled through drawers until I saw the packet, grabbed it and retreated to bed, glugging two caplets down

244

with a slug of water. Had we really drunk that much? It must have been the mix of wine and cocktails. Or maybe we didn't drink enough water – it had been hot. Why hadn't I made Mum drink more water? If I felt like this, how was she? Guilt oozed its oily way into my consciousness and I rolled towards the bedside phone, picked it up to dial Mum, then remembered she'd said she wanted a lie-in and put the receiver back down.

Propping myself up on the pillows with a large glass of water to sip, I faced the room, eyes half closed, and listened to the sounds of the ship. In the corridor outside, I could hear the Entertainment Manager's daily recorded message about the day's events burbling on in multiple languages. It garnered a sense of excitement about the day ahead – made me think that there were things out there to do and see and, twenty minutes later, I realised my headache was subsiding.

Opening the curtains a crack I peered out of the window: in the distance I could see mountains. A small boat was drawing a wake across a sparkling blue bay. In the distance, another boat appeared to be coming towards the ship – tenders. The buzz of anticipation distracted me from my physical woes. Maybe I could manage a gentle trip after all.

Santorini was a hidden gem – so hidden that I almost didn't get to see it. From the dock, it didn't look like much. Once I'd disembarked from the tender, I stood facing the crop of busy tourist cafés and souvenir shops that lined the water's edge. Behind them, inhospitable-looking cliffs towered, penning the dock, and exhausting me simply with the thought of how I'd get to the top. Heat radiated off the concrete road, sweat trickled down my spine, and the din coming from the crowds thronging the tourist shops made my head pound once more.

I wiped a hand across my forehead and thought, for a minute, about getting straight back on the tender and spending the day sunbathing on the ship; the thought of a quiet sun lounger and a cool swimming pool was tempting, especially if I could assuage the guilt I was feeling about letting Mum drink so much and stay out so late. I'd knocked quietly on her door before I left the ship and, when there was no reply, assumed she was sleeping. Would I get to see her if I went back? As I stood on the dock deciding what to do, an old man in a flat cap and a dirty blue shirt accosted me.

'Donkey?' he asked, pointing towards a path.

'What?'

'Ride donkey?' he pointed up to the cluster of white buildings that iced the top of the cliffs – the town of Fira, I guessed.

'Ride donkey up? To the top?' I pointed at the cliff in disbelief.

The man nodded.

'Really?' I tried to convey my scepticism through facial expression but even as I did, I saw a straggle of people setting off up the hill on donkeys, their handlers walking by their sides. 'Is that the only way?'

The man pointed at something. 'Lift.'

'Oh, okay. Thank you. Then no donkey.'

I crossed the dock and joined the long queue

for what turned out to be a cable car. At the top, I stumbled out of the cable car station onto a platform that was thronged with people looking over the edge. The glare was intense, even with my sunglasses on; the view, when I finally found a space not occupied by people taking photographs, was spectacular. Anchored on the bright blue of the bay, the cruise ship looked like a child's bath toy. I stared, entranced; I'd heard it said that the Lost City of Atlantis could have been under those waters. I stood for a minute or two, imagining what might lie beneath. Then I turned my back on the view and took a selfie, trying to get the ship in the background so I could show Mum if she didn't make it.

With a last look at the glittering bay, I made my way down the first street I came to; a narrow lane, riotously colourful with souvenir shops. Ahead, I saw a familiar cotton sunhat, a head and shoulders above everyone else. I ran a few steps to catch up with John and poked his arm. 'Hey!'

He spun around. 'Lexi. Isn't the view amazing? It's incredible to think we're standing on the top of an old volcano.'

'Isn't it?'

'Did you take a donkey up?'

'What do you think?'

'I did. Big mistake. I queued for ages, then I got what felt like a three-legged donkey. It was so uncomfortable I thought it was going to ditch me over the side. It stank of poo and I was covered in flies.'

I laughed. 'Anything goes in the quest for authenticity – right? So, what are your plans today? Did you see Mum at all?'

'Was I supposed to?'

'No. She said not to bother her. But I kind of hoped we might see her here.'

'I haven't seen her. Anyway...' he looked at his watch. 'I've got to find Gold Street: the buses to Oia go from there.' I looked at him quizzically – my reading about Santorini hadn't extended beyond Fira. 'It's "the most beautiful village on Santorini".' John paused, looked like he might ask me to join him, then carried on. 'So, we're due back by five? Shame I'll miss the sunset from Oia. Maybe see you back on board?'

I shrugged. 'I guess so.'

Bored with the souvenir shops that all appeared to sell the same items at the same prices, I sought out the side streets, which I quickly learned were home to more interesting boutiques and galleries selling handmade jewellery, handicrafts, and art. They were also cooler: the streets were so narrow they were in perpetual shade. Deep in the tangle of backstreets, a painting outside a small art gallery caught my eye and I stepped closer to look – smeared with the azure blues of the sky, the sea, and the domed top of a house set against the vibrant pinks and greens of palms and bougainvillea, something about the canvas reminded me of the one Mum and I had seen in Mykonos. I was staring at it when a sales lady emerged from the gallery.

'You like it?' she asked.

'Yes. It's beautiful. It makes me want to go to Santorini.' We both laughed. 'I love the way you

248

can almost smell the flowers and the trees. The way the artist manages to catch the light so perfectly.' I stopped talking, realising I knew nothing about art and that that fact was probably very obvious. 'Are you the artist? Did you paint it?'

'No. I just work in the shop. The artist sometimes works out the back. He has a few shops here.'

'Is he here today?'

She shook her head. 'No, not today. Usually he is – he lives next door.' She nodded towards a green door. 'But he's busy today.'

'What a shame.' I looked again at the painting, sizing up how difficult it would be to carry, and made an instant decision. Mum hadn't been able to make it here today; even though she'd said a gift 'wasn't needed', I was going to buy her the painting as a memento of her birthday cruise.

16 July 2013, 5 p.m.

I went straight to Mum's cabin when I got back on the ship. Hot and sweaty, I was desperate for a shower, but even more keen to give Mum her painting. Putting it gently down on the carpet, I knocked on the door and waited. Nothing. I knocked again, slightly louder, and realised, as I stood there listening for sounds of her footsteps coming towards the door, that I was holding my breath.

I heard a sound behind me in the corridor and

turned – it was the butler with the early evening canapé service.

'Did you see her today?' I asked, nodding towards the room. 'Mrs Templeton?'

The butler looked up in the air while he thought. 'No,' he said eventually. 'She was out when I came to service the cabin.'

'Oh. What time was that?'

'Ten o'clock? Maybe eleven o'clock? Later than usual because she hadn't put the "make up my room" light on.'

I nodded slowly. 'Oh okay. So she got up and went out. Maybe she went into Santorini after all.'

The butler stood poised with a plate of canapés. 'Is there anything I can help you with?'

'Are you delivering those? Can I just see if she's in the room?'

The butler knocked on Mum's door. 'Turndown!' he called. When there was no response, he unlocked the door and propped it open. Feeling strangely like I was trespassing, I peered in behind him.

'Is she there?'

'No.' He was setting up the canapés on the dining table.

'Not on the balcony?'

'No. Sorry Madam.'

I knocked on John's door before going for dinner.

'Have you seen Mum today?'

'No.'

'Me neither.' I started to turn away.

'Are you about to go for dinner?' John asked.

'Yes. Yes, I was. Maybe she'll already be there.'

'If you can wait a couple of minutes, I'll come with you.'

'Sure,' I said, and he opened the cabin door wider, indicating that I should come in. It was the first time I'd been inside his cabin and I stood awkwardly by the door, looking around. In contrast to my own cabin, where I kept the balcony doors open to catch the sea breeze, the air-conditioning was on and not a pin was out of place. Aside from the guide books on the table, the room could have been uninhabited; the bed pristine, no clothes or shoes lying around. I moved to the living area, hovered a bit, then sat gingerly on the sofa.

'I wonder where Mum got to today,' I said. 'I hope she made it into Santorini.'

'Probably.' John was fiddling in the wardrobe. I heard the rustle of plastic.

'She got up,' I said, 'I know that much. The butler said her room was empty by about ten or eleven, as he cleaned it. But whether she went into Santorini, I've no idea.' I paused. John said nothing. 'It's a shame if she didn't go in because she would have loved it. There were some beautiful art shops. I bought her a painting.'

'I'm sure she went into Santorini. Why wouldn't she?' John looked at me around the wardrobe door.

'Because she was tired? Maybe she had a hangover?'

'So maybe she had a lie-in first.' John shrugged.

'It's just odd, that's all. I'd have thought one of us would have seen her.'

'Lex. We're moving about in a pack of three

thousand people. Nine thousand plus on shore when other ships are in.' He disappeared behind the wardrobe door again and the rustling sounds recommenced.

'Aren't you worried?' I said.

'No! Maybe she went for a late breakfast ... maybe she went into Santorini; maybe she didn't. Maybe she lay by the pool. Stranger things have happened.'

I didn't say anything.

'Does it really matter?'

'It's just odd, that's all. Odd that we've not seen her around.'

'It's a big ship.' John emerged from the wardrobe with a bundle of clothes in his arms. 'She was tired. She had a lie-in. She had a late breakfast and spent the day on the ship. There are a million things to do on board and she'd probably had enough of Greek islands by now. She probably took one look at that mountain up to Fira and decided that it was too much for her to cope with without you. Remember, she is seventy. Anyway ... excuse me...' he waved a shirt at me. 'Need to get changed.'

'Oh. Okay.'

I slid open the balcony door and stepped outside. John closed the curtain behind me, blanking out the light that came from the cabin. The sun hung just above the horizon and the sea had turned golden, reflecting the colours of the sunset. From the height of the eighth deck, the water looked calm but I realised, looking down, that what appeared to be mere ripples on the surface were actually waves a couple of feet high.

Occasionally one broke and a mass of white foam appeared. I leaned over the edge of the balcony and stared at the water, scanning the surface for the dolphins I'd heard sometimes swam alongside cruise ships. In the far distance I could make out the shape of another cruise ship heading in the same direction as us. I imagined passengers on that ship sipping gin and tonics on their balconies, watching us watching them.

The door slid open. 'Ready,' said John.

'Coming.' I stepped back into the cabin. John looked uncharacteristically stylish. 'Wow,' I said. 'New clothes?'

'Yep,' said John. 'Well ... y'know...' He looked sheepish. My eyes widened as I realised what he meant.

'Seriously? Don't get carried away with this! It could be years.'

'Yeah, but ... I so needed a few new clothes. For goodness' sake, Lex, don't be so melodramatic. Right, shall we go?'

The buffet was circular, which gave me a chance to walk around the restaurant, surreptitiously checking the tables for Mum while I selected my dinner. Each time I stood up to get another dish, I did another round. Mum wasn't there. For dessert, I helped myself to some fruit and carried my bowl the entire way around the restaurant one more time.

'You took your time,' said John as I sat back down. He was already halfway through his apple crumble.

'I did another lap. She wouldn't have gone to a

formal restaurant on her own, would she?'

'Maybe she met someone.'

'Like who?'

'I don't know. Some other oldie? Maybe they met in the library, or at some oldies' class, and hit it off. Maybe she's been with a new friend all day. Maybe she's having dancing classes with Stavros. Look Lexi, you've got to stop worrying. We're on a ship, for heaven's sake. She can't have gone far.'

'It just doesn't feel right. Why hasn't she got in touch? She could have phoned one of our rooms and left a message.' John put down his spoon and glared at me.

'Stop. Worrying!' He emphasised the words, as if talking to a dunce. Then he shook his head and started to eat again. A piece of crumble trembled on his lip. I pushed my pudding to one side and sighed. Was I worrying unnecessarily?

'It's probably a plan,' John said, talking with his mouthful, 'to push us together. She's probably watching from some hiding place. You know how she's always going on about how we "only have each other". She probably wants to see whether we speak to each other when she's not here. I mean, pushing us onto this cruise together gives her the perfect opportunity to watch us. A social experiment, maybe.'

'I hope you're right.'

After dinner, I said goodnight to John at my cabin door but, after he closed his door, I walked quickly back to the lifts and up to the tenth floor. I rapped smartly on Mum's door, hoping beyond all hope that she'd appear at the door with an explanation of why she'd been out of touch. It would be so obvious! We'd laugh about how silly I'd been. But there was no reply.

I took the lift down to the lobby. I'd seen note-pads on the coffee tables there and I scribbled a quick note to Mum: 'Call me when you get this – A xx', took the lift back up, and left it tucked behind the room number on her door.

Back in my room I took off my shoes, sat on the bed, and flicked on the television: pictures, voices, but nothing went in. I shifted around on the bed, twirling my hair around my fingers, then I clicked off the television and walked over to the wardrobe. I opened the door, looked in, shuffled through my clothes, touched the life vests that were stored overhead, then closed the wardrobe. I stared at the deck plan on the back of my cabin door, hoping for inspiration. Where could she be? In the corridor outside, I heard the sound of someone approaching. I opened the door and stuck my head out, ready to see Mum, but a couple walked past, their arms entwined around each other.

'Evening.'

'Evening.'

I shut the door, went over to the table and poured out a glass of wine from the bottle I kept in my cabin. A rush of warm air greeted me as took the wine out onto the balcony and slumped into the chair, putting my feet up on the railing. I started out into the darkness. It was a clear night and the stars seemed to mirror the small breaks of the waves that caught the moonlight. It was diffi-cult to tell where sea ended and sky began. In the distance, the other cruise ship was still sailing parallel to us, lit up like a Christmas tree. I couldn't get comfortable. I shifted in the chair, tried different positions, then got up with a sigh, went back inside, and dialled Mum's number.

After a few tinny rings, the phone went to the messaging service. I dialled again, imagining Mum padding towards the phone just as it stopped ringing. Again – no reply. I threw myself backwards onto the bed and lay there for a minute, then I sat up and looked around the room. On the desk lay the pile of papers that had accumulated during the cruise: port information, itineraries, special offers, ship information. Rummaging through the pile of brochures and fliers, I found the full deck plan of the ship. Grabbing a piece of paper and a pen, I made a note of every place Mum could be: the spa, the gym, the champagne bar, any of the restaurants and cafés, the library, the internet café, the lobby coffee bar, the games room, the promenade deck, the theatre, the shops. I threw the paper down with a sigh. There were just too many places to search, but I couldn't sit here and do nothing; I slipped my feet back into my sandals, grabbed my key, and headed out.

I took the lift to the Deck 13 and started there. I walked to the front of the ship and made my way to the back, looking in every public area that I saw. When my search drew a blank. I walked down the stairs to Deck 12 and repeated the search. I did this all the way down to the promenade on Deck 4. Below that was the staff quarters and engine rooms – she wasn't going to be down there. On the promenade deck, I stood again at the railing and looked down at the water. Here, I was much closer to the sea and I could hear the sound of the waves breaking on the ship's bow as it sliced its way through the water. We were going fast and the wind whipped my hair around my face. I caught site of myself in the window: Medusa. A monster.

I turned and made my way back to the lifts. Back on Deck 8, I paused outside my room, then knocked on John's door. Inside, I heard shuffling, then some sort of grunt. It was apparent when John opened the door that he'd been asleep – the cabin was in darkness and he was wearing pyjamas.

'What?' he said, his face scrumpled up to the light in the corridor.

'I can't find Mum. I've searched the whole ship.'

'What do you mean "searched"?'

'You know: walked about looking.'

'Did it occur to you that she's probably in bed with her ear plugs in?'

I didn't say anything.

'You're seriously worried about her?'

'Well. Given I can't find her anywhere – yes.'

John looked at the carpet and sighed. 'Look. It's late and I want to go to sleep. She's here some-where. Trust me. She's fine. Go to bed. If we can't find her in the morning, we'll...'

'What? We'll what?'

'I don't know. Tell someone. Get them to do a proper search.'

'What if she's fallen down some steps and is lying hurt somewhere?'

'Someone will have seen her. It's not like this is a ghost ship. There are three thousand people on board. Even if she fell somewhere down below, the crew will have seen her. Did you check the sanatorium?'

'No.' I'd forgotten that – it was on Deck 1.

'Maybe she's there, and they just didn't know to tell us. Check it in the morning. Now, if you don't mind...'

'Night.'

I opened my door slowly, then sat on the bed, rifling through the paperwork until I found a number for the sanatorium. I dialled it and waited but there was no reply. Kicking off my shoes, I lay back on the bed and dialled again.

17 July 2013, 8 a.m.

I woke the next morning with a dry mouth, a stiff neck, and the phone still in my hand. I was still fully dressed, on top of the covers. As consciousness slowly returned, I remembered my search of the ship last night, and how I must have fallen asleep waiting for the sanatorium to pick up. But with daylight came logic; with a growing sense of embarrassment I went over how I'd woken John up to tell him I couldn't find Mum. What must he have thought? Of course he was right. Mum would be fine. What an idiot I'd been running all over the ship on my own looking for her in every bar, casino, lounge, and restaurant. It was probably just as well I hadn't got through to the sanatorium.

Still, I'd like to speak to Mum, to put my mind at rest. I picked up the phone handset and peered at the screen through eyes that were sticky with grit. The display was blank so I jabbed a button or two and it failed to spring to life: out of battery. I stretched across to the bedside table and replaced it in the cradle with a bleep, and caught sight of the clock as I did so: 8:00. We would already be docked for the morning in Katakolon, Greece. Now that posed a problem: Mum had said previously that there was a winery she was keen to visit on the outskirts of Katakolon. I'd suggested that we'd take a taxi up there together but, if she'd been trying to ring me she wouldn't have got through because the phone was dead. Would she have gone alone?

'For God's sake!' I muttered out loud. I pulled myself into a sitting position on the bed. 'This is ridiculous!' I shouted at the room, louder this time. 'It's like chasing a shadow!'

My anger spurred me into action and, shedding yesterday's clothes, I showered, made my face look presentable, and dressed in fresh clothes. I put my door on the latch and knocked on John's door and waited. Nothing. I leaned my forehead against the door, consumed by a sudden paranoia that Mum and John were deliberately hiding from me – playing some kind of game. I imagined them both sitting at breakfast, laughing. Breakfast. Of course!

I grabbed my key and hot-footed it down the corridors, charged up the stairs two at a time, and banged on Mum's door. There was no reply, but the message I'd left tucked behind her room door had gone.

'Yes!' I punched the air, then, with a big smile on my face, I headed quickly back towards the restaurant. Grabbing a squeeze of the regulation hand sanitizer without breaking pace, I marched into Ocean Breeze and walked around the restaurant, eyes swinging left and right as I examined every table.

'Have you seen my mother?' I asked a waitress whose face I recognised. She often brought us drinks.

'Morning, ma'am,' she sang with a cheerful smile.

'Have you seen my mother? Today?'

The waitress edged over to a counter and balanced the edge of her tray on it. She'd been clearing tables and it was piled high with dirty crockery and uneaten scraps of food.

'Let me see,' she said rolling her eyes upwards. 'I think so ... she is small? Brown hair?'

'No. Quite tall. Grey hair. A bit stooped. Walks like this.' I did a few steps' impression of Mum, realising as I did so how ridiculous I looked.

She nodded. 'Ah. I remember her.'

'Have you seen her this morning?'

'Umm ... I'm not sure.' She shook her head. 'No, I don't think so.'

'All right, thank you,' I said.

'But my shift only started eight thirty,' said the waitress. 'Maybe she came early? Lots of people come early, go to Katakolon before the crowds.'

'Okay, thank you,' I said. What the waitress said was true. Mum was an early bird. She could easily have finished breakfast before eight thirty.

'Anything else I can help you with?' asked the waitress, picking up the full weight of her tray again.

I shook my head. 'No. Thank you.'

'Have a great day!'

It was a short walk from the ship into Katakolon port; no need for shuttle buses. From Ocean Breeze, where I'd had a coffee, I'd seen a beautiful bay curving away as far as I could see. Close to town, people were splashing in the water. Squinting, I could just about make out horses pulling shady carts trotting around the curve of the shore. I wasn't keen to go ashore but, as I watched the scene on land, I convinced myself that, just minutes after disembarking, I was bound to find John and Mum sitting in a waterfront café, enjoying a coffee and a pastry, watching the world go by and wondering what on earth I'd been so panicked about. I ran the conversation through my head:

'At last! Here you are! Where have you been hiding?' I'd exclaim, weak with relief.

'What do you mean?' Mum would ask. She'd be looking particularly well, I decided, thanks to all the spa treatments and exercise classes that had kept her out of sight the last two days. 'I haven't been anywhere! Where have *you* been? You're never in when I call!'

We'd both laugh and I'd flop onto a chair at the table and order a welcome drink. John would tell Mum about my mad search of the ship and they'd both shake their heads and tut.

'What are we going to do with you?' Mum would ask, patting my hand. 'Sometimes I think you're more senile than I am.'

I smiled to myself at the thought of her safe and sound. After I'd finished breakfast, I went back to my cabin via Mum's. Still no reply and her butler was nowhere to be seen so, convinced she must already have got off the ship, I headed back to my room, got myself ready, and disembarked. As I walked through the port, the hot sun beating down on me, I almost believed that I was a few minutes away from finding both Mum and John. I practically skipped.

The main street was interesting but I was on a mission. Ignoring the lure of shops, I glanced in every café as I headed down towards the bay I'd seen from the ship. There, I circled around then sat on a bench under the shade of a tree and watched the world go by, eyes peeled for Mum's slightly awkward gait.

The cruise passengers were easy to spot: couples ducked in and out of shops, their faces reddening in the heat. The stop in Katakolon wasn't that long and many were nervous of going too far from the port. Families sank gratefully into chairs outside the cafés; children dug into pastries and tall glasses of frozen yoghurt while their parents leaned back in their chairs, fanned themselves, and sipped cold drinks. I doubted any of them were sitting there worrying about the whereabouts of an elderly mother. Even though the cruise had been Mum's gift to John and me, I started to think how different it would be if I were there with Mark instead of Mum. Maybe we'd have done a bit of shopping, and then we'd have sat in a café for a slap-up lunch, maybe strolled back to the ship hand-in-hand for a siesta. I wouldn't have spent the day searching for an old lady.

Unbidden, the thought entered my head that

there would, at some point, come a day when Mum would no longer be around – what would life be like then? I shook my head, trying to stop the thought from continuing. But once the idea had materialised, I couldn't get rid of it. For a moment – a scary, heady moment – I glimpsed a world in which I no longer needed to worry about my mother.

I stood up suddenly, deeply disturbed at the turn my thoughts had taken. Still, I couldn't stop them as I walked back into the busy shopping street. There would be a gap in my life without Mum, but there'd be nothing to worry about either; no arguing with John about who cared for her. I'd get used to it. Everything would be so much simpler. *And you'd have the money from Dad's will,* a small voice whispered. I thought about John's new clothes, his greasy smile. Is this how he felt? I walked slowly back to the ship, hating myself more with every step.

17 July 2013, 3 p.m.

Back on board, I went straight to Mum's room hoping the sight of her smiling around the door would assuage the guilt that was sitting in my throat like a physical lump. No reply. I walked slowly down to John's room, wondering what to say to him. I heard rustling from inside, then John, sunburned, poked his head out.

'Hi.'

'Did you see her today?' I asked.

John shook his head slowly. 'You didn't find her?'

I indicated the empty space next to me. 'What do *you* think? Would I be standing here asking you if I had? Can I come in?'

John opened the door wider and stepped back to let me in.

'It's been thirty-nine hours,' I said. 'I don't care what you say: something's wrong.'

John ran his hand through his hair.

'I've been going through what could have happened.' I said. 'One: she got off the ship and didn't get back on – maybe she had an accident or a fall or something in Santorini or Katakolon. Two: She had an accident or fainted on the ship and is lying somewhere on board. Three: She...' I swallowed. 'She's ... oh God.'

'Overboard,' said John. 'Look. She's either on the ship or not on the ship. We need to find out which.'

'My feeling is she's not on the ship. We'd have found her by now if she was. But we need to get the ship searched to be sure. And then we can look at the other possibilities.'

The balcony door was open and I stepped outside and leaned on the railings looking down at the people walking back to the ship in dribs and drabs. On the dock, crew members were trying to get passengers in the mood for the final sail-away party. Stewards and stewardesses in uniform were line-dancing; people were hanging over their balconies, drinks in their hands, watching, cheering and lapping up the atmosphere. Unconsciously, my eyes searched the dock for Mum. I turned to

John, who'd followed me out.

'I'm sick of searching,' I said. 'There's nothing more we can do. We need to raise the alarm.'

Now I'd said it out loud, all I wanted to do was call someone and get an official search started, even though a part of me felt that maybe I was being a melodramatic. I imagined the hassle of telling the crew my worries; the embarrassment of having them find Mum safe and sound.

'Who do we even tell?' I asked.

'Guest Relations?'

'Oh God. I don't know.'

'Okay.' John went back into the room and came out holding the ship Directory. He flicked through it. 'Yes. I think Guest Relations is the best bet. I'll call them. Does that make you feel better?'

I nodded.

'Come on then.' We went back into the room and John picked up the phone. 'Sure?'

'Yes. Just do it.'

'Okay.' He clicked a four-digit number into the phone.

'Yes, hello,' he said into the phone. 'This is John Templeton in zero eight sixty-two.'

I listened while he told the person on the other end of the phone the details of Mum's disappearance, then he was transferred to someone else, to whom he repeated the whole story.

When he'd finished speaking, John nodded a few times. 'Thank you,' he said. He replaced the handset slowly and turned to me, his face suddenly ashen.

'What did they say?' I asked.

'They're going to send the cruise director here

to talk to us, prior to launching a full search of the ship.'

'So what now? We wait here?'

'Yes. We wait. The cruise director – Doris something, I think she said – is on her way.' There was a silence as we both took in this development. John moved over to the dressing table, where he had a bottle of gin.

'I don't know about you, but I need a drink.'

17 July 2013, 3.45 p.m.

Even though I was waiting for the knock at the door, it still made me jump when it came. John and I had been sitting in silence; I lost in my thoughts while John nursed his gin. John jumped up and opened the door, ushering two people in to his cabin.

'Mr Templeton? I'm Doris Maier,' said the first person. 'Cruise director.' She was a short, stocky woman with dark skin, dark hair, and way too much red lipstick for the time of day. She held her hand out for each of us to shake. 'And this is Angelica Floros, director of Guest Relations. I believe you spoke to her on the phone?'

John nodded.

'May we, umm...' she pointed to the sofa.

'Yes, of course, please sit down,' I said. 'I'd offer you tea, but we can't...' I waved my hand at the lack of tea-making facilities. 'I can order?'

'We're fine, thank you,' said Doris. She settled

herself on the sofa while Angelica took her place standing with her back to the balcony window. She stood squarely, distributing her weight equally on both feet, and held her hands neatly in front of her body, looking not unlike a bouncer. It made me think her role was that of witness. Was this a legal conversation? Doris took out a notepad; a pen was already clipped to it.

'So, we're here to talk about Mrs, uh, Templeton?'

I nodded.

'Your mother?' Doris looked at John then me.

'Yes, both our mothers.' It sounded wrong. 'His and mine. Our mother,' I said.

'Okay, and you say you haven't seen her since when?'

'Since the White Night party.'

'Two days ago? Am I correct?' Doris flicked through her diary. 'Yes, White Night was after Mykonos. Yes, this will be the second night. So, two full days and one full night?'

'Yes, about to enter the second night,' I said. 'Thirty-nine hours, to be precise.' I gave a little laugh as if it was funny I'd added it up.

'And she is sixty-nine years old?'

'Seventy.' My voice was small. 'It was her birthday.'

Doris sat with her pen poised over a notepad. 'And this is the first time you have reported her missing?'

I nodded.

'May I ask why you didn't report this sooner?'

I opened my mouth but nothing came out. Suddenly I saw it through Doris's eyes: an old lady had been missing for thirty-nine hours and her children hadn't reported it. It sounded like we'd neglected her. Images of John and I dancing in the bars, drinking, eating, and enjoying shore excursions while our mother drowned flashed through my mind. Was this what Doris was thinking? Were we such terrible children?

'We didn't want to make a fuss unnecessarily,' John's voice was smooth. 'We weren't spending all day, every day, together, so it was easy for us to miss seeing her. We each had our own itineraries. When we didn't see her, we just assumed she was doing something else. It took a while for us both to realise that neither of us had seen her.'

Doris nodded. 'And disappearing is unusual behaviour for Mrs Templeton?' she asked. 'She doesn't often wander off?'

It took all my strength to rein in a sarcastic response.

'Yes,' I said. 'Highly unusual.'

Doris looked at John. He nodded.

'And you're positive you haven't just been missing her as you move about the ship? She in the library while you're by the pool? That kind of thing?'

'That's what we were saying. That's what we thought, why we didn't call you earlier. But now I've searched *everywhere!*' A sob caught in my voice. 'I've searched the entire ship from Deck 13 to Deck 4. Every restaurant, every café, every lounge, every shop. The theatre. The lobby. Everywhere.' Doris nodded and I felt she was finally beginning to understand the situation. 'I've knocked on her room door a hundred times.'

'And not got a reply?'

'No.'

'Forgive me for asking, but have you tried calling her room?'

I rolled my eyes. 'Yes.' I sounded exasperated, even to me.

'I'm sorry,' said Doris. 'I have to ask these things. Ninety-nine times out of a hundred, a so-called missing person turns out to be a misunderstanding.'

'Call her yourself, if you like.'

'I already have,' said Doris. 'I should also hear from her butler any minute. I sent him along to check if the bed had been slept in. In fact...' she punched a number into the mobile phone she had clipped to her belt and spoke rapidly into it. Then she looked up.

'No,' she said. 'The room hasn't been touched.'

I gasped. Not having seen Mum was one thing; having it officially confirmed that she hadn't been to her room was a shock. I'd assumed that the fact that my note had gone would imply Mum had been to her room but, even as I thought it, I realised, of course, that the butler would have taken it inside. John looked pale. He stood up and started to pace up and down the room.

'Could she have just got off the ship and not got back on?' he asked. 'Is that possible?'

Doris shook her head. 'No. As you know, every passenger must swipe their card out and swipe back in. We know exactly who's on board at any given time.'

'And she didn't swipe out and not swipe back in?'

'The captain would be aware had that been the

case, but I'll double check.'

John turned to face Doris. 'Is it possible that she's somehow gone overboard? Is that something that will be considered?'

Doris nodded. 'It is. And it does happen. But we mustn't speculate at this stage. First, I inform Captain Stiegman. Most likely, we will page for Mrs Templeton over the public address system, then we will check the CCTV. At the same time, with the permission of the captain, staff will perform a full search of the ship. This will take some time. If we find nothing, Captain will make a decision about reversing course and, or, deploying lifeboats.'

I looked at her in disbelief. 'You mean, we're not obliged to turn back? What if she did fall overboard?' An image of Mum treading water in her White Night outfit appeared in my mind's eye. For how long could she have lasted?

Doris shook her head. 'It's at Captain's discretion. The timescale is crucial. If someone witnesses an overboard,' I cringed as she used the word as a noun, 'we would reverse course and deploy lifeboats at once but...' she looked at me and then at John, 'in this case ... *if* we're talking about pax overboard ... *if* ... we don't know when or where she went overboard. It could have happened at any point between the waters off Mykonos to Katakolon via Santorini. It's a huge distance. I cannot speculate as to what Captain Stiegman will do.'

'But the quicker we know what happened, the quicker we can turn back,' I said. 'What if she's in the water? Alive? Waiting? What if she's hanging on, watching the horizon for us to come back? She'll expect us to come back!'

'There are a lot of factors to consider,' Doris said. 'The time she's been missing ... the distance we've travelled ... if there are any other ships in the area ... the tides ... many factors.'

'The main factor being that an elderly woman could be treading water in the Mediterranean.' I couldn't disguise my disgust.

Doris looked down and then I realised what she was being so coy about admitting: that the chances of Mum still treading water after all this time were slim. She didn't think she would have survived this long. I turned away.

'What about other ships?' John asked. 'Are there any other ships closer? Ones that could divert to have a look?'

'It is possible,' Doris said.

'There was! I saw another cruise ship travelling parallel to us. Maybe they saw something? Maybe they could go back? Can we speak to them?' Even as I said it, I knew the ship had been too far away for them to have seen anything.

'It will be in Captain's hands,' said Doris. She stood up, straightening her skirt as she did so. It was tight and it had ridden up when she'd sat down. 'But let's not be pessimistic. I will get the search of the ship underway and, with hope, we will find her. It will all be a misunderstanding.'

'And what do we do in the meantime? I feel like we should be doing something.'

'Wait. And try not to worry,' said Doris. She walked towards the door, Angelica in her wake. At the door, she turned. 'It would be helpful if you could stay in your state room this evening. So I can contact you.'

John nodded.

'Sure,' I said.

The door closed behind them.

17 July 2013, 5 p.m.

I turned on the public address speaker in John's room. 'I want to hear if they page for her.'

John didn't say anything. He was still pacing the room, his forehead furrowed.

'It's crazy to page for her,' I said. 'If she was able to hear that, we'd have found her somewhere. Either she's unconscious, she's locked up somewhere, or she's...'

John looked up. 'It's not wasting any time. That Doris woman said they'd do the search simultaneously, didn't she? So let them page her. Maybe it'll jolt someone's memory. Maybe another passenger will realise they've seen her. I don't know. It can't do any harm, can it?'

There was a silence, then the speaker crackled to life followed by the three-toned ping that preceded every public announcement. A female voice rang out: 'Paging Audrey Templeton. Paging Audrey Templeton. Would Audrey Templeton please go at once to the Guest Relations lounge on Deck 5.'

'Is that it?' I asked.

'They'll be starting the search now.'

I stepped out onto the balcony and leaned over the railing, scouring the sea. From the height of the eighth deck it wasn't easy to see anything. If Mum had gone overboard, the chances of her being found were miniscule. As Doris had said, it could have been any time since I left the White Night party until today. She would have been a weak, seventy-year-old dot in the ocean. My only hope was she'd have been picked up by another ship. But how would she have gone overboard? I tried to think of the different scenarios: she was tipsy, the ship lurched and she slipped. She climbed up to get a better view of something over a railing and lost her balance. She leaned on a gate or something and it gave way. She was pushed over. She was attacked, hurt, and thrown over.

I had to shake my head to stop myself from going down these avenues. Who would want to harm an old lady on her birthday cruise? This was the stuff of movies, not real life.

'What are you thinking?' John stood beside me.

'Oh – just...' I shook my head. 'If she fell ... God. We should have started the search ages ago.'

'We weren't to know.'

'But we did know! We knew she was missing. She's been missing thirty-nine hours now and what did we do? Nothing! I should never have listened to you.'

'We didn't know she was missing,' John spoke slowly, enunciating each word carefully. 'We knew we hadn't seen her since the White Night party. There's a difference.'

I thought back to the last time I'd seen Mum, dancing to Shakira. 'Stavros!' I banged my fist on the railing. 'I left her with Stavros. He might know something!'

I rushed back into the cabin and scrabbled with the papers on John's table for Doris's number.

'Thank you,' she said, politely, after I'd explained. 'I'll speak to him.'

I couldn't help myself. 'Any news yet?'

'The search has started. I will call you with any information. Please try to stay calm.'

I hung up and looked at John. He raised his glass. 'Well, cheers,' he said. 'The cruise certainly turned out more interesting than I'd imagined.'

A flash of anger ran through me. 'You want to watch what you say from now on,' I said. 'If they find out that Mum had just told us about Dad's will, they'll be asking both of us questions.'

'Lexi. Seriously? I was just trying to lighten the moment.'

'But look at yourself. Here you are, set to inherit a fortune, drinking gin and making jokes about your missing mother! It doesn't do you any favours.'

'Oh, for goodness' sake, Lexi. What else can I do? Weep and wail?'

'I don't know. Join in the search?'

'I think we should leave it to the professionals. They have a protocol for things like this. They have a drill. They know what to do. Besides, Doris said to wait here.'

I paced the room. 'Well I can't. I can't just sit here and do nothing. I'm going.'

John shook his head sadly. 'There's nothing you can do.'

'Maybe. But I can't do nothing either.'

I made my way to the back of the ship, to the promenade deck, where I had a good view of the ship's wake. It stretched out behind us, a white carpet of bubbles on the ocean. There was nothing else as far as the eye could see. A huge, blank, nothing. If I felt this small and insignificant on my towering ship, how must Mum have felt in the ocean, watching the ship sail away from her? A huge sob rose up inside my chest and I turned and marched back inside the ship.

I went straight to the Guest Relations desk and asked for Doris. 'Please tell her it's Alexandra Scrivener, about her mother, Audrey Templeton.' The woman looked blank.

'Was this about the upgrade?'

I snorted in exasperation. 'No! The missing passenger. The one you're currently searching for?'

Blustering an apology, the woman said a few words on a walkie-talkie and, before I had a chance even to sit down, Doris appeared, slightly out of breath.

'Mrs Scrivener. I'm afraid there's no news yet.'

'Did you speak to Stavros?'

'Yes. Yes, I've just been with him. He remembers her leaving the White Night party at about 2 a.m. He says he had no concerns about her safety going back to her cabin.'

'Was she drunk?'

'No. He says she was drinking only water.'

'Oh. Oh, well...' I couldn't decide if this was good or bad news. 'Anyway, look. I'd another idea.'

Doris used her eyebrows to get me to elaborate.

'You must have CCTV?' I said. 'Can we go

through the footage? See if we can see anything?'

'All in good time.' Doris spoke in a reassuring voice. I wondered if they taught it to her on her hospitality course: the 'dealing with unpleasant situations and difficult guests' module. 'Please understand that we're doing everything that we can. We have a procedure to follow and we are following it.'

'But I could help you. I could scan through the CCTV footage. I know what she looks like from every angle. She's my mother. I'd be faster than anyone else. Just put me in the room with the TVs and I'll do it. I know where to look. I know where she was, where her cabin was, what her favourite places were.' I paused. 'I need to help.'

Doris put her hand on my arm. 'We have it under control.'

I turned away from Doris, struggling not to cry. 'I just feel so useless.'

'Come.' Doris took my arm, steered me into a nearby chair and pulled one up next to it for herself. 'I know this is a very difficult time for you. But please don't give up hope. We are doing everything we can. Captain Stiegman is monitoring the situation closely. As soon as the search is complete, he will make the decision about turning the ship.'

'It's barbaric. I can't believe he wouldn't even consider not going back to look. The oceans are full of rubbish! What if she found something to cling onto and she's waiting to be rescued? And what? I'm supposed to sit here, on this ship, eating, drinking and making merry as we sail back to Venice leaving my mother to drown? Lost at sea? Just like that?'

But, even as I said it, an idea struck me. 'That's it! I could go back in a lifeboat! Why don't you ask the captain if he can deploy a lifeboat and I'll go with a crew member? If he won't turn the ship around, that's what we have to do! It makes perfect sense. You have those motorised ones, don't you? It'll be so much faster, too.'

Doris gave me a polite smile. 'It's Captain's decision,' she said.

'But you'll tell him, won't you? About my idea? If he won't turn the ship back?'

'Mrs Scrivener, Captain Stiegman is an experienced seaman. He will consider all options and choose the course of action he feels to be best.'

'Oh God, you sound like a parrot! "Captain Stiegman this, Captain Stiegman that. All hail Captain Stiegman!"' I parodied Doris's voice, surprising myself with the viciousness of my tone. Doris looked at the floor, taking my tirade in silence.

'Sorry,' I said. 'I just wish I'd realised sooner. I wish we hadn't kept thinking everything was okay. I should have trusted my instincts.' Tears sprang to my eyes and I swiped at them. 'What can I do? I can't sit about waiting. I need to be doing something. I just want to find her!'

'The best thing you can do is go back to your cabin and wait. If we have news, we'll be able to contact you fastest if we know where you are.' Doris stood up, pulled the hem of her skirt towards her knees. 'Now, if you'll excuse me, I will try to see how the search is progressing. See if there's any news for you. Try to stay positive.'

17 July 2013, 5.30 p.m.

My brother's door was on the latch so I let myself into his room, where I could see he was outside leaning on the balcony railings with a glass in his hand. The bottle of gin, now half empty, stood on his dresser, the smell of it pricking the air. I slid open the glass door and stepped out onto the balcony.

'Have they found her yet?'

'Yes! Here she is ... ta da!' I motioned to the space behind me. 'It was all a misunderstanding. She got locked in her bathroom... What do you think?'

'Keep your hair on.' John turned back towards the sea and stared across the ocean. He waved his arm loosely at the expanse. 'It's so big.'

'That's precisely my point.' I hissed, aware of voices on the adjacent balcony. 'She could be anywhere. How's she going to survive out there?'

'Well, she's not going to, is she?' John's voice was flat. 'Just got to face it. We're orphans.'

I wanted to smack him. 'How can you say that? How can you give up on her? The ship hasn't even turned yet. The lifeboats haven't even been deployed!'

'They're going to send down the lifeboats? I'd love to see that.'

'Maybe get some photos? John! What's wrong with you? It's not a spectator sport. This is our

278

mother's life we're talking about!' My voice rose.

John shrugged.

'Anyway,' I said. 'They might not even bother sending a lifeboat back. As I've been told a hundred times, it's the captain's decision. But obviously a lot depends on when she went over. If she went over.'

'Of course she went over. Where else is she?'

I sighed, my body crumpling from the inside out as I let the railing take my full weight. My head sagged down. 'It could have been up to forty hours ago.'

I heard John take a swig of his drink. 'In which case ... as I said: orphans.'

I turned my head sideways to look at him. 'How can you say that? How can you be so calm?'

'I've learned in life that there are some things you can't change, Lex.' John flung his arm towards the ocean, the sky, and I realised he was drunk. 'This is what it is. Whatever's happened has happened. I'll miss her as much as you will, but no amount of worrying's gonna change whatever's happened.' He looked at me and blinked slowly, his eyes taking a second to focus. 'Lex, you're gonna drive yourself crazy worrying like this and it's not gonna bring her back.' He raised his glass. 'I'm saying my goodbyes, that's what I'm doing. Cheers, Mum.' He took a swig of his drink.

Tears pricked at my eyes and I blinked hard to try and stop them from coming.

'She loved gin.'

'I know.'

We lapsed into silence. I looked towards the back of the ship, staring again at the wake that carved across the endless ocean. Then, far below us, a movement caught my eye and I peered over the railing: there was a flurry of activity around one of the lifeboats.

'Look! Look at the lifeboats! Something's happening there. Maybe they are deploying one.'

John peered over the balcony 'Yep. Looks like something's happening.'

'I'm going! I'm going to try and get on one.'

John turned to face me. 'Lex. Don't get excited. The captain's going through the motions. Covering himself legally. Don't get your hopes up. We're not gonna find her.'

'There might still be a chance.'

'She's been gone too long,' John closed his eyes and shook his head slowly. 'She couldn't have survived all this time. Chances are she hit her head on the way down and never knew what happened. She could already have been dead for nearly two days. To be honest, I think he's making a mistake to even go this far.'

I looked at him in disbelief. 'What?'

'Chances of us finding her? Very slim. It's almost cruel to get your hopes up.'

'Even when her life hangs in the balance?'

John leaned back against the railings and spoke slowly. 'Lex, her life ain't hanging in the balance. She's gone. The sooner you accept it, the better. Maybe they'll eventually recover a body. Probably they won't. You might be better off checking the lifeboats for signs that she hit one on the way down.'

I gasped, my hand clamped over my mouth as I looked down at the lifeboats.

'Just accept it, Lex,' John said. 'Mum believed in fate. Maybe this was her fate. We can't fight it.'

'Well I'm going to try. I'm going to find Doris. She seems to care about our mother more than you do!' I ripped open the balcony door and stormed through John's room, slamming the cabin door after me. The fact that it was still on the latch and bounced impotently instead of giving the shattering crash that I needed served only to fuel my anger further.

17 July 2013, 6 p.m.

Access to the lifeboats was from Deck 4. This I remembered from our pre-sail muster. I ran down the grand staircase and crashed through the sliding doors of Deck 4 onto the wooden promenade, hoping I'd got my bearings right and was on the correct side of the ship.

I saw the cluster of people at once: five members of crew fiddling with a lifeboat.

'Are you deploying the boat?' I asked, out of breath. 'Can I come too?'

Five pairs of eyes looked at me quizzically.

'What?' I threw my eyes towards the lifeboat. 'Are you deploying it? Letting it down? Can I come?'

'Madam ... I...' began one of the crew.

'What is it? Do I need to take off my shoes? Wear a lifejacket?' I flicked off my pumps and looked around for the floatation devices.

'Madam. You must be mistake.' The man who had tried to speak before shook his head. He was Filipino and struggled to speak to me in broken English. 'We making checks.'

'Okay!' I pointed to my watch. 'Five minutes? Ten? Then we go?' I pointed down to the sea.

He shook his head. 'No, madam. No going. Routine checks. Every day like this.'

I stared at the crew. Two stared back at me. The speaker fiddled with a cord in his hand. The other two almost imperceptibly started to edge away from me and back towards the lifeboat. Then it dawned on me. My face split into a huge smile.

'Oh!' I said, nodding. 'You don't know, do you? You haven't been told? You're performing the checks but you don't know why. I get it now! This lifeboat is about to be deployed to look for my mother.' I paused, waiting for a reaction but the crew who were staring continued to stare. 'We think she fell overboard.'

'No Captain orders,' said the first man.

'I know, I know! "It's Captain Stiegman's decision!"' I parroted. 'But if you haven't yet been told, you're about to be told. Call Doris. You know Doris? Guest Relations lady? Call her now. She'll tell you!'

The man looked blankly at me.

'You have walkie-talkie?' I mimed it. 'Call for Doris.'

'Okay.' The man nodded but did nothing. I stared at him, realising that he didn't have a walkie-talkie.

'Okay. I'll get Doris. Wait here. Don't move!'

I dashed back inside, stabbing the door button

furiously, and ran up a deck to Guest Relations. Doris was there, talking into her walkie-talkie, as I exploded into the lounge.

'Doris,' I called when she placed the handset back in its holster.

'Ah. Mrs Scrivener. I was about to go to your cabin.'

'You're launching a lifeboat?'

'Please. Take a seat,' she said, indicating the chairs on which we'd sat earlier. I sat impatiently, barely on the edge of the seat, leaning forward towards Doris, all ears.

'So? What's happened?'

Doris took a deep breath. 'We have reviewed the port exit and entry information and are confident that Mrs Templeton disembarked neither in Santorini nor in Katakolon. Furthermore, the entire ship has been searched, even the crew cabins so we can also say with complete confidence that your mother is not aboard the ship.'

I was so focused on the launching of the lifeboat that the immensity of this statement passed me by. Deep down, I'd known that Mum was no longer on the ship. The question for me was whether or not she was alive in the water; whether or not she'd been found by a passing ship.

'So is the captain turning the ship; or deploying a lifeboat? I saw the crew on Deck 4 preparing a lifeboat.'

Doris looked surprised. She shook her head. 'No, Mrs Scrivener. I have just spoken with the captain, and he will ask to speak to you very soon.'

'Do you know what he's decided?' I snapped. 'Lifeboat? I can see he's not turned the ship.'

'Mrs Scrivener,' said Doris. 'The captain is taking this incident very seriously. He is a very experienced mariner. He has been sailing cruise ships for many, many years.'

'When will he tell us what's happening? And what do we do meantime? Go to the cabaret show? Eat a five-course dinner? As we carry on sailing away from my mother? I can't. I just can't bear it!' I felt my face crumple. 'How long till we get ... where? Where are we headed now anyway?'

'We're *en route* to Venice,' said Doris gently. 'It's a direct run from here.'

I imagined us docking back in Venice – the same place as we had boarded with such excitement a week ago. I imagined John and me packing our bags and leaving the ship without our mother. It was grotesque. What were we supposed to do? Pack Mum's bag and fly home with her things but not her? Just walk away without knowing what happened? I put my head in my hands and sobbed.

18 July 2013, 9 a.m.

I dreamed that Mum was knocking on the hull of the ship. Weak and exhausted, she'd somehow caught up with the ship and was banging on the steel of the hull, her weak fists banging the metal as she croaked at me to throw down a rope for her. 'Alexandra! Alexandra!' she shouted. 'Throw a rope! Throw the ring! Lexi! Save me!' Bang,

bang, bang went her fists on the hull. 'Lexi!'

I woke in a panic, heart thumping, limbs frozen for the minute it took for me to remember where I was and realise that the banging was coming from outside my room. Someone was knocking on my door.

'Yes?' I croaked from my bed, then again, louder, because I clearly hadn't been heard.

'Lexi! I need to talk to you. Can I come in?' It was John.

'Have they found her?'

'No.'

'Is it important? Can it wait a bit? Half an hour?'

'No. It's urgent. Please.'

Sighing, I sat up on the side of the bed, still disorientated from my dream, then I shuffled over to the wardrobe, wrapped my dressing gown around myself, and opened the door. I sat back down on the bed, curling my feet under me, while John perched on the narrow sofa, his long legs looking scarecrow-like as they jutted out into the room. His face was grey; his eyes bloodshot.

'What's up?' I asked. My own eyes were scratchy from crying and tiredness.

'Doris just called. She said that Mum's cabin has to remain sealed until she's either found alive or, if she's not found, until the police come aboard in Venice.'

'Okay,' I said, failing to get what John was getting at. 'And what? Do you need something from in there?'

John lifted a box of cruise line matches out of the ashtray on the small coffee table, shook the box, put it back. 'Not as such...'

285

'What then? I don't understand what this is about. You're going to have to spell it out to me.'

'I just wondered,' again he picked up the match-box, studied it, 'if Mum has any valuables in her room. If we should take a look before the room's sealed. Ask if we can remove anything of value to us.'

'Like?'

'I don't know. Her jewellery? Those diamond earrings she had from Tiffany's were worth a fortune. Anastasia was always telling me.'

I stared at John, nausea rising in my gut. I spoke slowly. 'You want Mum's earrings?' I stopped short of saying 'for Anastasia'.

John tutted. 'Good God! I'm just being practical. If Mum's jewellery is lying around in the room, I'd rather we took it now than left it for some random member of staff or bent policeman to nick.'

I was empty with tiredness and getting dressed was the last thing I wanted to do, but I realised that regardless of what John was saying, I'd really like the chance to look around Mum's room myself.

'All right,' I said. 'I'll go.'

'Thanks.' John turned to go. 'Oh, and let me know if you find anything interesting.'

'Like what?'

'Oh I don't know. Anything that might give us a clue if this was … premeditated.' John stared at the wood of the door as he said this and something in his tone made me look harder at him, narrowing my eyes.

'Premeditated?' The word came out in a gasp.

'You think Mum planned this?' John's silence confirmed that was what he was thinking. 'Seriously? You think she might have jumped overboard? She wouldn't even jump into a swimming pool!'

'No,' said John, shaking his head. 'No, of course not.' He opened the door and exited, leaving me to get dressed.

Premeditated. I hadn't thought about that.

An image of Mum pulling a chair to the ship's railing, climbing up on it and preparing to jump overboard popped into my head. In the image, Mum was wearing her White Night outfit, her long white dress billowing in the wind. I couldn't picture her falling; the insignificant splash that her body would have made hitting the water. But was the thought that her disappearance – potentially her death – had been her own choice better or worse than the alternative?

I'd hardly been walking fast on my way from my cabin to Mum's, but my steps slowed even further as I approached the door to Mum's suite. While a part of me really wanted to see her things; another part was dreading it. Already there was a lump of solid emotion stuck in my throat. It wasn't lost on me that the last time I'd been into her suite had been on her birthday; I'd been singing *Happy Birthday*, drinking champagne for breakfast, and looking forward to a day in Mykonos.

When I reached the cabin, the door was on the latch but I stood for a minute outside, forcing myself to take a few deep breaths before I pushed the door gently and slipped inside.

Doris was in the living area, fiddling with a plastic gadget.

'Mrs Scrivener,' she said. She took a step towards me. 'You shouldn't be here. I'm afraid I have to ask you to leave.'

I heard the words but, in that moment, I was oblivious: I stood stock-still in the small entranceway that led to the living and dining area and breathed in the scent of night jasmine that still lingered in the air. Its familiar notes were a lynchpin of my childhood that triggered a flood of images in my head, and my knees buckled. I leaned a shoulder on the wall for support and fanned my face with my hand.

'Mrs Scrivener,' said Doris. 'I'm sorry. I must ask you to leave now.' She took another step towards me but I held up my hand.

'I just want to look. Please.'

'I can't let you in.'

'Why? Why not? I just want to...' I shook my head and waved my hand at the room, 'one last time.' Beyond Doris I could see Mum's sandals paired neatly by a lounge chair. I stared at them. 'Please?'

'It's against protocol. I was just about to seal the room.'

'Why?'

'Unless your mother is found before Venice, the police will want to come aboard and the room must be exactly as it was.'

An image of police tape sprang into my head. 'You mean it's a ... crime scene?' I almost laughed but Doris nodded.

'It will be treated as one, yes. We need to rule

288

out any chance of foul play.'

'Foul play?'

Doris pressed her lips together. 'We just need to make sure that we don't impede the police in any enquiries they might wish to make. That's all.'

'But I'm here now. Please? Just two minutes?' Doris shook her head. I ran over to her and took her by the arms. 'Please? I beg you. She was my mother!' My voice broke.

Doris closed her eyes and inhaled, then she gave a tiny nod. 'Okay. Two minutes,' she said. She moved over to the wall and stood with her back to it. 'But I can't leave you.'

'Thank you.' I gave her a weak smile and moved further into the cabin, wondering where to look first. Apart from the sandals and a pile of what looked like port guides, I couldn't see anything of Mum's in the living and dining area.

I walked slowly towards the bed. It was neatly made, the cruise line's signature pillows and throw arranged in the house style on top of the covers. There was nothing of Mum's on the bedside table: no book, no hand cream, not even the small silver alarm clock that she always took on holiday. Looking at the bed, it was as if Mum had never slept in the room.

I turned into the bathroom and immediately felt Mum's presence in a way that I hadn't in the main suite. Her scented candle – burned almost to the glass – sat on the edge of the bathtub. I picked it up and inhaled the scent deeply, then I touched the tip of my finger to the wax and rubbed it on my wrist: a little of Mum to stay with me. I moved to the wash basin. Here, Mum's cosmetics were arranged around the rim: deodorant, body lotion, face cream, toothpaste, toothbrush, and the face soap she always swore was better than any fancy cleanser.

I checked to see if Doris had followed me, then picked up the pot of moisturiser and quickly twisted off the lid, inhaling the scent I'd known all my life. The cream lay in peaks and troughs where Mum's fingers had touched it. I imagined her applying it to her cheeks – when would have been the last time? After the party on her birthday? Or, more likely, the night before her seventieth birthday. My insides clenched. The cream, bought no doubt in St Ives Tesco, had lasted longer than my mother. I imagined the checkout girl sliding it under the scanner, no idea that the customer buying it would be missing off a cruise ship – or dead – before the pot was finished.

I twisted the lid back on, put the pot carefully back and turned into the dressing area. Mum's suite had a large walk-in wardrobe and I couldn't avoid the sight of her clothes hanging on the rails, her shoes paired neatly underneath, the suitcase with its 'VCE' airline tags still stuck around the handle. I opened the top drawer of the vanity table. Inside, Mum's heated rollers and the hot brush she took everywhere. A glasses case – I picked it up and opened it – empty. Mosquito re-pellent. A little cosmetics case containing bits and bobs for First Aid: antihistamine cream, arnica cream, plasters, antiseptic spray, a strip of pain-killers.

The next drawer contained mum's underwear and swimwear. I closed it quickly, feeling like I was prying. As far as John would be concerned, there was nothing of any financial value here. These were the holiday essentials of an old lady. Guessing that all Mum's valuables – her purse, cash, jewellery, and passport – were in the safe, I checked the door. I stepped back out into the living room.

'Can anyone open the safe?' I asked Doris. 'I mean, without using her code?'

'We have a master key.'

Of course they did. 'Can I look?'

Doris shook her head, her eyes on the carpet.

I sighed.

'If you're finished...' she said.

'Yes. Yes, thank you.' I put my hand to my heart. 'I just feel a bit ... it's hard. I mean, she was here. We were on holiday. It was her birthday. The trip of a lifetime. She was so excited. And now...' Tears welled, and I dabbed my fingers along my lashes. 'I'm sorry ... I just can't believe she's gone. Where is she?' I pressed my hand to my face as if the pressure could stop the tears. 'I wish I knew where she was. And why.'

Doris put a hand on my arm. 'I'm very sorry. But, if you're ready, we must...' She motioned towards the door. 'You should not be in here.'

I nodded and followed her into the corridor, composing myself as I walked. Doris closed the room door with a click, checked it was properly shut, then placed the plastic gadget, which blocked off the card slot, over the door handle and padlocked it into place.

'This will stop any unauthorised personnel from entering the cabin,' she said. I lifted a hand

and touched the closed door, feeling bereft: locked both physically and metaphorically out of my mother's life.

18 July 2013, 10.30 a.m.

'How did it go?' John intercepted me as I returned to my cabin.

'I had to fight Doris to let me in. The room's now a crime scene.'

John gave a low whistle. 'So they've given up. Did you find anything?'

I shook my head. 'No. Anastasia will have to wait for her earrings.' I spat the words, my bitterness taking me by surprise.

John held out his hands, palms up. 'Whoah! Where did that come from?'

I got out my key card and slammed it through the swipe slot. 'From you!' It felt good to vent my frustration. The anger was a release. 'It came from you. Your whole handling of this ... this ... *situation* has been abysmal! I feel like I don't know you at all.'

'What do you mean?'

I pushed open my door but John was behind me, his foot in place to stop me slamming it on him. He shoved his way in and let the door bang shut behind him.

'What the hell are you talking about?'

I spun to face him, hands on hips, and he stared back at me, both of us breathing heavily. There was a hardness at the corners of his mouth; a coldness in his eyes, and I remembered the night in the Buzz Bar; how desperate he was for money; how scared he was that Anastasia might leave him and I stiffened, involuntarily recoiling from him.

'Oh my God,' I said, my voice quiet now. I backed away, getting the coffee table between me and him. 'You know what happened. That's why you've been so calm. Giving me all that "what will be, will be" rubbish! Refusing to admit she was missing! You know exactly what happened!'

John stared at me. 'Lexi, what's got into you? What kind of a monster do you think I am?

'You've already spent half the money!' I tried to edge around John towards the cabin door but he grabbed my arm, gripping me by the bicep. I shrugged him off and took a step back from him. 'The way you've been behaving since Mum told us about the will. The way you've been so *gleeful,*' I spat the word, 'about the whole thing!'

'Lexi!'

'Don't you remember asking me? That night in the champagne bar: "How long do you think she's got?" You asked me! You were practically counting the days. In Mykonos, you asked me if I'd finished her off!'

John started pacing the room. 'Oh, for God's sake. It was a joke. It wasn't like that.'

'It was exactly like that and don't you deny it. And then you refusing to believe she was missing. We could have started the search days ago. She might have stood a chance! I knew back in Santorini that something was wrong. I told you then but you ignored me.'

'You didn't need my permission. What stopped *you?*'

I shook my head. 'God. You've been like a vulture since she told us about Dad's will. It's almost like you *wanted* her overboard...' I stood there staring at him and then, with the sense that I was crossing a line, I let the thought that I'd been suppressing come hurtling out. 'It's just like what happened with Valya. There she was, about to go into an expensive home – and, suddenly...' I couldn't say it. 'My God, John! I don't know who you are!' A wave of sickness ran through me.

'Lexi! You think I pushed Valya? Oh my God!' John shook me by the shoulders. I jerked my face away, expecting him to slap me. 'Get a grip!' he yelled in my face, giving me a shake with each point. 'Listen to yourself. This has nothing to do with Valya. Valya fell down the stairs. I was in the kitchen doing the bloody washing up. I had no reason to push her. No reason whatsoever!' He suddenly let go of me and backed away, his shoulders slumped. 'Believe it or not, I actually liked the old mare.' Now he looked at me with all the vulnerability he'd had as a child etched on his face. 'Do you really think I'd do such a thing?'

I stared at my twin brother standing there and saw him as a boy: John shouting from the top of the apple tree, showering me with mushy apples; me dodging them, shrieking down the lawn to Mum. I saw the image; tried to reconcile it with the man he'd become.

'I don't know. I don't know what to think any more. All I know is that Mum was a nuisance to you. She got in your way. She was a hassle you could do without. Add to that the fact that you've got no money and you stood to get rich when she died and ... well!' I threw my hands in the air. 'Let's just say I wouldn't like to be you when the police come on board.' I spun on my heel, marched to the door and flung it open. 'I think it's time you left.'

I glared at John and he glowered back. Finally he moved towards the door. I stood back to let him pass and, once he'd crossed the threshold, he turned back.

'It's not looking so different for you either, by the way,' he said quietly. 'Don't you forget that.'

18 July 2013, 8.30 p.m.

I couldn't settle all day, nor into the evening as the row with John echoed in my head. I needed to clear my thoughts. I'd accused my twin of murdering our mother! How could we possibly move on from this? I spent a fretful day on the ship; settling in different areas before moving on. In the evening, I returned to my cabin. With the television droning on in the background, I paced again, sitting down for seconds at a time before jumping up and pacing once more.

I clicked off the television, grabbed a notepad, and went out to the balcony. Thoughts still racing, I stared out at the darkness and hoped the rhythmic sound of the engines might soothe me as I tried to get my thoughts in order. On the notepad, I put two headings: on the left, 'He did it'; on the right, 'He didn't'.

I filled the left side of the page up quickly. John had motivation by the bucket-load: he was fed up of looking after Mum; he wanted his inheritance; he was terrified he'd lose his marriage. Goodness, he'd talked about how long Mum had left; he'd been very specific about how she might have bumped her head on the way down – he'd certainly given the matter some thought.

He'd never been that close to Mum anyway. He hadn't been close to anyone – but did that make him a killer?

Although the motivation was there, when push came literally to shove, I had my doubts. Was my brother really devious enough to plan something like this? Strong enough to heave an adult over the chest-high railings? Brave enough to risk a murder, knowing the ship was full of CCTV cameras? Or was he clever enough to have found a spot that wasn't covered? I tried to imagine John plotting to kill Mum; staking out the ship, looking for the ideal location, planning how to lure her there. He'd left the White Night party early to go to bed. Or had he? I thought back: had John lain on the sun lounger planning his strategy while we watched Mum dance? Had he deliberately left early; lain in wait for Mum, knowing she'd be tipsy, and bundled her overboard then? On her birthday? Had he bashed her over the head first? With what? Oh please. This was my twin!

I stood up and paced the small balcony, trying not to see in my mind's eye Mum's surprise as she came across John lying in wait for her; her confusion as he lifted her up and struggled to get her overboard. Had she made eye contact with him? Screamed as she went over? Or fallen in stunned silence, her last emotions shock and confusion?

I picked up the notepad and, leaning on the railings, scribbled on the right-hand side. *'Too wimpy'*, I wrote. *'Wouldn't go through with it'*. But then I thought again about his financial troubles; how he'd started spending the moment he knew he was coming into a windfall. But, in the cabin just now he'd looked shaken. He'd stepped back, clearly shocked, when I'd accused him, and he hadn't had a defence ready. I suppose, like he'd said, to outsiders, I'd look as guilty as he did.

Maybe the police would think we'd been in it together.

I tore up the notepaper as small as I could and let the wind take the pieces. As I watched them scatter in the blackness, John's suggestion that Mum's disappearance may have been premeditated came back to me. If Mum had jumped overboard, what had driven her to it? Why had she invited John and me on the cruise in the first place? Was it for the pleasure of our company? To tell us about the will – or to say a final goodbye?

Had we driven Mum to suicide by pushing her to sell her house? I stared out to sea, shaking my head as I thought back to the conversations we'd had about Harbourside. We hadn't pushed her that hard, had we? Anyway, she'd come around to the idea. She'd said she'd consider it after the cruise – the 'last hurrah' as she'd called it; her last bit of fun.

Last bit of fun before what? Before she died?

With the thought came a sense of inevitability. Standing there on the balcony I realised this was the moment I'd been subconsciously waiting for all my life. I realised that the undercurrent of fear that had had run through my childhood wasn't so much a fear of Pa: it was the fear that Mum would leave. It was the sense of impermanence that had permeated the house. That night, when John and I had seen Mum packing her bag, I'd known – as much as a tiny child can know – that she was planning to leave. The essence of me had known, even if I was unable to comprehend it. And that subliminal fear, that sense that I might wake one day and find Mum gone, had never left me.

I rammed my knuckles against my temples. And now she'd finally done it! The conversation Mum and I had had in Corfu ran through my head.

'I used to worry what would happen to you – who would look after you – if I ... well, you know...' she'd said.

And I'd replied: 'Well, you don't need to worry about that any more.'

'I know,' she'd said.

Tears slid down my face.

I was startled by the screech of the telephone inside my cabin. Eyes puffy, I stumbled back inside, tripping over the door runners, dashed around the bed and sank onto it as I picked up the receiver.

'Hello? Alexandra Scrivener speaking.'

'Mrs Scrivener,' said Doris. 'I have...'

'News? Is there any news?' My mind filled with images of Mum saved; Mum pulled up from the ocean alive; Mum wrapped in a foil blanket. 'Did one of the boats find her?'

Doris paused and I knew before she spoke again that the news was not what I was hoping for; that she wasn't going to answer my question. 'I apologise that it is so late, but Captain Stiegman has asked to see you.'

I was buzzing with a torturous mix of hope and despair, my breath suddenly coming in rasps. 'Do you know what it's regarding? Do we have reason to hope?'

Doris paused again. 'Captain Steigman has asked to speak to you. That's all I can say.'

'But ... but ... if it was good news? If they'd found her? You'd tell me, wouldn't you?'

'Yes, of course I would.'

'So they haven't found her?'

Doris sighed. 'Mrs Scrivener. I haven't been told anything. The captain has asked if you can report to the ship's library at ten o'clock.' I looked at my watch, not taking in the time at all. 'That's in one hour,' said Doris. 'Ten o'clock. Do you know where the library is?'

I nodded into the phone. 'Yes. Pool deck?'

'Yes,' said Doris. 'Deck 12. Go to the pool and you'll find it there. Will you tell Mr Templeton, or would you like me to call him?'

I didn't say anything.

'Mrs Scrivener? Will you inform Mr Templeton, or shall I call his cabin?'

'Sorry. Please could you tell him?'

18 July 2013, 10 p.m.

With stuffed dark-leather sofas and armchairs scattered over carpets patterned in red, blue, and gold, the ship's library was reminiscent of a gentleman's club, the air within it stiller, quieter than anywhere else on the ship. Passing it on my way to the pool deck, I'd never seen anyone in there besides John. Now, I walked in in silence, nodded to Doris and the captain, who stood by the window, and sat down. John was already there. The tension was palpable as we waited for someone to speak.

The captain stepped forward. 'Mr Templeton. Mrs Scrivener. Thank you for coming at such a late hour, but I wanted to speak to you as a matter of priority.'

'Thank you,' I murmured, not sure if a reply was expected. John shifted in his chair.

Captain Steigman's gaze swept around the library, shifting like a search light until it had touched everyone in the room. He took a deep breath, steadied his hands on the back of a chair and spoke. 'The search has been called off.'

I pressed my hand to my mouth, stifling a sob. Even though I'd been primed to hear these words, the sound of them left me winded; until now I'd held out hope. There had been a mistake: Mum had been picked up by another ship. She'd been brought aboard, cold, weak, wrapped in a

300

silver blanket, but alive. She'd floated on her back; she'd clung onto some flotsam; she'd been rescued by a lifeboat. Failing any of those scenarios, her body had been recovered. Anything but this; this inconclusive conclusion.

Captain Stiegman stood motionless. He was waiting for a response. I looked at John. He didn't meet my gaze. He was looking at the floor, his thin lips pressed in a hard line, his expression inscrutable. The only part of my brother that moved was his hand, his fingers tapping a rhythm on the arm of the stuffed leather armchair. I wanted to speak but there were no words.

Captain Stiegman paced the library floor, his steps lithe in his rubber-soled shoes. Doris stood awkwardly by the bookshelves, her walkie-talkie in her hand, her lipstick rudely red. Outside the picture window, small whitecaps topped the ocean like frosting. I imagined my mother's arms poking desperately up from the crests of each wave, her mouth forming an 'O' as the lights of the ship faded into the distance. In the library, you couldn't feel the low rumble of the ship's engines that permeated the lower decks, but snatches of a Latin beat carried from the *Vida Loca* dance party taking place on the pool deck outside. Doris's walkie-talkie crackled to life then fell silent.

'The decision has not been taken lightly,' said the captain, his English curt with a German accent, his words staccato. 'We have to face the facts. Mrs Templeton has been missing for over forty hours. The ship was sailing at full speed on the night she was last seen. We have no idea when she went overboard, nor where – the search area covers thousands of square kilometres.'

He paused, looked at John and me, then – perhaps heartened by the absence of tears – continued, ticking off points with his fingers as he spoke. A band of dull platinum circled his wedding finger.

'As you are already aware, I did not turn the ship. This was because, with Mrs Templeton missing for thirty-nine hours before the search was initiated, I felt there was nothing to be gained by retracing our route. It is my belief that Mrs Templeton did not fall overboard shortly before she was reported missing, but many hours prior to that, most likely in the early hours of the sixteenth of July.'

I opened my mouth to speak – this was pure supposition – but the captain raised his hand in a request for me to be patient. 'However,' he said, 'tenders were dispatched from both Mykonos and Santorini, which is the area in which the ship was sailing when Mrs Templeton was last seen. A fleet of tenders traced our route from either end.' Now he paused and looked at each of us in turn once more. I gave a tiny shake of my head, eyes closed; there was nothing I could say to change the way in which events had run.

'The Coast Guard was informed as soon as the ship search yielded nothing,' continued the captain. 'Two helicopters were scrambled and all ships within a thirty kilometre radius of the course we took that night were asked to join the search.' He paused again, looked at his shoes, then up again. 'I believe there were five vessels involved. The search has been fruitless. Mrs Templeton could now have been in the water, without a floatation device, for up to forty-eight hours. She was...' he searched his memory ... 'seventy years old?' His voice trailed off and he looked again at John, then at me, his eyebrows raised, the implication clear: she could not have survived.

John closed his eyes and nodded almost imperceptibly. Captain Stiegman echoed the nod. I opened my mouth then shut it again.

'Thank you,' said the captain. He bowed his head; looked up again after a respectful pause. I felt the thump of the music from outside. 'With the engines on full power we should make Venice by dawn. I'm obliged to inform local police we have one passenger lost at sea. They will come aboard. They will talk to you. In a case like this, it is a formality.' He removed his captain's hat, held it to his chest, his eyes closed again for a second. 'I am sorry for your loss.'

'Well,' said John, when the door had clicked shut and silence once more filled the library. The look on his face said, 'I told you so'. He'd accepted before I had that Mum wasn't coming back, and now he'd been proven right. I felt beaten; empty. This was it: a five-minute speech, and our mother was no more.

'Well,' I said flatly.

I got up and left the library. Latino music jarred my ears as I yanked open the door and walked across the pool deck looking neither left nor right at the bikini-clad dancers swinging their hips in time to the beat. Without thinking where I was going, I walked along and down the ship until I reached the aft: the deserted promenade deck where I'd spent so many hours watching the foaming wake in happier times. I pressed my top rib into the railing. Mum was shorter than I was. I wondered, for the hundredth time, how it had happened.

Gripping my hands around the same railing, I cried out into the wind, but the endlessness of the ocean served only to show me my own insignificance. In the darkness there was no horizon. Black water gave way to black sky. Moonlight sparkled on the water; stars hung above my head. Drawing fresh air into my lungs, I breathed deeply and stared at the sea as the ship drew through the blackness. Even the hum of its engines, louder down here, couldn't drown out the soul-breaking sadness that thrummed in my chest. I realised my cheeks were wet. Somewhere out there was my mother. Only the ocean knew where.

'What happened?' I asked the sea. 'Did someone do this, or was it your choice?' My voice dropped to a whisper. 'Was it because of us?' I gripped the railing and looked up at the sky. 'Did we do this to you?' I paused. 'I love you. Wherever you are.' I said it again, louder this time. 'I love you, Mum.'

Behind me, the electric sliding door clicked and swooshed open. I turned, startled. John came towards me, a hand held out tentatively.

'I thought you'd be here,' he said. 'I came to see if you were all right.'

'How can I be all right? How can I ever be all right again?'

'She was my mother, too.'

'Maybe you should have thought of that before all this happened.'

'What?'

'She didn't slip!' I shouted, banging the railing with my fist, almost enjoying the physical pain. 'Look at this! Look how high it is. How could she have slipped? It's physically impossible!'

'Do you still think I did it? That I'm some sort of serial mother-murderer?'

We glared at each other and I understood that, for all his faults, he hadn't done it. Faced with him now, I just felt defeated. I looked away first. 'Maybe we drove her to it.'

'What?'

'Think about it. We made her feel like a burden. Neither of us wanted to look after her. We were always arguing about whose turn it was. She must have known.' I paused and John didn't say anything. 'And she was always so independent. She hated being a burden. And then that whole thing about Harbourside. Remember how upset she was that day in the pub? Did you ever question why she changed her mind so suddenly? She didn't change her mind. She had no intention, ever, of moving into Harbourside, or anywhere like it.' I paused. 'She's not stupid. She knew we didn't want to take care of her. We drove her to this. Her death is on both our hands.'

'But you moved to Cornwall to be closer to her. She knew that, too,' John's voice was surprisingly gentle.

'Mark lost his job because we moved to Cornwall. I took a pay cut. It was because of that move that we had so little money.' I shook my head, remembering the desperation. 'We were all right in London. I must have made her feel so guilty when I was going on about not being to afford anything. She knew we were struggling.' And then another thought hit me. 'She's done this so we could get Pa's money. She did it for us.'

We stood in silence for a moment, then John spoke.

'Even if she did plan this, she was happy. Did she look unhappy on the cruise? No, she didn't. Not for a moment. Whatever way you look at it, this is what she planned and what she wanted. I just wish we knew why.'

I could barely swallow for the lump in my throat. 'She called this trip her "last hurrah".'

John joined me at the railing and looked out to sea. After a minute or two, he put his arm around my shoulder. We stood there for a long time, in silence.

18 July 2013, 11.30 p.m.

Back in my cabin, I dragged my suitcase out from under the bed and heaved it up onto the bed. I had no will to pack. But we were due to arrive in Venice at 6 a.m. and I knew I had to be ready – for the police, the enquiries, the questions. Ready to face whatever it was that had happened to Mum.

I picked out clothes to wear the following day – travelling clothes – then opened my suitcase. Inside was the collection of bags I'd wrapped my shoes in. I fished them out and saw underneath them an envelope, 'Alexandra' handwritten on the front.

I hadn't put it in my suitcase; it hadn't been there when I'd unpacked at the start of the cruise. I sat on the bed, pushing myself back against the pillows, lifted the envelope to my face and inhaled: was there a hint of night jasmine, or did I imagine it? I traced my finger over the letters that made up my name, then I put the envelope on the bedside table and closed my eyes.

I knew who the letter was from; I recognised the writing, of course. What I didn't know was what my mother would have to say. I breathed deeply for a moment, then, with a sense that nothing would ever be the same again, I picked up the envelope with hands that felt drunk. I slid my finger under the flap and pulled out the letter my mother had written me before she'd gone missing. She'd written in Royal Blue ink using the Cross fountain pen she'd had all my life. I could picture her sitting at her desk in Cornwall, gripping the silver pen with her stiff fingers as she mulled over what she was going to say. The blue ink looped across the page, its twists and turns as familiar to me as the pattern of veins in my wrist. I started to read:

Dear Alexandra,
Yes. You're right. It really is me. That tells you one thing already: my disappearance was not an accident. Did you really think I would be so careless as to let myself slip overboard?
You don't have to answer that. But I'll say it again:

my disappearance was not an accident.

And I know you, Alexandra. I know you'll put this letter down now and start going over and over things that were said and done, looking for ways to blame yourself. Please don't. I've not done this because of anything you or John said or did. This is something that came from inside myself; something I needed to do for myself. It was time.

Promise me you'll move forward with your life, reaping all the success and happiness I know you deserve, secure in the knowledge that I love you, sweet Lexi.

Mum xxx

I threw the letter down on the bed and let the tears come. They spilled down my face, threatening to ruin the ink of my mother's handwriting. Thoughts churned in my head. Mum planning the cruise. Mum writing the invitations, inscribing the calligraphy on the envelopes, knowing all along what she was going to do; planning her suicide. Mum at her birthday dinner; at the White Night party; dancing with Stavros. *Look after yourself, darling.* She'd known she wouldn't see me again. Mum climbing over the railing, taking one last look at the ship, and making her jump down into the blackness.

Lying on the bed my body convulsed with sobs. The sadness was more than I thought I could bear. And among it all, among all that pain was one little word that, each time I remembered it, triggered a fresh round of tears: Lexi. Not once in forty-three years had Mum called me Lexi.

PART III

Before

September 2012

St Ives

Audrey sits back in her chair and flexes her wrists: if she's not careful she's going to end up that RSI thing as well as eye strain. She looks over the laptop screen out of the window, trying to train her eyes past the bright green of her garden and on the sea beyond. It's warm for September and today the bay is the same bright blue as you see on the covers of holiday brochures – she could be looking at the coast of Italy, Spain, France, or Greece. Audrey smiles at the view – there's not a day goes by that she's not grateful to be living in Cornwall, to have this view, even on bleak days when the sea is grey and menacing.

Today, though, with the warmth of the sun already making the garden buzz, is the kind of day that makes Audrey want to spend the afternoon doing nothing more than pottering about in the garden, then perhaps reading outside with a cup of tea. Audrey likes her solitude; being alone has never bothered her, not that her son understands that. His idea of showing her a good time is inflicting his family on her. Speaking of which, Audrey pulls her eyes back to her computer and checks the clock on the screen: 11.30. She's got about an hour before John arrives – he's taking her out for lunch. Audrey wonders for a

311

minute if there's any way that he might not bring Anastasia and the children, then dismisses the idea: it's customary for Audrey to foot the bill at these lunches and, if there's any idea of a free meal, her daughter-in-law will be first in line.

Audrey turns back to the computer and flicks screens to her email inbox. Still nothing. She's been acting like an addict, checking reflexively every time she comes to a break in what she's doing. But it's early days yet: she only sent the email last night, and it's impertinent of her, she tells herself, to expect a reply quite so quickly. She takes a deep breath. *Have faith,* she thinks. *Have faith.*

She clicks back onto her search engine. The internet has been a revelation for her; it's opened up her life. She simply can't believe how much information is available at the touch of a few buttons and she's spent the past month searching anything and everything that comes into her head, from holiday destinations and recipes to people she used to know. She laughs now to think how nervous she used to be of using a computer. But Audrey's treated her internet education as a project, forcing herself to learn something new each day from her bibles: *The Internet for Dummies* and *Computers for Seniors for Dummies.* She sees the internet as a friend now – she realises it's a bit like having the world's best library right there on her dining room table – and, now she's become more accomplished at refining her searches, she finds herself dwelling more and more in the past.

Audrey's favourite topic is India in the 1970s. She's embarrassed to admit how much time she's

312

spent poring over photographs and reading the personal accounts and memoirs of people who lived in Bombay around the same time as she did, or who travelled to India on the *SS Oriana*. She's stared at grainy black-and-white pictures of the ship, and lost herself in memories of that intense time she spent on board. It's not unusual for her to have tears running down her face as she posts a thank you to those who have painstakingly typed up their diaries and posted them online.

A ping from the computer makes Audrey catch her breath. She flicks the screen from her current search to her email and squints her eyes to see what's new in her inbox: it's not the reply she's been-hoping for, but it's still exciting. She's subscribed to a website for Indian ex-expats, and the new email is a message alerting her about a talk and photo exhibition on Bombay to be held at Truro Library. One of the pictures is included in the email and Audrey double-clicks it and zooms in so she can see it clearly – it's nothing special, just a typical view of a cluttered Bombay street but, as she stares at it, Audrey smells again the distinct smell of the salty, sweaty air; she hears the honks of the cars, the shouts of street hawkers; the thrum of a city living life to the full, and she feels the hum of life in her veins.

'Truro,' she says thoughtfully. Alexandra lives there. Without traffic, it's about forty-five minutes' drive away. The cogs of Audrey's brain start whirring and it's with an unfamiliar sense of excitement that she clicks the link to register her attendance.

The doorbell rings and Audrey jumps. She's

kept the last owner's electric bell that chimes the Westminster Quarters. Although its tinny sound is cheap, she likes the length of the ring – unlike a quick knock, it leaves her in absolutely no doubt that someone's at the door.

'All through this hour, Lord be my guide. And by thy power, no foot shall slide,' Audrey sings along to the chime as she makes her way to the door. It's not John yet, she hopes – first, she has an appointment with an art valuer. The picture – the one from the Barnes loo – is waiting on the dining table.

The art valuer is impressed. Clearly he knows his stuff.

'My heart beats faster when I see genuine pieces by this artist,' he tells Audrey. 'Would you like to sell? We could put it to auction. Collectors *fight* for pieces of his from this period.'

Audrey nods. 'Yes. Yes, it's something I would perhaps consider, maybe next year. You've been very helpful, thank you.'

The doorbell rings just as Audrey and the art valuer finish up. Audrey takes a deep breath, fixes a smile on her face, and opens the door to John, his wife, and her children. They make niceties as they pass the art valuer on the step. Audrey doesn't want to explain; she offers no introduction.

'Now, what can I get you?' she asks when everyone's inside.

'I'd love a beer,' says John. He walks into the living room and throws himself onto the sofa. 'But I won't because I'm driving.' The sentence is punctuated with the sigh of the martyr. 'But you go ahead,' he says to Anastasia. She gives him a sympathetic smile then turns to Audrey.

'A vodka, lime, and soda, please. Double.' Anastasia is not sitting down; she's doing the customary thing of walking about Audrey's living room, looking at her possessions as if she's cataloguing and valuing them. She reminds Audrey of a vulture circling a dying animal; the intent is so obvious. *If only you knew,* Audrey thinks as she mixes the drink for her daughter-in-law. *If only you knew your husband will one day be a millionaire.* Audrey could tell her, of course – put her out of her misery – but, for now, she enjoys the game.

'Is this the painting?' Anastasia says to John, pointing with a manicured nail at the picture that's still on the dining table. 'The priceless masterpiece you talk about?' She picks it up and looks at it critically; blows on the canvas, as if removing dust. 'Really?'

John looks over. 'Yes. That's it.' He looks at his mother. 'Why's it out? Why's it not hanging?'

'Oh ... no reason,' says Audrey. 'It was a little dusty...' She turns away from John, not wanting him to know she had it valued. She busies herself getting the drinks. The children unlock the back door and run out into the garden, where Audrey's installed a swing for precisely this purpose.

'Hold on, hold on,' says John. 'Is this to do with that man who just left?'

Audrey cracks open a can of soda water and pours it into Anastasia's vodka. She doesn't reply.

'Is it?' Nothing. 'Mum! *Is it to do with that man?*' John jumps up, comes over, pulls Audrey around so she's facing him. He's gripping her by her upper arms, and practically shaking her. She's a rag doll in his grasp. 'Did that man look at the painting? Is that why he was here?' Spittle flies from his lips and Audrey flinches as it lands on her cheeks.

'No,' says Audrey. She wrenches her arms. John lets go of Audrey's arms, almost pushing her away. He shakes his head vigorously, runs his hand across his brow. 'What did he say? God, Mum, please tell me you didn't give him the painting? Please tell me it hasn't left the house!'

'It's there,' says Audrey, nodding towards the painting. 'You can see it's there.'

'But it hasn't left the house? That man didn't take it away to "clean" it?'

Audrey shakes her head.

'Are you sure?' asks John.

'Of course I'm sure. The painting has not left the house.'

'Good.' John sits back down and runs his hands through his hair. 'There's a gang operating in the area. I saw it in the paper. They convince old ladies that their priceless family jewellery, antiques, and artwork need cleaning, then they take them away, swap them for copies, and hand them back. Most people don't even notice. You're absolutely sure he didn't swap it for another piece?'

Audrey nods, then takes the vodka and soda over to Anastasia. She pours herself a sherry, takes a sip, and sinks into an armchair. John's outburst has left her feeling quite shaken.

'Trust me,' she says. 'The painting hasn't left the house. Now. Let's move on. How are you?'

'Fine, thank you. How are you?' John asks.

Audrey nods. 'Fine, thank you. All good.' She turns to John. 'And how are you both? How's business?'

John sighs. 'Usual.'

'Building your empire.' Audrey smiles.

Anastasia gets up, rummages in her handbag for a pack of cigarettes.

'Excuse me,' she says. 'I just have to...' she nods towards the garden where the twins can be seen playing some sort of hiding game.

'Help yourself,' says Audrey.

She and John sit in silence for a minute.

'Don't you get lonely?' he asks. 'Here, all alone? It must be so quiet. I don't know how you don't go crazy.'

'Maybe I do,' says Audrey.

'Really?'

Audrey sighs. 'It was a joke. How would I know if I *was* going crazy? Presumably, I'd be the last person to spot it.'

John taps his fingers on the armrest. 'Are you planning to live here forever?' he asks. 'Or do you think you'll move again?'

'I doubt I'll move again. I'm very happy here. I love the garden, the view.'

'It's a big house for one person.'

Audrey snorts. 'Did you see my last house?'

John rolls his eyes. 'There were four of us there. I worry about you here. You know ... what if you had a fall? Like Valya. Who would find you?'

Audrey shrugs. 'People manage. I have neighbours.'

'If I were you,' says John.

'Which you're not.'

317

'If I were you, I'd want somewhere smaller. Safer.' He waits, but Audrey says nothing. 'It's better to move now,' he says, 'while you're still able to, rather than wait until you can't really do it yourself.'

'Better for who?' asks Audrey. She drains her sherry. 'In fact, don't answer that. Shall we get going? I'll call them in.'

November 2012

Truro

Audrey stands outside the imposing stone building that is Truro Library and takes a deep breath. Her tummy's a jar of butterflies, and she's no idea why; she's done the hard bit, driving along the A30, finding a parking space, and locating the library. She's spent the past month day-dreaming about the exhibition she's about to see, trying to recall the names and faces of various people she used to know in Bombay but now she's actually here, she's nervous.

She wants to go inside as badly as she wants to turn and run. Bombay was such an emotive time in her life. Her eyes are glued to the print-out that she's clutching in her hand. Staring at the little image on it, she's transported back to India so clearly she can smell it. But, at the same time, she's swamped by the visceral weight of the grief she'd carried there after her parents died; then the giddy excitement of meeting Ralph – oh, the naïve excitement back when she'd believed he was the perfect catch.

Audrey puts a hand to the wall for support and fans herself with the print-out. Footsteps tap along the pavement and suddenly Lexi appears in front of her.

'Hey, Mum,' she says. 'You found it okay?' Audrey nods and Lexi takes a step closer to her. 'What's wrong? Are you okay? Are you having a funny turn?' Alexandra's face is peering into hers, her eyes suddenly full of concern. She speaks slowly, enunciates the words carefully, as if Audrey's hard of hearing.

Audrey flaps the leaflet at her. 'I'm fine.'

'Do you need to sit down?'

Audrey shakes her head. The moment's passing. She straightens herself up and takes a deep breath; notices only then how tired Alexandra looks.

'Are *you* okay?' she asks.

'Me? Yes, I'm just,' Lexi flaps a hand and smiles coyly. 'I'm fine.'

'Excuse me,' says a voice behind them, and Audrey turns to see a couple of a similar age to her. They smile politely at Audrey and move towards the door, and Audrey examines them, wondering if they ever lived in Bombay; if their paths had ever crossed hers in a restaurant or a jazz club. Names and faces flit before her eyes – people she knew forty years ago. But what damage has time done to their faces, Audrey wonders. Would she recognise anyone after so many years? Janet, she knows, won't be here: her Prince Charming took her to Australia.

'Ready?' Lexi asks after the couple has gone inside.

Audrey nods. 'Let's do it.'

Inside, the library smells like every library Audrey has ever entered: a slightly stuffy smell of books, paper and ink. But, over and above the usual subdued hush of a library space, she hears the low buzz of conversation, unusual at this time of the evening. Audrey and Lexi register.

'Thanks for coming. Enjoy!' says the lady at the desk once she's put a neat tick by Audrey's name and asked if she'd like to leave her contact details.

Audrey turns to face the exhibition. It's not massively busy, not thronging with people, but there must be a good two score and ten. They look familiar – not that she knows them, nor can she identify what it is that makes these strangers look familiar, but there's just something about them that reminds Audrey of herself; an indelible mark, perhaps, of those who have India under their skin.

'Right, let's go,' she says. She glances around the exhibition, picks a board that's got no one standing at it and walks over. Within seconds, her nervousness disappears as she's transported back to Tilbury; in the photograph, a liner's preparing to leave. Audrey presses her hand over her mouth as if to suppress the intense emotions that wash over her as she stares at the picture. She remembers the sadness that had fuelled her flight to Bombay; the hollow grief and pointlessness that had been her existence since her dad had died; the unbearable sense of loneliness she'd felt as she'd realised there was no one in the crowd to wave her off.

Lexi moves quickly past the photos, lacking the

interest that she herself has. Audrey realises with sadness that Alexandra doesn't remember India at all. She looks at the faces in the black-and-white photograph and knows, without seeing the expressions on those people's faces, what they would have been feeling as they waved off loved ones on what, for many, was a one-way journey to a new life as far away as Australia. Overcome with emotion, she rummages in her pocket for her hankie and dabs at her eyes.

'SS Orcades,' says a low voice next to Audrey. 'Beautiful ship, she was.'

Audrey turns to see a woman standing just behind her. She's of mid-height and elegant in navy slacks and a peach blouse, her grey hair cut short, pearl earrings highlighting the lustre of her pale skin, a dab of lipstick warming her face. Audrey thinks she might be younger than she is. She assesses her in a couple seconds; although there's a familiarity around the eyes or in the bones, it's not someone she knows.

'Did you sail in her?' Audrey asks.

'No,' says the woman. 'Her sister ship. SS Oriana.' She's silent for moment. 'How about you?'

'Same,' says Audrey. 'Oriana.'

'Beautiful ship, wasn't she?' says the lady. 'They don't make them like that anymore.'

Audrey nods and the woman smiles back at her. There's another pause while both women turn back to the photograph and examine it intently.

'I remember it so well,' says Audrey quietly. She doesn't really mind if the lady's listening or not; it's just nice to speak about that time. 'The crowds, the noise. Well ... I think I do, and then I see something like this and it reminds me of so many of the details that I've forgotten. About life on the ship.'

'Me too. Quoits! Did you play deck quoits?'

'Yes! There was a league. I'd never heard of it before but – goodness – the hours I spent playing and watching quoits.'

'Well – there wasn't too much else to do, was there? The pictures, I suppose, in the evenings. And tennis.' There's a pause as both women remember their times on board. 'When did you sail?'

'1970,' says Audrey. 'I was twenty-seven. And you?'

'1960,' says the woman. 'I was twelve. I went with my parents.' She stops talking, then starts again, the words coming out in a rush. 'I don't know why I'm here, really. India wasn't kind to me.' She breathes in and closes her eyes, as if letting a wave of emotion pass before she carries on, her eyes fixed not on Audrey but on the photograph. Audrey strains to hear her words. 'My parents were killed in a car accident when I was twenty. I thought marriage was the way out. Married the wrong man.' She shakes her head sadly. 'I lost my children over it.'

'I'm so sorry,' says Audrey. She pauses, feeling the woman's sadness; wanting to make her know she understands. 'I lost my parents, too. And I also rushed into marriage perhaps not with the wrong man, but a difficult man nonetheless.' The women smile at each other; without words, they know. Then Audrey gives a little laugh. 'Yes, I don't know why I'm here either – except, well, there's something about India that gets under your skin.' She sighs. 'Do you remember the smell of the night jasmine? I used to love standing in the garden and breathing it in.'

'Oh, yes,' says the other woman. 'We had some in the garden, too. It was always my favourite.' The other woman smiles and Audrey realises that, after that small exchange, this stranger knows more about what's inside her than do most of the people who've populated her life in England, including John and Alexandra. All the things that Audrey's struggled to deal with in her life: the desperate pain of losing her parents; the experience of sailing to India; life in Bombay; the struggles of marriage – this woman knows all of those things too. Alexandra is nowhere to be seen. In silent understanding, the two women move on to the next photograph together.

'Well,' says Audrey, as she tears her eyes off the last photograph. 'That was incredible. What a trip down memory lane.'

'I feel like I've actually been to India tonight. I'm so glad I came,' says her new friend. 'I wasn't sure if I should or not – if it would bring back too many bad memories, but I'm glad I did.'

'I'm glad I did, too.'

As if on cue, Lexi appears.

'How was it?' she asks. 'Did it bring back lots of memories?'

'Yes, yes, it was really lovely, thank you. And lovely to see you, too.' Audrey stands awkwardly with her new friend, unable to introduce her because she doesn't know her name.

She turns to the other woman. 'It was a pleasure to meet you. It's lovely to meet people who've experienced the same things...' her voice trails off. 'I'm Audrey, by the way. And this is my daughter, Alexandra – born in India but she doesn't remember a bean of it, as witnessed by the speed at which she went through the exhibition.' Audrey holds out her hand but the other woman doesn't take it. She stares at Audrey, then her eyes swivel to Lexi, then back to Audrey.

'Born in India?' she asks.

'Yes,' says Audrey.

The woman is staring at Lexi. 'But you don't remember any of it?'

She shakes her head. 'No. We left when my brother and I were two. We're twins.'

'Ah,' says the woman slowly. 'No. I don't suppose you would remember.' She's still staring at Lexi. A mobile phone starts ringing and, without taking her eyes off Lexi, she fumbles in her bag, dragging her eyes away only once the phone's in her hand. 'It's my cab,' she says slowly. 'I've got to go.' She holds out her hand and Audrey takes it. Something appears to pass between the two women as they shake hands.

'It's been a pleasure. Thank you. For everything.' The woman squeezes Audrey's hand as she lets go.

'I don't even know your name,' says Audrey.

'Miranda,' says the woman. 'My name's Miranda.'

November 2012

Truro

Audrey tilts her head to one side as she watches Miranda make her way out of the library. There's something about the way the woman walks that makes her think of John; something in her bone structure that's pure Alexandra. But more than that, there was something in the way Miranda looked at Alexandra that makes Audrey feel faint.

For a second Audrey's body twitches towards the door as her mind wills its physical mass to run after Miranda, and she has to put out a hand to support herself on a book shelf. She shakes her head: her mind must be playing tricks. Seeing the pictures has been like reliving the intense time that she spent in India – those years feel like they were yesterday. Standing there in the library, Audrey is impervious to everything around her. She's remembering the intensity of the first time she met Ralph in Bombay; the strange shiver he gave her. And she's remembering the story of how his wife died – the story that Ralph had told her the night he proposed: the tragedy of the young mother with postnatal depression. Suicide. The pile of clothes on the shore. Ralph saying that she couldn't swim; that she knew about the currents. What was his wife's name? Audrey racks her brains. They had the same initials ... A ... that, she remembers.

Alice. It was Alice Templeton. She was missing, presumed dead, but had they ever found her body?

'No,' Audrey breathes. 'Impossible. How? How could it be?'

'Mum? Are you all right?' Alexandra grasps her arm, peers at her face. 'You look washed-out. Has it all been too much for you? Will you be okay driving back?' She pauses. 'You can stay with us tonight, if you want. I can make up the camp bed. Mark won't mind.'

Audrey takes a deep breath. 'Thank you. No, I'm fine.' Her voice sounds to her as if it's coming from the bottom of the ocean. Her head is too full of thoughts, gathering like storm clouds, to deal with Alexandra. 'You head on back. I know you've a lot to do. Thank you so much for coming.'

'Okay ... if you're sure,' Lexi says. She gives her mum a hug. 'It was great to see you. Drive safely.'

'Bye,' Audrey says as Lexi leaves. At least she thinks she says it – she's not sure if the words come out. Inside her head is a vortex of thoughts. She reaches out a hand towards a library assistant who's hovering by the door.

'Excuse me. Is it possible to see a guest list? From tonight?'

'Um,' says the assistant. 'I'm not sure.' He looks over towards the desk where Audrey had registered on her way in. The desk is unattended. 'I can go and ask?' His voice is weary. It's gone closing time and he wants to leave, not set off on a wild goose chase for a dotty old lady.

'If you could, I would appreciate it massively, thank you,' says Audrey, and there's something in her face that makes the assistant want to help. He heads off to look for the organiser of the night's exhibition.

Audrey moves towards the reception desk, fully intending to wait until help comes over but, as she approaches the desk, she sees the guest list lying on top. She edges around to the back of the desk and stands there, reading through the names as best she can without picking up the list. It's no good; although she can just about make out the word 'Miranda' her eyes aren't good enough to read the address or the family name. Taking out her phone, Audrey flicks it onto camera mode, hovers the phone over the list and clicks. Just in time, she slips the phone back into her bag.

'I'm sorry,' says the library assistant, returning alone. 'We're not allowed to give out details without prior consent. Security. I'm sure you understand.'

He picks up the list somewhat defensively as if realising a breach of security has occurred and Audrey gets the wild urge to laugh out loud. It's a list of old fogies who attended a photographic exhibition, not a list of terrorist targets. Still, she has what she needs in her bag.

'Okay, I understand,' she says. 'At least I tried. Thank you.'

Suddenly full of a surprising energy, she turns and exits the library.

Audrey doesn't know how she manages to open the car door, to start the engine, and find her way back to the A30. She's driving on autopilot, her head too full of Miranda to do much more than go through the motions of driving. She's aware, at a base level, that she probably isn't in a fit state to drive; that she should have stayed overnight at Alexandra's. But she wants to be alone. She needs to work out how it could possibly be that she's just seen Alice Templeton in Truro Library. Alice Templeton was dead; she had to be: Audrey married her husband and took on her children. How could she possibly think she'd just seen Alice Templeton?

Audrey remembers Ralph's words to her that night he found out about Mack: 'No one leaves Ralph Templeton,' and she shivers involuntarily. Audrey knows Ralph; knows what he's capable of; knows what can happen in the underworld of Bombay. What happened with Alice? Could the twins' mother really still be alive? Her thoughts race in circles but always come back to one thing: did they ever find her body? Audrey realises she's gripping the steering wheel so hard her knuckles are white.

And then she's at the roundabout. She sees, too late, a car speeding around the bend. Audrey slams on the brakes, skids for what seems like forever, tyres screaming as she tenses over the wheel and waits for the impact. None comes. Her car stops. The other car flies past. And then, from behind, a sudden screech of brakes and an impact that throws her head forward then slams it back onto the headrest and Audrey's no longer thinking about Alice Templeton.

November 2012

St Ives

John brings Audrey back from the hospital. She's stiff and she's shaken but she's all right. She barely slept a wink in the hospital bed; her mind was going over and over what Ralph had told her about his first wife. But always she stops at the same point. He hadn't said much at all, she realises now. Just a few lines. The bare outline of a story. Why hadn't she asked for more information? With a gush of shame, she remembers how thrilled she'd been that he'd proposed. Oh, sweet, naïve girl that she was, she'd taken his words at face value when he'd said Alice was dead. As he'd known she would. Her husband was a bigamist!

John plumps up the cushions, leads Audrey over to the sofa and settles her with the newspaper open to the crossword page.

'Now,' he says, 'the hospital wants someone to stay with you tonight but I need to go. The twins have a swimming gala this afternoon so I'll get Lexi to come down. Okay?'

'There's no need. She looked so tired last night. I'm absolutely fine on my own.'

'No, Mum. Someone has to be with you. The hospital said. I'll call her now, see when she can come.'

Audrey sighs. 'If you must. Thank you.'

She waits for the front door to close behind John; waits until she hears his car start and reverse out of the driveway. Then she eases herself carefully up from the sofa and walks stiffly over to her laptop, picks it up, and climbs carefully back onto the sofa, balancing the computer on a cushion.

She turns it on and stares at the screen as it whirs to life. She's well aware that she could walk away from this; could leave sleeping dogs to lie; live out the rest of her days quietly in St Ives without letting John and Alexandra know what she suspects. But then Audrey recalls the look on Miranda's face as she stared at Alexandra, and she realises that she knew. Oh, the courage it must have taken her to walk away. She feels awed by the generosity of the gesture; can imagine how much Miranda would have ached to let her daughter know who she was.

'Don't get ahead of yourself,' she says out loud.

The internet wasn't around in the '70s, but Audrey hopes there'll be something, somehow; some archives; someone's memories. All she needs is a photo. If she sees a photo of Alice Templeton, she'll know.

She Googles instructions on how to email a photo to herself. Then she opens up her email account and Googles instructions on how to download the picture she's just sent herself. Within minutes, the picture she's taken of the guest list is on her screen and Audrey enlarges it until the names are clear enough to read. She scans the list until she finds it.

'Miranda Smith,' she reads, testing the feel of the words on her lips. She pinches her bottom lip

330

as she stares at the name. Of course it's not going to be her real name.

Audrey opens another browser window, types in "Alice Templeton" and waits for a second while the results load. There are hundreds of thousands of entries. How would it be worded, she wonders? She types 'Alice Templeton+Bombay+drown' and takes a sharp breath as she sees what she honestly thought she'd never find: an archived article about the young mother called Alice Templeton, who went missing in Bombay. Fingers trembling on the mouse, Audrey looks for the date of the article: it tallies.

'Missing mother presumed drowned,' reads the headline, and Audrey's blood runs cold at the word 'presumed'. When someone tells you their wife's dead, you don't question it.

'Detectives today confirmed that a pile of clothes found folded on Juhu Beach belong to British citizen, Alice Templeton, who was reported missing four days ago. The victim's husband Ralph Templeton positively identified the items as clothes his wife had been wearing on the day of her disappearance. Mrs Templeton is presumed to have been washed away by strong currents off Juhu Beach.

The deceased is survived by her husband and three-month-old twins. At the time of her disappearance, Alice Templeton was said to have been suffering post-natal depression.

'"She was not a strong swimmer," Mr Templeton said in a statement. "She knew about the currents. I'm devastated."'

'But was there a body?' Audrey asks out loud. 'Was her body ever found?' It's a rhetorical question: she knows the answer. Audrey scrolls down the page and freezes. There's a picture. She can't click on it fast enough – her hand's clammy on the mouse – and then there it is: Audrey enlarges it as much as possible and stares at the eyes looking back at her. It's a young Miranda.

Audrey slumps back on the cushions, causing a ripple of pain to radiate from her neck down her spine.

'No,' she says. 'No, no, no!'

This changes everything. Everything. Audrey has the sensation of jigsaw puzzle pieces shifting inside her head; of tectonic plates moving under the surface of her life. For the first time in forty years Audrey allows herself to admit something that she's suppressed each and every day: the knowledge that she's not been true to herself. Every day she's lied to Alice's children; every day she's let them believe that she – Audrey – was their real mother. She's done it because Ralph had made her swear she would never tell them. There was no point in them knowing the truth, he insisted – *insisted* – since Alice was dead.

But now Audrey knows that John and Alexandra's birth mother is alive, everything changes. Surely the twins have a right to know? To meet her? To forge a relationship with her?

Audrey may be old and tired, but there's still time to make things right; time to correct the mistakes she's made. Flicking back to the photograph she took at the library, Audrey looks at Miranda's address: Truro. She stares unseeingly at the room. Like the ripples caused when a tiny stone's thrown into a millpond, the implications of what she's found out tonight are more far-reaching than she can even imagine.

A key turns in the front door lock: Alexandra's come to look after her. Audrey closes her eyes and feigns sleep.

December 2012

Truro, Cornwall

Despite her nerves, Audrey smiles as a car backs out of a parking space right in front of her. The car park is congested and this stroke of luck is just what she needs.

'Some things are meant to be,' she says, turning off the engine and gathering her things from the passenger seat. She takes a look at the map she's printed off the computer and nods to herself. Then she closes her eyes and takes a calming breath.

'Please be in,' she whispers. 'You have to be in. Please, let her be in.' Audrey is silent for a moment, her hands clasped in her lap. 'And please don't slam the door in my face.'

Audrey's low heels click-click on the pavement as she finds her way, map in hand, to Miranda's house. It's a modest house at the end of a run of white-fronted terraces. Audrey stops outside, double-checks the house number, and puts the map back in her bag before walking up to the front door and pushing the bell. At once she hears footsteps moving towards the door and she puts out a hand to support herself on the wall as her knees go weak. A bolt is drawn and Audrey takes a deep breath and stands upright again. The door opens and Audrey watches Miranda's face change as the woman recognises her from the exhibition.

Definitely, thinks Audrey. Now she's primed, now she's prepared for this moment, she knows what she's looking for – and it's there. She examines Miranda's face, taking in the shape of the eyes, the angle of the cheekbones, the turn of the mouth, the hue of the skin. It's more Alexandra than John; John was in the walk, the physicality of the body.

Miranda hasn't moved. She's frozen in the doorway, staring at Audrey. Audrey puts her hand to her chest, her fingers worrying a necklace at her throat.

'Alice?' The word comes out as a croak, but Miranda hears it. She presses her lips together and dips her head in admission.

'Audrey Templeton,' she breathes. 'You came ... you found me.'

The two women stare at each other across the threshold, then Miranda presses her hand to her mouth and Audrey realises she's crying.

At the same moment, both women step forward and hug. They cling together for a second, knowing their shared past. The emotion is there but the hug is awkward, the two women too unfamiliar with each other. Audrey pulls away.

'I just don't understand. I don't understand anything,' she says. 'I don't understand how you're alive.'

'You'd better come in,' says Miranda.

Audrey follows Miranda into a small living room. White linen curtains billow at an open French window; the air smells of coffee. Miranda sinks onto a blue sofa.

'Please, sit down.'

Audrey perches on the edge of an armchair. 'Is it Miranda? Or Alice? What do I call you?'

'Miranda. I've been Miranda for forty years.'

'But – how? You're dead. You drowned. Well, clearly not – but how?' Audrey's shaking her head, trying to take in the fact that her husband's dead first wife is sitting on a blue sofa in a little house in the middle of Truro.

'I didn't drown,' says Miranda.

'But what happened? Were you rescued? I just don't understand.'

Miranda's head drops into her hands. Her shoulders are heaving so Audrey waits for her to compose herself, her index finger tracing the grain of the fabric on the chair. After some time, Miranda looks up. Her face is wet with tears.

'I never got in the sea. He faked my death,' she says. 'The short answer is that I left him, and he faked my death. I didn't have postnatal depression. I didn't drown.'

'But why? What happened?'

Miranda wipes her eyes, stands up. 'I need some water. Can I get you anything?'

Audrey shakes her head and Miranda moves into the kitchen. Within seconds she's back with two glasses of water. She sets them down and takes her place on the sofa, more composed this time.

'Look,' she says carefully. 'I don't know what

your marriage to Ralph Templeton was like.' She looks at Audrey and Audrey closes her eyes and shakes her head, a wry smile on the corners of her lips.

'He didn't change then,' says Miranda.

Audrey waggles her head in that Indian way that means both yes and no.

'We both know what he was like,' says Miranda. A picture pops into Audrey's mind: it's Ralph standing over her in the kitchen, his eyes full of rage; of her cowering, absorbing his anger. She remembers the scene but not what she'd done to infuriate him. Something small. Her memory of Ralph is of him bullying her, of him belittling her, possessing her, controlling her – all of that, but also of him lighting her soul, in those early days, with his love. Her overall sense now – four years after his death – is of the complicated, exhausting schizophrenia of the marriage.

'I couldn't take it,' says Miranda. 'I was twenty-two. My whole life was ahead of me.'

'But the children?' Audrey asks. 'How could you leave your babies?' As she says it, she remembers the desperation of a night when she, too, was about to leave John and Alexandra. She'd justified leaving them by thinking she was only their stepmother; that it wouldn't make much difference to them to have another stepmother. But Miranda was their birth mother.

Miranda is pressing both hands to her throat. 'You have no idea how difficult it was. But...' Miranda's voice breaks, but then she looks levelly at Audrey. 'It's complicated. I didn't plan to have the children. I wanted to wait. Even early on, things

336

weren't good between Ralph and me, and I had a feeling the marriage wouldn't last so I didn't want to try for children, but...' Miranda looks at Audrey, changes the subject. 'Did he ever mistreat you?'

Audrey gives a single nod, her eyes closed.

'Badly?'

'It varied.'

'I'm so sorry.'

'Don't be. Did he...' Audrey struggles for the word. She's never told anyone about the times Ralph raped her. It seems odd to speak of rape within the confines of a marriage. She knows there's such a thing, but she can't imagine other people understanding how a husband can rape his wife.

'Rape me?' asks Miranda. 'Yes. The twins were the result of a rape.' She pauses. 'A brutal, degrading rape.'

Audrey leans over and touches Miranda's hand. Miranda takes Audrey's hand in her own and squeezes it.

'It affected how I felt about them. I never bonded with them. Every time I saw them, it reminded me.' She pauses. 'I tried. I tried so hard. But then, one night, he came home and he found the twins crying.' Miranda's eyes slide off to the middle distance as she recalls the events. Her voice is quiet and Audrey strains to hear. 'I was young. Alone. I had no idea what to do, no one to help. I'd tried to settle them but nothing was working. I was at my wits' end. As soon as I got one to calm down, the other went off. I was exhausted. I wasn't getting much sleep.'

Miranda shudders at the memory and Audrey,

337

too, remembers the frustration of the crying babies; the feeling of hopelessness when neither would settle, and wonders what she'd have done had she not had Madhu.

'Anyway,' Miranda continues, 'Ralph came home and found the twins crying and he called me a useless mother. He shouted at me – screamed at me – in front of them. He was drunk. I remember smelling the drink on him. Then he punched me in the face. In front of them. Broke my jaw. It was the last straw.' She rubs her jaw as she speaks, and looks at Audrey as if for validation. 'I know they were only babies but – oh, I don't know if it was the exhaustion or the hopelessness, but I waited for him to go to work the next day and I left.'

'Where did you go?'

'I went to an ashram.' Miranda shrugs. 'It was the seventies.'

'Were you planning to go back for the children?'

Miranda shifts awkwardly on the sofa. 'Maybe if I'd had some time and space to think; maybe I would have grown up a bit and gone back. I don't know. I'll never know. He didn't ever let me make that decision. We all had to do voluntary work at the ashram – *seva* they called it. I worked in the office. I used to see the newspaper. I saw the story.' She looks at Audrey. 'He'd faked my death. None of it was true. I didn't have postnatal depression.'

'Maybe you did,' says Audrey, and Miranda looks at her sideways.

'You know, I've never thought about it that way – but maybe I did. I always assumed I was that unhappy because of my marriage. But maybe there was more to it.'

'It's possible.' Audrey pauses. 'So why did he do it? Why did he fake your death?' Even as she says it, she knows the answer.

'He couldn't let me get away without making sure it was on his terms,' says Miranda. 'You know what he was like about losing face. I suppose he wanted to clear the way so he could marry someone else without the scandal of his wife having left him. People were still quite judgmental in those days, especially in the circles he moved in...'

'But why didn't you go to the police? You could have explained?'

Miranda shakes her head. 'You know what he was like. He would have paid off the police not to look too closely at the case. It was Bombay. You know how he operated. No matter what I said, this was a battle I was never going to win. And I was alone in India – no parents, no one to look out for me.' Her voice lowers. 'Things happen. You know what I mean? The police were in his hands. When Ralph picked a battle, he *never* lost.'

The two women look knowingly at each other. Audrey finds it odd to be talking so intimately with someone who was also married to Ralph. She feels like Miranda is her flesh and blood; a sister.

'You lasted way longer than I did,' says Miranda. 'Made of sterner stuff.' She laughs ruefully.

'I was older, I suppose.' Audrey pauses. She wants to say that she stayed for the children but she realises it will sound like she's competing with Miranda: *I stayed for them when you didn't.* So she talks instead about Ralph. 'And there were good times, too. There were. He loved me in his own way. I learned how to handle him. He mellowed as he got older.'

'I'm glad.'

The two women fall into silence. Audrey's processing all that Miranda's told her; rewriting history in her head. Ralph had romanced her and married her, all the while knowing his first wife wasn't dead. A secret he took to the grave. And the children! John and Alexandra missed out on knowing their real mother all because of Ralph's ego. She shudders.

'How do you feel about John and Alexandra now?' she asks.

Miranda dabs at her left eye and Audrey realises she's blinking back tears.

'I don't know. Guilty, I suppose. I used to wonder about them every day. But it's been forty years,' says Miranda. 'Forty years and I still feel guilty. I wonder if I should have stayed. I ask myself if it really was that bad.'

Audrey purses her lips.

'I even thought about going back – seeing if he'd take me back, just for the sake of the children. But then he married you – what? In six months?' She pauses. 'I came by once. Followed you to the Hanging Gardens and watched you with the children. You looked so happy. *They* looked so happy.'

'You watched us?'

'Yes. I saw that they were happy. I left India after that.'

'How? How did you even have a passport?'

Miranda rolls her eyes. 'This is India we're talking about. Anything's possible with a little money.' She rubs her thumb and index fingers together.

'Fake passport?'

Miranda nods. 'New identity. Easily done.'

Audrey exhales. 'Wow.'

There's a silence as Audrey takes in all she's been told. And then: 'But didn't you try to find us? It's easy these days. With the internet?'

Miranda purses her lips. 'I made a pact with myself not to track down the children. The last thing anyone needs is a mother who supposedly killed herself to get away from them turning up on the doorstep. Can you imagine? They'd need years of therapy. But ... oh God. There were days when I was longing with every fibre of my being to see them, to hold them. When they were young, I ached for them. Physically. Seeing Alexandra last night was ... oh God – weird.' She hugs her arms around herself. 'What does the boy look like? John?'

'He's the spit of his father,' says Audrey. Miranda gives an almost imperceptible nod, and the two women look at each other, understanding.

'Would you like to have them back in your life somehow?' asks Audrey. 'I mean, if that was somehow possible?'

Miranda sits very still; a slew of emotion crosses her face. 'I ... I mean, they wouldn't want to know me. They're adults now. They must be in their forties; have their own lives. They have you. You're the only mother they know.'

'You don't know how they'd react. Maybe they'd want to know you. Alexandra at least. If she knew.'

'But how? How would that ever be possible?'

'You're younger than me,' Audrey says. Her eyes glaze over and she stares into the middle distance.

It's as if she's speaking to herself. 'I've raised your children and I'm tired now.' She stares at the wall overwhelmed by the sense of things falling into place. 'I don't want to be a burden.' Then her eyes snap back to Miranda and she's present in the conversation once more. 'Let me think.'

April 2013

Audrey sits, as she now does every morning, at her computer, her breakfast dishes pushed to one side and a fresh cup of coffee beside her. It used to be that she read the papers in the morning, leaning over the broadsheets at the dining table as she caught up on the world's news and diddled her pen over the cryptic crossword in the hope that she might one day actually complete it but, these days, it's the computer that steals her attention. As she opens her email, Audrey feels the same thrill of anticipation she used to get on hearing the post drop through the letterbox each morning: a bubble of excitement; a fizz of hope.

'You have email,' says a voice from the computer and Audrey's heart quickens, as it does every morning. She makes a conscious effort to relax her shoulders, which she realises have hunched over the laptop. The page can't load fast enough for her and then, when it finally does, Audrey relaxes back in her chair, enjoying even just the sight of the name in her inbox. She clicks to open the email; reads it quickly, then reads it again, more slowly, savouring each and every word. She clicks the mouse, and her fingers fly over the keys as her reply takes shape. Every now and then she pauses and stares into space, a soft smile on her face. She's a method writer: as emotions bubble up inside her, she sighs, smiles, frowns, and even chuckles out loud at the computer screen. *Anyone watching would think I'm a lunatic*, she thinks. *Thank goodness John's not here!*

Email done, she presses 'send', then flicks to the research that's been consuming her for the past few weeks. The Mediterranean colours of the Greek islands fill the screen and Audrey's head tilts to the side as she lets the images wash over her. They resonate in her soul – she wants it so badly – but something's stopping her. Can she really go through with this?

'Audrey Templeton,' she says. 'You'll never know if you don't try.'

There's a young girl behind the counter at the travel agent. She looks still to be in her teens; a school-leaver perhaps. Audrey approaches the desk and sits in the vacant chair.

'How can I help you?' asks the girl, looking up from her computer.

'I'd like to go on a cruise. Around the Greek islands.'

'Okay, I'm sure that's possible.' The girl gets up and walks to the shelves of brochures that line one side of the shop. She picks a few and brings them back to Audrey.

'What sort of ship are you looking for?' She taps the top brochure with scarlet nails.

Audrey smiles brightly. 'A cruise ship?'

To her credit, the travel agent is patient, although her tone of voice does make it sound rather as if she's talking to a child. 'There are different sizes of ship. Different budgets. Some cater more for families; some don't allow children...' She looks at Audrey, mentally puts her into the 'oldies' bracket.

'I hope to be travelling with my children,' says Audrey.

'Oh.' The girl's eyes widen and, for a minute, she looks confused.

Audrey laughs. 'They're in their forties.'

'Oh, I see! Of course.'

'Um,' says Audrey. 'Maybe a medium-sized ship? Nothing too small, where everyone knows each other. I don't want that. And not too big either. My son would refuse to come.'

'Yeah,' says the girl, nodding as if she knows what Audrey means.

'Have you ever been on a cruise?'

'No. But I can imagine.'

Audrey smiles. The girl marks a few pages in the brochures with sticky notes. 'Why don't you go home and have a browse? See what's available and we can take it from there? This company's very good,' she presses a Post-it onto the top brochure. 'I get good feedback from clients about them and the ships aren't so enormous.'

Audrey picks up the brochures and places them carefully into her basket. She can't wait to get home and read them; see if she dares actually book this cruise. She remembers sailing to India: the endless ocean vistas; the sense of peace she got from understanding how tiny and how insignificant she was in the universe; the womb-like comfort of not knowing where the sea ended and the sky began. She's longing to be back on a ship.

It won't be the same, she tells herself as she drives. Oriana *was hardly a cruise ship.* She lets out a little laugh. Of course it'll be a lot more luxurious on a modern-day cruise ship; lots more to do than on that journey she'd made in 1970. Her first memory is of the heat – it had been cold, of course, as they left Britain, but she remembers the creeping warmth as they headed steadily south, the shedding of layers as they passed Lisbon, Casablanca – what came next? Then that relentless heat as they'd advanced up past Madagascar. She'd sat around on deck thinking she really, truly might expire. Audrey smiles to herself as she remembers the excitement as they headed up the final strait to Bombay. She shakes her head, a smile on her face.

Her mind still in 1970, Audrey turns into her driveway and almost crashes into a car reversing towards her. It takes a minute to realise that it's Alexandra's car; that she and John are both in it and, with a jolt, she wonders if she was supposed to cook them lunch today. She's sure it was next week but, to be fair, she's been so caught up in her plan that she's been ignoring everyday concerns. Even the house could do with a good dust and polish. The last thing she needs today is the pair of them fussing and fawning over her. She knows they think she's losing her mind; becoming a liability. John's been banging on about getting her to sell the house and now he's probably got Alexandra in on the act, and they're disguising their impatience with her as concern. Audrey sighs. If only she hadn't crashed the goddamned car.

Alexandra's moving the car back up the drive-way, so Audrey eases her car into the garage then takes a second to compose herself, breathing deeply. *Be patient,* she tells herself. *It's not forever.* She leaves the cruise brochures on the passenger seat, plasters a smile on her face, and goes out to face Miranda's children.

April 2013

Audrey's not a big fan of The Ship. With its bright décor and modern finishing, it's designed to cater to the tourists who wander up from the harbour looking for a slap-up lunch, and there's nothing about it that says 'pub' to her. But, since it's her fault she forgot the lunch with John and Alexandra, she can hardly complain. The place is busy when they arrive – Audrey would never come out for lunch quite so late – but John manages to find a table and Audrey sinks gratefully onto a bench seat with her back to the wall.

'Right. Drinks,' says John. 'I'll go. What does everyone want?'

'Nice of him to go,' says Lexi once John's disappeared off to the bar, and Audrey exchanges a look with her. She'll miss Alexandra. The girl has a good heart; always means well. Audrey's eyes glaze over as she thinks, again, about the pros and cons of her plan. Does she have the courage to do it? Does she?

'What do you recommend?' Lexi's question snaps Audrey's attention back to the crowded pub. She hasn't eaten here for over a year but one of her friends told her recently how good the veggie lasagne is, so. Audrey suggests that. Then John returns with the drinks and the news that he's ordered a roast dinner for them all.

Just like your father, thinks Audrey: you didn't even think to ask.

'Shall we call it twenty each?' he says, placing the bill on the table. Audrey takes in his gaunt appearance and the dark circles under his eyes and realises that things can't be going as well with his business as everyone assumes; understands that sixty pounds is a lot to fork out when you have a family to support, and is happy to reach into her bag for her purse, but Lexi whips out her bag and slams a couple of twenty pound notes on the table in a way that leaves no one in any doubt as to her feelings on the topic. Audrey watches as John nods his thanks and folds the money into his wallet. Yes, she thinks. The children need the money. How long should Ralph's control be allowed to continue? It's in her power to put an end to it – to tell the children about their real mother and to help them get the inheritance that's rightly theirs. Who is she to stand in their way? Ralph lied to her for their entire marriage!

'Cheers! To pleasant surprises,' Audrey says, raising her glass. The children clink glasses, assuming – as Audrey intended – that she's referring to their lunch today. Audrey laughs silently inside herself. *Just make up your mind,* she thinks. *Are you doing this or not? You're like a yo-yo. It's time to make a decision.* She takes another sip of her gin and orange and observes John and Alexandra. There's a strange energy between them today. John, she sees, is staring morosely into his pint and Alexandra seems nervous. Audrey tries to relax them both by talking about the recipe she'd been planning to cook for their visit the following week. She sees John roll his eyes when she says she found it on the internet.

'Anyway, Mum,' says John, and Audrey has a feeling that he's finally coming to the point; that she's about to find out what's going on. 'There's a reason why we wanted to see you today.'

What comes next – the news that they think she should sell her house and start looking for sheltered housing – doesn't come as such a huge surprise. She's known, of course, that John's thought this for some time now, but what surprises her is that Alexandra has allowed herself to be dragged into it; that they've both worked together to come up with this plan. She realises, as they speak, that the twins see her as something frail that needs to be looked after; as a liability beyond what they can manage. This, more than anything, surprises her. But it also crystallises things. It's the missing piece of the puzzle; the final thing she needs to see in order to make her decision. Audrey starts to argue with the children; says that she's fine in her house, then realises there's no point: they've made up their minds and, more importantly, so has she.

The food comes and Audrey stands up. She can't get out of the pub fast enough.

April 2013

St Ives, Cornwall

Audrey feels trapped in the passenger seat of Alexandra's car as they drive home from The Ship. Her neck's at ninety degrees, twisted as far away from Alexandra as possible as she stares out of the window, wishing with all her heart that she'd insisted on walking or taking the bus. But when Audrey had made to leave, Alexandra had jumped up and chased her out of the pub, adamant that she mustn't go home alone, and practically bundled Audrey into the car. Audrey wonders now if John's eating all three lunches.

'Oh look! That's new, isn't it?' says Alexandra, indicating to a shop front as they drive. Her tone is bright and breezy. 'Has it been there long?'

Audrey gives a noncommittal hmph of a reply and is glad when Alexandra puts the radio on. Staring out of the window without seeing the passing scenery, she's trying to identify the emotions that are running through her after what she feels was nothing short of a planned ambush by the children. She should be angry; she should be disappointed; she should feel betrayed – and she does feel all these things, but in far smaller measures than she imagines she should.

What she actually feels – what she's surprised to find that she feels – is relieved. Relieved to see that the twins, as adults and for all their differences, are getting on better than they ever have – relieved that they're working as a team; that they seem to be able to rely on each other. She also feels relieved that she finally knows the true measure of what they feel about her. She shakes her head to herself: after all she's done for them – after all those years bringing them up – they find her a burden. They're terrified of what the future may bring; they're trying already – when she's only sixty-nine – to contain it; to make things easier for themselves. What will they be like when she reaches eighty?

What Audrey really wants to do is thank them for giving her the final shove that she needed to launch her plan. She'd been wavering and now she knows one hundred per cent that she's doing the right thing. The thought terrifies and excites her in equal measures. With her face hidden from Alexandra, Audrey allows herself a tiny little smile; presses her lips together to stop it from growing too big.

'Here we are then,' says Alexandra brightly as she pulls into the narrow road that leads to Audrey's house. She stops the car and turns to Audrey. 'Look, about what John said...'

Audrey holds up her hand. 'Stop. Don't say anything. It's fine.' Her words come out in a rush as she tries to unclasp the seatbelt, pick up her handbag, and open the door. She's halfway out of the car by the time she finishes the sentence. 'I know you mean well.' She leans back into the open door. 'Really, it's fine,' she says, desperate to get indoors and start putting her plan into action.

'Mum. I'm so sorry,' says Alexandra, leaning across the car. 'I'm sure we can make things work if you want to stay here.'

'Don't stress about it,' says Audrey. Already she's fumbling for her keys. 'Bye!'

Inside, she makes herself a cup of tea and turns her attention to her cruise brochures.

The clock strikes eleven the next morning and Audrey puts down the pen and flexes her wrist, her eyes drawn towards the window and the perpetual view of the sea. Unlike the sunshine of the previous day, today it's difficult to tell where sea ends and sky begins: both are a dirty greige and Audrey watches a small boat make its way determinedly across the bay. It's too far away for Audrey to be able to see how it's being thrown around by the waves but, just by looking at the palm in her garden, she can tell how strong the wind is; imagine how big the waves are.

Her dining table is covered in discarded sheets of paper, each one decorated with the loops and swirls Audrey's made as she's tried to rediscover the art of the calligraphy she learned as a child. Her fingers are stained with ink and she's rubbed her face, leaving a grey smudge down the side of her nose.

The calligraphy has been a challenge, but Audrey wants the invitations for the holiday she's come to think of as her 'last hurrah' to have suitable gravitas; wants John and Alexandra to know that this is no normal invitation, so she's been practising. She picks up the latest piece of paper she's been working on and admires her handiwork. It's not bad, given she hasn't held a calligraphy pen for decades. Next to her lie two formal invitation cards and two envelopes waiting to be addressed.

Audrey opens her stationery drawer and rummages through her notepaper. Basildon Bond, she thinks. Nothing pretty. It's a serious letter she's going to write and she doesn't want Alexandra to be distracted by fripperies. She holds the pad, feeling the weight of it in her hand as she stares into space. *No quitting now,* she tells herself. *You've made your decision. This is for the best.*

There's a soft ping from Audrey's laptop, which sits next to her on the dining table, and she clicks the mouse to wake the screen. A new email. Audrey's heart quickens. She opens it and scans it quickly.

'Yes,' she says. 'Yes, yes, yes.' Audrey puts her fingers to her lips, then to the screen, stroking them tenderly against name of the sender.

'Not long now,' she says. After months of thinking and researching, the last piece of her plan slots into place.

Audrey looks thoughtfully out at the ocean. On the laptop, the screensaver kicks in. The image Audrey uses projects back at her the bright colours of a Greek island: azure sky, white-washed houses with blue-domed roofs cascading down a steep hill towards a sparkling sea. She sits for a long time, staring at the grey sea that she can see in her real life, then she pushes her chair back, grabs her handbag and her blue coat, wraps herself up against the wind, and leaves the house. She drives into town, and heads straight to the travel agent.

PART IV

After

September 2013

Truro, Cornwall

'Bye darling. Good luck today.' Mark put his arms around me and gave me a soft kiss. 'I hope it goes okay.'

I tried to relax in his arms; failed. 'Thanks.'

'Are you all right? I can stay if you want me to?'

'No. I'm fine. If I can't do it, I'll wait for you to get home. You've just got this job; you can't skive off in your second week.'

Mark squeezed me tighter. 'Thanks darling. Just put it in another room where you can't see it and wait for me. I'll be back in time for lunch.'

Mark left and I returned to the kitchen, gathered up the breakfast dishes, and put them in the sink. I turned on the tap, put in the plug, squirted in some detergent, and wrestled my hands into the rubber gloves but my eyes weren't on the washing up; instead, I looked out at the garden. A riot of semi-tropical flowers fringed my view of the sky: the colours today were so vivid, so glorious; everything was so very alive. The scent of flowers in full bloom wafted in on the breeze, and the sound of the birds almost drowned out the radio. Inside the kitchen, a fly circled lazily above the fruit bowl, alighting every so often on bananas that had seen better days, and I realised that, despite the hole inside me that ached for

Mum, I was happy; I realised that I loved living in Cornwall; that, even though there was no longer a need for us to be here, I no longer wanted to move back to London. Mark now had a job and, since the cruise, John and I appeared to have reached a different level of understanding. We were closer than we'd ever been, perhaps even as children, and, for the first time ever, I felt surrounded by family on whom I could count.

Hanging in the living room was a visual reminder of Mum: the painting I'd bought for her in Santorini. The splash of Mediterranean colour reminded me of the cruise but I tried to focus on the good bits: my last days with Mum; the conversations we'd had on board the ship; how I'd felt I was getting to know her; how happy she'd been at the White Night party. I'd joined an online support group for family of 'overboards' – they were far more common than I'd known – and drawn comfort from their stories. At least I had closure in the form of the letter: many of the relatives didn't even have that. I could look at the painting now without crying.

I put a hand on my still-flat tummy. 'What do you think, little beans?' I said out loud. 'Where do you want to live?' I waited, trying to feel some sort of vibe from the two balls of cells in my uterus; from the twin pregnancy that had, after all the time I'd spent worrying, snuck up on me, catching me by surprise when my mind was otherwise occupied. I imagined the embryos absorbing my voice and replying at a cellular level. In a way – a way in which I would probably never admit even to Mark – I thought Mum's spirit was somehow in the babies; that she'd somehow sent a part of herself back to me.

'Cornwall?' I said. 'Yes, I think so too. Your granny loved the sea.'

The sound of the doorbell jarred me out of my thoughts and, with a start, I tugged off the rubber gloves and hurried to the front door. As I turned the key in the lock – once, twice – I leaned on the door for support, my legs suddenly hollow. The courier had said he'd come between nine and five – it was barely nine now and, despite a fitful night, I'd had no time to prepare myself. I opened the door and there it was, wrapped in plastic: the unmistakable shape of a suitcase.

'Print and sign here, thank you very much,' said the courier, handing me a clipboard.

I did as I was told and, seconds later, he was retreating down the driveway while I pulled the bag over the threshold. The return of Mum's effects from the ship was the last of the formalities that had commenced with the involvement of the Italian police in Venice. Mum's death had been ruled a suicide; a death certificate issued. The will, however, was yet to be read – John and I were still none the wiser as to exactly how much we would inherit.

I dragged Mum's bag into the hall and looked at it. Then I went to the kitchen, took out the kitchen scissors, and cut away the courier company's plastic packaging. The suitcase still had its 'VCE' airline tag on the handle. I pressed my hand to my chest as I stared at it, remembering the excitement of the start of the trip: landing in Venice, taking the water taxi down the Grand

Canal to the cruise terminal. How annoyed I'd been with John that day; how irritated he was at having to go on a cruise with Mum. Oh, the trivialities that had bothered us then. How things had changed since that tag had been put on that bag. It seemed a million years ago – but it also seemed like yesterday.

I placed the suitcase flat on the floor and pressed the lock: it sprang open, releasing the zipper. Crouching on the hall floor, I started to unzip it, then stopped. *If you're going to do it, do it properly...*

I closed the zip, picked up the suitcase and dragged it into the living room, where I placed it flat on the floor and knelt in front of it. Carefully, I edged the zipper around the bag's perimeter and opened it. One of Mum's blouses lay on top. I reached out a hand and touched it then, without thinking, leaned down and put my nose to it, catching the faint scent of my mum: perfume, night jasmine, and a slight stuffiness from the garment's having been unworn for so long.

Slowly I peeled the blouse off the top, and started to make a pile of Mum's clothes, images of her wearing them on the cruise filling my head. The trousers she'd worn in Mykonos. The dress she'd worn for the dinner in Valentino's. The t-shirt she'd worn in Corfu. With a jolt I realised that I was holding in my hand the dress Mum had worn for her birthday dinner and the White Night party: so she'd gone back to her room after the party and changed. Frantically I looked through the clothes trying to see what was missing; what she'd been wearing when she jumped. I pieced the outfits together on the floor, laying them out like jigsaw puzzles, but, without knowing what she'd packed, I wasn't able to tell what was missing.

Underneath the clothes were her personal effects. Toiletries, cosmetics, the remainder of the scented candle, the papers I'd seen on the table in her suite. Slowly I lifted them out until my eyes fell on the jewellery box I'd given Mum on her birthday. I picked it up and, with sweaty hands, opened it: it was empty. I sat back, breathing hard, my hand pressed to my mouth as I tried to dispel the images that flooded my head: Mum jumping off the ship with the locket around her neck; Mum breathing water into her lungs with the photos of John and me next to her throat; Mum dying with it touching her skin. 'I shall treasure it always,' she'd said. Maybe she even touched the locket with her fingers as she died. Maybe she was thinking of us.

I jumped up and stumbled out to the garden, where I sank onto the wooden bench and breathed the fresh air deep into my lungs. I tried to focus on the garden, which was in its last blaze of colour before winter, looking in turn at my favourite trees, listening to the buzz of the bees, and inhaling the scent of the flowers. I closed my eyes and took some calming breaths, imagining serenity flooding my body with each breath. I could wait for Mark to get home and help me through the rest of Mum's bag, but letting him go through her suitcase seemed like a betrayal. This was something I had to do alone. I stood up, took one last deep breath, and went back to the living room.

Towards the bottom of the case were Mum's shoes. I rummaged for her handbag, her purse, but found nothing. Then, at the very bottom of the bag, I saw a book: *The Rosie Project* – a story I'd loved so much I'd given it to Mum to read. I stared at the familiar cover and it was as if Mum were speaking to me from beyond the grave. It was as if the book were saying 'I love you, Alexandra.' Mum had read it months ago. Had she liked it so much she'd read it again? Or had she known I'd be the one to find it? Had she put it there deliberately to give me some comfort; to remind me of her love when I opened her bag?

I picked up the book. It was large format, an early edition – a heavy book to carry on holiday. I touched the cover imagining Mum holding the book in bed, chuckling at the story of Professor Don Tillman that had so engrossed me. I flipped through the pages and two pieces of paper fell out. One was no larger than a business card. On it, Mum had written the contact details for 'Miranda Smith'; the address was Truro. Miranda. I remembered the name from the night at the library. It was the woman Mum had been talking to at the photography exhibition. *So you stayed in touch,* I thought, and, for some reason, the idea pleased me.

The other was a print-out of a newspaper article on A4 paper that had been folded into quarters. I unfolded it gently and read the headline: *'Missing mother presumed drowned.'* I wondered if it was about someone Mum had known; a friend perhaps. The quality of the reproduction wasn't good; the picture unclear, but, squinting at it, I realised it bore more than a casual resemblance to the woman we'd met in the library: Miranda.

Quickly, and with a growing sense of unease, I

read the article: a sad story about a young mother who'd committed suicide off Juhu Beach back in the '70s. But then I reached two names and I stopped understanding the words printed in black and white on the page in front of me. I couldn't comprehend what I was reading. Heart hammering, I read it again and again, and then out loud, as if that would help me make sense of the story. The picture was of Miranda but the dead woman's name was Alice Templeton; her 'devastated' husband, Ralph Templeton.

She'd left behind three-month-old twins.

September 2013

Truro, Cornwall

I was still sitting on the sofa, staring into space with the article in my hands, when I heard Mark's key in the lock. I felt the air pressure change as the front door opened; I heard a slice of noise from the street outside, then the bang of the door reverberated through the small downstairs.

'Hi darling,' Mark said. He took in the sight of the unpacked suitcase; me motionless on the sofa. 'Ah – so it came. Are you...?' Mark covered the length of the living room in two and a half strides and stopped at my feet. 'Are you okay?' He bent to kiss me and I looked up blankly, received the kiss without responding. Mark dropped to his knees and tried to look into my eyes. I looked at him without seeing.

'Was it difficult?' he asked gently.

'Look,' I said. I held out the article.

Mark took it. 'What is it?'

'You tell me.'

Mark's eyes moved left to right as he read the article. I watched his expression change as the words sunk in.

'What? Whaaat? No! How can that be?'

'So tell me I'm not imagining it. John and I are the twins, right? Our mother didn't die two months ago. She died forty-two years ago.'

Mark was shaking his head. 'Hang on. Hang on. Let me just read it again.'

I waited while Mark went over the article again, then he looked up and rubbed his eyebrow. 'Yes,' he said slowly. 'If this is true, that would appear to be the case.' He sank down onto the sofa. 'I'm so sorry, babe. I don't know what to say. Where did you get it?'

'It was in Mum's things. She wanted me to find it.'

'But why didn't she just tell you?'

'Maybe she planned to. And then – god, what-ever happened to her? Maybe she did plan to tell me. Or maybe she planned to jump off the ship and she wanted me to find this.'

'It looks that way. But why now? Why not just let it lie? There doesn't seem any point in telling you now.'

'Wait. There's more.' I passed Mark the piece of paper with Miranda's contact details.

'Miranda Smith,' he read. 'Who's she?'

'My real mother.'

'How do you know?'

'I met her.'

'What?'

'I met her. At the photo exhibition.'

'But it says in the article she's dead.'

'"Presumed" dead. Clearly there's a difference.'

Mark massaged his temples. 'I don't know what to say.'

I slumped back on the sofa. 'It all makes sense now.'

'What does?'

I sighed, searching for the right words. 'There was a time, when I was growing up, when I would have given anything to hear that I had a different mother,' I said slowly. I felt Mark flinch. He'd always been fond of Mum. 'No, no. Not that there was anything wrong with Mum. But – well – maybe there was something wrong with her.' I paused, struggling to find the words to explain. 'It's just like there was this distance. Almost like a force field around her, keeping me and John separate from her. It just felt *wrong*. I can't explain it.' Mark took my hand in his but I pulled it back and ran it through my hair, intent on remembering, clasping at memories I hadn't thought about for years. 'And, when I was little, I used to play this game – oh God, this is going to sound bad – I used to play this game where the front doorbell rang and it was this woman – she was always really beautiful and well dressed – and she said she was my real mother and she'd come to pick me up.' I remembered plainly this little fantasy I used to play out time after time; I remembered the yearning I'd felt for a mother who'd connect fully with me. 'It was like there was a part of me missing. I can't explain it. But now – oh my God – now … oh! I just…' I buried my face in my hands, tears seeping through my fingers. 'Mum knew! We talked about this on the cruise. She knew how I felt…'

'Come here,' Mark said. He pulled me into his arms and held me tight until I calmed myself. I grabbed a tissue and dabbed at my eyes.

'It all makes sense now,' I sobbed. 'It all makes sense.'

'But did you feel anything when you met this other woman? Did you feel like she could be your mother?'

I squeezed my eyes shut. In my mind, I went over the moment in the library when I'd seen Mum with Miranda. It was late and I'd been keen to get home and, bar noticing that the other woman was elegant and quite tall, I hadn't given much thought to her. She'd had a delicate bone structure, I recalled now; I remembered a deep voice and intelligent eyes. She'd seemed like a nice lady. But had I felt something when I'd seen her? A pull? A familiarity? I rubbed my forehead and thought, but the truth was that I hadn't. I hadn't felt anything.

The reality was that I'd been desperate to get back home to Mark. I'd been slightly irritated that it was late; that I'd had to offer Mum a bed for the night; and I'd been relieved when she'd said no. I'd thought I was pregnant. I was waiting for the results of the blood test; my mind was obsessed with the thought. Try as I might, there was nothing that had made me think that woman was my mother. But why would I go around thinking strangers were my mother? I had a mother!

'Do you think your mum knew all along?'

'My mum as in Audrey?' The name felt odd. 'No, she can't have done. But maybe she found out that night at the library. Something odd happened that night when I turned up – and then Mum had her accident. Oh God, yes! I think they both realised that night. But why didn't either of them say something?'

'How *could* they have? Miranda – Alice – was supposed to be dead.'

I picked up Mum's copy of *The Rosie Project,* folded the article and put it back in the book; I held it in my hand and looked at it as if for the first time. It was obvious that there was something inside the book. There was no doubt in my mind that Mum had known I would find it; had intended to lead me to my real mother.

'Why didn't Mum just tell me? She had all that time on the cruise. We had long talks; we talked loads about the past. She could have told me then.'

'Maybe she didn't know how,' Mark said. 'Maybe she wanted to nudge the ball into your court and leave you to decide what to do.'

'But what happened back then? How did this all come about? I just don't get it!'

Mark fingered the piece of paper with Miranda's number on it. 'You know, Lex,' he said gently, 'there's only one way to find out.'

Epilogue

16 July 2013

Santorini

Audrey walks to the edge of the cliff and looks down at the sea that's glittering below her in the early morning sun. The ship's anchored a way out and tiny white boats are starting to draw lines across the sea as Audrey's fellow passengers finish their breakfast and start coming ashore. Audrey smiles to herself. Even though she's tired from the White Night party, part one of the plan – disembarking without being noticed – has gone better than she'd ever dared to hope. She'd known that the suite guests would have a private exit to the tenders, but now Audrey says a silent thank you to the young family who'd been fussing there with life jackets, giving her the chance to slip past the officer on duty and onto a tender without swiping her ship card.

High up on the cliff, Audrey raises her hand to her lips and kisses her fingers, unfurls them, and blows the kiss towards the ship.

'Bye Lexi. Bye John. Good luck,' she says softly, and it reminds her of another sailing, another goodbye. She breathes deeply, filled with the sense that life has come full circle.

Audrey thinks of *The Rosie Project* left in her

case, her message to Alexandra buried within the book's pages. She imagines its progress as her things are bagged up and sent back to England. The bag should be with Alexandra in a few weeks. She's a smart cookie; she'll piece it together. Audrey recalls the conversation she had with Alexandra in Corfu. Maybe she'll finally get the answers Audrey now realises she'd been subconsciously searching for all her life.

Audrey's eyes mist with tears and, biting her lips together, she turns abruptly, takes a deep breath, and starts to walk away from the edge. She fumbles in her pocket as she walks; pulls out a folded piece of paper, turns it around until it's orientated, and starts to walk through the maze of streets that is Fira, her backpack weighing heavy on her shoulders. Apart from the cash she got from selling the painting, she's taken just three things from her old life: the delicate silver bangle her parents bought her, her silver travel alarm clock, and the locket the twins gave her for her seventieth birthday.

Audrey turns into a street and sees the art gallery at once. Someone's opening up the front as she approaches.

'*Kalimera!*' calls the woman, propping open the door. Audrey smiles and nods; hesitates while the other woman goes back inside, double-checks her piece of paper, then knocks, as instructed, on the adjacent green door. As she waits, images tumble through her mind: her passage to India. Bombay. Ralph. The desperate days learning how to take care of babies. Barnes. The house. Mack. A life devoted to children not her own. A life of duty.

'Now,' she breathes. 'Now, Audrey Templeton, it's time for you.'

There's a click and the green door opens. Mack stares at Audrey. His hair is still long, but it's grey now. His beard is full and his skin is tanned and craggy, but what Audrey notices the most is that magic light in his eyes: it's still there. A smile of pure joy breaks over Mack's face.

'You're here,' he says slowly. 'You're finally here.'

'Yes,' she says. 'Can I come in?'

Acknowledgements

A massive thank you to the wonderful people who helped bring this book to fruition: my inspirational agent Luigi Bonomi, Alison Bonomi, and my brilliant editor, Sally Williamson. Thank you, too, to all those beavering away behind the scenes at Harlequin to get the book produced, printed, marketed, publicised and sold. Thank you, too, to my friend and best beta reader ever, Rachel Hamilton.

A special thank you to all at the Emirates Airline Festival of Literature – in particular Isobel Abulhoul and Yvette Judge, and to Charles Nahhas of Montegrappa.

I'd also like to thank my parents-in-law, Natu and Niru Kantaria. It was with them that I first set foot on a cruise ship, and it was on that ship that the idea for this story was born (before you ask: yes, we all made it back to shore). Thank you, too, to all those who read and enjoyed *Coming Home;* and to all the wonderful book clubs who've invited me to join them for an evening of book chat.

Last, but not least, thank you to my cheerleaders: those wonderful friends who stand quietly behind me, cheering me on – you know who you are; thank you to my mum, and to my special little family: Sam, Maia and Aiman.

The publishers hope that this book has given you enjoyable reading. Large Print Books are especially designed to be as easy to see and hold as possible. If you wish a complete list of our books please ask at your local library or write directly to:

Magna Large Print Books
Magna House, Long Preston,
Skipton, North Yorkshire.
BD23 4ND

This Large Print Book for the partially sighted, who cannot read normal print, is published under the auspices of

THE ULVERSCROFT FOUNDATION